No One So Much as You

REBECCA GOSDEN

The Book Guild Ltd

First published in Great Britain in 2024 by
The Book Guild Ltd
Unit E2 Airfield Business Park,
Harrison Road, Market Harborough,
Leicestershire. LE16 7UL
Tel: 0116 2792299
www.bookguild.co.uk
Email: info@bookguild.co.uk
X: @bookguild

Typeset in 11pt Minion Pro

Printed on FSC accredited paper
Printed and bound in Great Britain by 4edge Limited

ISBN 978 1835740 187

British Library Cataloguing in Publication Data.
A catalogue record for this book is available from the British Library.

For the Cam Clan

ONE

The copper sky threw the winding lane into a haze of darkness. This was a part of the walk that she usually enjoyed, but the light was fading quickly now, and Charlotte found herself walking at a quicker pace through the copse of trees ahead. Space was so scarce, boughs and branches had grown over the road to form a tunnel of undergrowth. An uneasy sensation of intrusion and lurking menace seemed to rise from the earth itself, insidiously creeping up on her. Into the open again, with determined strides past the few residences and farm, she finally drew breath on the brow of the hill, rewarded with a view across the gently undulating fields as the land dipped and rose once more into the distance.

Skeletal January trees scored the sky with misformed calligraphic strokes on this top-land, the palate and composition fusing in muted shades of blue and grey compared with the fiery sunset behind. Charlotte sighed involuntarily as she looked down into the barren landscape, fields and hedges blurring together in the dimming light. God, this time of year was difficult. The ethereal winter beauty was a lie, trees portentous rather than scenic; no promise of the new, just the feeling of dwindling and that peculiar absence of sound and life that marks the passage between evening and night.

Everything was muffled; she felt emptied. Lost hopes, lost chances, the poignancy that she had kept suppressed, barely below the surface, threatened to submerge her should she move. A well-loved Hardy poem came into her head: 'Winter's dregs made desolate / The weakening eye of day'. The melancholy lines thrilled yet haunted her as she assessed the bleakness. Wrapped protectively in her layers of clothing, she felt strangely fanciful and reluctant to move from her spot, enveloped by the gloam as if caught between one world and the next. She was acutely aware of her own breathing, and the warmth of her body contrasted comfortingly with the chill that was settling on the land.

Random words and images from the last few days fussed and worried at her. She knew she had not responded in the best way or admitted her own erratic behaviour, but self-awareness didn't stop the thought that she may be at the end of her tether. Charlotte had 'escaped' from the fraught aftermath of a Seldon family gathering. It wasn't Daniel's fault that his family were, without exception, a bunch of complete and utter tossers (her own were hardly any better, but at least they had the sense to stay at a distance). However, he could take some blame for the fact that she had had to leave her own home to be able to draw breath finally and find release. Charlotte waited until she grew numb. Then a distant barking stirred her from her reverie, and she gave a shiver that seemed to spiral down to the depths of her spine.

"Jake, come on, boy! Jaayaake!" Charlotte's voice echoed futilely across the sparse land, and she felt that familiar helplessness. Shit... not again. Like she didn't have enough to contend with already. *That bloody dog* – what was he doing? She scrabbled about in her coat pocket and managed to extrapolate the torch, dropping gloves and dog lead in the process. Bugger, bugger and bugger again. Swearing audibly by now, she swept the gloves and lead up, dipping them into an icy puddle as she went.

"Jake! Jake!" *God, I hope there are no cars.*

It was a quiet country lane, Charlotte reasoned, but there was a farm and several houses further up all requiring access. *That effing dog.* Cats were far more her – artistic, aloof, self-reliant – but Daniel was allergic and so that was that. Jake was like a lovable but uncontrollable teenager. She turned and shone the torch onto the fields around her – nothing: no scrabbling, panting familiar black shape leaping across the ditch. Wearily, she turned to contemplate the way she had just covered, farm buildings and the looming shapes of houses in the distance. Better walk back the way she came then.

Scanning the fields either side and their intermittent hedgerows, she set off along the road, switching the torch off to preserve the beam and craning to see in the last vestiges of daylight. She could dimly see the outline of the footpath sign ahead on the right by a tall bramble-ridden hedge; perhaps the dog had got the scent of something down there?

She reached the corner of the hedge and was rounding it intently when a tall shape seemed to loom from nowhere in front of her. She knocked clumsily into something hard, moving and unmistakably human, catching a visceral odour of sweat and the bitter notes of some unknown masculine perfume. To her shame, Charlotte stifled a sound which was somewhere between a cry and a full-blown scream – she was notorious for her jumpiness – and her heart juddered unpleasantly against her chest.

"Oh… er… hey, are you alright?"

The figure seemed to materialise in front of her, and it became clear that it was male, about six foot and somewhere in the region of Charlotte's age, give or take five years or so. The voice was nuanced and appealing, both rich and deep yet tinged with… could it be amusement? A leather-gloved hand reached firmly for her arm in an attempt to steady her, but Charlotte recoiled in jerky embarrassment, squirming out of reach, and stumbling again as a consequence. Oh, the humiliation. She could see the scene as if it were playing out in front of her, as she struggled to gain composure.

"Erm… my dog's run off," she spluttered, re-positioning her left foot stubbornly on the muddy verge. "He's a black lab. Have you seen him?"

"Dog? No, I haven't seen anyone, man or beast!"

Charlotte could just make out dark hair and stubble, but determinedly avoided eye-contact. There was the slightest pause while both considered their next move.

"I've just come round that way." He gesticulated behind him, vaguely. "Sorry."

"No worries, I'll just carry on looking, sorry to bother you," Charlotte replied. Her voice was coming out all wrong – high-pitched and panicky – and why was she always so damned apologetic? She mentally crossed her fingers that the man was going the other way. Shit, he wasn't.

"Bit late, isn't it? I'm assuming you're from around here?" Max could see that the woman was embarrassed, but he couldn't help himself. He had been on his own now for forty-eight hours straight and the brief walk down to the village had scored precisely nil points for conversation even in the tired old pub which he had braved for a perfunctory pint; Nell really knew how to pick them! To think that he had had his arm twisted into signing a twelve-month lease – he doubted whether he'd make a month at this rate.

Not that he was able to see much of her in this light with the hat and scarf and whatever else she had managed to wrap round her. Face seemed very pale, and there was a bit of dark hair that had managed to escape between layers of wool. She looked cold. Couldn't tell how old she was; her way of speaking seemed rather prim and proper, but he liked her voice – it reminded him of an English teacher he'd had at secondary school who was great at reading aloud, and the bit of skin he could see appeared to be without warts, carbuncles, webbing or whatever else you might expect in these parts.

"The village," Charlotte answered shortly. Why was he expecting her to make conversation? This was painful enough already.

"I've just come from there. Quiet, isn't it? Not exactly buzzing with activity."

Charlotte almost snorted with laughter. "What d'you expect? The average patron is over seventy-five and anyone with any sense is probably on their sofa either sleeping off the Sunday roast or catching up on Netflix with something alcoholic!"

The man gave an answering chuckle, and Charlotte squashed the urge to join him. What did she care about his petty problems? She had plenty of her own to deal with! As if this wasn't excruciating enough already. They had walked for probably only thirty seconds or so and already Charlotte wanted the ground to swallow her up.

Christ, almost warmed her up there, thought Max, pondering his next riposte. "Do you normally walk the dog in the dark?"

Charlotte reflected bitterly that she was bound to think of a similarly witty, dead-pan response when she was back home with said creature hopefully but then, a second later, like a sign from on high, the lolloping outline of Jake slowly became distinguishable through the shadows. Charlotte felt light-headed with relief.

"That's him – oh, thank goodness!"

Feeling a love she hadn't realised she possessed, she ran the last few steps, half scolding and hugging the dog as she fumbled with the lead, managing to slip it round his neck but dropping her gloves again in the process. She gave up and swung round to face her helper. Typically, Jake was all over him – the treachery of pets; their dog greeting a total stranger with the adoration that she and Daniel thought was awarded only to them.

They were very close to the first house on the left now, an old farmhouse that had recently been renovated by some money-grabbing developer who, Charlotte and Daniel liked to speculate, had moved it swiftly on for profit. Behind that was a massive barn conversion that, if rumours were correct, even had a helipad in its grounds.

"Thanks for your help – sorry you got dragged into my mishap." Charlotte just wanted to get home now and put the whole sorry incident behind her. The awkwardness was palpable, and she yearned to walk away.

"No problem, I was just stretching my legs anyway.

You've dropped your gloves." He reached to deftly hook them up in one fluid movement. "Nice to meet you, even in these circumstances... er...?"

"Charlotte," she mumbled reluctantly, already turning to go.

Should I invite her in to warm-up? Max deliberated for a split second. Maybe not, it might come across as a bit predatory although, Christ, he was lonely enough.

"Well, Charlotte, I'm Max."

Absolutely no reaction. For a moment, Max felt bloody affronted; if she knew who he was! Then he berated himself for his hubris. *No one fucking cares round here, Max.* No one except Nell, and she was off on some jaunt for the next week apparently.

Charlotte was reluctant to make any further connection. She really hoped that she would never suffer the humiliation of meeting this human being again, let alone in daylight, but against her better judgement she allowed herself to look up. They were just outside the grounds of the farmhouse but the buoyantly positioned security light angled a beam of light in the direction of their faces. At the same time, their eyes met in the dreary half-light and Charlotte felt a sharp twisting sensation in the pit of her stomach, like something vital had been wrenched inside. Max's face was lit briefly and then shadowed again as the beam wobbled in the gathering wind. She wouldn't have been able to describe his features in any detail, but she couldn't help but notice that he looked annoyingly easy on the eye in an effortless, inconsiderate kind of way.

"Thank you," she faltered, and swung round abruptly, itching to leave.

"Hey, you can't walk on your own now in this dark. Let me just see you down the hill." Actually, that really did make him seem like some kind of stalker. Max groaned inwardly – the awkwardness was contagious.

"Don't be silly, I'm fine. I've got a torch. Goodbye." Charlotte set off at a pace. God, it was becoming weird... thank goodness she could now make her excuses and go.

Max gave her a few minutes and then silently followed his quarry – he could see the ridiculously weak torchlight bobbing in the distance. He knew it was unlikely but what if this strange woman had some kind of accident or fell in a ditch on the way home? He wouldn't put it past her; she wasn't acting exactly rationally, that was for sure. Besides, there was something about her, if you got past the rattiness.

Max sensed that she was troubled in some way; she seemed uneasy, and he had always had this sixth sense when it came to other people. Kirstin, his sister, called him an empath, and sometimes mocked him for it. At school, he had recoiled inside when he saw someone on their own in a line, or not being picked or undergoing one of the other myriad of agonising situations that follow us for a lifetime.

"For fuck's sake," Max could hear Charlotte mutter under her breath, as she stumbled on the uneven road surface. It was the stubbornness that roped him in, ironically. He may have left it had she not been so determined to avoid any kind of help. He kept well back but persevered in his quest.

Charlotte was focusing on walking as fast as she possibly could so that the ten minutes back to the main road was covered in just over five. As soon as she heard the familiar buzz of a lone car, she actually forced herself into an uneven jog to get down the hill and out of sight. She was conscious of the feeling of being watched abating. *I must be mad*, she thought. *What must he have thought of me?*

Max watched her dwindling figure disappear out of sight pensively. *What a strange woman! I wonder what was bothering her? Oh man, the gloves! Oh well*, he instinctively put them to his nose before stuffing them carefully into his pocket. Funny, same perfume as Nell, a lingering scent which was almost masculine with its intense woody smell and notes of pine. A souvenir of the encounter? Max sighed and began to stride back to the barn, trying to think about what he was going to fill his days with for the next fortnight and tonight – another evening in the vast lounge with only Netflix and the contents of the wine cellar for company. The irony didn't escape him.

TWO

"I'll see you then; a week on Wednesday, remember. When do you go back to school?"

Charlotte moved uneasily under the duvet. She opened her eyes a slit, feeling the shadow of a bent figure across hers.

"Er... um... Thursday?" she rasped. Her throat felt scratchy and constricted; perhaps she was coming down with something. Then again, she remembered dosing herself with several nightcaps of port last night before she eventually crawled into bed. What was Daniel hinting? She was only supply teaching at the moment, what did it matter when she went back? It may as well be never for all she cared, and she had nothing booked anyway. Had she told Daniel that? She couldn't remember. She felt a brief moment of contact as Daniel dropped his head to hers and then he was gone. A moment later the slam of the front door and low hum of a car engine. Then quiet.

Daniel picked his way over the puddled drive in his work shoes and clicked the unlock button on his key fob. Carefully positioning his suitcase in the boot of the car, he slammed it with a force that was heavier than he intended. The house stared judgementally back at him, curtains shut, borders unkempt and rubbish almost overflowing from the bin next to the house. Should he have reminded Charlotte to put the bins out on Friday? Oh, what was the point? He sank down heavily into the driver's seat, almost throwing the wallet that held his passport next to him, and sat without moving, his head fixed forwards but unseeing.

He knew that she felt low again; she always made it abundantly clear to everyone else, veering between wallowing or retreating into herself so she couldn't be reached by anyone, let alone him. It had been difficult yesterday. Mum and Dad had really gone to town over his birthday. He didn't know why they bothered really, and Sybil and the kids being there too hadn't helped. He wondered if they had remembered that it had been the anniversary of the first of the miscarriages? Hell, he hadn't remembered until, stony-lipped, Charlotte had made a single comment when Sybil had thoughtlessly commented on the size of the house.

"What do you do with all these rooms, Dan? Bit big for the two of you, isn't it?"

He wished she hadn't decided impulsively to give up her job last July. He felt that the rhythm of the school year bonded Charlotte to reality, gave her stability and purpose. Now she seemed transient: a day's supply here and there, never enough to forge links, never enough to answer his questions on the day with any more than, "It was alright, kids were okay," which anyone knew was a load of bollocks coming from a supply teacher. He had hoped she might take up painting again, but it was as if the creative urge eluded her. Ironically, the limitless freedom and leisure seemed stifling.

Mind you, sometimes he wished he could do the same with his job: chuck it all in and start from scratch. Property management had seemed new and exciting when he had begun as a junior manager twenty years ago. Now, even though he had been put in charge of the European division and was flying all over, he sometimes thought it was more effort than it was worth. Complications everywhere. He ran a hand through his thatch of greying curly brown hair and clasped both hands behind his neck for a brief moment, stretching and catching sight of the blue sky above. *Snap out of it, Dan, don't get sucked in. You're doing bloody well. You're flying to Portugal for work, for Christ's sake. Be happy!*

Daniel sighed, and put the car into reverse, edging carefully out into the road behind him. There was no real need for his extreme care, the neighbours were pretty much all retired or housebound. He put the car in first, moving forward slowly and then picking up speed. The radio intoned in the background and Daniel felt a sloughing off as he heard the familiar voice of the news anchor. He took a final farewell glance in the mirror; once upon a time, Charlotte would have been there waving. Straightening his back, Daniel trained his eyes firmly back on the lane as he came to the junction with the main road and the way out of the village.

***

Charlotte rolled over, the pretence of sleep slipping from her like a shed skin. To the right of the bed, the sky broached the panes of glass carelessly. Bright blue and garishly flamboyant, its abundance spouted disdain for the stunted winter foliage. She could be anywhere from what was visible. The sun lit the ceiling like a touchpaper. She thought of books, of pictures, of voyages and expeditions, all far away and devoid of human interference. She briefly imagined mountains or ice, sea lapping at the walls.

Then Charlotte caught sight of the box on the windowsill and felt the fracture inside her chest, something flimsily erected breaking once more. It was a whimsical box – a papier mâché affair made up of a misshapen fairy figure spread-eagled across the top holding a tiny wand topped with a star, *Teeth* written below. Charlotte had been given it by a well-meaning pupil who was of the mistaken but entirely understandable belief that she would one day be able to use it for her own children. Wrong, wrong, wrong. Hot tears came with a smart and Charlotte emitted a small sob. She felt herself wobble on that well-worn precipice between control and despair and rocked in a convulsive movement, once more giving birth to her grief and a guttural groan of anguish that mourned her lost children.

There had been hope at first; one loss was merely unlucky and there were plenty of placatory comments. Colleagues had been sympathetic, even her mother had gone through the motions of expressing her pity and the belief that it wasn't the right time. And she had so wanted to please her, to prove that she was capable of this most basic of accomplishments. Then the second, the third, the fourth, and lastly an experience so horrific that she finally could bear no more. To feel the pregnancy leave her body with a dull splash signifying weight and substance – her precious secret expelled in pain and disgust. She had recoiled into herself and built a wall of her shame.

Charlotte succumbed to her misery and sobbed firstly

without sound and afterwards with great howls of pain easing into a wracking shudder of grief. Then she started, interrupted by a scrabbling at the door. It swung open and Jake rushed in, his nose pushing into her face, front paws on the bed, trying to clamber on top of her.

"You silly dog," she murmured, feeling a rush of affection for him. Calmer now, she realised she felt ravenously hungry. Easing herself up, she wiped her eyes and blew her nose, leading the dog to the top of the stairs before she turned round and walked back to the bedroom.

Pulling on leggings and a sweatshirt, she realised there was nothing normal in the house, only displaced remnants from yesterday's entertainment or a hunk of dry bread and no eggs or butter. She craved some carbs and maybe the salty tang of bacon would help to fill the hollow space below her ribs. Pausing to pull on her boots and coat at the door and grab a tenner from under the coin tray, Charlotte ignored Jake's excited scamper and then downcast expression as he realised that he wasn't going to join her. She exited the front door, striding down the drive and then left along the small cul-de-sac, cutting through between the cottages opposite to reach the main road.

It was a crisp, beautiful morning and Charlotte felt inexplicably revived after a few minutes of being outside. She found her mind going over the events of last night, and that odd encounter with the man on her walk – Max, she supposed she should call him. Hopefully, there would be no further meeting. Perhaps she would have to avoid that walk for a bit. Reluctantly, as it was her favourite. From the few words he had spoken, he clearly wasn't local, so he might just be on holiday for a week or so.

"Morning." Charlotte forced a smile to greet a fellow dog walker coming towards her. She recognised him but didn't know his name; he sometimes volunteered at the local shop, she thought. To be honest, the male volunteers of a certain age faded into one – chinos, often red or dusky pink; open-necked checked shirt, usually with some blue; and then an assortment of what her dad would have called pullovers. Oh yes, and bodywarmers – they loved a good bodywarmer around here.

Charlotte pushed the door of the shop open, and the attached bell gave its customary tinkle. Ros, a sprightly looking retiree, who always boasted a carefully maintained set of gel nails, was standing guard by the till, inspecting them. Her head jerked up eagerly as she recognised Charlotte.

"Charlotte, isn't it? Are you on your holidays, dear? When do the children go back?"

"Yes, just under a week to go."

What is her name? Charlotte thought desperately. Should have been paying more attention when she introduced herself last year. People were so nosy – it sometimes felt that she was being scrutinised like a specimen on a slide at these village gatherings. Fatal to have admitted what you do – *they will never let me forget it, long after I have stepped out of a classroom for the last time.*

Ros smiled and turned her face back to the magazine she was reading half-heartedly. *Funny girl, that one. She has a discontented look about her. Shame – her face would be pretty if she smiled a bit more.*

"You're looking a bit peaky, dear – have you been under the weather?"

She's been crying, it suddenly came to Ros, and she felt a twinge of guilt for her garrulity. *I wonder what has upset her?* A certain amount of speculation had circulated about the childless couple in Brick House, but Ros doubted that much of it was true.

"Just hungry." Charlotte tried to engage with the woman, but she was mildly annoyed for having to make the effort. "It's…" Her voice trailed off as the door opened with a very decided jangling.

Ros's expression seemed to change, and her jaw slackened.

"Just these." Charlotte felt irritated; she really was increasingly hungry. Then she wheeled around too, wondering why the new customer was having such a strange effect on the woman. There was something familiar about the waxed jacket a few metres away from her and, as the man turned round from the refrigerator, she felt an unwelcome jolt of recognition.

Max beat her to it. "You again! Didn't think we'd be running into each other so quickly, Charlotte. I've still got your gloves!"

Again, his voice was melodious and disarming; this time she detected a slight hint of an accent – perhaps South London, the home counties? Charlotte felt her face growing warm – really, he was implying intimacy where there was none. Her eyes took in a now clean-shaven face but with the shadow of a beard; dishevelled dark-brown hair in need of a cut; and eyes that were lighter than they had appeared yesterday, more of a hazel brown, really. His nose was rather aquiline with lips unusually full and well-shaped for a man. She could see his pupils scrutinising her in return – she wondered if he was judging her also and flushed again.

He was grinning at her now, as if he knew what she was thinking, and she had to work hard to stop her face responding alike. It was rather strange, but he looked familiar in some other way also, reminded her of someone she was sure that she had seen recently – most odd. She turned back to Ros, to see if her shopping had finally been registered, and was surprised to see the elderly woman greeting Max like a long-lost friend.

"Ah, Mr. Collins, this is a treat. Are you on a break from filming then? How are you getting on at the barn? A bit lonely up there, I shouldn't wonder. What can I get for you today?"

"Max is fine. Oh, don't mind me, please serve Charlotte first. I only want some milk," Max's eyes twinkled at Charlotte. He made the few steps through the shop and came to stand at the counter next to her, feeling something akin to pleasure – someone he recognised, at least, despite not being his number one fan! He could actually have a proper look at her today, although there was still some kind of knitted beret thing on her head. A mass of brown hair spooled over her shoulders, and she had strong eyebrows with dark eyes beneath. She was younger than he had assumed yesterday – face unlined, clear skin, but there was a seriousness to her which closed her face off somehow. She was still unsmiling, in spite of his best efforts. He was going to give up soon. She was so bloody rude.

Charlotte took in the rest of Max's appearance, wordlessly. Tatty but probably expensive jeans; walking boots that at least seemed authentic; and an unusual, beaded leather bracelet which looked handmade – very hipster. Words and images were running through her mind as if they were being projected by a cinecamera. *Filming…* Who was this man? She was soon to find out.

"I really enjoyed the first season," Ros rattled on, passing Charlotte's bacon across the counter without conviction.

"You were marvellous! Just as I imagined him. Will you be making another? Surprised you haven't got anything lined up!"

There was the smallest of silences. "Quite a few projects this year, but I'm on a break at the moment," Max responded breezily. *What is her name?* He was sure Nell had said.

"Oh, yes, Nell told me," Ros answered, greedily. She wordlessly waved the card machine in Charlotte's direction. "Lovely girl, that one, and her last film was breathtaking – that romance, wasn't it, in the desert, with the army?"

Max grimaced inside, and saw Charlotte ineffectually suppress a smile as she rummaged intently for her switch card. Nell was always so two-faced, but he hadn't yet met anyone, apart from Bella, who wasn't putty in her hands. She had had a field day doing impressions of this poor old dear back at the ranch. He tried to avoid the word – Bella had hated it – but Nell could be such a bitch sometimes. The butter skidded across the floor as Ros absently fiddled with Charlotte's bag.

"Oh, I'm sorry, love, that's me not paying attention," she apologised, and all at once Charlotte and Max both found themselves bending and reaching at the same time. Inevitably, their hands brushed against each other, and Charlotte felt a frisson of warmth as their skin made contact. She could feel his eyes bore into her as she abruptly straightened and swept the rest of the items off the counter into her bag. She knew she was being rude, but she felt pugnacious. She didn't owe this man any favours.

"Thanks. Bye." She made a hasty exit out onto the pavement. Damn, no dog this time for camouflage. No time for processing. She walked quickly over the road and heard a car toot as it rushed past her. She resisted the urge to stick two fingers up, and continued to walk, ignoring the sound of the shop door clanging behind her. Thank goodness: the turning for the footpath. She slipped down it and a few moments later was unlocking her own front door, panting slightly.

No surprise that his behaviour had seemed slightly stilted at times and he projected a tangible air of entitlement. She conceded she was being uncharitable but there definitely had been something alien about him. At the same time, no wonder he had seemed vaguely known to her. Those eyes. She hadn't watched it herself, but she had seen him in a few other things, she thought. He had been younger, and the parts had been small – must have been prior to all this success. *Netflix*, she thought. *God, how embarrassing!*

***

Max cursed as the lorry blocked his view of Charlotte. Then she seemed to disappear into thin air. He crossed over and realised that a narrow footpath ran down between the gardens of the two pink cottages opposite. Should he go after her? He still had her ruddy gloves! Why was he worrying so much about what this woman thought of him? He couldn't explain and thought she would probably think him completely unhinged if he tried to follow her now. He didn't exactly mind being recognised when he was out – fame was too new for that – but he had felt foolish in front of Charlotte. He wasn't sure why. He could just about deal with the groupie type (*Rose? Ros?* He was still struggling to remember) but this woman's behaviour was something else.

He had been polite, he thought, charming even, but she had seemed totally preoccupied. He didn't know why he was getting so wound up about it. It was none of his business, was it? Sighing heavily, he turned and braced himself for the walk up the hill back home, then turned round again. *Fuck it. I've forgotten the milk.*

THREE

By Wednesday, Charlotte was feeling stir-crazy. She had drifted around the house for two days listlessly, reading a little here and there, tidying sporadically, staring outside and just regretting pretty much everything really. She couldn't paint – what was the point? It was too cold or wet to garden. All she could do was what her mother would have described as mope.

After the clear skies of Sunday and Monday, on Tuesday it had poured with a thoroughness that was almost admirable. The gutters ran, the puddles merged, and the greyness seemed to smother everything, including her mood. The dog had had to contend with being let into the garden to conduct his business and, by the mournful expression on his face, he too was thoroughly pissed off. Daniel was phoning zealously at 9.30a.m. and 10.00p.m., and Charlotte was starting to feel cramped and imprisoned. She was conversely filled with an impulsive wish to throw off her shackles and vanquish the inclement weather.

She had received several texts from her teacher friend, Emily, and tapped out terse replies to her enquiries, evading the questions on what she was doing at the moment and providing cursory responses when asked about her Christmas and New Year. There was also a WhatsApp from Claire, her university friend, suggesting a meet-up. Charlotte and Claire were polar opposites, but it somehow worked, or had up until Claire exiting the rat race. She had decided to opt out of the job market and immerse herself in her young family – three under four and a menagerie of animals to boot. The truth was that as Claire's brood had expanded, so had the distance between them. Charlotte was a generous godmother, but contact was now from afar and centred around occasional long weekend phone calls and the odd shopping trip. She felt sometimes, when she popped the latest banknote or voucher in an envelope, that she was paying not to see the children, the latest evidence of her failure rubbed in her face.

The final insult had come this morning at 11.00a.m. when she was interrupted from the terminal *This Morning* by a phone call from her mother, wondering when Charlotte would like to come to visit. Instantly, she knew that Daniel was behind this; she hadn't spoken to her mother since September.

"I don't think that would be wise, Mum," Charlotte had responded, almost choking over the unexpected invitation.

"Charlotte, dear, I don't know what you mean. We're both dying to see you. It's been months."

"The last time I saw you, you told me to pull myself together and get a job," Charlotte said coldly. "I had just made a momentous decision, and you made it clear that you thought it was the wrong one. Not only the wrong one, but one in a series of wrong decisions that have stretched through my entire adult life." Her voice was rising, and she felt her knuckles clenching.

"You're always so thin-skinned," her mother retorted, after a brief pause where Charlotte could have sworn that she heard the clicking sound that came with the trademark inhalation of breath every time Charlotte crossed or disappointed her. "I only want the best for you, Charlotte. Teaching is a lazy career… you were so talented. You could have done anything you wanted to, and now look at you. You don't think things through and then the rest of us have to pick up the pieces."

"Don't feel you have to pick up anything," Charlotte hissed and put the phone down as fast as she could. Her pulse was racing, and she felt a hot anger behind her eyelids. How could her mother be so foul? Why hadn't Daniel learnt in all this time? He expected mothers to be like his own – loyal to a fault, loyal to the detriment of judgement, loyal to him above anyone else, even her husband.

Her own father had died suddenly ten years before. He had been a quiet, insular, studious man. A print designer, she doubted his career aspirations carried the kudos her mother affected: she treated creativity like it was some kind of dangerous disease. Since then, she had made a habit of her failed relationships; although she maintained she was bemused when each new lover dwindled and lost interest. To be honest, Charlotte wasn't even sure Audrey Seldon really cared – that would have required emotional investment in another's existence.

A mildly successful businesswoman, she had made a reasonable amount of money through selling her first business – an interior design company back in the days when interior design amounted to little more than using Peter Jones for your wedding list. Then she had invested in the stock market at the behest of some former, unusually astute flame. This limited but tangible acquisition of material success had had a marked effect on a personality that already had little to endear it to her daughter. Charlotte valued nice things, of course, but she understood so clearly now that fulfilment had to be linked to more than possessions.

Some of the problem was her, of course; she often didn't feel very kind or empathetic herself when she had finished talking to her mother. Audrey was a person who polarised others. Common ground was a problem. Charlotte knew her tolerance levels for others' issues was far too low. It was frustrating to listen to her mother fussing with seemingly banal concerns whilst she was imploding, but she admitted inwardly that she had not had the patience to connect properly during the last few years. Their contact was sporadic, combative and normally made during times of high stress, disaster or general low mood. The trouble was that this only undermined the relationship further, made more vicious the circle.

Charlotte picked up the remote control and aimed it at the television. *Come on, I can do this. Forget Mum: I lost her long ago.* She patted Jake's head and lifted his lead off the hook by the front door, putting on her mac with the hood. She pulled open the front door, and braced herself for the wind that swirled around her as soon as she stepped foot outside. Tracing the familiar trail, she crossed the main road, and started straight up the hill towards the farm. She'd walk where she bloody well wanted. There was little chance she would see Max again, and so what if she did?

***

Max had spent an irksome two days glued to either his laptop or smartphone. Yes, he was contracted to his present series for a further four seasons, but he wanted to line up some other work in between just to prove himself, really, and lots of the initial castings now were by Teams. He knew that he could have taken a breather and just relied on the show, but success was too shiny and hard-earned for him to be complacent. The reviews had been in the main positive, but there was no way Max was going to rest on his laurels.

There were some interesting projects out there now he was 'known' in the industry. Della, his agent, was supportive in the main, although not always in the way Max wanted. She thought he should be capitalising on his success and wanted to book him in for appearances and social events left, right and centre. Max would have rather she focused on the business of acquiring reasonable scripts – another pilot or even an independent would have been appealing right now. He tried to not always be available when Della called, which was frequently, as Max suspected that her portfolio was somewhat less impressive than she had first advertised. He was happy to do a limited number of events – probably more than he wanted to as Nell loved an A-list premiere and often managed to tag along – but he was actually feeling a bit jaded by the recent press attention. Plus, there was nothing like being holed up in the back of beyond for a week to fuel his impostor syndrome.

"Yeah, Della, yeah, okay. I'll do it, I guess." Max inwardly groaned and wondered why some people were so oblivious to the fact that others were finding them intolerable. "God, the line's really bad – you know it really is the sticks here. I'll try and phone again tomorrow. Take care!"

He ignored the agitated noises coming from the other end of the line and firmly pressed the end call button. He could feel his heart rate gradually de-escalating as he chucked the phone on the sofa. Levering himself up, he crossed over to the big picture windows that faced down into the slight valley to his right and then the rolling fields to the left. It was an insipid kind of day, but the winds and rain had died down and the air looked clean and revitalising. His eye caught sight of an open barn to the far right where some dirty brown tarpaulin had been roughly thrown over a bulky shape. Max's eyes brightened and he cast a look at the sky.

"Well, it's hardly raining now, and the wind's dried the worst of the wet," he murmured. "Won't hurt to take it for a spin."

Ten minutes later and Max had donned his leather jacket and helmet, a cursory nod to safety but, as he assured himself, he wouldn't be going very fast. He didn't think his parents would forgive him if anything happened to him after Bella, and he certainly wouldn't forgive himself if he put them through that again. He hadn't got the full gear (Max would only have described himself as a fair-weather biker, really) but he had to get out of the house – he couldn't stand his own inertness a minute longer.

The bike really was a pretty fabulous beast. Max wasn't a petrolhead: he didn't love cars and could only barely tell one end of a spanner from the other, but he couldn't deny that the streamline combination of hammered shiny metal, tyres and engine had a certain appeal. It was his own reward to himself after winning the five-season deal eighteen months ago. A newcomer to American cable television, he had been the outlier, the casting director's gamble, but it had paid off and audiences had been riveted by the attractive newcomer from across the pond, an antecedent to the buffed and chiselled heroes that seemed so prevalent currently.

He had ridden it a couple of times in London, but it hadn't been particularly fun battling with the seasoned motorists of the capital, devoid of joy or empathy and well-versed to the tricks of bikers, moving across to block routes through traffic and honking noisily at any perceived violation of their space. Here, well, he found himself feeling oddly anticipatory – this might be what he had been waiting for.

Once on the bike, helmet snugly on, visor down, he felt strangely disconnected from the land beneath him. Revving the engine a couple of times, he felt the bike buck underneath him. It was a thrilling, heart in your mouth feeling and he braced himself as he vied with the bike to take control, jerking initially and then settling into the build-up of acceleration. He suppressed a gulp which turned into a sharp intake of breath as the sounds of the engine's roar shattered the tranquillity and a flock of crows spluttered into the air to his right. Turning left out of the small drive, he entered the tiny country lane which led a meandering route to either another bigger village or through a hamlet to the main road via long stretches of lonely lanes framing yawning expanses of Suffolk arable land.

Max sped down hills, hugged bends and coasted up and down, giving himself entirely to the pleasure of the ride. He met virtually no traffic on these tiny ambling thoroughfares. He found himself becoming more confident, speeding into corners, enjoying the sound of the air rushing past. Deciding to take the main road in a loop back to the barn and, ignoring the speed limit, he accelerated past houses with a screech, almost missing his turning. He pushed the throttle down hard as he increased speed again up the hill and over the railway bridge, then cruised along jubilantly into the open with the flat rolling farmland surrounding him once again.

Max rounded the corner by the first farmhouse too fast and rammed on the brake so that it gave an unholy screech. Shit, that sounded awful; he was painfully out of practice. The bike juddered and Max suddenly realised that there was a shape in front of him. Fuck, it looked like a dog. He swerved slightly and the outline of a woman came into view scrambling up the dip in front, holding the end of the lead. Max turned into the drive of the barn quickly but cast a swift look into his wing mirror and was amused to see her giving a swift unmistakable gesture after him, the vigour of the moment meaning that she stood upright with her hair whipping over her shoulder. His expression changed.

"Fuck… Charlotte!"

He switched the engine off but, not concentrating, found himself turning the throttle once again. The engine reverberated with a sudden mechanical growl and Max turned again to see the dog lunge out of Charlotte's hands, pulling her full length onto the uneven road surface. She cried out and lay there for an instant, stunned. Horrified, Max leapt off his bike, covering the eight or so paces in milliseconds.

"My God, I'm so sorry, are you okay?" His voice was louder and less controlled than he had hoped.

"You, you… you!" Charlotte was incandescent with rage. "You selfish bastard!"

She was raising herself gingerly from the ground, wincing and cradling her arm. Max saw at once that her hands and knees were marked from the stones – and was that rusty mark blood? Charlotte took an apprehensive step forwards and then her ankle seemed almost to fold beneath her. Her face suddenly assumed a sickly pallor, and he grabbed at her shoulders feebly as she crumpled to the ground.

"Owww!" she yelled as Max quickly released her arm, realising that he might be hurting rather than helping her. There was an odd silence, where even the air seemed to hold its breath. Then, "I feel so sick," she muttered, rage deflating like a punctured balloon. Max surveyed the situation and did the only thing he could think of.

"Come on, let's get you inside, then you can contact someone to come and get you," he said. *Lord, what a mess.* He just needed to get her off the road, so nothing else happened and they could assess the damage.

"But Jake? Where is he?"

Charlotte forced herself to open her eyes and look back. She closed them again quickly; that felt bad. Her head felt swimmy, and she thought maybe she had twisted that dodgy ankle that always turned when she overdid it or wore heels that it deemed unsuitable. As for her arm, Jake had really wrenched her shoulder when he had pulled the lead out of her hands. She normally withstood pain pretty well, but this was excruciating. She leant into the hard surface and wished desperately that the road would swallow her up.

"He can't be far," Max said firmly. "You need to sit down properly out of this wind."

He typed the key code into the gate, and they wobbled their painfully slow passage open. Charlotte tried to struggle to her feet, swaying slightly, still undecided as to whether to follow or not, but then was overcome by faintness. Max managed to lever her somehow towards the stable door and porch, which served as a main entrance to the barn. Charlotte was feeling too lousy to protest further and slumped against him as he guided her forwards. As luck would have it, the dog decided to wander over, trailing his lead and wagging his tail guiltily. Max half-hoisted Charlotte over the threshold and hoped that she wasn't bleeding anywhere; he couldn't stand the sight of blood – great nurse he was going to make. He was involved now; like it or not, he couldn't seem to get away from this woman.

FOUR

"Wakey, wakey. Come on, Charlotte… Charlotte? Lottie… Lots? Please wake up!"

Charlotte opened her eyes blearily to see a man looking intently at her, concern etched across his face. As he registered her awakening, his mouth broke into a grin, and she felt her own cheeks widen in response and recognition. Max! Images were jostling for space inside her head, and she felt hot and headachy.

"I think you fainted," Max said tentatively and then, with growing confidence, "thank goodness you've stirred, thought I was going to have to do some kind of actual resus for a minute. Are you okay? How are you feeling?"

He wondered whether to make some quip about acting as a doctor. Back in the early days, he had had a small but recurring part in a BBC medical drama and had quite fancied his bedside manner. *Oh, shut up and focus, Max.*

Charlotte tried to marshal her thoughts as she tried to think of a solution to the situation she found herself in. How had she ended up on a velvet sofa, no less, in a room of gargantuan proportions with this Adonis in front of her? It was the stuff of nightmarish fantasy. She felt slightly disorientated. She could dimly remember being helped through the front door and the discomforting feel of a stranger's arms. If only she was dreaming, but the throbbing of her limbs seemed to prove otherwise. Friend or foe, Max seemed to be making an effort to be pleasant despite the motorbike and everything else. She appeared to have little choice but to engage with him.

"It's Charlotte, actually, not Lottie." She finally rewarded him with a wary smile. *Lottie, ugh!* She squirmed uneasily, distracted by the many textures that were vying for attention; she seemed to be partially lying on some fur with a woollen blanket draped over her. There were numerous cushions squished at intervals along her back and she was sure there was a book digging into her thigh.

"I'm feeling... I don't know... aaahhh!" She tried to lower her leg to the floor but was prevented by a discombobulating twinge of pain. "Owww, my ankle." She closed her eyes. "It doesn't feel too good."

"I've got some ice in the fridge," Max said. Charlotte looked lost, bundled up on the sofa, and he found himself gabbling. "Ice and elevate, isn't it? I think we better have a look. You alright if I do the honours?"

He cursed himself inwardly for the bonhomie, but the more awkward he became, the more voluble.

"If you must." The pain was forcing Charlotte to dispense with any preamble. "Where's the dog? Is he okay?"

"Well..." Max disregarded further niceties and started to unlace her boot... *in for a penny*.

Charlotte eyed his actions with some apprehension, mentally registering in his long-fingered hands a sign of an artistic temperament apparently. She had always rather prided herself on hers, but at this minute there were more pressing things to consider. Had she shaved her legs recently? She racked her brain and then braced herself as her ankle was touched. Max noticed this with a frown.

"He says that he really enjoyed the chicken breast I had left on the side for my tea, and wants to know if there's any more where that came from?" Max looked at Charlotte sideways on, hoping to thaw her out further. The ankle didn't look too good. He should have taken the boot off sooner, but he didn't like to touch her when she was out cold. He carried on rolling down the sock but there seemed to be a lot of fluid around the joint.

"I can't see your other leg, so you might just have thick ankles, but I'd say that seems pretty swollen."

Charlotte met his eyes, heeding the joke a beat too late, too distracted to react. She struggled to sit up and failed, suppressing another groan. Her shoulder was agony, and she found herself fighting back tears.

"What an idiot I am. That stupid dog. He always does this when he hears a loud noise. Daniel's been pulled over before. Maybe I just need to rest. Did you say you have some ice?"

Max hesitated, trying to judge her reaction. "I have, but I'd rather get this checked out properly. Can I call anyone for you?"

Charlotte looked embarrassed, and then she couldn't stop the catch in her voice. Christ, what was the matter with her? He was just being nice!

"'Fraid it's just me at home at the moment. My husband left on Monday for a two-week business trip. My in-laws are in..." she named a neighbouring village, "but they've got relatives staying... I'm not sure..." Her voice trailed off.

Clearly a problem there, Max thought. "Look, I can take you to A&E – it's the least I can do. It was my bloody bike that caused the problem in the first place. I'm not doing anything, and you need to get that seen to sooner rather than later."

He looked at Charlotte and, for the first time, really looked at her face. Oval to roundish proportions with symmetrical features and dark, well-defined eyebrows. Natural, thank God, and not those hideous drawn-in ones. Her serious look wavered as she considered his proposal for a minute, and a more unguarded expression flickered across her face, lifting the years from her. A fleeting thought crossed his own mind – *Bella, she has a look of Bella*. He dismissed it quickly and focused on her eyes. They were so dark that he couldn't see the pupils. Bella had blue-green eyes the colour of an English sea on a stormy day – they weren't identical twins – but her contrasting black pupils had the ability to bore right into him. Charlotte's had that same unrelenting intensity of focus. He felt that same disorientating feeling that he had had before when their eyes met, like he was in freefall with just the one link keeping him from plummeting to the ground.

"Could you? Are you sure?" Charlotte was surprised at how grateful and relieved she felt that she wasn't reduced to calling Daniel's parents. They saw her as a chain round Daniel's neck, she was sure. She really didn't want to add anything else to the list of grievances. "Thank you."

Why was he starring at her like that? She turned her face to the side to wipe her eyes quickly. It all felt a bit overwhelming after the week she was having. She hated, above all things, going to hospital; it was the smell that got to her the most.

That sickly, chemical smell of disinfectant and the faint sweet aroma of decay. The last time she had been in hospital… no, she wasn't going to think about that now.

Max stood up and smoothed his hair away from his forehead, a gesture that at once felt both strange and recognisable to Charlotte.

"Look, I'm just going to get the bike in and get everything together, Charlotte. I'll get you a quick cup of tea too. You just relax for a minute."

He strode purposefully towards an archway at the end of the room. Charlotte leant back weakly and took in her surroundings. The sofa was in the middle of a large, vaulted room which seemed to be in the centre of the house. It was impressive to say the least, being the height of two floors, with what appeared to be a galleried landing running round three of the walls and a bespoke oak staircase leading up to the second floor. She spied a grand piano in the corner and several guitars displayed on the wall nearby.

A large wood-burner was impossibly positioned in the middle of the room with several other oversized, jewel-coloured easy chairs around it. Some newspapers had been chucked carelessly next to the fire, and much of the floor surrounding the sofa was covered with collections of other papers – they looked like some kind of booklets or… they could be scripts, she supposed. She strained to read the writing.

What she could see of the floor was a polished mahogany parquet covered with huge Asian rugs; likewise, the beamed walls were hung with several tapestries and paintings of an abstract nature. Huge patio doors led out to what appeared to be a lawn beyond. A thriller was open on the arm of the sofa beside her and a drinks trolley with half-full bottles of gin and vodka vied with the chairs for space. A few feet away, a huge pouffe acted as a coffee table with piles of rugs and the ubiquitous art house books that only seem to feature in Sunday supplements on ideal living. No photos or anything personal, as far as Charlotte could tell from craning her neck.

The intended effect was of comfort and easy opulence. However, the overriding impression that jumped out at her was one of chaos. More papers were thrown seemingly haphazardly on the pouffe and floor in front of her, and some magazines were spread over another chair. Several glasses and mugs were perched on furniture arms, and she was sure she could see some plates and cutlery sticking out from the side of one chair. No pets, that was for sure, because they would have mangled this lot. Speaking of pets, where was Jake?

The chink of china told her that Max was approaching with tea and, with some effort, she managed to force herself into a sitting position using her good arm. Max passed her a mug of steaming tea the colour of wet sand, just the way she liked it. She raised it carefully to her lips, took a sip and straight away felt a bit better.

Jake wandered through behind Max, sniffing at various piles and chair legs and then, recognising Charlotte, bounded up to her to push his face in hers. Charlotte put her good arm round his neck and buried her face in his damp, doggy smell, trying to ground herself in the familiar sensation. She still couldn't really take in what had happened in the last hour or so. She was starting to feel like a prize idiot, and she really didn't want to go to A&E for what was probably only a sprain. After taking another slug of tea, she tried to regain her composure; the situation seemed to be rapidly spiralling out of her control.

"Max, I'm feeling much better now. It's so kind of you to offer to take me to hospital, but can you just run me home after all? I think I probably just need some rest."

Max looked at her, his eyes widening. "No, I can't, I'm afraid. You're my responsibility, and there's no way I'm letting you go home when your ankle looks like that. Sorry, Charlotte, no can do."

He should have known that the hackles would go up again when she was backed into a corner. *What are you so scared of?* he thought.

Charlotte couldn't believe it; she was trying to be polite, to do this the right way. Why wasn't he taking the hint?

"Look, I'm telling you – I'm not going to hospital. It's stupid! We'll be waiting for years, only for them to tell me that it is fine."

Charlotte felt wrong-footed; she sounded angrier than she meant, but she wasn't having a virtual stranger telling her what to do. Daniel would have accepted this; he would have found the whole affair complete over-kill. He certainly wouldn't have pushed if she didn't want to go.

"I'm not asking, I'm telling you," Max answered with a hint of steel in his voice.

He could have rolled his eyes in frustration, but instead turned and walked out of the room, suavely avoiding the confrontation as usual. She was something else entirely. Nell would have lapped up the fussing. What on earth was her problem? He grabbed the keys of the Range Rover from the pot by the front door and walked back to the sitting room.

"Right, I think you'll have to leave the boot off, don't think we're going to be able to get it on again."

Charlotte bit her tongue and wordlessly started rolling up her sock while Max hovered awkwardly by the sofa.

"I'm sorry, look, I know you're trying to help. It's just… I… I don't particularly like hospitals. Who does? – I know. I've had a few issues recently," she said in a rush. "Sorry," she said in a smaller voice, then, "what about the dog?"

Max carefully helped her out of the chair and said, without eye contact, "I know what you mean, I'm not keen on them either. Jake can wait in the boot room – there's very little to damage in there – unless he's a chewer – and the owners even left a dog basket!"

In an uncomfortable silence, they managed to hobble to the car, both feeling a touch of embarrassment as Charlotte had to be virtually lifted into the passenger seat, sinking into the soft leather and swinging her legs across. She closed her eyes and hoped that the throbbing would ease.

"Addenbrokes is the nearest," she muttered.

"On it," Max responded.

They said little else for the next thirty minutes as Max followed the satnav, negotiating the increasing traffic skilfully and trying hard to make sure that the journey was as smooth as possible. Charlotte used the time to reflect on the novelty of the situation. It hadn't escaped her that Max was preternaturally good-looking, as well as being practically a celebrity, and of course that only made it all worse. She felt such a fool for taking this man away from whatever plans he had made for the rest of his day. What must he think of her? She had been so rude to him, and he was probably just trying to help. Why did she have to fight against everything? Why couldn't she accept that someone was just being kind? She always had to attach an ulterior motive or question whether she was worthy of another's good deeds. Why couldn't she just learn to deal with things gracefully? Some people would kill to be in her place! She was being helped by a film star, no less, who genuinely seemed to want to make sure that she was taken care of, and yet still she was complaining and being as awkward as hell.

She could feel her mood descending further as they rolled down the Gog Magog Hills towards the grey, dominating concrete of the hospital buildings. Despite the bustle of approaching people and the buoyancy of the entry signs, the assorted departments stood out grimly against the gentile 1930s housing that surrounded the hospital. Charlotte had had a university friend who lived on site at the hospital, and she could still dimly remember the labyrinth of hospital tunnels that lay beneath the surface. They had gone to the Flea, as the student bar was affectionately known, to dance and get trashed. She had been carefree then, although she hadn't realised it. Another set of worries, different friends long-since abandoned, but the same Charlotte essentially. *Now look at me.* Changed by some experiences, bowed down by others but still fighting against the current.

Max turned off the engine, opened the glove compartment and pulled out the cap he reserved for this kind of occasion. Charlotte looked curious but didn't comment as he stuffed it on his head, pushing his thatch of hair out of the way and pulling the brim well down.

"Sorry." He tilted his head and met her eyes with a crinkle. "Battle armour. Please don't think I'm being full of myself, but people can be so inappropriate. You wouldn't believe the number of times I've been approached in toilets, of all places!"

"Don't mind me," said Charlotte. "I don't watch it, I'm afraid." She waited, dead pan. "It's good though, or so I'm told." She gave Max what his mum would have called an old-fashioned look, and then a grin burst through like the surprising warmth of a winter sun, and Max realised that she was pulling his leg. He looked down and smiled to himself – that was unexpected.

"Wait here a moment, I'm going to try and wangle a pair of crutches."

He was back in a few minutes with a pair that looked like they had seen better days and worse owners.

They spent the next two and a half hours waiting to be seen by a doctor and finally were ushered into a cubicle by a distracted looking nursing assistant. Max was noticeably uncomfortable and kept shifting position and fidgeting with his hands. He kept adjusting his cap as they sat at the back, out of sight of prying eyes. His mind kept harking back to that last time that they had been in a waiting room with Bella. She had been so distressed; it had been heartbreaking. He had been so conflicted. To help her had felt like a punishment for both of them. He reached up his hand towards his hair and then realised he had his cap on. Charlotte's body was motionless next to him. He cast a look at her, and again was struck by the fleeting resemblance, that slight otherworldliness. He remembered a poem his teacher had recited to them in school and a line came to him now: 'Lying awake, with her wide brown stare'. He remembered that she had mentioned an aversion to hospitals and thought he would try to start talking – anything to escape the interminable boredom.

To begin with, their conversation was stilted, but time and tedium blunted their civility, and they began to make pithy observations about their fellow attendees and village life. Max deliberately tried to keep it light – there was a real prickliness about Charlotte. She clearly shied away from the personal, although she seemed to be interested in his opinions and, more importantly, laughed at his jokes. There were some silences, but neither felt the need to fill them. Charlotte was surprised at how easy it felt. She often felt self-conscious talking to strangers, especially men, and especially when they were this attractive. Maybe it was because there was often a particular kind of arrogance that accompanied those who had been favoured with above average looks. Max didn't seem especially aware of his own charms, however, and his relaxed manner and persistence were difficult to ignore.

"Do you want me to wait outside?" he said in a low voice to Charlotte, as the man covered the couch with the blue paper pulled from the roll at the side and sanitised his hands.

"No, no, please stay with me," she hissed in a voice that threatened to give way to panic. Max positioned himself awkwardly in a chair, as Charlotte was helped onto the couch, given a thorough examination and then instructed to make her way to the X-ray department. Once inside the doors, they found themselves in a new waiting area. A nurse appeared and instructed Charlotte to remove her lower outer garments and dress herself in a hospital gown. "Your boyfriend can hold your things when you're called in for the photo." She smiled at Max. Charlotte didn't even flinch this time; Max had variously been called her boyfriend and husband several times since entering the hospital. He didn't seem to react, and she was more concerned about the imminent removal of her clothes.

It was excruciatingly embarrassing to emerge from the changing room conscious of her bare legs beneath the awful blue tent. Charlotte found herself clutching the gaping flaps close to her skin at the back, thanking the lord that she had applied nail varnish only a couple of weeks ago in an effort to emulate something like a pedicure. Thank goodness Max had had to take a call at this point, murmuring something that sounded like 'Tom' and seeking sanctuary in the hospital corridor. Charlotte was relieved to be reprieved of the forced intimacy for a while.

Finally, after another half hour wait, they exited through the main doors that led to Accident and Emergency. Charlotte was now the proud possessor of a ubiquitous blue sling and an ankle boot that would have looked at home in a ski resort. Her arm was sore but only badly wrenched and she could already feel the pain abating after a strong dose of ibuprofen. The ankle was more awkward but at least not displaced. There was evidence of a crack and rest for up to three weeks had been prescribed by the doctor on duty. Max had long since taken off his cap as the waiting room had cleared and they were among the last to be seen before the evening rush.

"Your boyfriend can walk the dog for the time being," the doctor had joked, and then did a double-take as he recognised Max.

Charlotte almost laughed, his look was so comical.

"Would you mind signing this for my girlfriend?" He waved what looked like a prescription pad in front of Max, who gamely took the proffered pen and tried to conjure up a witty comment.

"Thanks, mate, and I hope your girlfriend gets better soon. Love the series!"

"Thank you." Max shook his hand. "You've got the hard work here."

"I'm not..." Charlotte began, but the doctor was already backing out of the cubicle with a smile as Max proffered a hand and gently helped Charlotte off the bed. "I really owe you." Charlotte looked him squarely in the face. "You didn't have to do any of this and having to do that autograph when you've tried so hard to go incognito... You are entitled to explore the countryside on your bike without being accosted by a mad woman and her dog!"

"You can repay me by buying us a takeaway," Max answered, pulling his cap firmly down as he yanked the curtain open and held out the crutches for Charlotte. "I'm absolutely starving, and I bet you are too. There's no way you'll be able to cook at home tonight, and it would be nice to find out a bit about the area from a real local, especially one who's under the age of fifty!"

Charlotte took the crutches he handed her, digesting what he had just said, and following his tall frame as he led the way out of the double doors at the front of the hospital. A brisk passage of thoughts made their way through her head... *a takeaway? Where? Back at his*, she supposed. *Hope Jake hasn't chewed anything; it wouldn't be unknown!* She was being pushed into a level of intimacy that would have been unusual for her with friends she had known for years. She suddenly realised that Daniel hadn't even passed her mind for the last few hours; she should really give him a call. *Still, I guess he'll be phoning me later.* A niggle of disloyalty passed through her as she met Max's eyes when he turned to check she was following him.

FIVE

"Soooo," Charlotte slurred, sloshing her drink vigorously as she plonked the glass down on the wooden floor beside her, "I've known you properly for lesh than a day, and you've probably seen me at my worsh, flat out and then in a hoshpital gown! Itsh not fair… I need some dirt on you now, or are you just a pretty facsh?"

As soon as the words left her lips, Charlotte knew she had perhaps betrayed more than she wanted to; she always went a bit too far when in this state. The wine was deliciously cold and crisp, and she felt very pleasantly inebriated, like she was floating on a cloud of cotton wool.

"And whash it like being a film star, an actor?" She was genuinely interested; reality seemed still very much in abeyance.

She had taken Max to the best takeaway in town, in hers and Daniel's opinion, and he had been suitably impressed, but she still felt slightly guilty that he had insisted on paying for the privilege of her treating him to pizza – did that even make sense?

"There's no dirt – I'm an open book." Max looked on from the chair he was sprawled in, entertained, but with slight trepidation. He wondered if the painkillers were reacting with the drink; that, or she was exceptionally lightweight. Should he be telling her to go easy? She didn't seem to have had that much. The evening had been fun, and it had seemed natural to open a bottle of wine to toast the safe return home. He hoped that his comments didn't appear too flirty; he had taken stock of the wedding ring during the first ten minutes of their acquaintance. Everything seemed to take on a double meaning after a couple of drinks.

"As for acting, well, you probably know it all. It's been a long slog, but now I've got a foot in the American market, the world will be my oyster." The last was said with a grandiose bow and some elaborate hand-waving.

Charlotte giggled obligingly though her eyes were half-closed.

The trouble was, Max speculated, he still knew pretty much nothing about Charlotte, despite what she had said and what had been left unsaid. And where was this husband of hers? She had ignored his call earlier, sending him a text and pretending not to hear Max when he offered to leave the room. How was she going to cope at home on her own? Should he offer for her to stay here tonight? He looked over and realised that the decision had been taken out of his hands. One hand was dangling limply over the side of the sofa and Charlotte's head lolled loosely to the side. He could hear her faint breathing and grabbed the dog as it looked like he was going to jump up and join her.

"Here, boy, you had better come with me." Jake was delighted to be reunited with them and had enjoyed his own slice of pizza. "Come on, let's spend a penny and then you can go back in your basket."

He pitched himself out of the chair as quietly as possible, draped a couple of blankets carefully over Charlotte, and adjusted some cushions to support her head.

He couldn't resist looking at her for a few minutes, although it felt a little voyeuristic somehow. She was the other type to Nell, one of those who didn't like to be looked at or admired. He guessed that she was about his age; it was always hard to tell with women. She hadn't got the stuff that Nell caked on her face, and he liked her better for it. She looked even younger in repose, and he had a strange urge to kiss her goodnight like he would have done to Dom or Vivi. Instead, he whispered, feeling more inebriated than he had realised, "'The brown / The brown of her – her eyes, her hair, her hair!'" She did look a bit like a pre-Raphaelite heroine with her hair all splayed out like that. He put a light hand out and touched it – slippery, alive somehow. A momentary shiver passed over him and he stepped away, the spell broken.

A few taps on his phone and the lights went into night-time mode with only the staircase and landing lit-up faintly. Another two taps and the doors were locked and alarm set. *I'll ring the kids upstairs*, Max thought. *They'll probably still be up, knowing Nell.*

***

My fucking giddy aunt. Charlotte dragged herself up to look in the mirror and was frankly appalled. She looked like she had the main part in a horror film – white skin, black eyes, hair everywhere and, let's face it, she was going to look a hundred times worse in the morning. Bursting for the loo, she had managed to navigate the humongous downstairs and find a huge bathroom, although that was only because the curtains hadn't been drawn and, as luck would have it, there was a full moon. She had had a frightening moment where she just had not known where she was. Now it had all come flooding back with a vengeance and it was possibly even worse than she had imagined – what the hell was she playing at?

It felt like she was stuck in some kind of surrealist nightmare on a loop, except that every single one of her senses were alerting her that unfortunately she was very much in the here and now. In some kind of millionaire's getaway with some actor she knew next to nothing about. Yes, he was kind and had helped her, but what was she doing passing time with him? She was nearly forty, for goodness' sake; this was the kind of thing she hadn't done when she was twenty, or thirty, or ever! God, she was so thirsty. *Wonder where the kitchen is?*

In the end, she had to content herself with drinking from the tap. The bathroom was one of those awful minimalist affairs where the cupboards appeared to be concealed and everything worked through sensors. Thank goodness the light came on when she walked in.

Charlotte hobbled back to the lounge and sank back into the warmth of the sofa with a mixture of gratitude and guilt. She hadn't phoned Daniel back either. She hoped he wasn't worrying. Mulling over quite what she was going to admit to him, she drifted into an uneasy sleep.

***

Charlotte awoke again to the smell of frying bacon and the cheerful sound of Radio 1. For a moment, she was taken back to childhood and Dad making breakfast at the weekend. She half-expected to hear his voice calling up the stairs for her to hurry up. She allowed herself the indulgence of missing him for a few minutes. Then a low buzz on her phone brought her back to reality. She checked the time and realised that her interrupted night had actually meant that she had slept in – it was nearly 10.00a.m. Then she remembered Daniel. Scrabbling for her phone, its screen confirmed that he was probably just a bit concerned. She quickly dialled his number, mentally composing what she was going to say.

"Hi, Daniel, sorry I didn't call last night."

"Charlotte, didn't you see I was trying to get hold of you?"

"Only really late at night. I had rather a dramatic day. I'm fine, but I did end up in A&E!"

"Whaat? Are you okay?"

"Yes, yes, luckily a neighbour helped me. It was bloody Jake again. He pulled me over up top near the farm but luckily there was this bloke on a motorbike and he took me to hospital."

"Hospital? On a motorbike?"

"No, not on the motorbike – by car. He's staying at the barn. So, anyway, I've just wrenched my shoulder. They gave me a sling, but it feels much better now," she lied. "I have a bit of a crack in my ankle, but they don't want to plaster it or anything because it's not out of shape. So I just have to wear this awful boot thing for three weeks or so."

"How are you going to cope with all this on your own?" Daniel tried not to sound cross, but his concern was coming out all wrong. He couldn't stop a trace of irritation creeping into his voice. He was at work, for goodness' sake. He had hardly been gone a day, and already there had been some drama.

"I'll manage. It's fine. They said that I can walk on it soon, just as soon as the swelling goes down. It feels much better today even. I can maybe ask Max to take the dog out sometimes."

"Max is the neighbour, is he? How come we've never met him before?"

"I think he's leasing the big barn." Charlotte lowered her voice. She really hoped that Max wasn't listening to any of this.

"Christ! Must be loaded!" Daniel's anger eased slightly. "Well, I've got to go and see a client now. I'll phone you again this evening. Do you want me to let Mum know so she can bring you some meals or something?"

"No!" It was Charlotte's turn to be sharp. "I'll be fine, Daniel. Not after last weekend. Please. It was bad enough that you got Mum to ring. Don't interfere. I'll be fine on my own."

"I'm just trying to look after you," Daniel ended with an exasperated sigh. "Gotta go now, anyway. I'm taking people out for lunch. Bye, Charlotte. Love you." As soon as he said it, it hung there, conspicuously present, like a habit he couldn't break.

"Love you," Charlotte said hurriedly and clicked the phone off just as Max came into the room.

"Morning! Do you want a bacon sandwich?" Max looked annoyingly chipper considering how much they had drunk the night before. He had a green hoodie on and running shorts and his hair was plastered back, obviously freshly showered. Charlotte tried not to look at his legs, holding the blanket as high as she could under her chin as if to ward him off.

"Yes, please," she croaked, trying to transmit a 'don't look at me, I feel like shit' vibe, but he had already left the room.

They ate breakfast in an uncomplicated silence. Max was scrolling through his phone, and Charlotte started picking through some of the papers at her feet.

"Do you mind if I have a look at these, or are they top secret?" she asked, seeing the odd word jumping out at her.

"Feel free," Max answered absent-mindedly, and Charlotte curled up as best she could with the padded boot and started to read. There were probably about twenty different scripts jumbled together, which someone had marked with post-its pointing out various sections – *Strong male lead*; *Anti-hero potential*; *LBGTQ+ appeal*.

"What do you think?" he asked her, after ten minutes had passed and she had paused only to sip her coffee and collect the last crumbs from her plate with a wet fingertip. It was fascinating seeing someone so absorbed in what they were doing. She was completely still apart from her eyes going back and forth across the page.

"Mmmm, not sure about this one, but the sci-fi film has a great beginning, a lot of human interest. The main character's got a really interesting back story." She trailed off to see Max looking at her with an unreadable expression. "Haven't you read any of these yet?"

Max looked away and made a split-second decision to air his well-rehearsed explanation. "I'm dyslexic, really dyslexic. I have to get someone to record them for me, so that I can listen to them and learn them like that initially. It's a bit of a pain, and my agent, even after working with me for five years, still hasn't fully understood yet that I just don't do words on a page."

So this is the real Max, thought Charlotte. This was the little hollow of vulnerability. It was alright; he wasn't perfect after all. She searched her brain for something to say.

"We always taught at school that being dyslexic was a bit of a superpower in some ways – you know, all those famous, highly successful people who are dyslexic. We did assemblies on it. It was actually quite inspiring."

"I don't know about that." Max seemed to know what she was trying to do and looked steadily at her with what Charlotte felt was close to irritation. "I don't need encouragement. It's just something that I have to deal with."

I've offended him, Charlotte thought, realising with surprise that part of her actually cared. What could she say to make him realise that she hadn't meant to be patronising?

"I love reading," she said slowly. "Painting and reading and drawing. Not necessarily in that order. I don't know what I would do if I couldn't read. I read the cornflake packets at the table if there is nothing else to do. Often, I would rather read than talk to someone else – usually, in fact." She tried to smile at Max and his jaw softened.

"Wow, I'm honoured then. You were talking a lot last night."

"You're easy to talk to." Charlotte felt a little embarrassed. This wasn't how she had expected the conversation would go. "Some people don't care about anyone else but themselves – it feels like an exchange of views with you, at least. Reading makes you live many lives, doesn't it? Well, stories, I guess. You must feel that too with what you do." How could she explain what she meant? "I feel that reading makes me appreciate life more, lets me experience things beyond myself. I suppose books have been a bit of a raft to hold onto when I have felt really down."

"I guess that's why I act. In my family, a lot of value was placed on academic success, but I was never going to be able to attain that. I felt I let my parents down in a way. I'm not particularly sporty, can't read properly, my writing is grim but, like you say, I can give people a sense of solidarity, make them feel a bit of empathy with others at least."

"They must be really proud of you," Charlotte said, with genuine admiration. "You've done so well."

"Yes," Max said flatly; he couldn't possibly explain the full picture, how his parents didn't even want to look at him. Charlotte watched a shadow pass over his face and wondered where the jovial Max of earlier had disappeared to.

"I'm sorry. You don't have to explain anything to me – I'm just being nosy. I haven't even got a proper job anymore, so you are immensely successful compared to me. The truth is I'm a supply teacher, so now you know what true failure is." Her tone was ironic, but with a raw edge of self-loathing. "You know, 'those who can, do, those who can't, teach'. Those who can't even teach become a supply teacher." Charlotte now tried to rise. "And I should get home, to have a shower if nothing else."

"Oh... yeah, okay." Max felt surprisingly drained. It felt like they had covered more ground in twenty-four hours than he had with some friends in twenty-four years. "I'll drive you."

He helped her up and went to grab Jake. "He's been walked. I took him round the garden this morning. It's like a small field, so he was happy."

"I'll bet. You've been so kind." Charlotte felt a rush of gratitude. "We don't know that many people here, you know what it's like when you are both in full-time jobs, not that I am at the moment. I guess I've been a bit of a hermit, really, for the past eighteen months."

"That's okay. I've enjoyed talking to you." Max meant it. He felt like he had been eviscerated, but in a good way. It had been quite cathartic really.

***

The drive down to the main village took less than five minutes. Both Max and Charlotte were quiet, not quite sure how to regain the easy companionship of last night.

"Let me know if you would like me to walk the dog at any time," Max said at the house. "I'll give you my mobile," he said in a rush of inspiration.

"Oh, okay, hold on." Charlotte rummaged round in the drawers next to the front door; a sharpie – great – but no paper.

"Give me your hand."

Charlotte hesitantly reached out her hand towards him with an unidentifiable look on her face.

Max took it firmly in his and wrote the twelve digits on the back. Her skin was slightly cold, and he felt an urge to grasp it tighter, to warm it somehow.

"Make sure you write them down somewhere else too," he warned, laughing.

Charlotte felt herself grow uncomfortably hot and pulled her hand back more quickly than she had intended. Max, normally at ease with himself, could sense a scarcely detectable undercurrent just below the surface. He tried to detract from the situation by pulling something out of his pockets.

"Your gloves, milady." He bowed with an exaggerated flourish. "'Twas a pleasure to be of service."

"Oh, them. I'd forgotten."

The walk of the week before seemed like a lifetime ago. Charlotte suddenly felt bereft. He was going to say goodbye in a few seconds and that would be that.

"Goodbye, Max, and thanks again." The words came out of her mouth robotically. The door shut like a full stop, and she collapsed in the hall chair while Jake ran off sniffing.

A minute passed and still she sat there, drained. Then, suddenly, there was a loud knocking and she almost jumped out of her skin.

"Okay, coming!" she raised her voice. It continued, and she stumbled with the lock. "Okay, I said… Max!"

"Charlotte, why don't you come and work for me?"

SIX

Several hours had passed. Charlotte could think of little else but Max's proposal. She couldn't decide whether it was a lifeline or if she had made the whole thing up.

"I need someone to scan the scripts and give me the main points, so that I can decide whether they're going to suit or not. Then it's a case of reading them out loud. It's quicker for me to learn it like that. You'd be ideal, being a teacher and liking reading. You could weed out the crap in no time. And it would be really handy if you could liaise with my agent, Della. She tries to get me involved in publicity – you know, the press and Instagram and all that rubbish – but I just can't organise myself. I need someone to handle my calendar, book flights, et cetera, be a kind of PA, I guess... that's if you're interested?"

"I- I don't know," Charlotte stuttered. He had completely caught her by surprise. "I'll have to think about it. Can I get back to you?"

"We can discuss pay later." Max was realising that this may be more complicated that he had first thought. The idea had literally just popped into his head when he had recalled how engrossed Charlotte had become in the script earlier. He couldn't explain why he had turned round and come back to the house; it was if he had been if he had been drugged. He could hardly remember the point at which he had turned or how he had got here. He felt somewhat dazed.

"Look, why don't you ring me tomorrow, or later? I'm not going anywhere." He wasn't usually this impulsive – Bella had always been the one who had acted instinctively, without thinking.

Even with crutches, Charlotte had restlessly paced the downstairs, her thoughts a maelstrom of ifs and buts. She eventually lowered herself in a scalding bathtub and lay back to work out what she was going to do. Financially, they weren't dependent on her income by any means. Daniel might have been put out when she had finally jumped the sinking ship of her teaching career, but she was pretty sure that that had more to do with his concerns about her mental health rather than disappointment over her lack of aspiration or resilience.

Could she work for Max? He would be her boss. She didn't know him well, but there was something there that made her feel an affinity with him, nebulous but undeniable. She was also intrigued; it was such a different life to her own. What did a film star do to make a living exactly, apart from the obvious? It seemed too exciting an opportunity to refuse.

But she was going to have to tackle the elephant in the room. Did it matter that there was a faint but definite attraction to her potential employer? How would Daniel feel if he knew that Max's eyes seemed to have the power to clench her stomach and that his touch seemed to fan a flame that had all but extinguished? She didn't mean romance or sex, even; it was deeper than that – a more unsettling emotion which had long lain dormant and which was causing her to make choices that took even herself by surprise.

She closed her eyes and allowed her mind to wander. A long, long time ago, she had made the decision to follow a postgrad degree in education instead of pursuing her childhood passion of art school and whatever might lie beyond. She wasn't a risk taker – she was too readily overtaken by anxiety, and it had taken a disappointing degree show for her to cast her back on what had absorbed her for much of her teenage years.

Now she painted in her spare time – or had done: trees and sky mostly – that certain light between branches, the contrast between sky and form, the elusive variations of blue and green, impossible to capture but incontestably visible. The landscape both frustrated and consumed her. She couldn't explain her obsession and cared not to anyway.

Charlotte opened her eyes and found them focussing on a small oil painting opposite the open door of the bathroom, painted when she was eighteen or so. Her tutor had told her that he foresaw a bright future for her, and she had been filled with hope and ambition. Could this be hers again, if she freed herself from the treadmill of teaching? She felt something akin to hope enter her veins, and dared to let her mind continue to wander for a few minutes more.

***

Max had been creating and then deleting an Instagram post when Charlotte phoned. He felt such a twat, trying to create pithy one-liners to accompany the over-posed studio stills that Della insisted form the bulk of his posts. His phone started ringing the familiar tune, and he picked it up without checking the number, assuming it was either Nell or the children.

"Hiya," he said nonchalantly, his attention half on the picture on his laptop, a toe-curlingly trite view of his bare chest as he worked out – in character, of course. Max found the gym excruciatingly boring and only ventured there if a role contractually specified it.

"Er, is that Max?"

Max's pulse skipped a beat, and he drew himself up. "Charlotte. How are you?"

"Yes, okay. Leg still intact, and better for a bath. I wanted to speak to you about the job. I will do it. How many hours do you think it will be for?"

"You will?" Max wondered if it was totally professional that he felt so pleased. Why should he keep the warmth out of his voice? "That's great, Charlotte. I guess it will probably just be mornings, generally. And I didn't mention pay. I was thinking about £17 an hour? I've Googled it and I think that's about right? I know it's not as much as teaching, but I could offer overtime if you had to work out of office hours."

Charlotte did a few figures in her head. She presumed that worked out as about £35,000 on full hours, having already looked up average pay for PAs herself. It wasn't quite as much as she earnt at the moment, but she would be free to paint in the afternoons, and it was so near to home. Sod it, it was up to her. She could always go back to teaching.

"When do I start?"

"Tomorrow? I know it's a Friday, but my diary really needs sorting for the next couple of months and you can see all the bollocks I have to go through and organise. 10.00a.m.?"

"I'll start at 9.00a.m. if you don't mind. I'd like to finish by 12.00p.m. Does that suit you?"

"Yes, of course." If Max was taken aback by her temerity, he didn't show it. "I'll look forward to seeing you then, Charlotte."

The phone clicked and Max realised that he was still holding it to his ear. He felt a little stunned. Had he really expected her to fall for his ruse? Yes, of course he needed a PA, but it had felt a bit more than that. Something had stultified within him since Bella's death. Yes, he had done very well professionally, but by playing one type of character alone: the anti-hero with a chequered past and equally flawed character. He was playing himself, the true self that he knew lay beneath the outer charm and light-heartedness. His mercurial ability to portray a completely different personality had dried up along with the flowers that had lain on Bella's grave. He had remembered crying when he had seen the solitary bouquet left by his parents, positioned on the earth before the headstone had come. The petals had dried to confetti like a sick joke for a lost future. Something in Charlotte spoke to him of his sister. It meant something and he couldn't ignore it.

***

It felt strangely formal the next morning when Charlotte phoned Max to ask him to pick her up.

"I feel so stupid; the ankle's much better, but I don't think I had better walk that far for a few days."

"Christ, no, I should have offered myself."

Max rolled out of bed hurriedly and dragged on a t-shirt, tracksuit bottoms and hoodie. In less than a minute, the

Range Rover was purring down the hill, and Charlotte was waiting anxiously by the front window.

"You're not overdoing it, I hope?" Max looked pointedly at Charlotte's ankle.

"No, Dad." She rolled her eyes. "The doctor did say that I could leave the boot off when I wanted. It feels much better today, and my shoulder barely hurts at all, lucky it was the left one."

That morning was a whirl of firsts. Charlotte was introduced to Della via a video call. Brightly coloured all over, with a rather nasal transatlantic drawl, an assertive pair of glasses and look of studied non-animation, she reminded Charlotte of the headteacher in her first job. Like Max, Charlotte detected a bravado in her manner. She was quietly amused to see Della's surprise and then poorly disguised delight that someone else was able to take over Max's schedule for her, although with an edge of jealousy – it was important that Charlotte wasn't able to do the job too well. Once she had realised that, although Charlotte had a degree, her academic background was decidedly unthreatening with no previous experience of the theatre or film industry, she relaxed a little.

"It's nice to see that Max is finally taking himself seriously," she confided in Charlotte. "With your help, we can get him out there properly. I'll send you a list of links to journalists who I think you should introduce yourself to. What's your email?"

"Er… I'll send it to you in a minute." Charlotte thought on her feet, realising that she would have to create a professional one now.

"Good, I'll also email you the list of guest lists that Max is on for the next four weeks. He's off the radar just until the end of this week, but I've got some important events lined up after that, and it's essential he's aware of these. There's an appointment with a stylist too. I don't want him turning up in a t-shirt and jeans again; that would be totally damaging."

"Would it?" Charlotte said limply.

"Max's image is very important," came the stern reply. "He's a serious player now – he could have his pick of parts if we play the next twelve months right. Although, I must say, he seems hellbent on putting every obstacle in my path he can."

"What…?" Charlotte began, and then tailed off as the subject of their conversation entered the main room, perspiring heavily and wiping his brow with a towel.

"Aah, Max." Della caught sight of her quarry. "Glad to see you've taken the character spec seriously. A run, was it?"

"Sadly, yes," Max said dryly. "Della, I'm going to steal Charlotte away from you now. I need to go through a few things with her."

"Oh… sure." Della couldn't hide the disappointment in her voice, but quickly covered with a gushing, "Bye then, darlings. Same time on Monday, please, Charlotte. I like to catch up with each of my crew at the beginning and end of each week. We can go through the diary and sort out any other appointments."

"No problem, Della. See you then." Charlotte pressed the 'Leave' in the corner of the window and shut the laptop carefully. She looked at Max expectantly.

"Sorry, she can be rather officious."

Max plonked himself down on the sofa and uncoiled like a cat. His t-shirt rode up slightly to show a lean pale stomach. Charlotte wrenched her gaze away and the bracelet on his wrist again caught her eye. It was mounted with turquoise and tiger eye stones not dissimilar to the colour of his eyes.

"You'd been on that call for almost an hour. Let me show you round the house, so you know where everything is. You can't work on the sofa. We'll have to find you a room. I'll just hop into the shower, I must stink."

Charlotte resisted the urge to sniff and busied herself with creating a new email – seldonpa@gmail.com – and a Google calendar for Max. There were a number of events to put in over the month: interviews; a premiere of a film – unusual title, probably a Sundance one; the appointment with the stylist; a hair-cut; even a medical examination.

Max appeared just as she had entered the last date and she gladly got up and followed him slowly up the stairs. He didn't turn round, taking two steps at a time with his long stride, but she managed to make her own way with no help.

"Oh, Charlotte, I'm so sorry. What a muppet." He palmed his head in a mock scolding and waited for her to get to the top.

"No, I'm fine." And she was if she kept the ankle rigid. Going upstairs was better than going down.

He went along the landing much more slowly, gesturing through open doors.

"Guest bathroom, spare bedroom, home office – this would be good for you, Charlotte."

She was led through the door into a generously sized room facing out to the view she loved.

"This is amazing," she murmured. "You can see for miles, can't you?"

She stood there reverently for a few seconds, tracking the lane as it glistened faintly in the feeble winter light.

Max touched her arm. "That's nothing. Take a look at this."

She followed him back to the landing and then through double doors into the master suite. Faint sunlight flooded into the large dual-aspect room, and, despite the unmade large bed, Charlotte's gaze was immediately drawn to the right of the room where a pair of open glass doors led to a balcony.

"Come and have a look." Max eagerly led her through the doorway and Charlotte was overwhelmed by the sudden immersion into the dipping landscape in front of her. An ancient copse of trees framed the private pasture, merging into the fields beyond, untidily delineated by meandering lines of hedgerows and shrubs. It was so peaceful here; they seemed to be in a slight valley cushioned from all other traces of human existence. Thick swathes of clouds were shot through with ridges of light from the January sun. Patches of shadow were suddenly lifted, and the white sphere was revealed with the shifting cumulus.

"I've seen deer in the morning." Max could feel her satisfaction. "Normal and muntjac; had to look them up. They look so comical with their tails in the air. Several times I've caught sight of a fox too. At night, slinking across the garden. I think the farm has some chickens."

"I don't think I'd be able to leave this spot." Charlotte breathed deeply. "You are lucky."

"I know," Max said ruefully, "I just didn't realise it was quite so remote. This view was what sold it to me."

He stopped. He had almost mentioned Nell. He didn't know why, but it wasn't time to cross that particular hurdle yet. It was simple and unspoilt at the moment; he was in no rush to complicate matters.

"I'd better get on." Charlotte suddenly felt uncomfortable. She sensed that Max was on the cusp of something. "I'll take my things up to the home office. I think that would be ideal, if you don't mind."

"Yes, sure," Max said hurriedly. "I'll also bring you the phone. There is a landline, but not enough handsets. There's one here, you can take it in with you, and I'll get you a mobile next time I'm out."

He turned and looked absent-mindedly out towards the grounds again. There were some slightly darker clouds in the east, the scarcely perceptible hint of a storm ahead. He reluctantly closed the doors and followed Charlotte out of the room.

SEVEN

The next few weeks settled into a pattern for both Max and Charlotte. Charlotte was surprised to find that she fell easily into her new role as secretary and something of a confidante, she felt. Contacts of Max were reassured by her direct and intelligent manner, and she found herself connecting with several of them. Occasionally, she had to pinch herself – she was working in conditions to which previously she wouldn't even have aspired, with a man who was both urbane and disarmingly down to earth, and liaising with people who moved in the cultural circles of which she had only dreamt. Yes, they had the same flaws as everybody else, but she was in an adult world and her mind felt occupied and on a new voyage full of discovery and self-awareness. She felt lifted out of her own mundanity and on the cusp of something new and bold.

Charlotte had always enjoyed the weekly round-up of media reviews and so it was no great leap to be interrogated by Della on these and the ubiquitous calendar. She was fascinated and appalled in equal amounts by the requirement of assisting Max with his scripts and screenplays. She was secretly impressed by his erudition: it was not enough for him to simply hear the words of the script, he liked to dissect the characters and language with almost visceral delight – making voice notes, dictating memos to himself and his director, until the background and motivation lay in pieces.

He analysed the writing to the point of argument. Then, if he was attracted to a part, he threw himself into the role with an intensity which was all-consuming. Gone were the light-hearted banter and repartee; Max walked round the house muttering darkly, preoccupied and distant. Charlotte was taken aback by this transformation. There was an edge to his humour at times, and he seemed to revel in the depths to which he was often asked to plummet.

"Why aren't you auditioning for anyone nice?" Charlotte asked, a week or two in.

Max had been preparing a monologue for a three-part BBC crime drama where he wanted to get the part of a particularly unpleasant sexual predator, albeit one with a nuanced childhood of loss and trauma.

"Oh, villains are far more fun," he batted back, lazily, although Charlotte detected a slight stiffening to his back. He looked at Charlotte with an apologetic grin playing at the corners of his eyes.

She pushed harder. "I mean, I don't know what would be more challenging. You're obviously not like these men at all, so I get that it must be fun to explore the darkness and all that, but this character is so revolting. Are you not revolted too?"

Max looked away from her. He spoke quietly. "I guess I must be plundering something in my own psyche then. Occasionally, I find it a release. Not the sex part, that's been difficult, but the fact that there are no limits. I am in control and yet I can be angry and behave as if there are no boundaries. Oh, I don't know, Charlotte. Don't psychoanalyse me, please."

They were strolling round the large back garden, which they had taken to doing at lunchtimes. Max had encouraged Charlotte to bring Jake with her each day, and she had gratefully accepted his invitation, feeling guilty at her own inability to be a fully functioning dog owner at present. It was a good excuse to stretch their legs at lunchtime and, besides, Jake reminded Max of his own childhood companion, Ludo, a boisterous and over-excited springer spaniel who oozed affection and disaster in equal amounts.

Charlotte had now put aside her crutches and was able to walk slowly but comfortably without the boot as long as they didn't go too far. She couldn't stop herself opening up chink by chink to Max and they had discovered a mutual love of music, art and the outdoors. Max was well-travelled and entertaining, but it was his genuine interest in others that made it easy for him to draw Charlotte out so that she hardly realised what she was divulging now that he had penetrated her armour. The tie she had felt initially to Max was slowly strengthening and binding them together. She sensed now that she had gone too far, pushing that newfound kinship towards fraying point. She knew she had hurt his feelings somehow, delved a little too deeply and uncovered something too raw.

She called the dog to her and busied herself putting him back on his lead. Max was standing facing the coppice at the end of the garden, monolithic and unusually introspective.

"Sorry, Max." She took a few paces towards him and touched his jumper tentatively. It was something she hadn't allowed herself to do as a rule; they were friendly, but he was her boss, and she tried not to forget it. The jumper was expensively soft in contrast with the solid mass beneath. "That was rude; I shouldn't have been so bloody nosy. I'm no psychiatrist. I was just thinking aloud, that's all."

Max swivelled round and looked at her without looking. It was as if something had been closed off.

"Don't worry, please. This is just how I get when I'm working on a role, cranky as hell." His lips smiled but his eyes were blank.

Charlotte walked by his side back to the house. The truth was that she had her own demons to face at the moment. She was painting again. Finally. Last weekend, completely alone and feeling more hopeful and at peace than she had done for a long, long time, Charlotte had ventured to the workshop-cum-summer house that Daniel once had optimistically described as her studio.

In the first years of their marriage, he had laid electricity and running water to the wooden cabin and inserted a large picture window facing the fields that lay beyond their modest garden. Now Charlotte had been taken aback when she had pushed open the slightly warped door and was met by the stagnating aroma of damp wood and mustiness. There was a thick layer of dust covering every surface. Abandoned canvases lay roughly stacked and her easel was spread-eagled on the floor, abandoned, she dimly remembered, in a fit of temper.

Charlotte had spent the morning collecting together her paints and making a list of supplies to order from Amazon. She cleaned the window and was rewarded by the pink lights of the late afternoon sky gently illuminating the trees at the bottom of the garden in a palette of rose, cochineal and lilac. The landscape was highlighted with a luminosity that set the foliage into relief.

Instinctively, she grabbed a pad from a stiff drawer and turned to a clean sheet of paper. She used a watercolour tray to wash and then capture the last lights of day. It took a mere half hour to finish the impression but, for Charlotte, this small picture represented a tiny but definite step forward. Twice more this week she had returned to the shed and had even started a larger oil piece, painting over an abandoned dystopic scene from that dark time when she thought her creative spark might have disappeared forever.

Friday was two days before Daniel returned home from yet another work trip, this one to Ireland of all places. Charlotte had planned to leave Max's promptly at 12.00p.m. in order to fit in some painting before a grand clear-up and re-stock of the house. She had warned Max of her intentions at the beginning of the morning. He had not said much, although she sensed that he was curious about her home life with Daniel, whom she had deliberately hardly mentioned.

Charlotte had had a long and entertaining three-way conversation with Davido, Max's stylist, that morning. There were some big theatrical awards next Thursday, and Max was presenting an award for best newcomer in a principal role. Max himself professed to be thoroughly bored by the prospect, but Della had briefed Charlotte thoroughly on the importance of this well-regarded event and she was taking it seriously even if he wasn't.

"I've boooked you in for a feetting at Paul Smeeth's on Saturday afternoon," Davido said sternly. "Don't bother questioning eet. You also need a treem and we need to dicide what you are doing with that truly 'orrific facial 'air."

Charlotte couldn't help but smother a giggle. She had tried to ignore Max's increasingly less designer and more vagrant-inspired stubble and was glad to see that someone else shared her opinion.

"Dave, you know I've got a perfectly suitable black tie suit already," Max said, blithely disinterested. "In fact, make that three."

"Are you sirious?" Davido spluttered. "They are out of date, and 'ideous, man. Do you want them to theenk you are a joke? Do you want to be taken siriously as an 'ollywood star?"

"Really?" Max raised his eyebrows. "For fuck's sake, Dave, they don't care what I wear! I could turn up wearing nothing! In fact, that's a good idea; they'd love that at the *Daily Mail*!" He threw back his chair in mock frustration.

"Davido is right, you know. A lot of people will be there or watching on television. I think it's important to look good, and Della has made her thoughts…"

Charlotte broke off as there came a sudden squeal of brakes outside, car doors opening and slamming and the sound of a child crying. She looked at Max with a growing sense of unease as she saw an anxious expression flit across his face momentarily before he regained control.

"Yes, yes, fine. Whatever!" He reached over and hurriedly closed the laptop, then got up and walked over to the window of the office. "Should have known Nell wouldn't be able to stay away."

"Nell?"

Charlotte got up and followed his retreating figure slowly down the stairs, hanging back not just because of the leg.

With a girlish squeal of 'Max!', a tall woman moved in a languid manner over the threshold, pulling a tear-stained child with her in one hand and a brightly coloured plastic suitcase in another. Following them was an older girl, probably around seven or eight, whom Charlotte recognised as being in that painful pre-adolescent stage with its accompanying emergence of self-consciousness. She trailed nervously over the threshold after her mother, her eyes darting to and fro. The woman was stunningly attractive, Charlotte saw that in a flash. The angular frame resembled that of a model's and her navy blazer and artfully frayed jeans could easily be part of what fashion editors loved to describe as a capsule wardrobe.

As she stood, her head given an aura by the light from the large glass doors to her right, her presence dominated the room. Facially, she was by any standards quite beautiful. Hair, delicately waved in Grace Kelly-style locks, framed grey eyes; a perfectly proportioned nose; and full well-shaped lips, all strategically enhanced by the kind of make-up that looks perversely as though none has been applied. Her skin was the honeyed shade that spoke of Caribbean vacations and expensive facials and the only blemish a slight, although suspiciously uncreased, frown as her gaze quickly took in the fact that Max was being followed by another woman. The three were clearly all related with striking flaxen hair and Charlotte realised, with a bolt of recognition, that the children shared the clear open features of their father.

"Max," the woman said, elongating the vowel like a caress, and her steely eyes met Charlotte's across the room. She stepped forwards and deliberately kissed Max full on the lips. "Gotcha!" she whispered under her breath.

He recoiled too late; the damage had been done.

"Daddy," the younger child cried, and Max scooped the boy up in a bear hug, glad to disguise the flash of anger he had felt as Nell once again manoeuvred him into an impossible position. He reached for Vivi too and clasped her to him. Nell and her endless games. He might have guessed she would behave like this.

Charlotte took the opportunity to step forward, hoping to exit as soon as possible. She was finding it hard to contain the feelings that were simmering within her. Children? Why hadn't he told her? And who was this woman – his wife? She looked familiar too, must be another actress. Were they still together?

Max got there first, gently setting down the children and measuring his words carefully.

"Nell," he repeated, recovering his poise. "This is Charlotte, my new PA. Charlotte, this is Nell, er, Dom and Vivi's mother."

"Nice to meet you, Nell." Charlotte could not meet her eyes. She felt out of place and embarrassed by her rising anger. "I'm sorry, I have to go, Max. See you on Monday."

She couldn't even look at the children. It was pathetic, but too painful. Pushing past the family, as she now termed them in her mind, she hurried through the still open door.

"Hey," Max called. "Wait for me, I'm just coming."

No, no, no, Charlotte thought frantically, *I don't want this. Not now.* She blinked furiously and strode determinedly down the gravel drive, clenching her teeth with each twinge of her useless ankle.

"Stop, *stop!*" Max overtook her in four strides and blocked her way. He didn't know what to do. He knew he should have said something, but this seemed more than just anger at being misled. Jealousy, is that what it was? Distress radiated from her, and he could have sworn that she was near to tears. *Damn it, Charlotte.*

He put his hands on her shoulders and half pulled her to face him, but she wrenched herself from his grasp like his hands were red-hot pokers, and hissed, "Just leave it, Max. I will be fine. I don't want to talk about it. Just drive me home and go back to your family."

***

The journey passed in silence but, as they drew up to the house, Max turned to Charlotte and addressed the back of her head.

"Nell is the mother of my children, but it isn't what you seem to think. We split up eighteen months ago, and I wouldn't have described it as a one-on-one relationship even before that."

Charlotte slowly turned and faced him. Her eyes were the blackest black, all light extinguished.

"It's not that." Her tone was cold yet there was a passion beneath her words. "You think I care about that?"

She was lying. There had been something as she watched the display of possession, but she wanted to hurt, as she had been hurt again and again when she saw other people with the one thing she wanted, had wanted more than anything in the world.

"Then what?" Max rejoined helplessly. His words were drowned out by a resounding slam of the car door. She was gone.

EIGHT

"So tell me about your new job." Daniel grabbed hold of Charlotte and drew her down to sit on his lap. She had been quiet since he had got home, but this wasn't uncharacteristic of her in the evenings, and he had been faintly encouraged by the revelation that she had started painting again. They hadn't really chatted about the job before. To be honest, Daniel wasn't sure that Charlotte would stick at it. It seemed so unlike her, so extroverted.

Charlotte twisted determinedly away, and then partially relented, perching beside him on the arm of the old grey sofa that had been his parents'.

"Well, you'd like the house. It's vast. And the views are fantastic. It's even got a helipad in the grounds, but it's all grown over now. I don't think it's been used for a long time."

"How the other half live, eh? Wonder what's he's paying for it? What's his name, the actor bloke?" Daniel prompted. "I hope he's not working you too hard or taking you for granted. He's bloody lucky to get you for that job!"

"Of course." Charlotte frowned, feeling offended, although she wasn't completely sure why. "What are you implying? I don't know if he is lucky to get me. It's obviously all new, but it is challenging, you know, and interesting too. His name's Max Collins, you know, the one who's in that fantasy series about the underworld. His partner turned up on Friday, or ex, I suppose, and kids. I've only just realised who she is too – Eleanor Jones." As she regaled the lines she had rehearsed in her head, Friday's events seemed far-removed from the present moment.

"Eleanor Jones, wow, he must be successful. She gets around, doesn't she? She always seems to be on the arm of someone in the news. She was in those films about the spy ring."

"I'm surprised you've heard of her!"

Daniel was hopeless with films and names.

"Well, she stands out, doesn't she?"

"Does she?" Charlotte picked up her phone and Googled the name. *Nell, Eleanor Jones*. Yes, unmistakably she and yes, she certainly did stand out. On the arm of a younger, curlier-haired Max who looked away from the camera with his gaucheness a foil to Nell's symbiosis with the unseen photographer. Charlotte flicked through the images with a feigned insouciance. However she stood, whatever angle she stood at, Nell radiated from the screen. She appeared to be everything about which Charlotte herself felt most insecure.

Daniel tried half-heartedly to sustain the conversation, but Charlotte had had enough and got up to go out to her studio. It was wearing to pretend that everything was alright when she felt that she had been pared away by recent occurrences. There was also the nagging guilt that kept surfacing; why did she feel that she could only share the merest outline of events with Daniel?

Mainly, she was frustrated with herself that she had reacted as she had in front of Max, exposing her vulnerability to an almost stranger. She also felt fed up with Daniel. She didn't feel in the mood to dissect her employer's life. It felt like she was relinquishing control again. Why couldn't she just be left alone?

Daniel got up and followed her. He stood in the open door of the studio, a seemingly insubstantial silhouette with the light behind him, new trainers nosing the dirty wooden slats. Charlotte had noticed them earlier and wondered idly when he had bought them; she couldn't remember seeing them before. They were an unusual choice for Daniel, a little less sensible than usual, a little too much effort.

He said softly, "Charlotte, are you alright? Do you think that you are making too many changes all at once? I'm worried about you. It's good you're painting again, but this new job? It's all a bit sudden, isn't it? Just because he's helped you with your fall – you don't need to repay him!"

"No, you've got it all wrong. I need the change!" The words came out louder and more aggressively than Charlotte had intended. She picked up a brush and looked out of the window, searching desperately for the lucidity that resisted her. "I need something to take my mind off everything. It's something different, a fresh start."

Daniel walked over and stood behind her. He put his arms round her, and she felt his familiar touch, sensing an unspoken invitation. His body tensed behind her, and it felt like an invasion.

"I need to get on, Daniel. I want to get in a few hours' painting before the light goes."

Wordlessly, he detached and walked away. Charlotte

shrugged and sighed simultaneously. She knew what Daniel wanted but she couldn't physically surrender to that level of closeness. It felt like he no longer understood who she was; she wasn't even sure that she wanted him to understand her. Hell, she didn't fully understand herself either.

Daniel returned to the house, hands in pockets and frustration coursing through his veins. He felt rootless; Charlotte just didn't seem to need him anymore. Initially, he had thought that the loss of so many hopes and dreams would bind them closer but, as the months had passed, he had begun to sense in her an alienation which he couldn't bypass. He thought he loved her still, but he was feeling tired. Tired of the barely submerged conflict, tired of trying to humour something he could not understand and that seemed oblivious to his own needs and desires. He got out his phone and opened his text messages. It was Valentine's Day tomorrow.

***

Despite everything, Max had had an enjoyable weekend with the children, once Nell had gone. When he got back from taking Charlotte home, he had found her standing by the door and a pile of toys and bags dumped on the sofa. She wheeled round when she heard the car, phone to her ear, ending the call and stowing the phone in her handbag on his approach.

"Sorry to disturb you and your PA, Max, but you had remembered that we had arranged for you to have the children this weekend, hadn't you?" Nell's silvery tones managed to be both delicate and threatening, a thin skein of self-control connecting her words.

Max was fairly sure that the arrangement had been for next weekend, but he knew that this was a typical Nell tactic to paint him as the disorganised and selfish father, and he wasn't going to rise.

"No problem, Nell," he said easily, "the bunk bed hasn't come yet, so Dom will just have to sleep in with me. Vivi, I'll show you where you're sleeping in a minute. You are going to love this place. There's all kinds of animals, and a dog we can walk, too!"

Vivi was lingering close to Nell and Max, as if waiting for permission to be released. Max softly whispered something to her and gave her a little push towards the main room.

Nell narrowed her eyes, always jealous of the intimacy that Max made look so effortless every time he reconnected with the children. She shot her closing barb.

"Dad will be back to pick them up on Sunday. My parents are having them for the week, as I'm off to Antigua for a short break."

"Why didn't you let me know? I'd have had them; you know I would." Max was tight-lipped and furious. This time he had no doubt this was a deliberate move on her part. Her parents were dire, absolutely dire, and had been brainwashed by Nell pretty much from the word go, or vice versa – it was a bit like the chicken or the egg.

"Oh, Max," Nell said sweetly. "I just wanted to make sure that you were settled here. I wasn't sure if you would be ready to have them just yet. Bye darlings!"

She dropped a kiss on Vivi's head, and rumpled Dom's curls. The children gave her a cursory look behind as they became braver and started to explore the house. She leant into Max, ostensibly to kiss him again too, and he took a step backwards, shaking his head in disbelief.

"I think that's enough of your games, Nell. What's happened to the latest squeeze?"

Nell laughed airily, looking after the children with a thoughtful look on her face. "Neil? Oh, yes, we're still seeing each other, but he is just a teensy bit boring, Max. Doesn't have your more obvious charms. You still not seeing anyone? What happened to that make-up artist?"

"I don't think that's any of your business," Max retorted, determined not to take the bait.

The make-up artist, Kasia, had been a brief, mostly enjoyable interlude after Nell's duplicity, but she had actually dumped him about a month ago. He had managed to string it out for about four months this time but, although the sex had been exciting, he had had little in common with Kasia beyond her endless supply of revelations about the vast array of actors she had transformed. And she had felt that he was preoccupied, his heart not really in it, which was true, of course.

"Oh well, must be off. Neil's taking me to The Savoy Grill for dinner tonight. Don't want to be late. Gramps will pick you up on Sunday, darlings," she called into thin air.

Max followed her to the door and watched her leave the premises with a hardened expression on his face. He knew Nell far too well and suspected that more was at play than just an unexpected visit. She had been determined to become involved in his planned sabbatical, bullying him to rent this barn because it was easily accessible from London, and insisting on inspecting the house for its suitability.

Why do I let her do this to me? Max reflected helplessly.

He knew the answer already. Nell had readily taken Bella's place as Max's chief protector, and he had given Nell what she had wanted at the time – kudos and a child, in that order. He turned rather wearily to face his whooping children. *Better all go to Tesco's*, he supposed.

They got back late, having not only been shopping but incorporating a detour to a chain restaurant that served hot, vaguely palatable food and was less than fussy about its patrons, particularly if they were under the age of twelve. Tired and comfortably full, the children surprisingly went to bed with very little fuss, Vivi tucked up in the spare room bed, and Dom curled up looking small and angelic in the left-hand side of the super king bed, at which point Max sent heartfelt thanks to the previous inhabitants for having let the barn furnished.

He couldn't sleep. It felt strange having the children here rather than at his London flat which, although cramped, was something of habit. This still felt like he was on holiday. He got up and walked over to the balcony, letting himself out of the sliding door with a gentle click. Looking down at the garden below, he was amazed to see that everything was bathed in bright moonlight, the moon was indeed shining as bright as day. He chuckled inwardly at the recall of the nursery rhyme and then something caught his eye to the right of the patio.

The lithesome figure of a fox crept silently across the open pasture below, pausing for a minute a few paces from the edge, ears pricked up and body tense with exertion. Then it scaled the fence in one fluid movement. Max suddenly felt the chill of the night air and shivered involuntarily. Which poet had identified with foxes – Ted Hughes, wasn't it?

Max felt more pursued than pursuer these days. He found himself wondering what Charlotte would have made of the sighting. It would have intrigued her, of that he felt sure. He wondered whether the full moon had stopped her sleeping too.

"'*Will you come? / Will you come / If the night / Has a moon / Full and bright? / O, will you come?*'"

When you had to learn everything by ear, words came unbidden to your mind when you were least expecting it. He couldn't remember who had written the poem. He pulled the doors to and padded over to the bed. The next thing Max was aware of was a hot sticky body getting in beside him when he really could have done with another few hours' sleep.

Saturday was a pyjama day with movies and popcorn and then they went out to a local park on Sunday. Max again found himself thinking of Charlotte when they saw a Labrador exactly like Jake.

"I know a dog like that," he told Vivi without thinking.

"Do you, Daddy?" Vivi looked up at him quizzically and he found himself retracting from those trusting blue eyes.

"Would you like a dog, Vivi?" he pondered, then kicked himself mentally for giving the child false hope.

"Can we, Daddy? Really?" She looked up at him with her open guileless expression and he really looked at her back. He saw, with a painful leap of his heart, her poker straight hair, plaited haphazardly herself, the light smattering of freckles on her nose, and the increasingly anxious look on her face as she looked at her father, trying to work out whether he was being serious or not.

"Maybe, Vivi, maybe." He held her hand tighter, and they ran to join Dom as he splashed in puddles and oozy mud, wholly absorbed in his own world.

The weekend ended successfully enough with Max attempting a roast at home and then handing the children reluctantly over to his ex-father-in-law, a man bigoted and retentive enough to scare away a thousand refugees but whose ignorance was marginally redeemed by his clear delight in his progeny. Nell's parents were self-made and proud: their lives revolved around the leisure pursuits of the well-off retiree, but the lives they had created were a curated façade.

John played golf, dabbled a bit on the stock market, and enjoyed holidaying in France but, in poor secrecy, was a regular at the local betting shop and never more at home than in a slightly dodgy pub on the outskirts of the town where they lived, greeting regulars and taking a keen interest in any underhand transactions that took place. He had been a local businessman, owning a small chain of body shops which had expanded throughout the South-East. Sarah, his wife, had done the accounting for the firm – off the books, of course, cash in hand.

Sarah placed a high value on appearance – no surprises there – and did not appear out, ever, without a veneer of make-up just pushing the boundaries of good taste. They both tolerated Max, as he had at least provided them with the grandchildren of their dreams, but clearly were bemused by his and Nell's choice of career. In turn, he abhorred their materialism and narrow-minded attitudes. They could be kind, and loved the children, but he knew that Nell had shrugged them off like last season's coat as soon as she had reached the age of sixteen.

They had barely been able to control the teenage Nell, and had focused instead on her younger brother, Steven, who had fully realised their hopes and dreams by following his father into working at and then taking over a prestigious local car dealership. Max didn't hate them; he just had nothing in common with them. He guessed he and Nell were lucky to have their support; the irony was that his own family unit was the one fractured and dysfunctional beyond repair.

John stood there now, a smile breaking out over his face as he spotted Dom hovering behind Max. He was wearing very crisp blue jeans, a labelled polo shirt stretched tightly over his paunch and some rather dubious looking deck shoes. He and Sarah generally sported a year-round tan (Max suspected some help here) and he failed to disappoint with a patina resonant of antique walnut. He was good-looking for his age still, an imposing six-footer with a thick silver head of hair that had been carefully tended and styled. Nell called him 'Bill' when she was pissed off with him; Max thought privately that there were probably a few more things the old man had in common with Clinton.

"Grandad. Have you come to see our new house?" Dom tried to grab hold of the man's hand, but John broke away awkwardly with an embarrassed chuckle. He patted the little boy on the head, glancing at Max as he did so.

"Not today, Dom. Nanny's waiting for you at home. Come on, we need to get you tucked up back at our house and it's getting late."

"Viv!" Max called and got hold of some of the children's belongings to load into the back of John's Mercedes SUV– nice, obviously one acquired by Steven, and wasted on the old man who was a perennial lane hogger. Still, Max was pleased to see it was obviously one with the latest safety features if it had to transport his children. Finally, Vivi and Dom were packed into the car, and it was purring out of the drive. Feeling the customary pangs of guilt and relief, he made a show of waving enthusiastically as the car retreated out of sight.

Max turned and faced the house again, reluctant to re-enter it. He would get a breath of fresh air. It had been a pretty sedentary day so far, and he needed some space to breathe after the intensity of the children. A stroll into the village might blow away some cobwebs.

As he went, he couldn't help revisiting the encounter between Charlotte and Nell. He felt guilty; he knew he should have at least intimated to Charlotte the true state of his mangled family situation. They had seemed protected from the rest of the world, and he had enjoyed shrugging off the pitfalls of fame for a week or so. He tried to rationalise why he even cared. Charlotte was good at what she did. He knew that early on. Christ, even Della had commented on her efficiency and skill with organising his affairs. But it was more than that, a trust growing between them. He had enjoyed that sensation but, ironically, he had no one else to blame for jeopardising it.

Max had reached the railway bridge and he could hear the odd car speeding through the village. It was only 8.00p.m. and he considered nipping back to the pub and drowning his sorrows with a pint. There was a shorter route, but he thought he might walk past Charlotte's house just to see where she lived. He used the same short cut that Charlotte had taken when they had encountered one another in the shop, and he walked quickly through the dark passage to emerge almost in front of the Seldons' house, slightly taller and more imposing than the older cottages to either side.

Lights downstairs lit up the sash windows and exposed the interior to prying eyes. Max was on the other side of the lane, but he was struck immediately by the personality and individualism of the furnishings… and the artwork. He found himself moving nearer to get a closer look. The house seemed to be drawing him in despite its slightly forbidding exterior.

Several large paintings hung on the wall opposite the road, and he could see even from a distance how they dominated the room. They seemed to be of skies, scudding clouds with windswept landscapes beneath. Max was bemused: so Charlotte was an art aficionado as well as everything else. They looked like originals, or perhaps not with their size.

Moving to turn away, he noticed a movement in a doorway to the right of the front room. A man came into view, and he realised with a jolt that this must be Charlotte's husband. He was about Max's height, maybe an inch or so shorter, with sandy, greying hair and a medium stature. Pleasant looking, a responsible face, intelligent even, Max acknowledged, but probably not in the league of who he was dreading. The man made as if to walk towards the window and Max hurriedly moved on.

Later in the pub, he realised that he had been relieved. Already, it had felt like he was in competition for Charlotte's attention with a faceless opponent. *This isn't good*, thought Max, as he downed his IPA. He wasn't playing a game. This wasn't Nell and him – he wasn't someone who would willingly meddle in another's relationship. Charlotte was his friend.

Perhaps he'd phone Kasia tonight. She might have forgiven him in the time that he had been away. He sipped his pint and tried to block out the image of Charlotte's face when he had chased her out of the house. He could identify now the blank expression that she had worn – he tended to react to Nell in a similar way – defeat and betrayal blended into one. He realised it was Valentine's Day. The jaunty blackboard to the left of the fireplace proclaimed the bar meal offer of two steaks for one, and he spotted a few solitary couples in the eating area trying to chew on the steak and still look attractive for their partners. He offered them a silent toast and tried not to think of his own failed love life.

NINE

Charlotte let herself into the house on Monday morning, resolved to keep matters professional at all times. Daniel had given her a lift up the hill on his way to work, and she was pleased that she hadn't had to rely on Max for once. Daniel seemed cheerier and she was relieved that she wasn't required to bolster his mood, making a point of leaning in for a kiss, and wishing him a good work trip.

Her ankle was very nearly better, only the odd twinge here and there, and she had abandoned the boot and crutches altogether. In celebration, she had donned a black flippy skirt from her assistant headteacher days with black tights and a favourite chiffon blouse covered with peonies of various pinks on a black background. It had a jaunty pussy cat bow, and she teamed it with a sheepskin gilet and her favourite chunky Chelsea boots. She had taken more time with her make-up that morning, carefully drawing on winged eye flicks and eschewing the nude lipstick she normally wore for a bolder cochineal, picking her favourite gold locket to finish it off. It seemed important that she appeared credible and self-possessed today. She needed to be able to hold her head high.

"You look nice," Daniel had commented as she got in the car, quashing the suspicions that were floating in his head. She had forgotten to get him anything yesterday, or that's what she had told him. He had bought her a card and felt dreadful all day.

It was a mild day for the middle of February and, unusually, there was no breeze, just the faintly warming glow of the transient sun. The fields and paths were a sepia brown with tinges of dull green here and there. Everything seemed on hold and poised for the advent of spring.

Charlotte had acquired a key to the barn last week and was glad that she had accepted.

"I can't always sleep," Max had explained, "and this will mean that you can come and go as you like, even if I'm not up yet."

She had taken several transatlantic calls, booked a hotel room for Thursday night, and arranged for a cleaner as Max had requested, before he emerged from his room, tousle-headed and bleary-eyed. He was clad in a rumpled sea-green t-shirt and tracksuit bottoms and was pulling on a checked shirt as Charlotte looked at him, thinking he looked more boyish and less put together than normal. She found herself visualising him waking up in the bedroom next door. It was faintly disturbing.

"Do you want a coffee?" she asked as he stood in the doorway of the office, unsure of how to greet her.

"Yes, morning, sorry, my head's killing me. Had one too many last night. I guess I was more tired than I thought. Child..." Max's voice died away, and he made a show of checking his phone. He was slightly perturbed by Charlotte's appearance this morning: her stature seemed to have grown since he had met her only a few weeks before. She looked more polished and assured somehow. He noticed that she had done something with her eyes, he wasn't sure what, but he acknowledged for the first time that she was quite attractive in her own way. He liked that she seemed to forge her own style; her quirkiness gave her an individuality that he found lacking in the acolytes that tended to frequent the sets he worked on. She wasn't beautiful by any standards but, after his experiences with Nell, he wasn't sure that beauty had the edge on authenticity. Plus, beauty, in his experience, was something that often had to be maintained, worked at. He was heartily over beauty.

"I'm sorry about Friday." Charlotte had been agonising all night about what to say and had decided that she was going to be as honest as possible. Max was a friend as well as her boss, and she owed him that much at least. "It was nothing at all to do with your family. I just find that kind of thing difficult. Seeing other people's children. It's so stupid, and it makes me feel very screwed up. I've had a lot of... disappointment in the last couple of years. I mean, I've lost... I've had several miscarriages." She felt clumsy, it was so difficult to express what had happened. "They were all very unpleasant, but I found the last one particularly traumatic." She focused on a tree in the distance, making a conscious effort to fend back the tears. "I know it's not the same as losing a child, but it makes me feel horrible and behave horribly. I feel awful as I'm doing it, but I can't stop myself. I'm eaten up with jealousy and what-ifs."

That was it. She had done it, presented herself to him, a flawed and faulty human being who felt like a failure. It felt like a pivotal moment, now all she needed was validation.

Max stood stock-still in the doorway. Charlotte mistook his stance for embarrassment. She blushed, a deep red staining her skin.

"God, I'm so sorry, it's too personal, I don't know why I told you. Take no notice of me. I'll just get on with this." She bent over the laptop, trying to block out her surroundings.

Max walked over and put an arm around her; he was so close that she could smell his shower gel and the distinctive aroma that she had come to associate with him. He paused for a moment and then spoke quietly and sincerely.

"Thank you for telling me, Charlotte. I'm pleased you've explained. I did wonder and I appreciate you trusting me. I'm so sorry for you... and Daniel. That must have been so difficult, must still be difficult. I'm really glad you told me," he repeated. "Is that why you left teaching?"

"Some of the reason, maybe a lot," Charlotte admitted. She sat back in her office chair and breathed deeply. It felt good to talk to someone about it. There had been no one whom she felt she could properly confide in. Her mother had dosed her with platitudes and Dan's mum had been too busy looking after their physical needs to worry about her mentally. They had both shown concern, but Claire would never properly understand with her umpteen full-term pregnancies, and Emily was more interested in talking about her Tinder dates.

"You know what it's like in schools, especially primary schools. The endless pregnant mothers, that chair in the staffroom that everyone jokes about. The demographic of primary school teachers is just a joke. They fall pregnant one after the other... all except me. Except that the problem I have isn't with falling pregnant, it's just with keeping it."

Are you still trying? Max wondered. He moved back, perching on the edge of the desk, and said, "I feel so sorry for you having to go through that, especially more than once. We were very lucky – sorry, I don't mean to be insensitive. That was a tactless thing to say."

"No." Charlotte looked up at him and met his eyes. They looked directly back at hers, warm and sympathetic. "It's probably easier talking about it to a man, if anything. I don't feel my ovaries have failed in comparison with yours." She tried to smile. "Go on."

"Well, you obviously know that I'm not with Nell now." Max shuffled slightly and avoided her eyes as he spoke. "We had been together for about six years when Nell decided she wanted a baby. I was a bit unsure to be honest – my home life was... well, complicated at the time. Hadn't even really agreed – it was just something she had mentioned a couple of times and, well, you've seen what she's like. When she wants something, she usually finds a way. I could hardly believe it when she told me she was pregnant.

"Then Vivi was born, and, well, you've seen her. She's an angelic child – we don't deserve her." He looked at Charlotte and decided to go on. "Nell found it difficult straight after the birth. I think she expected to blast her way out of it like she does everything else, but Vivi was unsettled, not that you'd guess it now. Nell loved showing her off, but she wasn't so keen on the rest of it. You've seen how gorgeous she is – Nell, I mean. Image is everything to her, and some parts fitted, and some parts didn't. I probably didn't help enough, or didn't help with the right things? Who knows?" He shrugged and looked tired.

"I guess some couples are brought together through it, but Nell and I were precarious anyway. It was all getting a bit easier when she discovered she was pregnant again, and then all hell broke loose. Turns out she had only wanted the one, to say she had done it, really, and one drunken night later, we were suddenly steering towards being a family of four.

"By that time, I had suspected that Nell was seeing other people anyway. I wasn't even one hundred percent sure that Dom was mine at first. She managed to keep it behind closed doors for the duration of the pregnancy and then left me almost as soon as he was born. Usually, it's the other way round. You have to admire Nell in some ways; she plays games but she is true to herself at the end of the day. She wouldn't stick with something that wasn't going anywhere."

Charlotte was stunned. "I guess it shows that no one knows what really is going on in anyone else's life. You told me you had split up, but it all looked so perfect... Nell, you both look so perfect with the children. I'm sorry too. That must have been awful."

"I know, I know." Max raised his eyebrows and sighed. "It's complicated and difficult and I feel that we both use them as a weapon at times, but I do really love them, and I know Nell does too, and I try to put them first when I can."

"Why hadn't you told me about them though?" Charlotte turned back to her computer screen and tried to ask the question casually.

"I suppose I was enjoying feeling a bit free-er – is that a word? – than I usually do." Max had lost sleep thinking the very same thought. "Nell is quite controlling, even though we're not together, and you didn't seem to have any preconceived ideas about me. You have no idea how many people put on this big fake grin and persona when they are introduced to me. I get sick of it; it's one reason why I'm out here and not in London at the moment. You seemed different, caught up in yourself. I was interested and I didn't want anything else to get in the way."

"Well, now you know why I'm such a selfish bitch," said Charlotte dryly.

Max met her eyes; he could feel the oppressiveness of her self-loathing. She looked back at him steadily; her lips were slightly raised but her eyes were unsmiling. Again, he felt the presence of Bella in the room.

"Don't say that!" he said more loudly than he had intended. "You're grieving and you've got to get through it in your own way. It's like PTSD. It takes years to get over trauma like that. You have a right to be selfish. I'm not going to tell you to snap out of it. It will get easier, but the pain will never completely leave you."

Charlotte put a hand to her face and blotted a tear with the back of her hand. Max's words fell on her ears like a benediction. The hurt, damaged layers had been stripped back and all that remained was her sadness. She had been seen. It was a relief, being given permission to grieve. Perhaps she should be more kind to herself. Perhaps it would get better.

"How do you know so much about it?" Dabbing her eyes with a tissue from her bag, she turned round but realised that Max had gone.

***

Towards the end of the morning there was a phone call from Della, a rarity as she usually stuck to Teams conversations and angry WhatsApp messages, often punctuated by expletives and an unsubtle array of emojis. Charlotte was on another call at the time to a designer jeweller who was hoping to get Max involved in an advertising deal. She could see the incoming phone call but thought Della could wait for a few minutes as she finalised the details of the initial meeting. She cursed as she could then hear the sound of the landline growing louder and louder from Max's room.

"Yes, Thursday morning at 1.00p.m., sure. I'll pencil it in, Nina. Sorry, I've got another call coming in." Charlotte hurriedly made her excuses and darted out of the room and along the corridor.

She paused for a moment before knocking on Max's door. No response, and she needed to shut that phone up before she spoke to Della, otherwise she would go mad. She pushed the door and spotted the phone chucked carelessly in the middle of the unmade bed. She grabbed it and plonked herself down on the covers, trying to ignore the intimacy of the scene and the slight perfume of Max's aftershave.

"Hello? Charlotte Seldon," she spoke politely into the phone, trying to recover her breath. There was the faint static crackle of the phone line and then a click as the person at the other end hung up. Charlotte felt unsettled. A prank phone call? Some kind of scammer? Her mobile was still vibrating on her legs; Della could be ignored no longer.

"Do you want me or Max?" she said without her usual preamble.

"Both," snapped the voice on the other end of the line. "Has Max got a date yet for Thursday? I'm sick of asking him about it."

"I've no idea." Charlotte had taken care of all the domestic arrangements. She was pretty sure it wasn't part of her job description to have to consider Max's love life too.

"It is ee-sen-tial that Max has someone on his arm on Thursday night, do you hear me, Charlotte? The paps are going to be out in full force, and he was on his own at the last two events. Another mistake could spell disaster!"

"I think you better talk to him," Charlotte said firmly. This was spilling over into uncomfortable territory; it wasn't her place to bring this up, particularly after recent events. As purging as the conversation earlier had been, she and Max had made sure their paths hadn't crossed for the rest of the morning. Unburdening herself had been draining and the one-sidedness of the confidences made her uneasy.

She headed thoughtfully down the stairs to find Max in the kitchen, throwing some chicken and vegetables in a wok for lunch. The kitchen was full of stainless steel and minimalist surfaces, a nightmare to clean and one reason why Charlotte had made it a priority to source Max a cleaner.

"I'm making pad thai; do you want some?" he called over his shoulder. The previously spotless worktop was now a mixture of packets, gratings, condiments and lethal-looking knives.

"Here, I'll take over. Can you talk to Della, please... now?"

Charlotte passed the phone over as Max wiped his hands on a tea towel and took it from her. She could hear Della talking loudly, and then Max walked out of the room and she caught the odd word and phrase drifting out of the hall.

"...for the sake of it... Christ, no, Della... how many times... it'll be fine... yes, she won't mind, I'm sure... no, I can't... no, not even for this... I'm not going to pretend, Della!"

Charlotte tried to focus on the food as Max re-entered the kitchen and hovered behind her.

"Hey, it's done, I think. I've added the noodles and the soup."

She divided up the contents of the wok into two bowls and carried them over to the polished concrete island where Max was putting out two mats and some chopsticks.

"Do you want cutlery too? No, good."

They started to eat, and Max racked his brain with how he was going to present his case to Charlotte. Trust Della to have put him on the spot like this. Still, it would be nice to have company, and it would be a lot more enjoyable going with Charlotte than anyone else.

"Charlotte, I've got a proposition for you."

"Another one?" Charlotte raised her eyebrows in mock concern. She put down her chopsticks and gave Max her full attention.

"I need a partner for the event on Thursday. As you've probably gathered, Della is convinced that the press will paint me as either a closet homosexual, mummy's boy or possibly both, if I go on my own again. I don't really care either way, but I'm wondering if you should come to the appointment afterwards with the Circanis. And I don't really know what I'm doing with that meeting beforehand – a watch is just a watch as far as I'm concerned. I need someone to sound out the financial arrangements, and then you may as well come to the evening too, if you're there."

Charlotte looked as if she was going to respond, but Max carried on hurriedly.

"They provide all the outfits, hair, make-up, everything's laid on for you. I think it would be useful to see what I'm up against, as my PA of course and, besides, I think you'd enjoy it, and I'd enjoy going with you." He ended by looking at her beseechingly, and Charlotte couldn't help but laugh.

"Well, I don't mind attending a very swanky premiere – you're not going to need to twist my arm – but I'd like to just stay in the background, obviously. I don't want to have to meet anyone and pretend I know what I'm talking about."

"Strange girl." Max smiled. "Others would kill to meet all those celebs."

"Well, it depends who it is, of course! What will I need to wear? I'm not sure I've got anything suitable for that type of event, not exactly red carpet material anyway!"

"Weren't you listening? They provide the outfit. You don't need to worry."

"And you're sure you haven't got anyone else to go with? No one you're dating?" Charlotte looked at Max under her eyelashes. She had the feeling that he wasn't entirely single. There had been a few texts at different times, and even the phone call today had been a bit odd, and... how could he be single looking like that and with what he did for a living?

Max dismissed the fleeting thought of the voluptuous and supremely well turned-out Kasia, and patted Charlotte on the hand.

"You'll be fine. I'll look after you." Then, almost as an afterthought. "I like what you're wearing today. That colour really suits you." He was thinking aloud, but realised his mistake as soon as the words left his lips. The words hung there without preamble or explanation, a sudden dip into his thoughts. Charlotte's reaction was immediate, and he mentally kicked himself for his thoughtlessness as the blush spread to the tips of her ears. She hadn't been fishing for a compliment; they always made her feel so awkward. Did he really like how she looked, or did he just want her to go to this thing with him? She had met Nell now, and that bar was set so high that she would need stilts to reach it. Thinking about him assessing her appearance caused an unexpectedly visceral impact. She felt shaken; she wasn't ready to engage with these conflicting emotions.

They ended the meal in silence and Max went to throw a few balls for Jake in the garden. Charlotte saw the phone on the kitchen counter and went to return it to Max's room and collect her bag from the office. She quickly entered the bedroom and spotted the cradle on the left-hand bedside table, a one-drawer, bleached oak affair. She put the phone back on the stand but knocked a small silver frame to the floor in her haste. It clattered on to the floorboards, also bleached, and she reached down to pick it up, praying that nothing had broken. Luckily, the glass was intact but loose. She carefully pushed the velvet casing back and twisted the little clips back into place, turning it around to look at it as she placed it carefully back on the side.

Charlotte had assumed that it would have been a picture of Vivi and Dom, or even of Nell with the two children, but she saw that it was of a teenage girl and boy. It looked old, perhaps twenty years ago or so. She picked it up again to look at it more closely. The pair were under a big tree, the boy with his back to the camera, his head thrown back in laughter, sitting at the feet of the girl, who was leaning against the trunk with her arms reaching round the back. They looked to be about seventeen and were very similar builds with curly brown hair and slim, almost gangly limbs.

The girl was looking directly at the camera as if to

challenge the bearer; a smile played on her lips, but her eyes were focused and intent. Charlotte felt a glimmer of recognition, although she could have sworn that she had never seen her before. She put the photo back carefully, so it looked undisturbed, and walked away from the room with questions buzzing in her ears.

TEN

Charlotte had assumed that Daniel would have thought of some reason why it wasn't sensible for her to attend the awards ceremony with Max, so she was surprised when he voiced his approval at the dinner table that night.

"Yeah, why not?" he said, absent-mindedly winding spaghetti round his fork. "It'll be something for you to do. I'm away again, I'm afraid. Newport this time. Got to visit the Welsh office."

He looked at Charlotte and thought that she looked more animated than he had seen her for a long time. In contrast, he felt jaded, weary of fighting the tide that seemed to have turned against him. He had arranged the trip to Newport. Head office had thrown a few names around, but in the end, he had suggested that he do the honours himself. He needed to think some more before he made a final decision. Alone.

Charlotte had almost wanted him to react against the idea; the more she thought about the night ahead, the more she felt anxious and full of trepidation. This was completely out of her comfort zone. The job itself was one thing but attending an event with famous people who all worked in front of a camera for a living... she must be mad to even consider it.

Images scrolled through her mind relentlessly: all the beautiful women – slim, gorgeous, highly maintained women at that, the cultured, brilliant mothers. She didn't go to the gym, didn't even manicure her nails as a rule. She liked make-up and dressing up, but she wasn't foolish enough to compare herself with the illuminati who graced these events. Could she hold her own when she would be at such a cellular disadvantage?

Then, on Wednesday, Max had carelessly mentioned that they would need to stay at the hotel for the night; they would both want to drink, may as well take advantage of the free champagne, et cetera, et cetera. Charlotte was flummoxed; she hadn't prepared herself for this further test. She felt pushed into a corner and wrong-footed, even emailing Della about it, as if it wasn't above board or something. Back came a flippant reply a few hours later:

Sure. There are loads of freebies at these things. If it's at the Grosvenor, pinch one of their robes for me – they're amazing!

There was only one small consolation... at least she would have the hotel as an escape if she needed to make a sharp exit.

***

At 9.20a.m. on Thursday, a mere fifty minutes later than planned, Max's Range Rover crunched into the drive. Charlotte, who had been waiting anxiously by the phone, felt her heart touch the bottom of her stomach as she grabbed her suitcase and shoulder bag and opened the front door.

Shushing Jake away, she stood back uncomfortably as Max took her case and bag, berating herself for her impostor syndrome. Max stowed the holdall in the boot of the car and took her shoulder bag round to the front as he opened the passenger door.

"No Daniel?" he queried, as he carefully shut the door behind her.

"Er, no, he's already left. Some kind of meeting in Wales for a few days."

"Busy man, your husband. Who's got the dog?"

"Daniel's parents are collecting him," she replied shortly, sidestepping the first comment.

Something in Charlotte's tone made Max drop the subject. Meanwhile, she seemed to be trying to look for something in her bag.

"Lost something?"

"No, no, aah – here it is! Your checklist!"

She proceeded to reel off a list of items and things that Max was supposed to have looked up or checked prior to the awards ceremony. Max grinned inwardly. It was so obvious that she was a newbie. Generally, everyone was too pissed to notice when you couldn't quite remember either the name of their partner or the project they were trying to promote. Still, it was sweet how she cared so much. They settled down into a comfortable banter involving Charlotte mock-scolding Max for his ill-preparedness and him gently teasing her efficiency for the rest of the journey. It took the sting out of the M25, Max thought, and it beat Nell nagging him to keep his speed down.

***

"Nice," said Charlotte numbly, in response to Max's, "Is this okay?" as the porter opened the door of her room. Inside, she was thinking a lot more than that. It was one of those whiter than white luxury bedrooms where you wondered how on earth they kept it so clean. Not enormous by hotel standards, but this was London after all. It was certainly comfortable, personality-less perhaps, but that's how they probably liked it, those who could afford to frequent this kind of establishment.

"I'm next door, if you need me. Otherwise, shall we have something to eat in about an hour in the bar? They don't feed you until later at these things, and I suggest we build our strength up now."

I know where you are, I booked the bloody thing, Charlotte thought. This felt weird – the Zen-like hotel room, the assumed deference of the porter who mutely melted away with their luggage when Max had handed him their bags.

"What about the interview, Max? Didn't they say they were coming at 1.00p.m.? We've also got the clothes fittings booked in at 2.45p.m. How are we going to fit it all in?"

"Don't worry, I can ask them to come straight to the hotel. They're not shooting today, are they? We may as well appreciate all this. You deserve a little relaxation after all you've done to organise everything."

"But…?" Charlotte raised her eyebrows. Max just laughed at her and batted her hands away.

"I can speak to them; chill, you. They're used to celebrity types being right arses – this will seem a minor request, believe me!"

"Okay, okay, I'm going."

Charlotte retreated to her room and decided to have

a bath. She had had a shower the night before, but she felt
sticky with tension. She fancied slathering over herself some
of the complimentary products and she could also see if the
bathrobe lived up to the hype! The bath was divine. It was
marble and sunken, a decent length with taps in the middle.
She could feel her eyes closing as she inhaled the delicately
scented steam, invoking some eastern bathhouse with a hint
of neroli and orange blossom, bubbles covering her body.
She couldn't help smiling… this was probably as film star as
she would get! She let herself steep for a few minutes in the
hot water and then her daydreams were rudely interrupted
by a knock at the door… already? *Shit!*

She slithered out of the bath dropping water all over the
tiled floor, patting at herself at speed with an impossibly fluffy
towel and then grabbing the bathrobe. Opening the door to
her room, she was astonished to see a bellboy looking coolly
at her, unabashed by her attire. He was wheeling a trolley
with an ice bucket and two glasses.

"Errr… I haven't ordered anything!" Charlotte felt
her voice go higher with embarrassment. She clutched the
infamous bath robe to her, conscious that it was gaping
slightly, and she had nothing on underneath. Presumably he
had seen a lot worse in his time, but she really didn't want
to make it into a story passed around the staff on a cigarette
break. Actually, no, she was here with Max after all – perhaps
it would make it into the Daily Freak show. She grimaced
inwardly.

The bellboy met her eyes and smiled evenly. He was
probably well used to these kinds of situations.

"It's from Mr. Collins with his compliments. He wanted
me to tell you not to rush, take your time."

Charlotte stood back, wordlessly, as the man skilfully laid out a cloth and mats and popped the cork into a napkin. He poured one glass half full and smoothly exited before Charlotte had even had a chance to say thank you. *Ah well.* She grabbed the glass and downed the drink in one before she remembered that she had had nothing to eat all morning, not even breakfast, given her last minute nerves back at home.

Decidedly more relaxed after her soak and drink, she put her favourite jeans back on, but exchanged her checked shirt for a soft salmon-pink cashmere jumper that had been in the sale at TK Maxx. *Should I get a glass ready for Max?* she wondered. There were two, after all. He must have expected that she would ask him to share this. She idly picked the bottle up... *fuck... Bollinger...* what was he playing at?

She reached into her bag, which she had put on the desk chair near the bed when she had first arrived, not liking to besmirch the virginal snow-white landscape of the eiderdown.

Thks 4 champers. U going to pop rd for dk? she texted Max hurriedly, already feeling a slight fuzziness around the edges as the bubbles continued to work their magic.

In what seemed like seconds, there was another knock at the door and Max bounded in. In truth, he had been sitting bored for the last twenty minutes, wondering what Charlotte was up to. It felt liberating being in this neutral territory together. Normally, he found these events draining; he had been to so many of them that they no longer felt special. But seeing it through Charlotte's eyes, he felt some of the gratification of giving a child a special treat.

"Mmmm, you smell nice." He lifted his nose and sniffed the air like Jake would.

Charlotte giggled and replied, "Too right, I've doused myself in the free smellies, and already had a glass of champagne. Of course, that was before I realised it was Bollinger. *Max!*"

Max smiled, unruffled. "You've got to splurge sometimes, and besides, most of this is free. It's all good advertising for them. The sponsors of the ceremony cough up for the rooms and practically everything else, seems almost unfair on the hotel not to get a few extras in return for all their efforts."

"Well, thank you." Charlotte met his eyes, raising her glass to Max and then hurriedly pouring a generous glass of champagne which she handed to him. "This is lovely, but don't spend too much money on me, please."

Max hesitated and then shut up. He enjoyed treating people, and he wanted to make Charlotte smile, it was as simple as that. But perhaps it was inappropriate, is that what she was inferring? The lines were blurred, he realised that. He had come to think of Charlotte more as a friend than as an employee. And he had to admit that one of the images that had passed lingeringly through his mind nigh on twenty minutes ago was definitely something that crossed out of the friend territory. He wasn't even sure what the appeal was; she wasn't the type he went for at all. He guessed it was something to do with how much he had grown to value her companionship. Familiarity had meant that they had become attached somehow. And there was something that drew him in also, some elusive quality that he struggled to name. It didn't hurt that she wasn't displeasing on the eye, quite striking really, but looks for their own sake were problematic to him after the likes of Nell.

"Cheers," he said, "bottoms up, let's hope we don't do that on the red carpet tonight," and then he proceeded to entertain Charlotte with a story of how his good friend, Remeil, had tripped up and split his trousers whilst high and partnered by an escort. Max told the story predictably well, and Charlotte was doubled up with laughter at the thought of Remeil and his date straddled over each other on the main walkway of the theatre with four hundred pairs of watching eyes, plus assorted TV crews, enjoying live coverage of his backside.

"I can't think what on earth possessed him, but he was wearing yellow boxers that night – his lucky pair, apparently!"

***

The afternoon passed in a blur of fine food in a salmon-pink salon – Charlotte blended with the furnishings of the avant-garde dining room rather too well – listening to the sales pitch of the high-end watchmaker with Max emerging with one on loan for the ceremony. Then came the moment of truth as they were taken to a side room and asked to pick the outfits they were to wear that night.

"You first," Charlotte insisted as Max started to protest. "What happened to the Paul Smith fitting?"

"I cancelled it." Max looked sheepish. "Can't stand them faffing about with a tape measure. An off-the-peg suit is so much easier."

After a few had been held up by the sales assistant and Max had resigned himself to trying them on, she commented, "I think the Rokhsanda. Do you agree?"

Max wasn't surprised to find that he did. If he had to be trussed up in evening dress, then this one still felt vaguely comfortable and even had a rather fetching matching waistcoat in a patchwork of jewel-coloured hues. He had noticed that Charlotte had a good eye for form and colour. Must be why her own clothes always seemed to draw him to appreciate her dark eyes, hair and contrasting complexion.

"Now you…" He emerged from the screened-off changing area looking expectantly at Charlotte.

"Are you sure we don't pay for this? I don't understand; how does it work?" Charlotte felt anxious. Much as she liked Max, there was no way she wanted to be indebted to him for an event and trimmings on this scale. She already felt slightly inebriated, not from the drink as much as the names that were being sallied to and fro like the commentary at a tennis match… Erdem… MiuMiu… Chanel… Versace… Amanda Wakely.

"Don't worry, babe, we'll sort you out with something lovely." The Harrods assistant had taken to Charlotte instantly. *Must be because I've got plus-size tattooed on my forehead*, thought Charlotte grimly, surveying the creations being held before her. *She probably feels sorry for me. Perhaps she thinks Max is taking part in a charity event and I've won a competition.*

"You're lucky, the hideous ones are funnily enough the ones that go first. Celebs like to make an impression and some of them know jackshit about colour or cut." The stylist was from Newcastle and Charlotte found herself warming to her instantly.

"What about my size though? I must be twice as big as most of the women."

"Y'look fine, hon, honestly, and, like I say, the more normal dresses are the ones that seem to get left to last as a rule. Even at this kind of awards ceremony, you get the numpties who seem to think that baring a bit of flesh, even past forty, is their ticket to a place at the Oscars and a handprint on the walk of fame. When Max told me he was bringing you, I had a feeling you were going to be a bit more sensible – I mean that as a compliment – and I put a few dresses I thought you might like to one side, before anyone else got their hands on them."

The assistant was already unzipping some gowns from their plastic sheathes, and Charlotte was relieved to see that they did look classical rather than garish or revealing. She started to relax a bit; maybe this wasn't going to be as bad as she feared, but there was no way that she wanted Max around when she tried clothes on. They definitely weren't on the friendship level, or any level for that matter, where they displayed parts of their body to each other. A million different body hang-ups dragged themselves laboriously through her mind.

"You go," she said to Max, feigning breeziness. "You'll need a shave and a hair-cut. I can sort myself out here."

"If you're sure." Max could tell Charlotte was nervous, but Tash, the stylist, was one he had had before, and he knew she could put even Charlotte at ease.

"Thanks, Tash," he silently formed the words on the way out of the room and blew her a kiss.

She gave him a wink and mouthed back, "She's great, Max – well done!"

Inexplicably, Max felt himself blushing and shaking his head as he made a swift exit from the room. *Get it together, Max*, he told himself. It was an honest mistake. But he knew he needed to heed the warnings floating around in his head. *She's your employee and married. Don't complicate things. You're lonely, that's all.*

ELEVEN

Max absent-mindedly downed a whiskey on the rocks in one fluid motion. He had kept his curly thatch at the front, a nostalgic nod to haircuts of yore, but the back and sides had been shaved, and the designer stubble was gone in a few skilled swipes. He'd got his mate, Tony, to visit the hotel. Tony didn't mind; they'd been friends for years and he refused to take payment anymore. When Max had met him, he had been a seventeen-year-old chancer, only a few years younger than Max himself. Tony had been travelling with a girlfriend and had broken up with her and run out of money. Too ashamed to return to his fiercely proud Italian parents, he had taken a risk and rented a spot in a collective near Borough market.

Dashing to his first audition, Max had seen his sign advertising an all-over for five pounds and hadn't thought twice. He'd got the job and been a loyal customer ever since. Tony liked to say that as he'd lost his own hair, Max's hair had seemed to rejuvenate. A year or so ago Max had flown Tony out with him to the set in Iowa. That had been fun. Tony had been so starstruck that he had hardly spoken for the first few days. Now, on the back of this, he had been able to open his second salon in South London. Max counted him almost as a relation; they had each other's backs, and he was godfather to Tony's three bambinos.

He checked his watch. Five past seven, and the car was getting here at twenty past. Charlotte had better be quick if she wanted a drink. The bartender glided over and exchanged his empty tumbler for another. The service was benignly anonymous here, just as he liked it. No embarrassing chit-chat, just action. Mind you, he felt a little apprehensive himself tonight, perhaps he could have done with some gentle camaraderie. He suddenly wished that Tony had stuck around for a beer.

It felt a bit like he was on some kind of excruciating first date, he reflected as the spirit hit the back of his throat. He was reminded of his sixth form prom where he had escorted a bookish girl called Natalie to the local town hall. Bella had gone with a group of friends instead and he had felt jealous all evening as he hung round wondering how far he could go with the silent Natalie, whilst Bella and her mates had become increasingly raucous. He leant on his elbow a minute, lost in his memories, when he heard a small cough behind him, and wheeled round, startled.

"Charlotte!" For once, words failed him. She was facing him, looking hesitant, of course. The colour saturated his senses... where had he seen it before?

She was wearing a flowing dress of teal-green satin, a chiffon layer creating undulating ripples of fabric looking rather like the sea itself as she moved towards him. Her shoulders were bare; he couldn't stop his eyes being drawn to the exposed skin. Below them were long sheer sleeves gathered at the wrists with matching ties. Then a halter neck gathered by another tie. Her hair had been pinned loosely behind and dark tendrils escaped down the back of her neck, seemingly entwined with the fastening like some kind of waterfall.

The lack of structure pleased him; the dress matched her somehow, skimming the curves which were an antithesis to the lean angles of Nell and enhancing rather than disguising her. She seemed almost illuminated, her pale skin iridescent in the overhead lights. That colour, yes, he remembered now. Their eighteenth birthday, a family party, Bella dancing on her own, a slip dress that had brought out the blue-green of her eyes. Her laugh, eyes almost closed as she stayed on the dance floor the longest. Eyes meeting his briefly as he clapped and cheered with the others. He closed his eyes for the briefest of seconds.

Charlotte had been assessing Max's reaction intently. Her own pulse had skipped a beat when she had seen him waiting at the bar in his dinner jacket and bow-tie. She felt slightly giddy when she surveyed him. He was perfect; this had the hyperreality of a dream, a strange parallel universe where she had been mistaken for another person without her past. But now Max was looking away, and she felt a sudden cold fear. Was he was embarrassed by her?

"Too much?" Her nerves and mild inebriation meant she found herself gushing. "I told them to go easy on the make-up, but they insisted on this whole smoky eye thing and then they wanted to curl my hair, and look." She held out a sapphire pendant for him to see. "They even had jewellery for me to wear too, and they've got me in heels – which I'm not quite sure about, knowing my clumsiness – and they bloody insisted on this whole complimentary drink thing too so, between you and me, I need a packet of crisps at least if we're not eating till later." Charlotte trailed off, realising that she was filling in the silence.

She looked down at the bag she clutched, feeling self-conscious and cumbersome. Perhaps tonight had been a mistake after all. Who did she think she was? She had been fooling herself with this illusion that she could reinvent herself, inhabit this alternate reality. She clenched her hands tightly, and wished fervently that she was on her sofa, or better still in her studio with a paintbrush in hand and no one to please but herself.

"No, Charlotte, you look… you look amazing," Max interrupted her, trying to inject some warmth into his voice, struggling to get his own feelings under control. He signalled to the barman, turning from her abruptly.

Charlotte put a tentative hand on his arm, wobbling slightly on the unaccustomed heels. Then she leant in more closely with a concerned look on her face; he could smell the heaviness of her perfume encircling him.

"What is it, Max? Is there something wrong, are you alright?"

"I'm fine, I'm fine. Let's get some crisps then. What do you want to drink?"

Charlotte asked for a mineral water and perched on the very edge of the stool next to him, trying desperately to focus on regaining some of her lost composure. As Max waved his card in front of the machine, his shirt sleeve inched up his arm slightly. She registered that Max was still wearing the tatty turquoise bracelet. It seemed out of place with the sharpness of the dress shirt and gold cufflinks. She was about to mention it, but something had changed. They had lost that easy intimacy of earlier. She paced her breathing and felt her shoulders hunch slightly. *Just get through it, Charlotte, just get through it.*

***

"Oy, Max, over here, mate!"

"Max, who's your lady friend?"

"Hey, Max…"

A moment out of the womb-like interior of the saloon and the bright lights of the cameras showered on them like an array of fireworks. Max, practised and efficient, grabbed Charlotte's hand. She felt herself become limp and pliant; there was no time to protest.

"This is what Della wanted; just do as I do." He slid an arm around her waist and guided her along the red carpet in front of them, up the steps of the hotel to a roped off area outside the revolving doors of the main entrance. Charlotte concentrated on balancing in her heels and planting her feet squarely on each step.

"This is where we have to pose," he said out of the corner of his mouth, throwing the photographers a rictus grin, but Charlotte couldn't respond; it was utterly overwhelming. She fixed a smile on her face and looked unseeing out into the sea of media.

"What's your name, love? Where did you meet?"

Max pulled her towards him, ostensibly in a closer embrace. "Don't answer," he hissed. Then, before she had time to react, he swooped and kissed her hard on the lips. Charlotte, stunned and then appalled, was caught between a wave of revulsion and desire. Still feeling the pressure of his mouth, she could feel a slow flicker of rage curl up the corner of the touchpaper and creep through her body. Finally led by Max towards the hotel entrance, her hand wooden in his, every fibre of her body was both alert and repelled. She could hear catcalls and whoops from the photographers but she would not look up, would not face them.

Then it was over, and they were through the doors of the hotel. The Grosvenor Park Hotel was a traditional late Victorian building with ostentatiously high ceilings from which hung elaborate cut-glass chandeliers. Eclectic gold, origami-style decorations swung at intervals with the name of the sponsor – some elite banking service – and waiters could be seen circulating gold trays full of old-fashioned champagne glasses. There were people everywhere one looked, walking up the stairs to the theatre doors, thronging the entrance hall like the pulsating feathers of some tropical bird performing a grotesque mating dance. A band was playing somewhere but the noise seemed incessant to Charlotte, the sounds jarring and competing for attention.

There was a large table in the foyer laden with gold boxes fashioned with the same origami ornamentation, being handed out by androgynous assistants clad in gold catsuits.

"Complimentary gifts," Max said, not managing to fully hide his disdain. "Take a few, why don't you, give them as presents to people. The stuff inside often adds up to hundreds of pounds." He took several parcels almost absent-mindedly and handed them to a waiter as he hurried past. "Put these somewhere for us, please."

Charlotte felt that she was being towed around the floor. Max hadn't let go of her hand since they had stepped in, and she took this chance to pull away. He stopped and faced her, only having to take one look at Charlotte's stony face, for his own appearance to falter. He tried to take her hand again but let it drop, realising his mistake.

"I'm so sorry, Charlotte. I just wanted to shut them up. I should have asked, I know. It's inexcusable. I don't know what came over me." He ran a hand through his hair. "Please accept my apologies. I'm not normally a big fan of these occasions, and that's putting it mildly."

He turned and looked for a waiter. *Fuck, where's a drink when you need one?* A tray hovered near his arm, and he took two glasses, downing one immediately. He was breathing more heavily now and realised that he was very heightened; this wasn't going to end well.

Charlotte still stared at him, not trusting herself to speak, shaking her head when Max tried to pass her the other glass. Internally, she was at war with herself. The pressure of his touch had flicked a switch inside: below the surface, some kind of chemical reaction seemed to be taking place; she felt simultaneously aroused and ashamed.

"You used me, Max. I thought you liked and respected me, but clearly not."

"You're right." Max couldn't even look at her. "Sometimes I disgust myself." He took a swig of the other drink without tasting it.

"I work for you, but that doesn't mean that you can pretend we are something we are not. I came here as a favour, and certainly not for you to act out some part with. I don't want to embarrass you here, but please don't behave like that again."

Max looked at her standing there in front of him, flushed and angry. Yet again a memory of Bella flashed in front of his eyes. Bella shouting at him not to go, not to leave her behind; he'd promised not to leave her!

He swung around as if on autopilot, taking a few steps forwards into the throng, and Charlotte stepped after him in a sudden panic. Was that it? Why didn't he say something?

Suddenly from a staircase to their right came a clarion call: "Why, Max, fancy seeing you here!"

For fuck's sake. Max could feel his body tense and become rigid. His palms were clammy and he felt that huge patches of his back were swathed in sweat. The treacherous syncopated pulsating sensation was taking over his body; he knew that he was having a panic attack, the first one in ages, and he was helpless before its onslaught. Christ, he could feel his heart beating now like it was competing to stay alive… It was happening, that sudden skewing of direction just before the fatal nosedive and… Nell arrived by his side.

"Max, come with me." She grabbed hold of one arm and turned to her male companion. "Neil, I'm just going to show Max and, er… his friend the thing, you know."

Her partner, slightly glazed already, gave her a cheery wave and picked up another drink.

"Come with me." Nell spoke authoritatively, and Charlotte followed her, hardly aware of what was happening but dimly registering Nell's gold slip dress and matching sandals and gloves; she looked like some kind of celestial being. They ducked down a passage tucked behind the gift tables, and up another smaller corridor, Nell's heels clacking as they then went down a small flight of stairs, Nell leading Max ahead, leaving Charlotte to scurry behind. They reached a fire exit door at the end and Max pushed at it blindly, sinking to his heels and then, humiliatingly, hands and knees. They were outside in a yard-like area where they could see the lights and sounds through the open kitchen doors screened by panels of fencing and big industrial bins.

Nell was bending over Max now. She unbuttoned the top of his shirt and loosened his bow-tie. His shoulders heaved, and Charlotte realised that he was shaking uncontrollably.

"Breathe, Max, breathe. Count to ten slowly. You're okay. No one's noticed." She stood there patiently, rubbing his back as he fought for breath.

Charlotte hung to the side, not knowing what to do or say. Eventually, Nell straightened and looked at Charlotte.

"Sorry about that, I couldn't let him go through it on his own. I'm assuming you probably don't know about them?"

"No," Charlotte protested, defensive. "No, he hasn't... didn't mention them."

"Guess he wouldn't." Nell looked contemplative. "He hasn't had one for a while; they started at the funeral – Bella's still having an effect on him."

She gave a hollow laugh. Charlotte stood there, mute and expressionless. There was nothing to say, and she wasn't going to give this woman the satisfaction of revealing her ignorance.

"I am here, you know." Max levered himself up and started straightening his clothing. His heart was starting to behave itself and his breathing had almost returned to normal.

Nell said dispassionately, "You've been drinking too, I expect – you look awful."

"Of course," Max responded with a tired cynicism. "Christ, Nell. What else does one do at these things? I'll stop now. Have you got a cigarette?"

Nell wordlessly fished a vintage cigarette case out of her evening bag. It was a drill, Charlotte realised, movements honed by muscle memory, revealing an affection that had lasted despite the dents and scratches on the surface.

"Thank you, Nell. What would I have done without you?" Max muttered with a self-deprecating trace of irony and took a long drag. "Not having one?"

"You know I've given up." Nell looked at Charlotte. "He'll need water, plenty of it, once you're sitting down at your table."

She paused as if she wanted to add something and took a step towards Charlotte. Charlotte noticed her take a final look at Max with an unexpected tenderness that she suspected Nell would rather not have revealed.

"If you want to talk... either of you. *Brrrrr*, but it's freezing now. I had better get off back to Neil; he won't be coping without me." She raised her eyebrows archly and flowed through the door as smoothly as she had come.

Max silently contemplated the red tip of his cigarette. He felt like he had just taken part in a ten-mile run.

"I- I'm so sorry, Charlotte. I really did want you to enjoy tonight. It's not turning out as I planned."

Charlotte stood there, shivering. "You've been acting strangely since the hotel. I know something is on your mind. I need to understand, Max, what you aren't telling me, but this isn't the time. Let's just get through the rest of the evening."

"I will tell you. I want to tell you. Fuck it, how I hate these things." He aimed a kick at the fire door. Charlotte took a step back, stumbling slightly, and he was overcome with self-disgust. He threw the cigarette on the floor, grinding it with his heel. Holding out his hand, he willed Charlotte to take it, but she hesitated. He felt such a fool.

"Please forgive me, Charlotte. I know I should have said something, but it's something I've locked away. I've had to do that to get through it. The problem is that it doesn't always stay locked away, as you can see."

He met her eyes and held her gaze. Charlotte resisted taking his hand; the urge to hold Max to her, to stroke his hair and tell him that it would be alright was vying with her determination to maintain a professional distance. He looked so broken standing there. She wanted desperately for him to go back to being calm and cocky, even, but he looked older, fatigued.

More than ever, she felt the past weighing in on the future. She was blinkered by her own sorrow, and she knew that it had made her selfish and insular. Who knew what had happened between him and this Bella? It was clearly devastating to have caused this visceral physical reaction and this was by no means the first time it had happened, according to Nell. Now, however, their positions were reversed somehow. She had the authority, and she must use it.

"Look, I'm just your PA, Max. You don't owe me anything. Let's get on with the evening and you can do what you came to do."

TWELVE

Despite everything, the rest of the night passed smoothly enough, and Charlotte even came close to enjoying herself and the novelty of the occasion. The compère, a florid, ageing comedian, welcomed each prize-giver with a similar bitchy little speech belittling and disparaging their achievements with the predictable effect that it made the audience roar with laughter.

The venue was formerly a Victorian ice rink, and the circular arrangement of tables festooned with the same origami-like gold décor took her breath away. The walls were replete with sconces and wooden panelling with more chandeliers suspended from the ceiling like giant jellyfish. She was reminded unexpectedly of a childhood outing with her father, some kind of ballet, was it *Copelia*? She remembered being transfixed by the lights playing on the dancers' faces and the tiny Copelia pirouetting across the stage as if by clockwork. It felt a bit like that now, like they were all merely an assortment of puppets who would cease movement as the clock chimed thirteen. Her father back then had been both amused and gratified by the intensity of her concentration;

and she drank in the details greedily now, committing them to her mind's eye.

Thankfully, she had been seated next to an extremely charming film director and his actor wife. They were both American and effusive in their friendliness and interest in her life, which they had interpreted as enchantingly eccentric rather than humiliatingly mundane. Her stomach twisted disconcertingly whenever she met Max's eyes. She could feel him scrutinising her at intervals but, when she looked up, he kept his gaze resting on her lightly and she tried to meet it as casually in return.

Max managed to mount the stage, crack a few scripted jokes, announce the winner of the best newcomer without incident, and exchange air kisses with the bodacious recipient. Inside, he was counting the minutes until the end of the evening. It was only by treating the presentation like a part in a film that he was able to get through it at all. Charlotte got a few well-chosen snaps for the Instagram account, which she proceeded to upload in real time partnered with enthusiastic comments detailing Max's wardrobe: the watch, obviously; the sponsor (awareness of future deals); and of course Max standing with the proud winner.

She noted that Max had taken on the insouciant air that he gave off in character, and wondered whether he was as relaxed as the image he was portraying. He paused professionally for the laughter that met his gentle dig about one of the other nominees (a co-star), and the self-deprecating comment about his own lack of suitability in presenting the award. It was a slick performance, though without heart.

Nell was sitting several tables back, glowing like a beacon even in this glitter, and Charlotte saw her glancing away on several occasions when she realised that she had been spotted. *She still cares for him*, Charlotte thought, feeling some sympathy towards her. Neil was a buff and chiselled man with a weak jaw, questionable dress sense (loafers without socks) and the distinct lineage of *Made in Chelsea*. He bore a mild resemblance to Max, but it was Max with his features distended and slightly blurred, and Charlotte recoiled from the slightly braying laughter she could hear him emitting. To have lost Max and gained Neil felt like a massive loss of capital in life's lottery, and she had no doubt that the perspicacious Nell would have agreed.

On the table were other presenters, many of them slightly older actors who had made their careers originally on the stage rather than the screen. Charlotte started to relax as they involved her in their conversations.

"You teach, you paint... you look after this one... is there anything you can't do?" An avuncular character actor to her left appeared to be particularly enamoured.

"Paint?" Max turned round from the conversation he had been reluctantly having with a young ingénue who had been hovering, complimenting him on the latest episodes of the Netflix drama, desperate to follow the same route.

He addressed her directly across the table. "I didn't know that you painted seriously, Charlotte!"

Charlotte turned round to face him. "I wanted to paint professionally after I finished my degree, but I decided to do a teaching course instead. Good to know you don't know everything about me."

Charlotte had the smallest amount of satisfaction in her response. Petty, she knew, but she felt like she had regained some agency.

The elderly actor stifled a grin and patted her on the back. "Well said, young lady!"

"No, I don't suppose I do." Max turned back to the young actress before him and immediately thought how vapid and tiresome she was. Small, blonde, almost a younger version of Nell. He had seen a hundred of these women in America; porn star pneumatic and clad in something akin to a negligée. She ticked all the boxes yet satisfied none. He dimly registered the ripple of laughter passed round the table.

Max stared unseeingly at the girl in front, his face giving little away. Inwardly, he felt like he had been slapped hard across the face. He had wanted to impress Charlotte this evening, he knew that now, but all he seemed to have done was to reveal his insecurities. Charlotte registered the minute change in his expression and instantly felt guilty. Then she dismissed this feeling. People were actually talking to her for who she was, and for once she was feeling seen. Not a failure of a woman who couldn't become a mother, but an interesting individual in her own right. She felt emboldened, reinvented.

***

Back at the hotel room, she dismissed his request to talk.

"I'm tired. We can talk in the morning. It doesn't matter now."

Max looked at her standing there outside her room, leaning against her door; he wasn't sure what he was asking for – a promise? A bond? But he was struggling with her proximity; he needed physical contact in some form.

"May I kiss you goodnight?" he said coquettishly; it was a calculated risk after earlier events.

"I suppose so." Charlotte was taken off-guard; the evening had gone well, and she did not want Max to change that. Hell, she wasn't sure what she wanted apart for him to go so she could sleep, and then think some more. She suddenly felt light-headed and weary. At the moment there were possibilities; anything more risked disappointment and the failure of expectation.

He dropped a gentle kiss on her cheek. "Thank you for coming with me tonight. It was a big ask, even as my employee." A pause. "You looked stunning."

Charlotte coloured. "You didn't need to say that. It was the clothes, the make-up, not me really." She could feel her pulse throbbing as the heat entered her body.

"You did look beautiful. I'm not saying it for the sake of it. It was that which threw me earlier on." Max looked at her steadily, but his heart was pounding. He hadn't meant to do this now, but he seized the opportunity gratefully. "You reminded me of someone: Bella. Did you hear Nell say her name? She knows how it makes me feel still. Bella is— was my twin. It's why I wear this bracelet. She had a matching one. It was buried with her. Wearing it makes me feel that I'm near her still. I want to talk to you, Charlotte. Please let me explain. In the morning."

Her gaze held him; he was drowning. Her eyes were his lifeline. Charlotte stared without seeing, events slowly shuffling and reordering in her mind. She laid a hand on his arm for a second but said nothing. Max checked his breath and met her stare without looking away. The very air seemed suspended for a moment, taut and anticipatory.

"Yes, good night." Charlotte walked into her room without a backwards glance and the door closed with finality.

Her mind was roaring; she couldn't quite believe what she had just heard.

Max watched her go and imagined following her. He could feel a powerful pull, he just wasn't quite sure of its nature. He wrenched himself away and threw himself on the bed in his own suite, still fully clothed. Sleep came over him like a fog, forgiving and dispassionate.

THIRTEEN

She couldn't sleep that night. Long after she had heard Max's footsteps padding to the other side of the corridor, she tossed and turned despite the 400-thread count. She was being presented with a reality that she wanted to absorb but her mind was fighting against her. Why was Max showing such interest in her? Was it solely because of this twin, this presence in the background that seemed to consume him? Had she room to accommodate his frailty as well as her own? She wanted to know him fully, but at what expense? She was scared, scared of being humiliated, of being used, even, although she wasn't sure how he could need her. What could she really give him?

Images of the night rushed before her eyes like camera stills. The candelabra catching the lights of the golden decorations below; Max on the stage, confident, a golden boy amid his peers; Nell bent over his prostrate body, her hair bright against the night sky; the blinding flash of a camera as they exited the theatre so that the photographer's shape was seared into her brain for moments afterwards.

***

She woke up later than she had intended, having finally dropped off in the first light. For a moment, blissful forgetfulness meant that she spent a few luxurious seconds relishing the softness of the mattress and the fug of sleep slowly lifting. Then she reached for her phone and registered that not only was it after 10.00a.m., but there had been a number of missed calls and messages. Dan, obviously, but Max had been busy too and it was these she opened first.

Shall we meet for breakfast at 9.30? Then, *I've overslept [sorry emoji] – typical. Plse eat if ur up. Will be down in 20.* Lastly, *U okay? Shall I order u something?* This was only fifteen minutes earlier.

Charlotte slowly raised herself up and then sank back down against the padded headboard. She allowed herself a blush-inducing few minutes to replay the events of the night before. She couldn't hide from herself any longer. She was attracted to him, terribly attracted. But what should she do? Carry on in a state of denial, pushing him away, punishing him for being kind, whatever the reasons behind this? And what had happened to Bella? She supposed she would find out at some point before they left for home.

There was a shoot scheduled for today, a bloody stupid idea, now she thought about it. Some aftershave brand wanted Max to star in a series of screen adverts. He was going to be their face for the summer campaign. It was studio-based, which is why she had agreed to pencil it in for today. She sighed and started to move.

***

Max was lying on his bed staring up at the ceiling when he heard a tentative knocking at the door. He hadn't had any breakfast. He felt like he was floating, precariously connected to the land like a rowing boat moored in a storm. He had listened to his current script a couple of times, but the words lapped at him without meaning.

He bounced off the bed with one agile motion and opened the door. Charlotte stood there, and there was a moment when they were both unsure of what to say. How did one return to the confidences of last night in the cold light of day? Max moved first, his usual aplomb struggling to surface. He felt embarrassed of how he had behaved. As much as Nell looked after him, he knew there was a part of her that exploited his weakness, the dent in his psyche. And he let her. How would Charlotte react when he told her about Bella? How would she judge him? Could he trust her? Outside the family, they had managed to keep the matter almost entirely out of the public eye. His stage name was different to hers; there was already a Max Hollinsworth in Equity, so Collins, a nod to an astronaut he had completed a project on as a child, had seemed a reputable choice.

"Are you ready to go? Have you had something to eat?" He seized the mundanities gratefully.

"I'm not sure that I can face anything yet, but I hope you have."

"Yes, I've cleaned out the buffet," Max lied. He couldn't eat. He felt too wired. "Are you ready to go then? Shoreditch, isn't it?"

They picked up their car at the front of the hotel after Max had paid. Charlotte hovered uncertainly a few paces away. She supposed that this was all tax deductible. Should she be collecting receipts or investigating VAT? Oh well, that was the least of her problems at the moment. Outside the hotel were several hardcore autograph hunters who came alive as soon as they recognised Max. He posed for some photos and signed some arms. Charlotte marvelled at how he turned this persona on and off and, for the hundredth time that morning, she wondered how well she really knew him.

The car took them straight to the entrance of the company headquarters. The journey passed in silence and Max sat slumped and brooding for the duration, making monosyllabic returns to Charlotte when she ventured to pass any remarks. She was struggling. He had managed to put on a face with the fans, so why not with her? She steeled herself not to react and loaded the headlines up on her phone. Oh shit, there were pictures of the night before in glorious technicolour. Thank fuck Max's head blocked her view... Oh crap, there was even some video. *The dress at least suited me*, she thought, relieved, *and at least the papers didn't seem to know who I was*. Small mercies. She contemplated what to say to Max and then decided she wouldn't. He could look for himself if he was interested.

There were several WhatsApp messages from Della, which Charlotte chose to leave unopened. She could see the beginnings of them and had no wish to explore further.

FFS, Charlotte, what have...

Can you get back to...

I insist you contact me...

It was up to Max to deal with her; she just didn't have the energy right now.

The car slid into an underground carpark underneath the offices of the company, and Max peeled himself off the upholstery. The driver came round and opened the door for Charlotte, and she smiled her thanks, inwardly groaning as her head protested when she stood. She followed Max to a glass door with a logo embossed across its front. Max buzzed and said shortly, "Max Collins and PA to see Marco Circani."

"Please come through, Mr. Collins."

The door clicked and Max held it open for Charlotte. She missed her step as she entered and lurched into Max's side. He held out his hands to steady her, and she registered his grip but did not acknowledge it, quickly righting herself and keeping her expression fixed. They both entered a small vestibule and were greeted by a girl hovering by a lift, all eyes and legs: tiny skirt, bared midriff and slogan t-shirt with long, long hair and deer-like limbs.

Charlotte realised she had been wise to wear the fashionable slouchy biscuit-coloured suit with a silky ivory t-shirt underneath and white trainers that were much more edgy than she would have normally picked, a doubt-fuelled last-minute online purchase for this trip. She had teamed it with a chunky gold chain and matching earrings and left her hair loose, but it was behaving itself today at least. The remaining curls from last night had given it a slight wave which was taking the edge off the lack of washing. She couldn't really do smudgy eyeliner so had settled with some hastily applied wings which at least seemed to draw attention away from the dark circles under her eyes... well, with a large amount of concealer on top.

She cast a sideways look at Max, but he was looking at his phone, frowning as he scrolled. He looked decidedly worse for wear this morning, and he hadn't yet shaved. Charlotte felt oddly protective. He looked up at her suddenly and caught her eye. She felt that odd sensation of being penetrated beyond the surface level, her stomach twanging like it had been plucked. Painful and pleasurable all at once.

The girl had an expensive-looking laptop perched on a standing desk and made a show of locating their names on it.

"Okay, guys, please come this way, the shoot's scheduled for 1.00p.m. and Marco wants to say hello before we start selecting outfits, et cetera."

Max rolled his eyes at no one in particular and followed the girl into the lift. She tapped in the floor and Charlotte raised her eyebrows after the first four storeys.

"The penthouse," explained the girl.

The lift chimed and stopped, and she waited for them to exit. A far cry from the artificial lights of the basement, this floor was filled with sunlight from the ceiling to floor windows that lined the walls with a view of the London rooftops stretching out beyond. It was furnished lavishly with huge, outsized sofas and chairs in cream leather, and a fifties style bar area at one end. Looking out of the outsized windows were an olive-skinned man and a woman who exuded an air of relaxed wealth. He was in his fifties, in a black polo neck and grey tailored trousers, and she wore a charcoal loose-fitting suit with a laundered white t-shirt underneath and metallic trainers. From a distance, she could have passed for much younger with her athletic frame and thick hair; close up, Charlotte would have said that she was nearer to sixty.

"Max, Max, *ciao, caro mio.*"

The woman warmly embraced Max who, to Charlotte's surprise, leant in and accepted the hug with enthusiasm.

"Adriana, Marco, it's a pleasure. How are you both?"

"All the better for seeing you! And who is this?" The man clapped his hand on Max's shoulders and leant towards

Charlotte, who visibly stiffened. How was she supposed to greet them? "Relax, my child." He double kissed her on both cheeks, and she tried to smile.

"Charlotte." Max gestured towards her airily. "My PA. Thanks to her I'm here today. She's now managing my diary and I am actually getting things done in the right order!"

"*Si*, Max, the communication was much more prompt that usual, very efficient!" Adriana smiled and her tanned skin wrinkled and dimpled. "She must be one clever lady to have taken in hand your – how do you say it? – disorganisation. *Che pasticcio!*"

"What can I say? She is a blessing—"

Marco interrupted impatiently, "So we shoot you today for the aftershave, *chico*? You've seen the ideas, and I 'ave some great clothes. We're going for urban chic, you know? A little *farsi la barba*, perhaps?" He cocked an eyebrow, and Max made a wry face.

"It was a late one, Marco, do what you like with me – I'm all yours."

Charlotte stepped in tentatively, eager to show her preparation yet aware of her inexperience.

"We've seen the storyboard and we feel that Max could mix it up perhaps, a bit of a nod to his character at the moment?"

"You've done your 'omework. I'm impressed!" Marco gestured to a rack of clothes at the side of the room. "Why don't you pick a few things that you feel comfortable in? Ajay will be shooting you today. Abigail will get Jonno to give you a lovely close shave – *bellisimo*! You remember Ajay? He did the shots for *Esquire* last March with…" He named another big name from the world of film. "Why don't you sit there, Charlotte? Max can come and show you each outfit, yes?"

Charlotte sat down on one of the vast sprawling sofas that were angled out to the skyline. They were so big as to be almost impractical for mere sitting and she perched uncertainly as Max was led off by the assistant who had directed them earlier. Marco gestured towards the bar area.

"A drink, *cara mia*?"

Charlotte hesitated, and then, "Why not? Do you have a gin and tonic?"

"*Si*, very English! You like this one?" Marco smiled and then proceeded to mix the drink with an expert hand.

Adriana wandered over from where she had been taking a phone call, "One for me too, Marco. Abigail," she called to the girl who had come back with some olives and lemon, "run out for a charcuterie tray too. It's way past *il pranzo*."

Charlotte smiled at Adriana and then she too started scrolling through her phone. At long last a message from Daniel had arrived and she texted back eagerly but it was ambivalent, anonymous, and she wondered whether he had been offended by her lack of communication. A couple of minutes later and Max appeared in an oatmeal linen suit with an ivory shirt and tie. He looked very unsure, and his discomfort was obvious. He walked over to her and said under his breath, "God, this is horrific, Charlotte – I wouldn't be seen dead in this get-up."

She could see Marco's eyebrows slowly rising and eyed Max critically for a few seconds before deciding what to do. He was right, this wasn't Max right now, this sophisticated, cultivatedly relaxed image – he needed something a bit more undone, more human, less perfect.

"Let's have a look, Max, don't worry, there must be something a bit more you."

There were several darker options. Charlotte was mindful of the fact that this was for the late summer campaign, so she thought they might just get away with a faded shade of navy, and she selected a pale cornflower linen shirt that contrasted with Max's eyes. The trousers were sharp and flattering but Charlotte sensed that something still wasn't quite right. The assistant was hovering nearby, looking at her watch.

"Roll your sleeves up, Max, and undo another button. Then hold the jacket, but don't wear it."

Max nodded and did as he was told just as the photographer coughed from the other side of the screen.

"You ready, mate?"

"Leave the stubble, it looks good. Let's see if they go with this."

"Coming, Ajay."

Max started taking his bracelet off.

"No, Max – it's you, and that's what they want."

Max stared at Charlotte and then looked down at his wrist. She was right. It was part of his skin now, under it, even.

They walked round the edge of the screen where Marco and Adriana were hovering, bent in conversation. Adriana saw Max first and her face broke into a smile.

"There, *caro*, you look wonderful. That is what we want – *the uomo moderno*. Marco, look…"

Marco turned. His face registered surprise and then he nodded appraisingly.

"Much better, thank you, *cara*." He winked at Charlotte. "You have an eye for this… the sleeves, *si*, *tagliente*, he has an edge here. This way, Max. We're using a green screen, technology, eh?"

They were both shown through a doorway into an anteroom which was windowless and set up with a green screen across the opposite wall and white photographer's base. A round metal table, of the kind that you might find outside a restaurant, and some metal chairs were positioned in the middle. Ajay and Max stood by, talking presumably about the posing. Max settled in the chair and Ajay started taking test shots. Charlotte stood for a few minutes, ill at ease. Suddenly she heard voices behind her, and a string of French.

She swung round and saw what could only be a model being ushered into the room by Abigail. She had on a cream linen sundress, the bodice of which clung to her figure as if she had been sewn into it. Her long muscular limbs were the colour of mahogany, and a coil of blue-black hair was slicked back into a tight bun, skin and hair both shining like they had been oiled. Her figure towered above Charlotte, who hurriedly moved to one side. She was like some kind of goddess.

"Max, this is Onuala. I think you two have met before?" Adriana whispered some words to the woman and then ushered her forward.

Max looked up and he greeted Onuala amiably enough, but his face took on the slightly set look he adopted when he was preparing to film. Onuala was given some instructions by Ajay, and she perched against the table initially and then leant against Max's lap. Ajay came to consult with them again, and Adriana joined them – they seemed to be having a heated debate. The couple got up and assumed the pose of a tango, Max throwing Onuala's upper body back tautly across his arm. They did this a few times, twisting inwards also with Ajay throwing out encouragement. The images would be visually arresting, Charlotte reflected, the contrast of the skin colours and the drama of the dance movements entwining them in a passionate embrace. She wondered if he found Onuala attractive. Who wouldn't have enjoyed having her body thrust against them?

Charlotte decided to leave them to it. She wandered back into the main room where a huge tray of Italian meats, cheeses and olives had been left on the coffee table with napkins and sparkling water. She picked at a few olives, realising that she had regained her appetite after her lack of breakfast this morning. Marco and Adriana were nowhere to be seen and she leant back, feeling suddenly exhausted. The next thing she knew was the sound of Ajay and Max talking close at hand. She opened her eyes and saw Max grinning at her, looking more relaxed than he had done since they had arrived.

"You were sleeping like a baby!"

She sat up hurriedly. "Where's Onuala?"

"She had to go – another appointment. I don't know how she has the energy. I'm bushed." He plonked himself down next to Charlotte and felt immediately the intimacy of his position. He could feel the softness of her thighs; she seemed diminutive after the model. He suddenly wished that they were on their own, in the garden at the barn with Jake running round outside. The shoot had been tiring, although Onuala was aways a laugh. He had worked with her several times before and she always regaled him with stories of her recent conquests, both male and female. She enjoyed a bit of flirting as well, grinding into him suggestively during the closer dance moves and making sure that she took overly long to find her position when on his lap. He had never taken it further, although he couldn't help but admire her audacity.

He started wolfing down the food, realising he was ravenous. The aftershock of the evening before was starting to retreat. Adriana and Marco joined them and started chatting about past shoots with Max, peppered with affectionate questions about his children and work, and trying to involve Charlotte in the conversation where they could. They both started to relax, and Charlotte felt her reserve begin to slip away. She hardly noticed that Ajay had started snapping again, but then suddenly he exclaimed, "Yessss, that's it. It's a wrap, guys – great job! Marco, Adie, you need to see these."

"Ajay, don't you ever stop?"

Marco got up, glass in hand, and went to look over Ajay's shoulder. His eyes widened and he started to beam.

"Ajay, you're a master, these are amazing! Max, you are animated! We'll have to use these for another part of the campaign, Adriana."

The camera was passed round, and Charlotte had to admit that Ajay had captured something that she herself would not have seen. A group of friends, spanning the years, the effervescence of the boy with the film star looks holding his audience. She was in profile in many of them or looking down to disguise a smile. In some, Max looked at her, and she studied his gaze, wishing she knew what to make of it. Adriana started a slow handclap, and Max shushed her quickly, laughing.

"I feel like you'll be paying me for nothing, and you've fed me too!"

He changed quickly and Charlotte was left with Ajay while he packed his camera carefully away.

"Max seems happy, you must be good for him."

"Oh, we're not together," Charlotte spoke quickly. "I'm just his PA."

"My mistake." Ajay smiled and carried on polishing and undoing lenses. "It's just the way he looked at you back there. Are you interested?"

"I'm married," Charlotte responded immediately. She turned slightly so she wouldn't see the flush that stained her cheeks in betrayal. Why did people keep assuming that this was the case? Had they seen her? Had they seen him? "He's a film star... I'm a... a... different circles, you know?" She tailed off lamely.

"So? Max isn't like that." Ajay laughed at her embarrassment. "Truly. You're misjudging him if you think he cares about any of that crap."

"It's not relevant anyway," Charlotte said stiffly and pretended to fiddle with something in her bag.

"Most women would die to be in your position," Ajay persisted.

"Well, I'm not most women then." Charlotte snapped her bag shut and walked towards the exit. "Goodbye, Ajay. It was good to meet you." Was this how it worked – the more that she denied it, the more obvious it became?

"It was a pleasure," Ajay retaliated.

She was good, but it was obvious that she was falling for him. You didn't have to work long in his industry to work out who had chemistry and who had not. He could see something growing between these two. It was subtle but there, nonetheless. He wondered what had happened, or would happen, between them. Max deserved a break. She wasn't his obvious type, true, but he wasn't exactly renowned for choosing well in the past.

FOURTEEN

It had gone 4.00p.m. before they left the building, still light with the promise of longer days in sight. An English March had delivered a sunny day, although cold, and the sun had brought an eclectic mess of locals and tourists out onto the London pavements: joggers, tourists, families, parents with prams vying for space on the pavements with commuters. Charlotte stared, cocooned in the car: so many lives lived simultaneously, all bound up in their own stories. When you stopped to consider it, it became dizzying.

She was brought out of her reverie by Max speaking: "I'd like to pop in on my flat before we leave for home, and I thought I might call in on my parents, if you don't mind hanging around. I haven't seen them for six months or so, and Dad's had a hip operation."

Max apparently had a small two-storey flat in Hampstead. Still disconnected, she mumbled an affirmative. He began to drive the car more aggressively, hugging the bus lanes and leaving just a touch too little distance between him and the car and front.

The mass of concrete started almost imperceptibly to soften into tree-lined Edwardian avenues. Charlotte, her face dulling, spied a Bugaboo here and there; school children hunched over their mobile phones; an elderly man clutching a bag of shopping.

"Thank fuck, a parking space." Max drew up at speed and manoeuvred the car into the slot outside. It was a squeeze, and he swore again as the car nudged the kerb. Rummaging in the glove compartment, he drew out his permit. "Some luck at least. Can't believe I was sensible enough to stow it where I could actually find it."

Charlotte caught sight of an expensive lipstick case rattling against the sides and resolved to say nothing. It was none of her business.

The flat was part of an early-twentieth-century semi and there was a short walled garden leading up to the navy front door. Ornate brass door furniture and a tiled step suggested illusions of former grandeur. Max fiddled with the key and then stepped back to let Charlotte enter first. She stepped over the pile of takeaway menus and junk mail, finding herself in a comparatively airy hall with black and white tiling, sage green walls and big wooden doors leading off.

Charlotte took in the details of her surroundings with interest. Although she would never have admitted it, she was intrigued to see what a film star's pad looked like in the flesh. It all appeared rather Nell-like to her. She could almost see the Insta posts: *Thrilled to have finally finished our townhouse reno #townandcountry #moderncitychic.* There were a few carefully placed side tables and some floating shelving. Monochrome pictures of Max and the children in matching lacquered frames formed lines up the stairs.

"Let's grab a drink," Max said, feeling the adrenalin ease slightly. "This way."

He stepped down the hallway to the door at the end. It led to a spacious kitchen-cum-diner, enjoying the last of the late afternoon light. It looked out to a long and narrow strip of a garden typical of the style of property. There was a bird table leaning forlornly on the other side of the window and a seat just visible at the end, overshadowed by trees and hedging. The actual kitchen was fairly traditional and needed some updating, but it had a homely feel and she could see Max visibly relax.

"Did you live here with Nell?" Charlotte asked curiously. The house seemed a strange mix – the traditional and the intimate juxtaposed with something that was trying a bit too hard.

"Nell lived here for a bit when we first got together; she even started doing some decorating and such," Max replied, filling a kettle and getting a couple of mugs out of a cupboard, "but she couldn't bear it after a while – all the crumbling and unevenness, I mean." He laughed without humour. "A bit like me. We found something together in Kilburn. Much more modern, more Nell. No, this was my parents' flat. I used to rent it from them, bought them out a few years ago. Bella and I both lived here when we were students. That's why Mum and Dad got it… thought it was a financial investment and would give us one less thing to squander our student loans on. Tea? Coffee?"

"Tea, please, strong – have you got milk?"

"That's a good point." Max opened another cupboard and pulled out a carton of long-life milk. "Is this okay?"

Charlotte nodded and he handed her the drink. She took

a few sips and felt revived. It was funny how tea could do that to a person.

"Biscuit?" said Max and met her eyes. They both giggled suddenly. The stress of yesterday, and the incongruity of the present situation seemed ludicrous somehow.

There was a sofa in the dining area of the room: old, leather and covered with a rumpled throw and cushions that felt soothingly worn and squishy. They both sank down, thrown together until Charlotte firmly shuffled a few inches to the left. A faded Indian rug covered the centre of the floor, and some plastic toys were spilling out of a painted cupboard that stood unjudgementally in the corner. Children's pictures had been blu-tacked to it haphazardly. *To Daddy* had been painstakingly spelt out in an uneven hand on a drawing of an elephant. Another life. Charlotte turned away and saw that Max was watching her with a tense, constrained look on his face.

"Were you at the same place, you and Bella?"

She could tell that Max had something he needed to get out; she just needed to find the key to opening him. Like a child with a confession to make – she was used to that.

Max exhaled slowly and stretched his legs out in front of him. Where to begin, how to do her justice? *Here we go, Bells, for you.*

"I went to Central Saint Martins, the Drama Centre; Bella was at UCL. She studied English and Philosophy. She was very brainy, you know, instinctively, much more than I was, and driven too. We thought she would go and do something big; she was so opinionated and mouthy. We all felt she was the one with the bright future." His voice faded away, and he felt the dormant anger once again seep through him.

"What happened?" Charlotte said quietly.

Max could feel his breath inch out slowly. Saying it never stopped it feeling wrong, unreal, like he was plummeting the depths for some god-awful role.

"She killed herself, Charlotte. My brilliant sister. She had a breakdown and couldn't stand it anymore. It happened when she was in hospital. They let her down and we let her down too. We all failed her." The tension in his voice was grating.

Charlotte held her own breath; she hadn't expected this. He continued in a torrent, hardly aware of her now.

"People going on about mental health and wellbeing. They frustrate me. Most of it is a joke. When someone is really mentally ill, so mentally ill that they think they are actually the only sane ones, you can't always see it coming. We didn't really understand it until it was going really badly wrong. Sometimes it's so much a part of someone that you accept the unacceptable. You love them so much that you don't want to believe something is so intrinsically skewed, that they're completely fucked up." He rested his elbows on his knees and put his head in his hands.

Charlotte waited; it was all she could do. It was worse than she had feared. She had thought maybe an illness or disease perhaps, or some tragic freak accident. She dimly remembered a conversation with Emily, long-since forgotten. Em had been talking about her dad; he had depression, highs and then terrible lows where he was almost catatonic. The family just got on with it, but she remembered Em raging about her mum, who she accused of encouraging her and her siblings to think that by ignoring it, it might just go away.

"She won't admit there's a problem; she puts her head in the sand until the next time when it happens all over again. I can't stand it, Charl. No one will tell him that he needs to get help." She had left home as soon as she could, and privately admitted to Charlotte one drunken night that she considered herself emotionally damaged as a result, permanently.

"He just wasn't present, he couldn't be. I don't blame him, but it was a hideous existence, for all of us. He was there one moment, helping us with our homework, and the next he wasn't speaking for four weeks."

She could see that Max had entered a world of his own pain. He walked over to a drawer and wordlessly handed Charlotte a photo. It matched the one she had seen by Max's bed, but here the girl was caught in laughter, her face transformed by mirth. The young Max was laughing too but his eyes were on the girl, and she filled the frame.

"When we were children, I was always the quiet one. Bella led in everything, and she used to take risks, stupid risks. She would be the one to try the rotten branch, to race the car on her bike, to drink the illicit drink. And I hurt for her. I was terrified for her at times. She seemed to have no fear. She was always laughing, laughing about everything. She could be such fun to be with, but often it wasn't fun after all. As a child, I was the one who was always scared, scared of being found out, scared of being last, scared of her anger. But I also loved her so much. She was like part of me, the strong daring part that was hidden. She did things so I didn't have to… at least that's what I told myself."

Charlotte murmured a word of comfort.

"Then she did well at our sixth form college. Our background was fairly average, but she loved reading, and

I loved the stories. Our parents encouraged us; we were the spoilt surprise arrivals. I have an older sister too, Kirsten, but she's six years older and didn't want much to do with two little brats. We were inseparable. We both wanted to go to university and Bella decided that we were going to have to relocate to a city. I'd appeared in a few advertisements, nothing big, but it helped out with getting onto my course. I think the model scout twisted a few arms so that they waived the normal entry requirements – my A-levels were pretty shocking.

"Bella decided to read English and Philosophy; of course, she could do brilliantly without having to do too much work, whereas it was much more of a slog for me. You can imagine, with the dyslexia. That wasn't even diagnosed until my teens. Bella went to my teacher to complain about how I was being penalised. She was the one who identified it.

"We both moved in here, after a bit of convincing Mum and Dad that we would be able to cope on our own, and at first it all seemed to be okay. We were out a lot, separately by this stage. We crossed each other in the kitchen late at night or on the sofa in the morning watching daytime TV. You know what it's like. You're selfish at that age, aren't you? Caught up in your own social bubble." Max was quiet. The truth was, he had discovered girls and they had discovered him. It had been quite an awakening.

"Looking back now, I think that was the first time that Bella entered a manic stage. I began to hardly see her. She literally didn't stop for several days and then she would bomb and hardly move, staying in her room, wearing the same clothes, not washing. I hadn't tried anything much myself, but there were small signs that she was probably taking all sorts: weed, poppers, coke. Windows were left open at sub-zero temperatures, there were plates with weird debris by the side of her bed.

"She lost quite a lot of weight, and that's when I really noticed her personality changing. She started having these strange theories about all kinds of things, but she was particularly obsessed by the belief that one of our neighbours was stalking her." He looked directly at Charlotte with a weary expression. "Do you want me to go on? There's so much crap that I have a problem filtering it. Do you really want to hear this?"

"No, no, go on, Max. I want to know. She sounds like she was an amazing person. I mean, she sounds pretty exceptional."

Max laughed bitterly. "She was, and she wasn't. The illness started to attack her. She became fixated with the idea that she was being followed. Paranoid, I can see now, but then I didn't know what to do. The awful thing was that she sounded so lucid, so rational when she spoke about this neighbour. I almost started believing in some of it. I'm surprised that he didn't go mad himself, poor bloke. I had to apologise several times when Bella started to jump into hedges when she saw him, and she even called the police twice. I took a bottle of whiskey round after that. But then she started to go AWOL for a night or two at a time and I began to get really worried. I realised that I couldn't deal with it on my own.

"The final straw came when she was brought home in a panda car with one of her mates. The girl was distraught. Bella had tried to jump into the Thames off Southwark Bridge. She had been drinking and was on her way home in the tube with her friend. She saw someone and thought that the neighbour had put some kind of hit on her. She panicked and did a runner. The friend was beside herself. Luckily, some good Samaritan managed to grab her before she went in.

"I lay in Bella's bed with her that night and I remember being rigid with fear. I didn't dare sleep. Bella admitted that she was hearing voices in her head. We got the train home the next day. Mum and Dad took Bella straight to the GP and he told us to take her to the mental health unit at the local hospital. She was admitted but it was voluntary that time. In between bouts of delusion, Bella recognised that she needed help and she felt guilty – we were all so obviously terrified. She tried to explain herself to me, but I didn't want to hear. I felt responsible – I had let her become who she was. It was always easier for me to be led, to give into her.

"She was discharged after a month and seemed much better, on meds and calmer. She wasn't quite the Bella of old, but we knew she needed the drugs and, frankly, we were just pleased that she seemed to have everything under control."

Charlotte listened intently, imagining the shadowy rows and heartache that had happened here, so at odds with the heavy silence that bore down on them now.

"Mum and Dad couldn't stop rowing about it all summer – what to do for the best. There wasn't much family support then; don't know if there is now, to be honest. They danced around mentioning it to her; they thought they could cure her by wrapping her up in cotton wool. She stayed at home over the break, working at a local supermarket and going out with her old school friends. Then autumn came and she begged Mum and Dad to let her rejoin her university course – she was so bright that she had been allowed to defer. They couldn't stop her, could they? She was a grown woman. So she started again. I was in my second year, and it was all okay for a while, until it wasn't.

"The second time seemed much more sudden and terrible. Bella barricaded herself into her room after a weekend drinking herself into oblivion. I had to ring the police to help get her out. They wouldn't come out at first – she was over eighteen, apparently not a risk to anyone. They couldn't hear what she was saying. Rubbish most of it, but she was totally convinced by what she was spouting out. I had to say that she had threatened to kill herself." His voice was hoarse.

"Mum and Dad turned up and we took her home. She was angry and frightened, and we were desperate for help. We took her to the hospital again, and this time they decided that she had to be sectioned. She was spouting a load of shit about the neighbour, tutors, even friends. She was livid, screaming at us, and then begging for us to take her home. It was the worst moment of my life. She accused us of abandoning her, of tricking her to get her into hospital." Max's voice broke. "I can't get that image out of my head. They had to drag her off me. She knew that I was the one who would break first." He banged his fist against his head. "I let her down, Charlotte. I let her go."

"You did what was best for her, Max. She needed to be there," Charlotte said softly, feeling tears come into her own voice. "How could you deal with that? She must have been so ill by that point."

Max put both palms on the window facing the garden and stood still for a moment, his muscles rigid. "No, I did let her down, Charlotte. That was the last I ever saw of her. We got a phone call the next day. She had managed to hang herself with the strap of her shoulder bag."

Charlotte's face widened in horror. "Wasn't she checked before she went in? Wasn't she put on suicide watch? I thought they had cameras in these places."

"It was a catalogue of errors. She was admitted on a Sunday, and we found out at the inquest that they were massively short-staffed. They hadn't done the full checks on arrival, and she had actually been handed the bag back by an orderly who was new to the job. None of us had really taken her threats seriously. Not even me. That's what I can't stand. That she couldn't share with me why she was feeling that way."

"I'm so, so sorry." Charlotte went and stood next to Max awkwardly. She wanted to hug him, to soak up the grief from him like a sponge, but instead she put a tentative hand on his arm. "What a terrible, terrible thing to happen to your family. It must be unfeasibly awful having to go through something like that."

She realised now why he had been so understanding of her own issues; how could he not have been with what he had gone through?

"She sounded unusually brilliant, your sister. Don't they say that the largest stars last the shortest time because they burn themselves up? It's not your family's fault – it sounds like a destructive cocktail of genetics, nature and circumstances."

"I don't know." Max looked out to the bird table and blinked his eyes furiously. "The birds don't really come anymore."

He had long ago stopped putting out food, despite Vivi being desperate for him to do it. "Too many urban foxes," he had said far too paternally but the truth was that Bella had loved that bird table and it had been her daily routine to empty the crumbs from her breakfast plate onto the flat surface. Even when she was really ill, that had been the one thing she had managed to do.

"Come and look at this." Max turned towards the hallway.

Charlotte followed him, wondering where he was taking her. He came to the foot of a staircase and took the stairs two at a time. At the top of the landing were several doors. Max walked to the end of the corridor and paused before the last one.

"I didn't like to change it. I couldn't do it in the end. I pulled down the awful photos of the neighbour and maps she had stuck everywhere but the other stuff reminds me of her, that first term before she started losing it. Another reason why Nell couldn't wait to get out. She thought it was macabre and kept nagging me to sort Bell's things out."

Several books were still scattered on the bedside table, along with a dreamcatcher hanging from the drawer knob and a lava lamp. CDs were out of their covers on the stereo and a tie-dyed skirt hung in front of the cupboard door.

"You remind me of her, a little," Max said, from the doorway. "Not in the mad way," he interjected hurriedly. "You don't look that much like each other either, but it's something about your eyes and your expression. I can't really explain it. Your directness, maybe. Your strength."

He gave a hollow laugh. It was more than that; when he felt her eyes looking into him, it was like he couldn't hide.

Charlotte picked up a silver frame that had been placed on a heavily laden bookshelf over the bed. Was she strong, direct? If strong was knowing what the hell you were doing, then she didn't feel she met the description. Then again, she was here, wasn't she? She was trying. As for the directness, she really struggled with that. Half the time her words didn't match what she really meant, and she felt she was putting her foot in it, but perhaps that wasn't what Max meant.

She looked at the photo in the frame. It was a formal family scene, with Bella and Max in their early teens by the looks of it, seated with their mother and father either side and a taller, fuller-figured girl between them.

"How have your mother and father coped? I mean, it must have made them very overprotective over you and Kirsten?"

"Overprotective? Quite the opposite. My parents can barely look at me. Every time they see me, they are reminded of her, I suppose. I can't even blame them. I blame myself. We should have kept her at home. We should never have let her go into that place again. I didn't listen to her. I didn't listen to her when she needed me most."

"Max." Charlotte could hold back no longer. She reached her arms out and put them round him hesitantly. Max stood there, tall and angular, and then bent his head to rest on her shoulder, folding himself up and letting his body relax. She felt him heave with a choking gulp of air.

"Do you know what the worst thing was? The night before I took her home, she had this one moment of clarity. She asked me if I thought she was going mad? I lied and said no, of course. And then she said she was so sorry." His voice broke and he shuddered.

Charlotte realised that she was stroking Max's hair, and pressing her own head against his as if she could drain the emotions from him. She was conscious of his body leaning against hers. Not as soft as Dan's but more sinuous and wiry. She could feel his breathing; he felt so warm and alive. He stiffened slightly and the atmosphere altered subtlely. An indefinable energy seemed to be coursing through her and she pulled apart reluctantly, not meeting Max's eyes. He stepped back, brushing a hand against his cheeks.

"What about your parents? When are they expecting you?" Charlotte asked, trying to gain traction.

"Sod them, seeing me just unsettles them anyway." Max shrugged his shoulders, and the spell was broken. He couldn't face them now after reliving the worst days of their shared experience. "Let's just go; I want to go back to Suffolk."

***

Much, much later they pulled up again outside Charlotte's house. Max got her case out of the boot and then appeared again, shamefaced, thrusting some bags into her hands.

"I asked the waiter to go back and collect them. I was looking forward to you seeing what was inside. Sorry I spoilt it," he said softly.

"I had a good time, Max." Charlotte looked up at him and meant it. "It was fun to be a part of that world just for a bit. It's important for me to see what kind of thing you are involved in. And thank you for telling me about Bella. I won't forget what you said." She held his eyes for a minute, looking steadfastly at his face, seeing the thirteen, seventeen, twenty-year-old Max and his sister. They were still there, part of him. Then she went to move towards the door.

Max put a hand out to slow her movement and bent and pecked her cheek. The warm exhale of his breath grazed her – their faces still only a few inches apart. On impulse, she leant forward and kissed his cheek. She felt his rough stubble and smelt his closeness – an unidentified cologne mixed with something else. She couldn't explain why this gesture felt appropriate, but it sealed something between them. Her stomach retracted and she fumbled with her key.

"Goodbye, Max."

The door shut with a louder slam than she had intended, and she leant against it, her heart hammering her ribs. What had got into her? What would Daniel have thought?

On the other side, Max touched his cheek thoughtfully. He was taken aback but touched. He hadn't told many friends the full story about Bella, couldn't deal with his own conflicting feelings about what had exactly happened in those last few months for her life to culminate as it did. He had made a leap of faith today, because it had felt almost like a quid pro quo. Charlotte had been brave enough to share her own problems with him. He didn't want to feel that he was hiding something anymore, burying his soul. There had been enough of that for a lifetime.

He walked back to the car on a different plane; her acknowledgement was forcing him to see the situation differently, see himself as a victim as much as Bella. He closed his eyes before he got in the car and felt the evening sunlight on his face. Something felt loosened within him. He took a deep breath.

FIFTEEN

Charlotte tried to phone Daniel that night, racked with a nagging guilt that she daren't put into words. She kept trying to push the image of Max stooping over her out of her mind; the trouble was, the more she dismissed it, the more it lingered. She was mildly surprised that she hadn't heard anything. It was unlike Daniel to become so self-absorbed that he forgot her, and her guilt became compounded by a nagging anxiety. She sent a few texts and tried ringing finally as it got towards evening, but the phone went straight to voicemail and she was left with a feeling of abandonment. At last, the phone rang, and Charlotte rushed to answer it then noticed with annoyance that it was Daniel's mother. She hung back and then picked up the phone. Maybe Barbara would know why Daniel hadn't been in contact.

"Charlotte, is that you?"

What a stupid comment, thought Charlotte. *Who else was it going to be?*

"Hi, Barbara. How are you?"

"I'm fine, dear. Are you okay? I hear you were off to something rather exciting yesterday?"

"Yes, it was very exciting. I had a great time." Charlotte squirmed inside, deliberately avoiding details. Barbara was being her typical saccharine self, all sweetness on the outside with the acidity hidden within. "Do you know why Daniel isn't answering his phone?" she ventured.

"Oh, he spoke to us earlier, I think he was going out with some clients tonight. Taking them all out for a posh dinner somewhere. He'd been asked to entertain them by the big boss, I think. He must think a lot of Daniel. Didn't he mention it?"

"He might have done," Charlotte lied through gritted teeth. "It's difficult to keep track of what he's doing sometimes. Okay, I'll try again tomorrow. Guess he probably won't be able to answer tonight."

She sensed surprise from Barbara and hoped she couldn't detect her own embarrassment over the phone. Why hadn't Daniel told her what he was doing? She couldn't help but feel like he had excluded her from his schedule on purpose.

They exchanged a few more pleasantries but Charlotte couldn't be bothered to make much more effort. Daniel had phoned Barbara over her; some things never changed. She felt hurt, but not surprised. It was probably her own fault, after all. Maybe he was punishing her for ignoring him yesterday, although it wasn't like him to be so petty.

Surprisingly, she slept deeply but with disconcertingly vivid dreams in which Max featured large. She was searching for something, and Max was helping her, but she needed Daniel, and he was nowhere to be found. There were other more disturbing feelings too, that faded in and out and that she only remembered partially. Max holding her and a deep feeling of attraction enveloping her, pleasurable and shameful in equal measures. Daniel hiding something, burying it; she wasn't sure. Was it a baby? Had she lost another baby? She was scrabbling desperately in mud beneath the tree in the garden. There was a storm; the rain was lashing down, and her clothes were plastered to her. Max was calling for her to stop, or was it Daniel? She awoke drenched in sweat and got up to get a drink.

As she padded through to the kitchen, she saw a light flashing on her phone. A message! It was from Daniel.

Hope you got home safely. Sorry I didn't call. Will phone tomorrow.

Bland and impersonal. Charlotte felt angry; he must have understood that she would be worried.

Then she realised that there was another message, one from Max.

Thanks for today. Sorry for dumping that lot on you. My baggage [confused face emoji]… I feel better though.

She noticed that he had sent it only ten minutes before. So Max couldn't sleep either. She sat down and wrinkled her brow. She didn't do emojis.

I'm pleased you wanted to share with me. It's a lot to carry round on your own.

A couple of seconds then a message pinged back:

U up still? Difficult to wind down after these events.

Charlotte thought for a few seconds and then replied:

Yep. Lots on my mind at the mo.

Almost immediately another ping:

Anytime YOU need to share – payback etc. U doing Anything tomorrow night?

Sleeping!

Apart from that? Do u want to go 4 drink?

The dog is back tomorrow. Why don't you come here?

Charlotte paused before sending. There were so many reasons why this was unwise. Daniel wasn't back until Tuesday, so she wasn't worried about him, but she quizzed herself on whether or not he would approve. She couldn't help feeling deceitful somehow and, given their poor communication at the moment, that it probably was not a good idea. Despite her qualms, she closed her eyes and let her mind indulge in the feeling of the weight of Max's body leaning into hers in her dream. In the morning, she wouldn't remember it. It didn't matter; she wasn't hurting anyone. She missed that feeling of intimacy; she hadn't felt capable of it for a long while. She knew it wasn't real, but it had been so satisfying. She pressed send before she could bottle out.

The message came swiftly back:

Why not? I'll bring dessert.

Great. Any time after seven. I get hungry early. Night.

Charlotte resolved to postpone her moral quandary until tomorrow. It was just a dinner with a work colleague stroke friend. She fell into a dreamless sleep.

***

Max woke late the next morning. The moment he opened his eyes he was filled with the kind of anticipatory feeling he had had as a child on Christmas Day. Then he remembered Charlotte had invited him over for dinner and she knew everything – well, almost. He felt lighter and unencumbered. She hadn't mentioned whether or not her husband would be there, but he was assuming he would be. *Better bring some beers*, he thought to himself.

He realised that he hadn't stopped thinking about her since he had dropped her off yesterday, and yet he still wasn't sure what it was all about. Only that it was disruptive, potentially dangerous. He wasn't used to this kind of complication in his love life. Yes, there had been a whole raft of problems with Nell, but he had never felt that his own conscience had been compromised. When Nell had had, what he knew now, were probably two or three different affairs before and, he suspected, during the beginning at least of her pregnancy with Dom; he had been in the dark, a cuckolded spouse himself. There was no way he could even come close to getting in the middle of a couple. *We're friends and I am her boss; I just need to make sure that the lines are clear*, he told himself unconvincingly.

He drove to the nearest market town and trailed around a deli that looked vaguely appetising. He bought some ice cream, unsuitable probably in these colder months, some kind of gateau, and then a decent bottle of wine and some craft beers. Flowers? Chocolates? Why not? There were a dozen reasons, but Max managed to push them out of his mind.

He dithered among the flowers, in the end selecting a pre-wrapped bouquet of pink and red roses, peonies and freesias. He knew Charlotte liked peaches and salmon pinks – he couldn't remember how, but it had stuck in his head. Oh yes, he remembered now, the meal in the hotel. They had been talking about sunsets. It had made a change. Nell had made it quite clear that she was not intellectual in any way and would tell him off if he became overly sentimental or maudlin. His mates would have laughed, apart from maybe Remeil.

When Bella died, it had seemed safer to shut away his emotional core to some extent. He admired the way in which Charlotte treated him as an equal, without pretence or artifice. Most women he met either threw themselves at him (a few fans, quite literally) or became coy and flirtatious in a way that they presumed he found sexually alluring. Of course, sometimes he couldn't help his body's response, but that was all that it was at the end of the day in these cases: a skin-deep reaction. When he was talking to Charlotte, the interest felt mutual. There was nothing so off-putting as a one-way conversation, a woman being disingenuous, but sometimes it felt that that was the sum of all his failed relationships.

The afternoon petered away. Once home, Max made a half-hearted attempt to address his correspondence and emails – about twenty from Della that he hadn't bothered to respond to yet. He registered that he had an interview with a Sunday paper coming up on Monday. He recorded himself reading a monologue for a new play that was planned to open on the London stage next March, arty but fun, and he fancied that it may be something to do during the end of season break from filming.

He took a long shower at about 5.00p.m., shaved and then dressed with more care than normal, choosing a casual shirt in a pale blue and his favourite pair of jeans. He was getting butterflies; it was ridiculous. *For fuck's sake, Max, her husband will be there – what exactly do you think is going to happen?*

He let himself out of the front door with his clinking bottles in a backpack and started off on the walk down the hill. Thoughts were coursing through his mind. What would Daniel be like? How would she behave after the events of yesterday? He ran his hands through his hair and then told himself again: *she is happily married, and you have enough on your plate at the moment.*

Charlotte was similarly unsettled. She had decided to roast a chicken – it was easy enough and would leave her with time to whip together some lemon tagliatelle with a cream sauce and prepare some roasted vegetables with pesto; easy but always a crowd-pleaser. At least she didn't have to worry about pudding. The house was cleanish, but she cleaned the loos again nevertheless and ran a hoover round. Finally, it was pristine and tidy and even the dog looked a little anxious and expectant.

What to wear herself? Charlotte decided in the end on a burgundy sleeveless shift with tights and pumps. She brushed her hair out and applied some make-up. *You look okay*, she addressed herself in the mirror, but there were dark shadows under her eyes and her skin looked almost ghostly as her reflection looked back at her dubiously. *Pull yourself together, Charlotte*, she said sternly to herself.

At ten to six, the smell of roasting chicken was wafting fragrantly through the downstairs and Charlotte was already savouring a deliciously cold glass of white Burgundy. Daniel had been saving it for Easter, but Charlotte was past caring about that. She was hurt and upset that he hadn't contacted her. A few sips of the drink and she could feel its limb-relaxing qualities already take effect, easing her resentment. She put the last finishing touches to the table and then the phone rang, and she rose unevenly. Perhaps it was Max, perhaps he couldn't come.

As she picked it up, relief poured over her. It was Daniel's number on the screen.

"Daniel, are you okay? Why haven't you phoned?"

"Charlotte, I'm sorry. I didn't know what to say." There was an odd pause, and they both started speaking at once, then Charlotte was stalled by Daniel repeating, "We need to talk. We need to talk about us."

Charlotte felt confused, befuddled. What was he saying?

"Charlotte, do you understand? I want a separation. I want to split up. I don't want to be with you anymore."

Charlotte could hear the words, but they seemed to be coming from a long distance away. She held the phone away from her ear, still listening to the tinny words fading gradually. He was leaving her. He was leaving her. The tinny sounds became more insistent, and she pressed the red button, feeling the silence bearing down on her.

Max, he could arrive at any minute. She picked up her mobile phone and started to text.

I'm ill, have to cancel. Very sorry.

The bottle was next to her, and she poured herself another glass of wine. She felt completely and utterly alone. What did anyone ever really know of someone else? She had been a fool and was now paying the price. She had largely ignored Daniel's behaviour: the signs, the missed moments. Everything had been processed through her own sensibility, and her instincts had let her down. She had trusted him wholly, trusted him to put up with her, to hold on for when it got better, only he couldn't hold on any longer.

Max was about to descend the hill down to the main road when he got the text. He looked in disbelief. What the hell was she playing at? Cold feet? Why? What was going on? He tried to call her. The phone rang and rang. He texted:

Are you okay? What's wrong?

A text came back after a few minutes:

Some kind of stomach upset. I'll be okay. Sorry to let you down.

You and me both, Max thought as he trudged back up the hill, lobbing the flowers into a ditch. He didn't know why he suddenly felt angry, but he did. Let down once more. Why was he giving anyone the power to make him feel like this again? Why did he feel bereft?

SIXTEEN

Charlotte didn't get out of bed on Monday. Or Tuesday. On Wednesday, she heard a banging on the front door, and she forced herself to get up. It was her mother; unbelievable. She stood to one side to let her in. Audrey took off her sunglasses and surveyed the interior of the house with a bemused look on her face. Charlotte looked at her in dull wonderment and reflected that the slightly pillowed contours of her face must mean that she had just had her monthly helping of Botox.

Audrey took a step towards Charlotte and then reconsidered. None of the family were natural huggers, but surely this occasion called for a modicum of affection. She reached out a gym-honed arm and rested it on Charlotte's shoulders. Charlotte looked down, helplessly, and felt the familiar prickle of tears. There was nothing worse than being pitied. The phone rang again and she groaned. Every few hours it rang and rang, and she put a pillow or the nearest soft furnishing over her head, trying to shut it out. Her mobile had run out of battery yesterday morning, and she was glad that she was finally truly unreachable.

"Daniel, I assume?" Audrey quizzed with latent amusement. "He said he was trying to reach you. You really must talk to him, darling. He just wants to know that you're okay. You haven't been answering any calls. We're all worried."

"I'm not okay." Charlotte almost spat the words out. "And he can fuck right off."

"Alright, Charlotte. Don't shoot the messenger."

Her mother tripped delicately towards the kitchen. She had kitten-heeled boots on, faux leather jeans and a cream trench coat. Charlotte thought that she looked like some kind of high-class escort from behind. What on earth was she going to make of the mess in the kitchen?

To her credit, Audrey restrained from commenting and managed to put together a credible cup of tea and find some biscuits. Charlotte heaved books, remote controls, washing and tissues off the sofa and they contrived to sit alongside one another. Her mother offered her a biscuit and she shook her head.

"Not eating, Charlotte? Try not to be so predictable."

"Predictable? This doesn't feel predictable!" Charlotte exploded.

What were the stages of grief? Denial, grief, anger, acceptance? She was definitely stuck on the anger part. She felt like a ball of bath salts – drop her in water and she would fizz away to nothing. The only person who could truly understand was the very person who had rejected her. To hear her mother judge her in that heartless, tinkly tone was more than she could bear.

But Audrey was used to Charlotte. She blinked, snake-like, and moved a few centimetres away.

"I think you should speak to him."

Her voice was firmer now, and she set Charlotte in her gaze over the cup of tea. Jake had come into the room and was nuzzling Charlotte's arms. She hid her face in his fur, not wanting Audrey to witness the collapse that was now threatening.

"You may feel at the moment that he is the biggest bastard in the universe, but sitting here in limbo is going to help no one. You say he has someone else? What do *you* want? Are you ready to fight for him, or is there nothing left? Daniel said something about you working for some actor."

Charlotte almost laughed as she heard her mother elongate out the last syllable.

"What's going on there – should he be concerned?"

Pure anger surged through Charlotte, and she spluttered out her words. "Firstly, I would never go behind someone's back. Secondly, why would I want to fight for someone who has so obviously gone behind mine? He was so cowardly that he told me about this over the phone. Over the phone, Mum! I hate him, I hate him!"

Tears streamed down her cheeks unchecked, and Audrey carefully levered herself nearer to Charlotte, rubbing her back and patting her hands as if she were an errant child.

"There, there, Charl, it will be alright. It seems unbearable now, but it will sort itself out in the end, believe me. You don't know how many times I have been spurned and come out the other side. And there is another side, trust me!"

Charlotte looked at her mother in surprise at the fervent tone and words. Audrey didn't own failure or wrongdoing; it undermined her invincibility. She felt the anger leave her in one brutal lunge, hollowness engulfing her once more. She looked at her mother though watery eyes.

"I know it was my fault. He wanted me to look to him for support, but I couldn't. I wanted to wallow in my grief alone."

"We can only react as our personality allows," her mother responded simply. "You have been through a lot, and perhaps you have grown apart. Who knows? If your father had lived, my story may have been the same. But equally, you may feel you owe him a chance to explain. This may just be a crush, after all, or a fleeting passion."

"He hasn't told me there's someone else," she said tentatively, her mind exploring the possibility with mounting disgust.

"Darling, don't be so bloody naïve. There is always someone else. Sorry to have to break it to you, but I am somewhat of an expert in these matters."

Charlotte leant back into the sofa and contemplated the ceiling. She suddenly felt tarnished and embarrassed too, even with her mother's record. How could she have been so gullible? She was talking almost to herself.

"We were children. And I enjoyed growing older with him, making those new discoveries, playing at setting up house, playing at being independent. But these last ten years. Loss after loss, and I couldn't talk to him. He didn't understand or didn't seem to feel what I was feeling." She tried to be honest with herself. "I guess I have felt trapped at times. Playing a part, trying to be something I'm not. The pregnancies... what little there was of them..." Her voice broke. "It would have been different if I had been able to have a child."

"Charlotte, I know that we sometimes haven't seen eye to eye." Audrey looked Charlotte directly in the face. "You do feel things very deeply. We always joked that you had inherited Charles's artistic temperament. You are sensitive and highly strung and that can be difficult to live with for us lesser mortals. You can't keep berating yourself for the miscarriages; that is a completely different issue, and it relies upon two committed individuals. If he has felt unsure, then you must take heed of this."

"I know. But I've been hard on him too. He has been trying to support me, in his own way."

Charlotte looked out of the window, pulling a blanket over her. She thought on the time wasted, the time given over to trying, to waiting, to hoping, all in vain. Her heart hardened.

"But how could he do this to me? I never thought that he would actually leave me. I really didn't see this coming. I don't care how fleeting it may be. He has betrayed me. Betrayed my trust. How can I love someone who has not been loyal to me?"

But inside, she couldn't help mulling over thoughts that refused to go away. *He was in it for himself, just like I was. The irony of Daniel finding someone while I have been preoccupied these last few weeks.*

Audrey looked at her daughter, seeing her as someone else might. There were inky shadows under her eyes, her body was swamped by the baggy clothes and blankets, but she spoke with clarity and spirit. Perhaps the marriage had not been as good for her these last few years as it once had. She couldn't say that she was a big advocate of marriage herself. It might have been different if Charles had lived longer. They could have got over that middle-aged hump and supported each other into old age. She felt a tickle at the back of her own eyelid and dismissed it instantly. She had made her choices, and she was quite satisfied, thank you very much. Her relationships were based on equal transactions. Unfortunately, she had learnt from experience to be scrupulously careful with whom she was involved.

There was a banging at the door. They both started. Audrey got up and looked at Charlotte.

"Are you expecting anyone?"

"No, only you know, and Barbara obviously, Daniel would have told her."

"It might be one of those awful cold callers. I'll soon see them off."

Charlotte picked up the mugs and biscuit tin and walked towards the kitchen. She could hear the dull murmur of voices; she craned to hear. Was the newer one faintly recognisable? It sounded male. She walked down the hall so that she could listen unseen to the conversation. She had barely made three paces before she had identified the source of the noise, who else?

"…personal emergency."

"So she's not ill? Why did she tell me that then? Can't I see her?"

"Not now."

There was a brief pause and Charlotte could sense Max's charm working its inexorable magic.

"But it is nice to meet you, and I will pass on your best wishes."

"Well, the same to you, and I would be grateful if you would give her the flowers."

"I certainly will, and I'm sure she will let you know when she is ready to return to work."

"I'm away to Morocco at the end of the month. She'll

know that. It would be good to make contact as soon as she can, but please tell her that I just want to support her."

"I'm sure you do; I'll let her know. Goodbye, Mr. Collins, and keep up the good work."

The front door closed firmly, and Audrey almost pranced into the kitchen carrying a rather ostentatious mixed bouquet of pastel-coloured freesias, tulips and roses. Charlotte couldn't remember telling him that that sunset shade of peach was one of her favourite colours. Her favourite memories were under skies of that shade; she felt the sadness saturate her as she remembered. How could something once so strong suddenly be rendered so fragile?

"I wondered whether you were listening. Well, he seems most concerned, that's for sure. He also seems very reliant on you, Charlotte. You must be good at that job, that's all I can say!"

"I can't think about that now," Charlotte retorted. "I don't want to see anyone. I just want to be on my own. Forever probably." But did she really mean that? She couldn't really imagine not seeing Max again. And as for Daniel, did forever mean forever?

"You're being silly, Charlotte. Life goes on. I will stay for a night or two and then you must sort yourself out. Now, let's see what is left in that fridge before I nip to Sainsbury's. I trust you have wine?"

***

Charlotte's mother stayed for a week. She was still Audrey, and the shared intimacies of late didn't cancel their rocky history altogether. But strangely enough, her unique blend of remoteness and self-centredness was exactly what Charlotte needed at the present time. Audrey borrowed a pair of Charlotte's walking boots and took Jake out each day for a walk, since Charlotte refused to set foot out of doors except under cover of darkness. She cooked for her a strange combination of nursery food and convenience meals. But crucially, she gave Charlotte space.

One effect of this was that Charlotte gravitated back towards the painting shack. She had a couple of large canvases she had previously started that had not come to fruition. On one, she started a study of a single silver birch with the wuthering winter landscape behind it, not fully spring but a gradual burgeoning of new life. Daffodils in a ditch. A few snowdrops sheltering by a fence. A touch of cornflower blue dragged across the sky. Far in the background she painted the outline of a lone figure, slightly bowed against the wind. She felt cleansed when she finally laid down her brush. Her mother brought a cup of tea out to her and clapped her hands when she had put the mug down on the bench.

"Charlotte, that is superb. I feel like the picture is moving. The wind!"

Charlotte said nothing, but quietly viewed her labours with satisfaction. She felt oddly replenished.

"Perhaps this is what you needed," her mother commented more brusquely, and turned and walked back towards the house.

An unpaid mortgage, a house full of someone else's belongings and a broken heart, Charlotte reflected. How typical of her mother to select the parts she wanted to see. But it had been positive, and she relished the praise.

During that week, Charlotte painted five canvases in total: the tree, a triptych of a moonlit field and, lastly, a self-portrait. She rarely painted people, but she remembered that her favourite professor at art school had told her about Frida Kahlo's famous explanation of why she painted so many self-portraits: "I paint self-portraits because I am so often alone. I am the person who knows myself best."

When she had finished, she thought it had a touch of Yvette Coppersmith. She looked doll-like, her porcelain skin accentuated and a perfect foil to her dark eyes and hair. She was filled with overwhelming contentment for the first time in she didn't know when. Everything continued despite what choices she had made and would make, insignificant in the great scheme of things.

That night she plugged her phone into the charger and waited until she was able to fire it up again. She sent clipped messages to Claire and Em and ignored the calls and messages that came back. *Not yet*, was her internal mantra, *not yet*.

As she kissed her mother goodbye at the end of the week, she resolved to return to her job the next day. And meet Daniel at the weekend, if necessary. She was strong, stronger than she had thought.

SEVENTEEN

"You're here!"

Max got to his feet as he heard the door being unlocked and, by his confusion, Charlotte realised that he hadn't been expecting her. He took in her appearance quickly and was shocked by how diminished she appeared somehow. Her clothes were muted and bland, lacking her normal panache. However, she looked resolutely at Max and held her nerve, quelling any questions with a fixed, impenetrable expression.

If he only knew how psyched up she had needed to be to get here. She had probably slept only a handful of hours in the last few nights. Questions kept gnawing at her, jumping through her mind until she had to escape herself. She hadn't particularly wanted to face Max, but she couldn't stay in that house any longer on her own.

"Why wouldn't I be?"

She knew it had been a mistake to tell him, even as she had typed the words into the phone. *Daniel has left. Not sure what's going to happen. Will see you soon.* But she hated lying, and as the week turned into two, and his messages had become more probing, Charlotte had felt more and more compromised. In the end, the truth would out anyway.

She stepped over the threshold and scrutinised the room in front of her. Lego pieces were spread out over the floor as far as the eye could see, and a small boy was sitting in the middle, bent over a tower-like structure. Good, she didn't want to see Max on her own. She knew that it would only take one kind word, and she would overflow with grief. She tread delicately over the blocks and knelt down near Dom as he looked at her warily in return. Charlotte looked back without flinching. She could do children. Their needs were simple enough: attention and food, not necessarily in that order.

"That's really tall," said Charlotte. "But I think it needs an aerial. Can I help?"

Solemnly, Dom nodded, and offered her some bricks. "You have these ones. It's going to be as tall as me, Daddy says."

"We better get cracking then," Charlotte answered him, sitting down as he shifted to one side. She started lining the bricks up, grateful for a focus.

Max sat down on the settee beside them and put a hand on Charlotte's shoulder.

"How are you, Charlotte?" he began to say.

She reacted as if she had been touched by a red-hot poker. Turning her head towards Max, she hissed, from the side of her mouth, "Don't! I don't want to talk about it."

Max sat back and took stock. Of course, back to the prickly, defensive Charlotte he had met initially. She had got a point; it really wasn't any of his business. But he had been asking as a friend and it felt like his concern had been thrown back in his face. He immersed himself in surfing the web, listening intently to the snippets of conversation between the two, primarily Dom asking questions about Jake.

Gradually, Max found himself coming round to her position; this was the problem when you always saw both sides of an argument. It must have been hellishly difficult to face him today. He remembered how emasculated he felt after Nell left him. He couldn't face any acquaintance for at least a month, more in some cases. Who was he to judge? She wasn't the only one to put up a protective barrier when something happened that was too raw to deal with. He lay back on the sofa, picking at his iPad, feigning disinterest, and watching the two of them stacking the Lego bricks out of the corner of his eye. She played very naturally with Dom, no baby voices or put-on charm. Dom was relaxed with her, leaning against her side and handing her bricks.

At length, Charlotte stretched and moved back towards the sofa, rubbing her back.

"Dom, I'm going to have to go and do some work now. I'll come back and help you later. See if you can build that next layer on your own."

The child clung to her, and she touched the top of his head lightly. "I will help you again soon, I promise. I've really enjoyed it."

She unfurled herself and looked down at Max. He wondered what she was going to say.

"Where's Vivi?"

"In the bedroom, reading," Max tried to answer casually. "She's a real bookworm. I've had to put her in the office, actually. The spare bedroom was too far away from mine. I'll go and tell her she has to move."

"Oh no, I can move, if there's a problem. I'll see what she wants to do."

They walked towards the stairs and there was an awkward moment as they both moved towards the banister at the same time, brushing each other's shoulders.

"You don't need to work today, Charlotte, I wasn't expecting you to."

"If you don't want me here, I'll go. You've obviously got to look after the children. I can always go through the calendar from home."

Charlotte tried to sound calm and measured, but she was a mess inside. She needed to work, to bury herself in something. Surely, he could see that.

"Of course I want you here. Come and say hello to Vi, and then we can make a plan."

God, it was so difficult ascertaining the right thing to say. She was upset now; he could feel the open wound of her words. Max took the stairs two at a time and knocked on the office door.

"Come in!" a child's voice rang out in stertorous self-importance.

Max peered round the door and then opened it fully. Charlotte stepped tentatively into the room after him. An airbed was lying on the floor with a duvet and blankets draped across it, plus several cushions Charlotte recognised from the lounge. Vivi was leaning against the wall with a book in hand that Charlotte recognised it as one her Year 5 and 6 classes had enjoyed.

"You like Anthony Horowitz, Vivi? Have you seen the film?"

"Dad won't let me see it yet," Vivi said politely. She was

wondering who this stranger was, before she identified her as the lady she had seen before with Dad, who had disappeared so quickly last time she had come. "Are you Daddy's assistant?"

"Yes," Charlotte returned gratefully, thankful for an easy question. "I help him to organise himself. Are you an organised person, or a bit all over the place like Daddy?"

"I don't know." Vivi returned to her book. She hoped this woman wasn't going to criticise Daddy like Mummy did. It was so difficult when that started, and they began to quarrel. She looked up again and was surprised to see her daddy laughing at the lady.

"Vivi is a lot like me," he said, sitting down next to her heavily and pulling her towards him with a hug and a kiss on top of her head. "She loses herself in her books, don't you, my love? But Vivi can actually read them properly. I loved the stories but couldn't access the wretched books!"

Vivi looked up again, smiling shyly at her father, grateful for the snatched moment of closeness, and the lady smiled too. Vivi thought how her face transformed when she smiled. She was pretty in a nice to look at kind of way and she made you smile at her back, different from Mummy, who was very beautiful but definitely had a look-but-don't-touch vibe going on. Mummy had already made a few comments about why on earth Daddy needed a jumped-up secretary, but this woman seemed okay – better than okay, actually. She would make up her own mind about her.

Meanwhile, Charlotte was thinking of how the scene warmed her. Max didn't shy away from affection, and she sensed that shy Vivi needed that affirmation of his love. She could see how she lit up with the attention that she suspected the younger Dom monopolised. She had memories of time with her dad like this. Walks, mostly. Audrey was never keen, but Charlotte clamoured to accompany Charlie, to get the uninterrupted focus she craved and that went some way to balance the feuding between mother and daughter.

"I like reading too, Vivi. Don't worry, we won't disturb you now."

Charlotte turned and exited the room. She waited on the landing until Max joined her.

"Sorry, Max, I had no idea you had the children here. I can see it's not convenient. I can come back tomorrow or later in the week."

"I didn't know that I was going to have them this week, but it's still the Easter holidays, and Nell has started rehearsing for a play," Max answered ruefully. "Of course, I love spending time with them, but it was a bit unexpected. Please stay, Charlotte, we can have a chat about the next few weeks, if nothing else. Are you home alone?" he added perceptively. "I take it that your mum's gone home now?"

Charlotte hesitated. She hated that Max was clearly feeling sorry for her, but she didn't know whether she could go back to the house, either. The dog was mournful without Daniel, and she kept catching sight of his things lying around and feeling fresh tears well up. Her sleep had been interrupted since Daniel had phoned. She had arranged a meeting next weekend with him, but she was dreading it. The thought of actually speaking to him rather than holding imaginary conversations in her head was making her feel tense and like she had weights placed on her. She had been torn over whether or not to see Max again, but right now she wanted to feel that there was some kind of purpose to her existence.

The children had been a welcome relief, but it was bittersweet to watch Max with them. Daniel would have been good with children, she knew. He could be overly fussy; she teased him for being old before his time, but she knew that he would have been proud of a son or a daughter. She felt that loss had prevented her from knowing him fully. Perhaps she could have been more tolerant towards him if she had sometimes been an observer rather than the sole recipient of his attention. Of course, they had also avoided the excess, the irritation, the intolerance, but Daniel had been limited because of their lack of children, of that she had no doubt.

"I'm not sure. I don't want to intrude. The children won't want me here. They don't even know me really."

"Don't be silly," Max said gently, willing her to engage with him. "You'd do the same for me. Dom's already taken to you over the Lego. We can go and collect Jake later and take him for a walk. It will be a good excuse to get them out of the house."

Charlotte finally looked at him, her swollen, red-rimmed eyes evident. He could see that she was on a knife's edge. Did she say they had got together at school, or had he just surmised that? What exactly had happened? Some couples seemed to do this on an endless cycle. Oh Christ, a tear was rolling down her cheek. He put his arms around her helplessly, and she stood woodenly for a second and then he could feel her shaking. He put his arms up and stroked her hair softly. The children were here, thank God. He was acutely aware of the need to temper his own reactions. His personal situation was too recent for it not to feel personal. In a way, it felt that he was living through elements of his own separation again.

He felt a dart of anger against Nell. *This is what happens, Nell. There is fall-out; you take people down with you.*

Charlotte felt overcome with emotion. She had felt a volcano building inside, and then the intimacy of Max's gesture shocked the fury out of her, and she clung onto him as the grief threatened to subsume her. She wanted him to keep holding her, to be submerged so completely that she lost consciousness of everything else.

"Daaa-aaad?" A call came from downstairs, and Charlotte and Max sprang apart.

"Get into the car, and we can go and collect Jake." Max wasn't an actor for nothing, disguising his confusion in imperatives. "Vivi, Dom, get your coats on. We're going to meet the dog I was telling you about!"

***

It had been the right thing to do, as far as Charlotte was concerned. For the next hour and a half, she was forced to pay service to the two children as they (Dom) asked her endless questions about the old railway, and she recounted Jake's life story to an entranced Vivi.

"So you chose him?"

"Yes, he was a rescue dog and my, er, my friend said that he was the only dog in the rescue centre who wasn't howling. He just sat there, looking up at us."

"Did he have any brothers or sisters?" Dom asked, putting his hand through Charlotte's.

Charlotte smiled. "Probably. I often wonder if he is related to any of the other Labradors I see. Although, I think he is the best."

"Even if he has managed to pull you over once or twice!" Max laughed, and Vivi looked curious.

"He's pulled you over, Charlotte?"

"Quite a few times, but recently he was a bit nervous and pulled me over so strongly that I fractured my ankle."

"Bad dog!" Dom said sternly.

"No, he didn't understand, Dom." Max lay a reassuring hand on his son's shoulder. "He was upset when he saw Charlotte."

"How do *you* know he was sad?"

Vivi, ever astute, sensed an imperceptible sea change in the body language of the adults.

"Oh, it was when I first met Charlotte," Max said lightly. "Well, what do you think of the view, guys? How does it compare with London?"

"I love it here." Dom sighed. "I like the rabbits, and the deer and the foxes, and the tractors!"

Charlotte laughed. "You have seen a lot of animals, Dom. What about you, Vivi?"

"I like Suffolk and London," Vivi responded diplomatically. She felt disloyal, somehow. She couldn't imagine Mummy living here. It was so quiet. She would go – what was it she said? – stir-crazy.

"Right, we had better turn round. You two run ahead and call Jake. Let's see how long before he notices he's been left behind!"

The two children ran off ahead. Jake, meandering in the distance, suddenly realised that he was no longer accompanied by his people, and bolted towards them at top speed. The children, screaming with excitement, ran as fast as their legs would carry them and Charlotte couldn't help smiling. She had actually managed to forget about her problems for a few hours. Life was so simple when you were a child – brutal, yes, but simple. The worries were out of your control – you were not responsible for them.

***

Back at the house, she quickly logged on in the spare room. Della had arranged some press interviews for the second season trailer before Max resumed filming in Morocco. When was he going away? Oh, blimey, the week after next! Della had also scribed some acerbic one-liners about a lack of care in communicating with the press. Then Charlotte noticed another email from Marco and Adriana with some attachments. Oh, the photos and the ad – they were on a timed link so that Max could view it. She clicked it and settled back into her chair.

The room filled with the distinct sound of Amy Winehouse, and she could see the reclining figure of Max backlit by the evening lights of the city – it was amazing how they had superimposed the scene so realistically. She could see why they had used the green screen. There were some imaginative fantasy touches which seemed to broach on Max's current role: flames licking the edges of the table, sparks coming off their heels. It was cleverly done; Max's clothes even seemed slightly ruffled by the evening breeze.

Charlotte was pleased that she had advised Max to roll up his sleeves and let loose a little. He exuded a relaxed air of contentment, like someone winding down at the end of a long day. Charlotte was impressed with the way he could put on a persona like a clean shirt; this certainly wasn't the vibe she had got from the small section of filming she had seen.

Then Onuala appeared, sashaying in from the corner of the screen. Exotic and sensuous, the camera tracked her moves and cut to Max staring at her intensely. The drama and repetition of the refrain matched the climax of their dancing, and the mood became more dangerous and edgy. The light changed so that shadows were thrown on faces and the space around them. Max allowed himself to be pulled to his feet and then the music crescendoed and he became the lead, twirling and tossing her so that they finally were spent in the iconic closing pose of the tango. The voice-over came on at that point, Max again, amused, louche and laughing at himself.

Charlotte closed the computer and stared at the blank screen. She must be crazy. What was she thinking of? And that was probably just it; it was typical of her to be caught up in a fantasy world. Reality had always seemed mundane, boring. She had woven a fantasy around this man, but she was providing him with a service and there was no more beyond that other than what was in her head. He just felt sorry for her. It was likely, let's face it. He was kind, and he thought she looked a bit like his sister. A pity shag may even be in the offing if she really span the evidence so far. He probably thought she was easy pickings. And why was she fantasising about this anyway – shouldn't she be trying to get back with Daniel if she truly loved him?

"Do you want to stay for tea, Charlotte?" Charlotte turned swiftly to see Vivi standing behind her. She must have crept in without her noticing. "Was that Daddy in that advert?"

"Yes, it was. It looks good, doesn't it? He's done an excellent job."

"Yes." Vivi wrinkled her nose. "But it's a bit silly, not like proper acting."

"I know what you mean." Charlotte got up and put her phone back in her bag. "I won't stay, Vivi. I've got to take Jake home and feed him or he might end up helping himself to your meal!"

"Oh, okay."

Vivi looked momentarily disappointed or perhaps she was imagining it. She followed her downstairs and broke the news to Max's back.

"I'll go through your calendar tomorrow at home."

Max turned round, pasta server in hand, and grimaced. "I'll give you a ring, if I manage to win the battle with this spaghetti."

Charlotte felt that she was intruding. She wasn't part of this domesticity. Her relationships were fractured; she belonged to no one anymore. She heard the children squabbling in the distance and realised afresh that she was going home alone to a house with just her in it. It hadn't bothered her before, when she knew that Daniel was returning at some point. In fact, she had relished her solitude. Now she just she felt pathetic.

Max noticed her hesitation and his expression changed. He did feel sorry for her. He had been there, undergone the confusion, the humiliation.

"Let me know if you want anything, Charlotte. I'm here if you need me." He understood enough to know that they were on precarious grounds at present, caught in a delicate equilibrium. He deliberately wasn't pushing anything. Anyway, he knew how she worked now. You entered at your peril. He had never met anyone more stubborn, apart from Bella, of course.

Charlotte nodded unconvincingly. She wouldn't ring.

EIGHTEEN

April showers. On and on it had rained. Alun Lewis would have sympathised. She was meeting Daniel tomorrow on neutral ground: a pub outside the village. Her mother had actually phoned to wish her luck.

"Don't lose your temper, darling, just listen to what he has to say."

She was going through the accounts now, the ones she could access, that is. The credit card account was saying that she wasn't able to look at the statement as she wasn't the main card holder or some such crap.

Charlotte thought she may have been able to manage on her own if she still taught full-time, but of course that ship had sailed, and her current position seemed so precarious. She had clearly been a fool to ditch it all at once. Had that set events in motion – the babies, her job, now her husband, next the house?

She got up from the dining table and started pacing. She had a fleeting memory of Daniel and herself locked in an embrace in this room when they had first moved here, looking out at the view beyond and congratulating themselves on their good fortune. Charlotte beat down the urge to scream with fury and sorrow. Was she mourning the past, the present or the future? She made an incomprehensible groaning sound, and the dog came and pushed his muzzle into her leg. Charlotte sank to the floor and buried her head into his neck. He groaned in ecstasy, burrowing into her and rubbing his body against hers. *At least the dog loves me*, she thought in mock-despair.

***

Charlotte arrived at the pub in plenty of time. She waited in the car, applying a fresh layer of lipstick and checking that her eyeliner had remained intact. It seemed important to her that she looked at least as though she had not lost the will to live. The rain had passed, and the countryside looked lushly verdant with a mackerel sky inexplicably overhead. So many hues of grey-blue.

Charlotte was jolted from her contemplation by the sound of a car pulling in next to her. She instantly recognised Daniel's silver saloon, out of place with the battered Land Rover on her other side. She exited the car awkwardly, fumbling for the keys and almost dropping her bag on the gravel. Daniel walked round and stood in front of her, glancing about him as if for witnesses. It was windy and a gust of wind took her hair and twirled it round her head almost deliberately. She tried to smooth it to no avail. It was playfully vicious, like a cat toying with its prey.

"Sorry I'm late, got stuck behind a tractor."

"Shall we go in?" Charlotte replied, at once irritated but compelled to greet him as usual. She was willing this to be over. Daniel looked appallingly normal, albeit with some kind of beard pending. She didn't recognise the jumper, though. It was brighter than his usual attire, with a branded logo on the breast, burgundy with a jarring orange stripe running round the neck. She wished she had made the effort to wear something other than jeans.

They sat down at a table near the window, studiously avoiding the table they had used before on several occasions. That one was by the fire, which today was unlit and hidden behind a big vase of dried grasses and flowers. The pub had had some kind of makeover again; it seemed to regularly change owners and they each seemed to subscribe to a slightly different view on hostelry décor. This set were leaning towards Scandi-chic. Someone had painted the beams overhead in a whisper of grey so that they almost looked limed, and the walls were matching. They had thankfully left the furniture alone, perhaps having run out of money. Prosaic and soothing, the chunky oak bar tables stood their ground, complete with mismatched chairs, their surfaces marked and scratched by years of wet glasses, children and nervy partners fiddling with cutlery.

At least it's quiet, Charlotte thought. A few elderly men were standing by the bar at the other end, chatting to the bar hand: typical farming types with Barbour jackets and tweed caps. There was a middle-aged couple eating lunch in the corner. Charlotte felt a twinge of sadness; once they had thought that that would be them, twenty years from now. She looked away quickly.

Apart from that, it was pretty empty. The waitress hovered nervously as they both looked at the menu. She looked young and unsure. Her ears had pricked up as they came in and she started bustling round the cutlery table and collecting menus together. Charlotte suddenly felt sickened by the whole affair.

"I don't want food, Daniel. I'll just have a coffee. Let's get to the point, shall we? What's going on? Had you been planning this?"

Daniel put down the menu and looked at her gravely. His face took on his customary slightly concerned expression and she thawed slightly. She was coming at him from the offensive; it wasn't fair.

"Charlotte, I don't want to hurt you. I know I have, and I'm sorry. Let's order the coffees first; you sure you don't want any food?"

Charlotte beckoned to the waitress. "I'll have a medium Americano, please."

"A double espresso for me. Thanks… no, thanks."

The waitress scuttled off and Daniel looked at Charlotte with a more apprehensive look. *What is he trying to say?* she thought. *He looks terrified.* Suddenly she knew. It hit her like a punch in the stomach. He had met someone else. Her mother was right. Charlotte was concertinaing the paper napkin in her hand, backwards and forwards she kneaded it, then she scrunched it together. She felt a fluttering in her chest like her heart was trying to escape.

"Charlotte, you know it hasn't been like it used to be for a long time. I know you've been struggling, but we seem to have been growing further and further apart. I have needed to talk to someone too. I've needed support too."

"And I expect you're going to tell me that that's not all they've been giving you?"

Daniel looked shocked and his face turned a satisfying

shade of puce. Charlotte almost felt sorry for him; she had shocked herself.

"How did you know?"

"I didn't. Not until today. How long has it been going on for?"

"About six months. We met in September. She's a PA to the main boss. I'm so sorry, Charlotte. I've felt so guilty, but I didn't know how to tell you. We were just friends to begin with, and then it just seemed to evolve."

Charlotte was feeling the sensation that had become commonplace over the last few months; there seemed to be a voice coming from somewhere distant to her, and she looked at Daniel as if she was seeing a stranger. September was only four months after that final miscarriage. She had stopped working, and Daniel had encouraged her to take time to look after herself. While she was lurking listlessly around the house, Daniel was out liaising with this other – *no, let's call it what it is, screwing this, this…*

"How could you? Why didn't you tell me how you felt? I assume you're sleeping with her? How could you betray me like this?"

"Do you really want me to spell it out?" Daniel was spitting with the force of his reply. It was all about her as usual. He was an afterthought, an appendage. If he had had just one fragment of love during those months, a sign that there was hope, that he was still valued. "Because you're cold, Charlotte, you're frigid. You don't give me warmth; you don't love me! Don't try and pretend you care for me anymore. I'm just a convenience, someone you've got used to!" Daniel's voice was beginning to raise, his defensiveness mirroring aggression.

Charlotte felt strangely animated; she was glad he was angry, that their relationship was worth a reaction. Her response was lacerating.

"That's not true. It's just you. I don't love you." She wasn't sure that she was capable of anything more than a desire to wound before she was wounded further.

The waitress returned, rattling her tray as she set it down in front of them. Charlotte helped her place the crockery, her hand trembling slightly as if in sympathy. The milk spilt, and Charlotte told her not to worry. *Just go*, she thought, *leave us alone.*

Daniel leant back in his chair, looking towards the other tables, his face set and furious.

"You're shagging that bloke then, that actor. I thought you must be. That's what Angela said too."

"What?" Charlotte feigned a high mocking laugh. "Don't judge me by your own lack of self-control. I do – did take my marriage vows seriously. I have been faithful to you through and through. I am cold. Perhaps I am frigid, but I'm in mourning, I'm depressed. I needed your support. Do you remember, Daniel? In sickness and in health, not buggering off to fuck your secretary as soon as life gets difficult!" Her heart was racing, and she hurled the words at him, steeling herself for the next parry.

"I can't do this." Daniel pushed his chair back and Charlotte winced as it grated across the tiled floor. "I thought I would do the right thing and try and be honest, but you're impossible as usual. You are self-obsessed, Charlotte. I can't give you any more. Do you understand?" His voice cracked. "I'm done." He got up and stood by the table a moment longer, grappling with his emotions. "I do want you to be happy, Charlotte, I just don't think I'm the one who can help you to be happy anymore."

Charlotte was the one to look away now, fighting back tears, as he walked through the bar to the exit. Thank God she was facing the wall, so she didn't have to see the curious or sympathetic looks of the other customers. She lifted the coffee cup, and her hands were shaking. The young waitress came over to the table.

"Excuse me, er, are you alright?"

Charlotte suspected she thought that she was in the throes of an abusive relationship.

"Yes, yes, sorry. Can I pay?"

"I'll bring the card reader over."

Charlotte felt the first tear roll down her cheek, and then the second. She looked down and waved her card over the machine.

"Can you put it in?" the girl said.

Shit, the world really was against her. Once done, she grabbed her bag, and wiped her eyes roughly with a napkin. Taking a deep breath, she walked purposefully to the entrance. Damn, more customers coming in. She kept her head down. Children laughing and the deeper voice of a man. *Oh, it couldn't be.* She flattened herself against the wall.

"Charlotte!"

"Daddy, your friend."

"Hi, Max, hi, Vivi. I'm sorry, I'm in a rush."

She caught a glimpse of Vivi's face as she squeezed past them. Then she heard Dom: "Why's she crying, Daddy?"

Max saw Charlotte and in his first glance felt a rush of sensations come tumbling together. She looked a mess. Her eyeliner had run, and her hair looked dishevelled. She wasn't holding it together as she usually did, and this had a destabilising effect on him; he wanted to comfort her, to protect her. He seized the children's hands and turned round. He couldn't let her go home alone. She looked like she hadn't recognised him or the children to begin with. In fact, she looked, well, he had been shocked by her lack of composure.

Why hadn't she confided in him properly? How could he help her and be a friend to her if she hadn't actually admitted to him what was happening? He knew what it was like. Yes, it had been a long time coming with Nell and they got on now – in fact, ironically, he felt sometimes closer to her now than when they had actually been married – but he could still remember those dark initial days of separation when he felt such a failure and that he wasn't worthy of fatherhood. He willed her to stop and meet his eyes, but she pushed past him blurrily and he pulled the children after her.

Charlotte made it over the gravel and got into the car as quickly as she could. She rammed the keys in the ignition and started the engine. Tears were streaming down her face. It was over, it was really over. What's more, she knew he was right. There was something wrong with her; she couldn't connect. She was cold. She had punished him for not understanding her grief.

There was an urgent tapping on the driver's window. Charlotte looked to her right and saw a male figure gesturing frantically. For a split second she was unsure, half-determined to ignore him and leave but he was blocking her exit, and she turned the ignition off and said almost venomously, "What? What d'you want?"

"Roll the window down. We're all here," Max warned, "I couldn't leave the children on their own."

"Oh, Max, please just go and have your meal."

She couldn't look at him, couldn't let him see her defeated like this.

"I'm not leaving you while you're so upset." He peered into the car. "Have you got some tissues?"

Charlotte welled up again and she then caught sight of the children standing a little behind Max. They both looked big-eyed and worried. This was clearly not a standard Saturday outing for them.

"Look, I'll be okay." She hesitated. "I've just met Daniel and it's all been a bit of a shit… shock."

The bastard, Max thought to himself. He could at least have hung around to make sure she got home okay.

"Right, you're coming with us. Come on." He opened the door and she let herself be helped out of the car. "We're going to get the biggest takeaway pizza we can find, everyone." Charlotte managed to smile at the children. "We'll pick your car up later, Charlotte. You'll feel better when you've got some food inside you. Won't she, Dom?"

"Yes, if it's the monster pepperoni pizza!" Dom was jigging up and down on the spot. "Can you sit next to me, Charlotte?"

"I'll sit in between you," Charlotte said weakly. She let herself be walked to the Range Rover and numbly got into the middle of the backseat. She let Dom take her hand and felt a bit better.

"It's our goodbye meal," Vivi said quietly to her left. "Daddy's going to Morocco tomorrow."

"Is that tomorrow? I didn't even think. I'm sorry, Vivi. I didn't mean to gatecrash. Your father's hard to say no to."

She tried to smile at Vivi who looked uncertainly at her.

This was all she needed; the child clearly thought that she was making moves on her father. What a mess it all was.

"Max, I'm sorry, *Max*." He turned round and she leant forward. "Please drop me at home. I'm in no state to be good company for anyone, and the children were looking forward to having time with you. I had forgotten about tomorrow." She could see he was wavering, and she seized her chance. "Please," she said quietly, "this is so... humiliating. I don't want your children to see me like this. It's not fair on them or me."

Max was ready to protest but then he caught sight of Vivi in the rear-view mirror. She looked tired and pissed off, uncannily like Nell, in fact.

"Of course, if that's what you want. How will you pick your car up?"

"I'll manage, don't worry. You're leaving early in the morning, aren't you? Did you get the itinerary I emailed you?"

"Yes, right down to the filming schedule on day fifteen – I think you've covered every angle, Charlotte."

She smiled in spite of herself. At least she was doing something right.

They drew up in front of the house. Max lifted Dom down and Charlotte clambered out. He strapped Dom back into his seat and firmly shut the door.

"I'm worried about you, Charlotte. I know you don't want to talk about it now, but will you promise me that you will phone me tomorrow?"

"Of course, I'll be checking that you've followed that itinerary minute by minute." Charlotte spoke lightly in spite of herself. She really didn't know what she was going to do without him there. She unlocked the front door, made sure that the car had really left and then finally collapsed on the floor and sobbed without restraint.

***

She didn't hear the sound of the car's engine as it drew up outside. Daniel stepped onto the gravel and took a deep breath as he sized up what he was about to do next. He couldn't leave her like this; he had to check that she was okay. It had always been thus. Eighteen years of marriage couldn't be wiped out in the space of a few weeks. He undid the door with his keys and then knocked a couple of times as an afterthought. Charlotte jumped to her feet with a jolt and opened the front door a crack. Then she realised who it was.

"Daniel. Why are you here?"

He took one look at her tear-stained face and felt the familiar cloak of responsibility settle on his shoulders.

"It's alright, Charlotte, it will be alright."

He took her to him without preamble and hugged her hard. He felt the tension and rigidity in her body and longed for it to run away, for him to absorb some of her pain and anger. Neither of them had meant for this to happen. Neither of them had really wanted to hurt the other. Her sobbing eased and he found himself kissing her face, lips, more forcefully than he meant to initially. He needed to stop the hurt, to show her he hadn't meant to harm her, didn't blame her for what they both had done. His kisses blotted her tears. She found herself seeking his lips in return, blocking out consciousness with the immediacy of physical sensation. Then negating thought altogether.

He sought redemption, forgiveness. It only took only a few minutes for their caresses to progress into the well-practised moves of their lovemaking, and finally there was something darker, something final that lay below, more exciting and risky. He cried out and the line between anguish and ecstasy was indistinguishable. All qualms abandoned, transient feelings secured for that last what the hell, last chance, last ditch, whatever. There was finally no agenda, no ulterior motive, just the need for complete obliteration.

When it was over, he pulled himself up from the sofa – they hadn't even made it to the bedroom – and pulled on his clothes, doubts starting to filter through him, making him clumsy as he fumbled at fastenings.

Charlotte watched him through half-closed eyes. She had nothing left; she felt heavy, spent. Her pride held her back from saying anything. If she had begged, would that have moved him? She couldn't bring herself to even utter his name. He had rejected her, but this was her one last satisfaction.

Daniel was already cursing his weakness. Angela would kill him if she suspected that anything had taken place.

"This can't happen again," he said bleakly. Charlotte looked corpse-like on the sofa, all white limbs and dark hair. It was a mess. As quickly as that, he didn't feel lust anymore, just regret and confusion.

Charlotte turned her face towards the sofa. She heard the front door bang behind him.

NINETEEN

The next week was up there with the most difficult that Charlotte had endured. She was still finding it hard to sleep and kept replaying Daniel's comments over and over in her mind. She acknowledged that the majority of what he had said was true but, ultimately, it was his faithlessness that was abhorrent to her; whatever else, she had been loyal to him. On the other hand, if she was totally honest with herself, she could see why he could have looked for solace elsewhere. She had punished him by banishment, had built a fortress inside her head. That wasn't his fault, it was hers.

She tried to push that last encounter out of her mind. It had felt hyperreal, an impassioned release which had no place in real life. Perhaps it had only happened because the ties had been truly severed. Afterwards he had walked away, left her once again. The rejection had a finality that it had lacked before.

She couldn't paint in this mood, she felt too unsettled. Instead, she went for long walks with the dog, anywhere but near Max's house. Emily tried to ring and texted messages on WhatsApp, but Charlotte still hadn't told her anything other than the initial separation. Her mother rang each day, or when she remembered.

Then, when she went to the shop at last on the Wednesday to get some essentials (loo roll, bread, milk, dog food), she was surprised to be greeted almost as soon as she had opened the rattling door and the bell started clanging.

"Charlotte, Mrs. Seldon, oohh, I wanted to speak to you!"

"Oh?" Charlotte was taken aback. She had wanted to creep in here quietly, gather her small items and escape as easily as possible. She had pulled a hat over her unwashed hair and still had her pyjama bottoms on, disgusting. It was Ros, of course – she didn't think the others knew her name. She was waving bright fuchsia talons at her now. How did she manage to get anything done with those? They seemed incongruous with the weather-beaten complexion and baggy fleece. The object of her attention leant over the counter with a conspiratorial air, narrowly missing a box of eggs.

"Fella asking after you. Wanted to know where you lived! Well, I didn't tell him, of course. Were you expecting someone?"

"Noooo," Charlotte answered, gripping her bag more tightly. "Did he say what his name was?"

"No, he didn't dawdle. Was he a friend of Mr. Collins? I think you've been seen a couple of times with him out and about in the village. He was on a motorbike, quite smart it looked, too!"

Ros looked hawkish and Charlotte recoiled inwardly. She refused to be drawn into any further conversation, paid hastily for her purchases and left the shop. That felt a bit odd. Had Max got some friends who might be looking to contact her? Or maybe Della had sent them?

She walked slowly home, concentrating on the road. Not many cars passed, and she looked at the ones that did thoughtfully. It was unsettling.

She went to bed early and passed much of the small hours watching TV, Max's show in particular. She hadn't actually seen many of his films or TV series, and definitely not the one that was premiering at the moment. Fantasy had never particularly been her thing, but she had to admit that this series was peculiarly addictive. For a start, the actors played it straight, which was effective as the premise was that they were leading double lives as humans with a salubrious underworld co-existence. Max was doubling as king pin in a gang and an immortal ruler of Hades. He was cruel and menacing, but ruthless in a beguiling, inveigling way, leaving a trail of conquests in his wake.

Charlotte had to admit that he was mesmerising on the screen. The first few episodes introduced his childhood and exposed certain vulnerabilities which gave the watcher an affinity with the character, exposing the reasons behind his sadistic behaviour. This, of course, only added to his charisma, and Charlotte found herself involved in spite of her scepticism at the series' mass appeal.

Max became romantically involved, of course, with the direct descendant of his nemesis, a demigod who became aware of her powers throughout the season. The sex scenes were fairly tasteful but disturbing to watch, as Charlotte compared the man to the character. She felt voyeuristic; Max's sexuality packed a visceral punch as portrayed on screen. The cinematography was aimed to arouse a vicarious pleasure obviously. Charlotte couldn't help but relate the character and behaviour to the man she knew. She turned off the television and found herself imagining what had not passed between them.

She awoke late and disorientated, uncomfortably hot and sticky. There was a strident knocking coming from downstairs accompanied by frantic barking. Charlotte grabbed her dressing gown and put her feet in her slippers. Must be some kind of delivery, but they were being bloody rude. Normally they just left it by the front door if she didn't get there in time. She fumbled with the key and tried to shush the dog who was whining and pawing at the door. She bent down, held his collar and pulled the door ajar. Two youngish blokes stood there, one with what looked like a camera bag, and one who stepped forward with what was clearly meant to be a disarming smile on his face. To Charlotte, her senses jangling, it seemed more like a leer.

"Charlotte Seldon? It's lovely to meet you. I'm Tom Steele, senior entertainment reporter at the *Daily Mail*. We'd love to get your thoughts on how Max Collins has settled into country life." He paused and started getting a card out of his breast pocket.

"Wha-at?" Charlotte was stunned. She took a step back, pulling the dog with difficulty as he tried to sniff the shoes of the journalist. Both men looked so reasonable and patient standing there on the doormat, she was having difficulty adjusting to what was happening. The first man gave an apologetic smile and cleared his throat. The other man, clean-shaven and more smartly dressed in a jumper and collar, spoke in a polite tone to her, much as a doctor might address a patient.

"Mrs. Seldon, I understand you're closely acquainted with Max. Would it be possible to have a comment on the nature of your relationship, please? We'll pay well for an exclusive interview, and we can be very discreet."

The words started to form meaning to Charlotte and she could feel her adrenalin rising with the audacity of the situation.

"No, no comment!"

She heaved the door shut and jammed the bolt across with unsteady hands. She was totally taken aback. How had they found out where she lived? Was this after those photos at the premiere? Had Max said something to someone about her?

They banged on the door again and she shouted angrily, "Go away, or I'll call the police. I don't want to speak to you!"

She sank into a chair and realised that her heart was pounding against her chest. What should she do? This was totally unexpected. She felt like she should have been warned, could have been better prepared. They had come out all the way here to try and speak to her... it was madness. She would call Max. Perhaps he could explain to her how this had happened. And what if Daniel heard about it? It would confirm what he suspected. It couldn't have come at a worse time. Nothing had happened, or was going to. She picked up her phone and with shaking fingers pressed Max's number. The phone went straight to answerphone, and she put it down immediately, unsure of what to say. Then she tried again, trying to think rationally.

"Max, it's Charlotte. Please would you ring me. I need some advice."

She walked upstairs to the landing and peered outside. Sure enough, a car was parked opposite her house, and she could see the two men hovering by it, unloading some equipment and looking up. She ducked. Shit, she still wasn't dressed. What were they hoping to see? Some kind of exposé on how low Max had sunk? Care in the community?

She tried Della, again; had no reply. She left a message for her too. There were unopened messages from Em on WhatsApp. Charlotte felt irritated; it felt like more harassment. She muted her messages and tried to control her growing panic.

She got dressed hurriedly, rejecting the tracksuit for her more reasonable jeans and shirt just in case she was interrupted again, and went out to the shed to paint. After half an hour of bodged starts, she gave it up. It was impossible for her to focus. Every bang or noise from one of the neighbouring properties sent her head into a spin. She went back inside and walked to the front lounge window. There were now two cars, and she could see someone approaching the front door. Fuck! She ducked and crawled along the carpet. There was knocking at the door again. Charlotte ignored it. Then she heard the letterbox being opened and something dropped through it. The post! Christ, she was becoming paranoid.

Another hour passed while she made herself tidy the house. Looking out of the window again, the cars had gone, and she wondered if she had been overstating the situation. She had panicked, understandably, but now she could relax again. She needed to calm down. She decided to take Jake for a walk, and grabbed his lead, bunging her phone into the nearest bag. *Perhaps I'll go out of the backdoor*, Charlotte thought, *and I can nip up the side of the house, just in case*. She grabbed a thick hoodie and a pair of sunglasses. It was just about warm enough to leave her coat off. Jake was predictably bouncy, and he whinnied and groaned appreciatively when he saw her start to get ready. Charlotte crept up the edge of the house and opened the side gate as quietly as she could. She inched it closed and cut down the neighbours' path; they weren't in so there would be no complaints there. Then she heard a call behind her.

"Mrs. Seldon? Charlotte?"

Without turning round, she kept walking faster, her heart pounding against her chest. Suddenly a woman blocked her way. She was youngish with beach blonde choppy hair and a phone held in front of her.

"Hi, Mrs. Seldon, I'm from *The Mirror*. We'd love to get an exclusive from you for the right amount. Would you mind clarifying the nature of your relationship with Max Collins?"

Charlotte backed away in shock; she managed to turn left to cross to get to the cut-through to the main road. To her horror, she almost barged into another man getting some camera equipment out of a bag. Were they everywhere? She heard a shutter click and tried to block her face unsuccessfully with her right hand.

"Leave me alone, go away!"

Another shape appeared to her left and she broke into a run, stumbling painfully on her weaker ankle. The dog, excited, pulled her forwards and she almost fell.

Pushing through the pain, she jogged up the path and onto the main road. Looking quickly, she pulled the dog across and then heard a horn blare as a car swished behind her. She kept up the pace and then turned into the lane that ran up towards Max's house. Once past the railway bridge, she felt exposed rather than on top of the world as she normally did. Her feet kept walking towards the barn on the horizon. Jake looked up at her quizzically, and she realised that she hadn't let him off the lead. She slipped it over his head and paused while he ran off elatedly. She stared after him for a minute enviously; not a care in the world, all energy and freedom. Her pocket started vibrating and she groped for her phone.

"Max!"

"Are you okay? What's wrong?"

Max's voice travelled across the air waves, kind and concerned; Charlotte suddenly felt alone and emotional. She wished he was here.

"Journalists, I think. Outside my house. How do they know where I live, Max? They've taken photos, and they keep trying to get me to speak! I had to run away from them just now. My stupid ankle went again." Her voice faltered.

"Oh, Charlotte, I didn't know whether to mention it or not. There's some stupid speculation on the internet after that black tie event. I guess they want to find out who you are. I should have warned you. I didn't want to alarm you with everything else that's going on."

"Okay, I understand. It's not your fault, but they seem so persistent. It's made me feel scared, to be honest."

"Where are you now?"

"On the lane past the railway bridge. I've taken the dog for a walk. I didn't think they would notice me, but of course they did. They're not here now. They don't seem to have realised that you live up here."

"That was Nell's idea," Max explained, and she could hear the jaded note to his voice which she now associated with his ex-wife. "We rented the house in her dad's name. She always thinks ahead to do with things like that. Protecting the kids, you know."

Charlotte didn't want to talk about Nell. "Thanks for phoning back so quickly. Are you filming?"

"Not quite, I've been shown the set, and we've met the extras and the director of the next two episodes. We're at the foot of the Atlas Mountains for a week, and then in a hotel in Essaouira. Very trendy. Actually, it's great. I think you'd like it; very authentically Moroccan and the scenery is absolutely beautiful. The outdoor scenes are going to look fantastic."

"It sounds perfect. Do you get a chance to explore?"

"Not really, there's too much to do at the moment, and they don't want anything to happen to me. I feel like I'm in a glass coffin at the moment. Oh, they're calling me now." Max's voice became more hurried. "Look, Charlotte, why don't you stay at mine for a few days? I think this will blow over, but you should lie low for a while. They never take rejection easily. There's plenty of food there, and you can keep in contact with Della and me. You haven't got the key with you, by any chance?"

Actually, miraculously she had. It was attached to her key ring: car keys, house keys and the key. She had felt funny about using it the first couple of times. It had felt like a liberty.

"Are you sure? What about Jake?"

"Of course I'm sure. I feel responsible, and I don't want you having to run the gauntlet with that lot again. They're like animals circling their victim. Use my Amazon account. The bed's got clean sheets on it. Get some clothes delivered for a couple of days. Then they'll give up and you can go home."

Max could almost hear Charlotte hesitating. He felt irritated; this was no time to be stubborn.

"Go on, Charlotte, please."

"Alright. Just for a day or two."

She didn't want to feel any more indebted to Max but, equally, there was no way she was going back down that hill while those photographers were there. She supposed she did work for him, and the house was empty. It couldn't do any harm for a day or two.

"Great. Now, I'm going to have to go. Text me if you need anything, and I'll phone you later."

"There's no need…" But Max had already gone.

TWENTY

It felt empty in the barn without Max. He had left it more than a little untidy, which Charlotte didn't mind. The detritus spoke of Vivi and Dom, their warm, reassuring bodies, and the safe mundanity of family life. She fussed around a bit, picking up some odd bricks of Lego, rifling through some of Max's business deliveries and sorting them into piles for him to deal with on his return. Most of the time she sat in front of the television watching old films, Max's back catalogue, seeing him grow from boy to man in front of the camera. Fantasising about all kinds of things. What if she had pursued painting from the beginning? What if she hadn't married Daniel? What if she had kept the pregnancies? What if something had happened between Max and her at the premiere?

It felt odd sleeping in Max's room. She settled eventually but then slept fitfully, waking up at about 1.00a.m. to see the silver sheen of moonlight infiltrating the room through the gap in the curtains. She felt instinctively for the trailing cable of her own bedside lamp and then remembered where she was. Her hand brushed between the wooden cabinet next to the bed and she felt some paper. Turning on the light fully, she pulled the paper up so it was visible. Photo proofs. Oh, the aftershave advert, but not of the advert itself – they seemed to be of the meal with the two executives, and these were close-ups... of her... laughing, captured in animation and then repose, listening intently, looking. One of her asleep on the couch beforehand – Ajay must have given it to Max. She looked relaxed in sleep. Charlotte was taken back to that day. It felt like another world. Why were they here? Max must have been looking at them. She felt that odd tugging again in her gut, that nagging feeling that something just below the surface was happening that was managing to evade her understanding.

She got out of bed and padded over to the balcony. Pulling the curtains gently aside, she unlocked and opened the door. It was nearly May but there was an acuity to the night air that cut her to the quick. Grabbing her cardigan from the easy chair near the window, she walked onto the balcony and looked down. Her breath caught, trapped within her throat. Something stared up at her from the centre of the garden, frozen in its paces. A fox. It stayed a second more and then carried on in its tracks with an impenetrable resolve. A calmness descended on her as she watched it continue on its path below the stars. She turned away into the caress of the bedroom, succumbing to a dreamless sleep.

***

In the morning, she decided to return to her house, at least to get some clothes and art things. This was ridiculous. She was sans underwear today; she hadn't been so organised as to order anything, and she still felt soiled despite a long soak in Max's en suite. She was sitting at the kitchen island, scrolling through a fan page, when she heard a car pull up on the drive. On high alert, she jumped up, knocking over her coffee. Grabbing kitchen paper, she threw it down on the surface and darted back as she heard the front door being opened with a key. A silvery voice called into the hall.

"Helloooo! Charlotte, are you there?"

"Nell!"

Charlotte stepped into the hall and wished that she wasn't naturally so much at a disadvantage. Nell was in some kind of exercise gear this morning, soft lilac yoga pants draped becomingly round her taut limbs, and a matching hoodie. Her hair was tied back today, and she had the barest hint of make-up on, or so it seemed. Charlotte was acutely conscious of her scruffy attire and complete lack of visible self-care.

"I was just having a coffee before I went home. Did Max let you know I was here?" She walked back into the kitchen, mopping up the spillage. "Can I get you a cup?"

"A herbal tea, please. They're in this jar."

Nell perched herself on one of the counter stools and looked Charlotte up and down.

"You do look rough, darling. I bet you're not sleeping. Those journalists can be utter bastards. Not all of them, of course, I've made inroads with several, but I've learnt the hard way who it pays to be pleasant to."

Charlotte handed the tea to Nell and sat across the island from her. She was unsure of what to say. She really didn't know how she had found herself in this position.

"I'm just the personal assistant. I didn't even want to go to that event. It was just to help out."

"Didn't you?" Nell's eyes glittered. "You're a bit strange then, if you don't mind me saying. Most people would bite off their arms and legs for an opportunity like that." She fumbled in her bag. "Do you mind if I smoke? I'll open the door."

She went and stood in the doorway and took a long drag.

"It was the kiss, of course. Unlike Max, I'd say. He's not usually impulsive."

"Oh, that." Charlotte could feel her cheeks burning and looked down at her hands. "That was Della's fault. She had been going on and on about him needing a date. I think he just lost his temper with it all. I felt a bit used, to be honest."

She could feel Nell looking at her intently. She had an odd expression on her face; Charlotte had seen it before on children at school. It was as if she was sizing Charlotte up, weighing up the competition. Charlotte checked herself; that was ridiculous.

Nell shrugged. "I'm still quite protective of him, I'm afraid. I like to check out his acquaintances, both personal and business. I have to think of the kids too. Their wellbeing is of the utmost importance, you understand."

"Oh, I understand."

Charlotte hadn't meant to be flippant, but she could see Nell's back tauten.

"Do you? You haven't got children, have you, Charlotte?"

It was though she had received a punch in the stomach. Charlotte felt winded. She should be used to the routine by now. After all, she had been through it hundreds of times before. She folded her arms, and then unfolded them.

"No, did Max tell you that?"

"I asked, yes."

Nell looked around for an ashtray. Seeing none, she pushed the stub against the mug and dropped the remainder in it. Charlotte felt a flicker of distaste. For such a meticulously groomed woman, the gesture was grubby. Oblivious to Charlotte's musings, Nell came and stood next to her, ostensibly to put her mug by the sink. She plucked at her fingernails nervously. Charlotte had a small burst of satisfaction in seeing that they were unmanicured and sore around the edges.

"Charlotte, can I give you some advice, a warning, perhaps?"

"If you like," Charlotte said reluctantly. She felt as ill at ease and uncomfortable as Nell clearly did. She didn't want to hear any revelation or dark secret about Max. It was complicated enough already.

"Don't get too involved. Max has a lot of baggage. You've seen some of it already. It wasn't easy being married to him even before he was an A-lister. I was a lot younger than you, and I found myself getting sucked into it all. He also has the children to think of now."

"When did you meet?" Charlotte couldn't resist asking curiously.

"On the set of a film, some kind of independent. Max was one of the leads. He had just been 'discovered', you know, fresh out of drama school. I was an extra, but I had a massive stroke of luck – well, for me anyway. The woman playing against Max dropped out at the last minute, some kind of illness, and I begged, practically bribed, the casting director to give me a go." She dimpled mischievously at Charlotte. "I didn't have to sleep with her, but it was a near thing. Max and I hit it off and moved in with each other more or less straight away. We didn't have much money at that stage, and it was cheaper to share in London on our wages anyway. Max needed someone to look after him. He was holding it together remarkably well really. Not many people guessed that something was wrong, and I like to think I got him through the worst of it. He was very resistant to taking prescription drugs at first – Bella had made him very distrustful – but I got him on anti-depressants and the panic attacks stopped. Those years were fun!" She sighed wistfully. "We could both up sticks and go where the work was. There were no ties. Then we both started getting bigger parts, and I fell pregnant with Vivi. By this time, Max had decided to cut down on the medication, and we started to row. I'm sure he's told you the rest."

"Sort of. Why did he come off the medication?"

"To be fair, he had been on them almost constantly for ten years or so," Nell replied, her face darkening. "I think he was worried that he was turning into Bella. He went and saw a couple of shrinks, but he felt that the acting was his way of dealing with everything, you know? I suppose I was envious; I love everything about acting, and what's attached. That's the bit Max hates. Two children under three and Max to contend with. I felt desperate. I love the parties, the events, the media. I'm an exhibitionist really."

She stretched her legs out in front of her as if admiring them and there was a contemplative pause.

"I didn't treat him well. I'm not proud of that, but it always felt that there were three in the marriage, to be honest. And Max can be very intense. Do you understand, Charlotte? I don't mean to be cruel. I am as I am. I care for Max very deeply, but I also know that he needs support. I've always been there for him."

"You needn't worry. I work for Max, and that really is all it is." Charlotte laughed brittlely. "Please don't believe what you read on the internet. It's rubbish. I'm ma—" She stopped. Thankfully, Nell didn't seem to have noticed.

"Well, I've said what I came here to say. I hope those bastards clear off and leave you alone soon."

Nell's tone changed, and she switched to the light, careless tinkle. She had seemed sincere, but now she was evasive again. She picked up her bag and walked out into the hall with Charlotte following. Charlotte took in more details of her appearance as she walked; the tracksuit fitted her gamine figure like a second skin, the colour matching the trim on her trainers. Then she said something which Charlotte didn't catch.

"I beg your pardon?"

"We're still sleeping together, you know."

Charlotte couldn't be certain that she had heard Nell correctly but, from the needle-like dart from her eye as she turned to say goodbye, she thought she probably had. It didn't matter; she wasn't going to walk into this… it had nothing to do with her and her problems. It had been revealing though, to hear Nell's point of view. She didn't think any more of Nell, but she did appreciate better how caught up they had all been in an impossible situation, and the damage that had been wrought, reaching through the years.

"Goodbye, Nell, I appreciate you coming to check on me."

"Goodbye, Charlotte, and good luck… with everything."

***

After lunch, she and Jake took a fast walk down the hill and nervously crept up the passageway so that they were standing opposite the house. It seemed clear. They sprinted over the road and Charlotte fumbled with the side gate. Once through and into the back garden, she emitted a sigh of relief. She let them into the house quickly and immediately closed the front curtains, but something caught her eye.

Someone was standing at the window watching her in the house opposite. There was an elderly couple living there, and Charlotte hadn't had anything much to do with them before apart from the barest of greetings. It looked like they were getting their revenge now. By the stature, it seemed to be a woman who was looking at the house, and then the shape of a phone materialised and was raised to her ear. Charlotte resisted the urge to raise a finger, and rearranged the curtains so that they were shut tightly without a chink of light showing through. The phone rang.

It wasn't a number she recognised. She put the receiver to her face and held her breath.

"Is that Charlotte?"

An unfamiliar female voice sounded breezy, friendly even. Charlotte started to relax, probably some appointment she had missed. Then the woman's voice rose, and the timbre changed completely.

"Hi, Charlotte. Are you sucking Max Collins off, you dirty slut? How much is he paying you to blow him? Why don't you crawl back under the stone you came out from, you skank."

There was a click and the dialling tone sounded. Charlotte replaced the phone in its handset and sank into a chair on autopilot.

She realised that her hands were shaking uncontrollably, whether from anger or fear, she couldn't say. She was sweating. Maybe she should call the police? She rang 1471 but the number was unrecognised. The phone rang again. Charlotte jumped up and pulled the phone out of the wall. She didn't know what to do. Should she contact Max? How was she going to explain this to him? Yes, it was ludicrous, something from out of the playground, but how the fuck had they got her number? What the hell were they putting together to get to this? They might know where she lived! She could phone her mother, but she would probably just offer to stay for a couple of days, and she couldn't carry on with that indefinitely.

She would check her mobile, maybe Max had rung. She fished it out of her shoulder bag and saw that Max had indeed been texting her.

How are U this morning? Did U find everything U need?
Can you call me, please? No rush. When you get a minute.

She had barely finished texting when the phone rang. Max? It was a different number and she hesitated before answering.

"Charlotte, are you alright? I can't speak long. We're shooting halfway up a mountain – quite literally, I'm afraid. The signal's crap – I'm on one of the sound guy's phones."

"It's you." Her voice shook. "Thank goodness, I thought it was, oh Max, I've had a horrible phone call. It was obscene."

"What?" Max's voice hardened. "What exactly has happened, Charlotte? Are you at home? Are the paps outside still?"

"No, but they soon will be. I think the neighbour opposite may be speaking to them. I'm not one hundred per cent sure, but it looks like she could have been the one who called them. And I've just had this awful phone call. This woman sounded normal and then she accused me of… of… well, let's just say it was pretty grim. Her voice was foul, Max, full of hate. Do you know who she is?"

"Could be the stalker." Max sounded grimly humorous. "Sorry to drag you into this, Charlotte. I really didn't think she would target you this quickly. Haven't seen her round for a few months, but I guess the pap attention has stirred her into action again."

"A stalker?" Charlotte sounded calmer than she felt. "Should I call the police?"

"Yes, I'll send you the incident number. Should think they've got quite a dossier on her now, to be honest. If I were a woman, I think they may have encouraged me to take her to court, but Della thinks it will take something a bit stronger to galvanise them. Fuck, sorry, Charlotte, I don't mean to scare you. The woman's unhinged, that's all. She's never tried to touch me or anything." Max could have kicked himself for being so thoughtless. "I've had enough of this, anyway. I'm getting you out here with me. You can work from here as well as you can from Suffolk. We can do some interviews, and I need you to help me practise the script. The director's doing my head in. He thinks we're on course for a fucking Emmy."

"I can't come out there, to Morrocco! What about Jake?"

"Get Daniel to have him; he's his dog too. Jake won't mind you being away for a couple of weeks. Then the pap frenzy will die down and you can get on with your painting. I'm only out here for another six weeks, anyway. Then we've got a month's break before we're back in LA."

The words were rushing over Charlotte's head and she felt disorientated. This was surreal. "Where would I stay?"

"We're in trailers at the moment, but then they're putting us up in hotels in Essaouira and Agadir tonight. They'll be plenty of room to work and de-stress. Go on, Charlotte, I need you too, and I don't want you on your own with all that going on." He tried to make his tone sound plaintive.

Charlotte laughed, despite herself. "I guess it's an opportunity I can't miss."

"Great. I'll send the tickets across. How do you fancy travelling first class?"

"No, no, it's better for me to just blend in. I'll buy my own ticket and claim on expenses later."

Max knew better than to argue. "Yes, ma'am. See you tomorrow some time?"

"Ye... es. Max, there's something else I need to tell you. Nell came round today."

"Oh yes? What did she want?"

"She warned me to stay away from you. She's worried about the children. She said that she doesn't want them to be caught up in any publicity. She said that she was worried about me too." There was a slight pause and Charlotte strained to hear. The line was crackly. "Max?"

"What total bollocks." Max snorted. "She knows that I wouldn't let the children anywhere near a reporter. No, more like she's concerned that your unwelcome bit of media notoriety will detract from her column inches. She loves it that the press still speculate that we're involved in some way. It guarantees her press attention and means that she can still command a fairly healthy social media following. Sorry, Charlotte, I don't want to drag you into this, but she's gone too far this time."

He was furious; how dare Nell go behind his back like this? He was trying to keep Charlotte apart from all of their shit. He bet that wasn't all Nell had told her either. He'd heard it all before from mutual acquaintances: Nell's version. Where she had propped him up and kept him going until he shrugged her off with his success. She just didn't want to let go. Charlotte didn't deserve to put up with all this.

"Okay, take no notice of me, then. I'll be out as soon as I can."

Charlotte felt slightly mollified by his comments. Nell had been very persuasive, but what Max had said did make sense. Of course, they still could be sleeping together, but it was none of her business anyway. There was something nagging at her about Nell's general demeanour. She definitely seemed on edge. Was there a hint of jealousy there? How on earth could a woman like Nell be jealous of Charlotte?

On the other hand, Max had definitely paused before he had replied. Did she trust him either? Probably not in the light of Daniel's affair. Daniel was the last person in the world she would have thought capable of infidelity. *How well do you really know anyone?* she mused. Max probably understood that better than most.

"Charlotte, take care, won't you? I'll get the film company to send a driver to the airport."

"I will, promise."

TWENTY-ONE

Charlotte shifted uncomfortably in her seat. She was on the aisle at least but, inevitably, a small, cross child behind her had been kicking her on and off, off and on. It was an afternoon flight, and the clamour and light felt relentless. Positioned where she was, it was difficult to blank out the hustle and noise of the other passengers. She always found this was the way of flights; you spent the time wondering about the lives and motivations of the people round you. She was particularly sensitive to the family behind, the truculent seven-year-old with footballer's legs who assiduously refused to respond to her parents' increasingly bleating requests to focus on her iPad and stop kneeing Charlotte in the back. She tried not to judge, well-aware that she was anything but impartial.

Meanwhile, Charlotte was trying to not make physical contact with the man sitting next to her, unnervingly sprawled diagonally into her foot space. She had already made up a whole back story for him. The flashy watch, t-shirt, designer jeans and expensive-looking black bomber jacket suggested some lucrative business interests and she decided that he must be some kind of investor, checking in with his clients. On the other side of the gangway was a girl a few years younger than herself. Travelling alone, she kept rummaging in her bag, fumbling for her phone or this or that. Was she, poor schmuck, like her, the assistant, rushing to help?

She sighed and fiddled with her own phone, impatient with herself. She should be grateful. This was an opportunity of a lifetime. The podcasts were irritatingly similar, celebrity after celebrity keen to explain that she or he had captured the zeitgeist of contemporary living or the meaning of happiness or whatever. They were all desperately trying to feign ignorance of their good fortune or talent, pretending that they were just like anyone else. Success was played down – it had either been foisted upon them in a burst of luck or a long hard slog which had finally reaped rewards. Few and far between, you came across one that was more witty than inane or where you could sense an honesty that probed a little deeper, became more profound.

Her mind returned to the call that she had made before leaving for the airport. Daniel had arranged to come to the house in her absence to pick up his clothes and items which he needed. There was so much that was his in the house that neither of them had really addressed the mammoth task ahead of separating their possessions. As it was, the conversation had been stilted and strictly functional. Charlotte had insisted he look after Jake, about which he had responded unsurprisingly reluctantly. She speculated on whether the girlfriend had an aversion to dogs or perhaps was particularly houseproud. A few slip-ups in his speech had intimated that they were living together at the moment.

Charlotte couldn't help but hope that the advent of Jake would put a spanner in those works, then chided herself for being so petty. She was still angry with Daniel – there was a large possibility the hurt would never ease – but she liked him still, even after everything. She would probably even want him to be happy in the distant future, but not yet, not when she woke up every morning and was taken aback by the realisation once more that she was on her own.

She sighed and let her mind wander to whether or not Max would meet her flight. She was still feeling quite uncertain about whether she had done the right thing in coming to Morocco, but it was way too late to chicken out now and, besides, she had been through too much to get here. She had braved the queues at check in – thank God, not in any school holidays, but still far too full of young families for her liking – the departure lounge, and the trawl through customs. Luckily, the flight was comparatively short and no time lag, so even better. She supposed she had been rather stupid in refusing the offer of first class. It would have been good to have tried it, she reflected, blast that wretched pride again. She dozed for some time, the faint voices lapping at her ears. Then the seatbelt sign came on.

Charlotte fastened the tray and fumbled with her shoulder bag, rearranging phone and EarPods and checking for the hundredth time her passport and boarding pass. Landing was something she hated. She could only remember travelling alone once before: a flight to join Daniel for a work do in Madrid and she had only just stopped herself from clutching the hand of the stranger next to her as she prepped herself psychologically for crashing. She braced herself now, and shut her eyes, shoving in a sweet. She knew it never worked but frantic sucking distracted her a little as the noise outside changed timbre.

Half an hour later and they had finished their protracted descent, bumping onto the runway at 7.20p.m. Moroccan (and British) time. Charlotte managed to get her rucksack from the overhead lockers and rummaged beneath her seat for a soft toy that the girl behind her had dropped, narrowly preventing a scale nine temper tantrum. The mother thanked her warmly and Charlotte smiled thinly, ramming her sunglasses on quickly as she sensed the woman pause a bit too lingeringly. Charlotte herself had immediately clocked the mother's face, with an artist's eye for detail. She looked worn out and harassed: hair curled but frizzing stubbornly with the air-conditioning, forehead furrowed as she heard the strident refrain next to her: "Mummy, Mummy, hurry up!"

In another life, that could have been her. She felt the push and pull of her grief again, still ebbing and flowing below the surface.

Stepping off the plane, there was a fresh breeze blowing the heat of the desert away. Charlotte sniffed the air and assimilated the faint yellow aura so different from the myriad of grey at home. A subtle change of mood came over her; she felt a whisper of liberation and marvelled again at her own bravery. Who would have thought it? En route to a film set!

It took another forty minutes to pick up her suitcase from the juddery conveyer belt and get through passport control. Not everyone was as quick as her; a handle of a suitcase had looped the loop several times before the man next to her had let out a cry and pounced on it, cursing audibly as he marched towards the flight attendants standing nervously at the gate.

Clutching her shoulder bag, rucksack and suitcase, she walked cautiously out through the entrance, unsure of whom to look for. She had texted Max on the flight but had had nothing in return. Then, as she felt her phone vibrate and started fumbling for it, she felt a tap on her arm. A youngish man in a Manchester United football shirt and track pants, teamed with the leather slip-on slippers she would learn were typical of Moroccan male attire, was hovering by her side. He smiled, revealing white, even teeth, and his whole face was split in two.

"Charlotte? Yes?"

"Er, yes," Charlotte stammered, struggling to keep her case upright.

"Nice to meet you, Charlotte. I'm a runner for the production company, and Max asked me to come and meet you. He sends his apologies but they're trying to get this big scene right, and it has to be early evening. There's been enough continuity errors so far, and he's not in the best of moods, hence you have me!"

His grin was infectious, and Charlotte couldn't help smiling back. "Thank you, that's very kind, er?"

"Oh, yes, sorry, I'm Hassan. Max should have messaged you, if you want to check."

Charlotte fiddled clumsily with her phone and caught the name 'Hassan' in a message. She smiled affirmation, and Hassan continued without skipping a beat.

"I've got a car if you'd like to come this way. Let me help you with that."

Still talking, and now gripping her case, Hassan led the way to an ancient, off-white Fiat which was parked right in front of the airport and being inspected with interest by a policeman. Charlotte felt her senses stretching. There was so much to take in, the background of tooting horns, faint sounds of distant traffic and mysterious, unidentifiable odours in the air. She apprehensively inspected the outside of the dusty vehicle. Hassan proceeded to talk loudly, with a lot of arm movements, in response to what were clearly some heated requests to move the vehicle. Eventually, Charlotte was ensconced in the back next to her bags with the suitcase across the seat as Hassan drove in an indomitable fashion out of the airport.

"Bastard police, they act like we are in a dictatorship!" he proclaimed, banging on the horn a few times to salute the official as they flew past.

The policeman shook his fist at the car and Hassan laughed. Charlotte found herself unexpectedly triumphant too, despite her fear. Hassan seemed to read her mind and slapped his hand on the steering wheel.

"Not what you were expecting, eh? Never mind, it is safe and reliable, like me!"

He laughed again, and Charlotte tried to smile in return, her fingernails gripping the door rest. They wove in and out of traffic with little regard to other road users or speed limits.

"Have you been to Morocco before, Charlotte?"

"No, no, I haven't."

Charlotte searched for some kind of comment to make, but Hassan beat her to it.

"It is both the best and the worst of places. Morocco is a capricious lover, but impossible to forget once you have tasted her hospitality!"

I see that, thought Charlotte. She drank in the yellow minarets with their distinct decoration of lapis lazuli tiles.

Cerulean doors lined ancient passageways and the roads were edged in all manner of buildings, some ramshackle, some more permanent. Then, the people – where to begin? The women's dark eyes just visible from their hijabs contrasting with the men's cool white robes and sandals, children gazing wanderingly as they drove past in clouds of dust. It was like stepping back in time, as far as she could see in the dwindling light. The evidence of poverty was everywhere, malnourished children running barefoot with snatches of clothing, but intermingled with modernity – advertisements for perfume, beauty products, fast food, petrol stations. A beggar by the side of the road with matted hair and skull-like features. It was like the spinning top she had had as a child, the scenes changed so quickly. She was riveted.

Hassan looked at her curiously in the rear-view mirror. "You work for Max long?"

"Not really, just a couple of months." Charlotte couldn't believe it herself.

It transpired that Hassan was a film student at the local university and was doing some kind of work experience.

"I'm a novice too," Charlotte assured him. "You'll have to show me the ropes when we get there. I'm a bit nervous, to be honest."

"It's all good." Hassan assumed a relaxed position with one hand on the wheel and the other draped over the passenger seat.

Charlotte had elected to sit in the back, and she now wondered whether this had been a good idea or not. Probably for the best not to view the driving at close hand.

"Max is great," he continued, oblivious to Charlotte's concern. "He has been very helpful actually, introducing me to some of the more experienced crew. Yes, he's good, but some actors... *phff.*" He gestured with his hand. "They are difficult. You have to get this, get that, change lights, dress wrong, dress right, you know?"

"It sounds like I'm going to find out. What area are you studying?" Charlotte felt a growing affinity with Hassan. She guessed it was probably a big deal here to get into university, like winning a ticket to a different life.

"Oh, I want to be a producer, shoot with the big guns – Steven Spielberg and all that." He smiled and Charlotte could see his white teeth, lighter in the evening shadow. "You have to aim high, right?"

"Yes, yes, you do," Charlotte found herself responding fervently. She guessed that she also felt that or why else would she be here? A leap of faith, a leap into the unknown. She and Hassan did have something in common.

"Aaah, we are here."

"Already? That was quick!" Charlotte peered out. The light had dimmed quickly now that it was 9.00p.m. or so. Hassan had already disembarked from the car and was heaving her bags out of the opposite door. Charlotte got out slowly, anaesthetised from the journey, but noticing immediately the imposing entrance to the hotel. It was big, at least twice the size of the one in London. Although it was dark, there were a number of people at the front, several guests arriving, met by porters, and a few smokers, tourists by the look of their dress. The air was disconcertingly cold. She had read about the unique contrast in Morocco between the hot day and the windswept desert chill of the night.

Following Hassan in through the pillared entrance, Charlotte was distracted by the looming pillars and ornate carvings on the sandstone walls. He led her to the reception desk, clearly visible with bright lights overhead. Smartly dressed hotel staff, all gleaming hair, pristine make-up and smartly creased uniforms, were easy to identify, and Hassan had a brief conversation with the receptionist in French. Charlotte could only pick out a few words of the rapid dialogue.

"I'll show you to your room, madame." A short, buxom woman, with hair in a well-coiffed bun, came round to the front with a key card. "The porter will bring your bags up shortly."

"See you tomorrow, Charlotte. Sleep well." Hassan raised his hand in greeting and strode off towards the entrance.

Charlotte followed the woman through several cavernous hallways resplendent with more sculptures, marble floors and walls, domed archways, large vases and plants positioned suggestively in every orifice. They entered a lift, and Charlotte looked nervously at the blurred reflection staring back at her. She felt rumpled and travel-soiled, and longed for a shower. They were on the fourth floor. The place really was enormous.

"'Ere is your room, madame, and Monsieur Collins wanted me to tell you that 'is room is on the second floor, number twenty-one, and please to call on him when you 'ave refreshed yourself."

"Thank you." Charlotte gratefully took the proffered card and pushed the door open.

Amazingly, her bag and suitcase were already there, stacked neatly by the suitcase stand in a small dressing area which led to the main bedroom. She collapsed on the bed and surveyed her surroundings. The bed was large and soft, surrounded by the ubiquitous mahogany-style bedroom furniture. She spied a balcony through the muslin curtains that had been pulled across the glass doors. She opened them and slid the doors open. Beyond was a large swimming pool and sunning area decorated with palms and bougainvillea.

Back in the room, she shut the doors again and registered the slight humming of the air conditioning. Tiredness enveloped her like a blanket, and she found her eyes closing. She must have dozed for about twenty minutes, hazy images floating in front of her eyes while she tried to rouse herself unsuccessfully from her torpor. Finally, she managed to galvanise herself into action. The shower was powerful and effective. Finally, she was cleansed and mentally refreshed. Now to find Max.

TWENTY-TWO

Charlotte took the lift down two floors and thanked the heavens for the clear markings on each corridor. The hotel was, as she had suspected, palatial. She passed several couples and an older family, perhaps Italian or French, going down to dinner. The teenagers were uniquely European, at once beautiful and resentful with their luxuriant dark thick hair and smooth olive skin, slumped and awkward on the stairs, unaware of their quiescent power. Their parents followed, the mother svelte and stylish but with a bored, discontented expression on her face, escorted by her silver-haired husband in a jacket and open-necked shirt. His eyes met Charlotte's as she stared; she felt the weight of his appraisal and looked away, embarrassed.

She was apprehensive now, but also incredibly hungry. It was after 9.00p.m. and she hadn't eaten since the airport in England. Hopefully, Max would have food. She knocked with some trepidation at the door of No. 21. It was opened by a tiny blonde woman in jeans and a black t-shirt with pixie-like features and a mat of thick, frizzy hair.

There was a brief silence, and Charlotte took a step back

in embarrassment. "Oh, I think I may have the wrong room," she stuttered.

Inside Max heard her voice and jumped up, almost knocking over a glass in his haste. He had been on high alert since her flight got in three hours ago, checking and re-checking the two tiny ticks on the WhatsApp screen.

"No, darling, this is the right room, don't panic. You're Charlotte? Max's expecting you." For a small woman, her voice was bell-like. She smiled and her eyes scrunched up at the edges, so that she looked even more elfin. She moved to one side helpfully, and Charlotte attempted to elegantly squeeze past.

"Steady, mate!" Remeil's eyes followed Max as he made for the door. Was this the PA that Max had been so evasive about? Unlike him to take his admin arrangements so seriously. She must be good! Remeil took another sip of his wine, and pondered on what she looked like. Nell had been texting him with various warnings to let her know if the relationship was anything but professional, so he was expecting her to be something special. He wouldn't expect anything less of Max; he knew how to pull the ladies, that was for sure.

Max got to the door but, annoyingly, Maxine had got there first. Typical, she could sniff a lie out at ten paces. She had been badgering Max for the last two days to go through his lines with her, but he had found it difficult to focus. He had blamed himself for getting Charlotte into this mess, especially when she had had to deal with all the marriage stuff on top. He thanked Christ that he hadn't been actually married to Nell. It had made it easier to walk away, without a doubt. Probably too easy, his parents would have said, but then they hadn't had to live with her.

He could see Charlotte now next to Maxine. She looked tired but still unmistakably herself, her pale skin flushed from the confusion. He hadn't anticipated how torn he would feel when he saw her, relieved but nervy at the same time. She was here with his people now; it was important to him that there was mutual approval. Right now, he was feeling like a coiled spring inside: tight and not quite confident that he was fully in control. He felt sheepish, as he met her eyes, fraudulent somehow. What a shit time she was having, and now she had to put up with his shit too. *Okay, get your act together, Max. You can do it.*

"Charlotte!" His voice bounced resoundingly along the narrow entrance corridor and Maxine grinned at Charlotte's confusion. "I should introduce myself. I'm Maxine, one of the voice coaches. Nice to meet you."

Max, by now, was in front of her. "Found it all okay?" He put a hand on one arm, and Charlotte appreciated its reassuring pressure as she drank in his appearance.

"Just about. Hassan was helpful."

His hair was shorter, and he had a goatee beard. She wasn't sure if she liked it or not. It looked too groomed, too sharp.

He touched it nervously as he saw her eyes look questioningly at him. "For the part… Helix's devilish good looks, remember?"

"Hmmm, I think Helix can keep it," Charlotte started to say, but they were interrupted by his name being called raucously from the inner sanctum. She followed him through to what seemed to be a suite of rooms. "Wow, this is… spacious!"

Four or five people were lounging in various attitudes on sofas or on the floor round a large coffee table on which were placed various plates of food and bottles. They greeted Charlotte without ceremony, and several resumed the animated conversation they were having. There was a pleasant fug in the air of drink and the slight drift of cigarette smoke. An external door was ajar, and she could see tips of cigarettes being waved about as people chatted on what she assumed was a balcony. Beyond that were the faint red watermarks of a setting sun.

"Charlotte, you've met Max 2, then El and Steve are assistant directors and Beth over there is a scout." Max pointed to the three on the sofa. "Mira and Zach are outside having a smoke; Remeil is an assistant producer and, incidentally, one of my oldest friends."

"Oh." Charlotte suddenly remembered the red carpet anecdote. "Nice to meet you."

Remeil looked at her for a moment, registering her slight intake of breath, and his face creased with exaggerated dismay. "Shit, man, you've told her too?"

"Had to be done, mate, had to be done!"

Remeil put his head in his hands in mock despair, and Charlotte hovered a moment between not knowing whether to smile or not.

Then Max pulled her down on the sofa beside him in an easy gesture which covered her embarrassment.

"How's it going?" he said quietly to one side.

Remeil was giving him the thumbs up behind Charlotte's head, and Max stuck two fingers up in response.

"I'm fine. We'll talk about it later. It's just nice to be here." Charlotte looked into his warm brown eyes without interruption at last. It was like returning home. The lights were reflected in his pupils, highlighting their tawny glow and he crinkled at her, taking pleasure in the sincerity of her words. She became acutely aware that their hands and hips were touching, and they glanced apart simultaneously, the absence of contact imprinted like an ache.

The hangings cast shadows against the walls and the terracotta shadows cast a mellow spell over the watcher. Charlotte could hear the muted drone of chanting and, somewhere in her subconscious, realised that she was hearing the call to prayer. She felt her limbs become heavier and let the hum of conversation pass over her. Max had resumed a conversation with Remeil and then went to get her some food. She answered a few questions from Max 2 but mainly focused on trying to stop her eyes closing.

"You must be starving. Here, have some of this." Max had stacked a plate up with food and she had a few stuffed vine leaves and some pastries flavoured with the rose water. She felt herself drifting into a warm swathe of softness and could fight sleep no longer.

***

Clink, clink. Knock, rustle. Consciousness gradually infused Charlotte's limbs and she endured the crick and pull as she came to. For a moment, the faint sounds she could hear in the room were unidentifiable, and then she realised it was someone clearing plates and glasses from afar. For a few minutes, she sat there curled up in the corner of a sofa, blanket draped over her. She stretched her aching limbs, realising that her shoes had been removed and a jumper placed under her head. She cleared her throat more loudly. She was alone in the room, but she could see a doorway off to the right and hear more clinking intermingled with a few choice expletives. Max – she could easily identify his rangy silhouette – seemed to have dropped a glass.

Gingerly, she cast the coverlet aside and, feeling her body protesting all over, she walked over to the open door.

"Hey, Max."

"Ah, you're awake. Thought I'd let you sleep, seemed cruel to wake you." Max was stacking plates next to the safe and fridge. "I can't be bothered to call room service to take these now. They can deal with them in the morning, lord knows I've tipped them enough."

He felt shattered now that Charlotte was actually here. He was now able to relax, he supposed. She looked up at him, slightly dishevelled and still with that muzzy, unfocused quality one has after a deep sleep. Her features seemed more prominent, eyes dark and mysterious, lips full. Her shirt was open low at the neck, and Max couldn't help but notice a hint of more insubstantial fabric dipping between her breasts. He took in the curve of her hips and the way her neck seemed to arch as she yawned, pushing her body towards him as her arms stretched behind. He looked away quickly as their eyes met; *think of something else, think of something else.*

Max knew that he had probably had more alcohol than was good for him. He felt frustrated and empty. Every instinct in his body was telling him to make a move, but still something stopped him. With other women, he had been happy to act first and ask questions later, but Charlotte was his friend and employee. He liked her, more than liked her, but he felt keenly her confusion and vulnerability. Was this why all his relationships seemed doomed to fail? No doubt Nell had already seen to that anyway. He felt a gloom descend over him. Did other people analyse their behaviour to this degree? No wonder he felt in an emotional limbo half the time.

"I think I better go back to my room." Charlotte felt embarrassed. Why was Max behaving so peculiarly, peering at her like that? She started rummaging in her pockets for the key card. She felt in her trouser pockets, and then in her cardigan. Why hadn't she brought her bag with her? Or had she? She stepped back into the living room and towards the sofa and plunged her hands down the sides of the chair where she had been lying a few moments before. Some gritty crumbs which she rubbed between her fingers nervously but nothing else. *Shit! Shit! Shit!* She remembered now… her bag. Lying next to her on the bed as she had slept. The card slipped hastily into her jeans pocket, now discarded on the floor of the shower room.

Max walked towards her, a million thoughts going through his head.

"Fancy a nightcap?"

Charlotte looked back at him and considered her response. Why was everything so difficult? Sometimes it felt like everything she touched was doomed.

"I'm so stupid, you're going to think this is some awful set-up, but I really have left my key card in my room. I think I'm going to have to get another one from reception."

Max stared at her fallen face and let out a bellow of laughter. "Charlotte, I thought it was something serious. I must have mislaid my key card four times at least already. Remeil has threatened to tattoo the QR code on my backside. You know what I'm like, Charlotte, or you should do by now at least."

Charlotte tried to smile but felt herself grimace. "I'm just stupid, no excuses for me." She brushed a hand across her eyes, and Max watched her helplessly. She wordlessly put her hands over her face, and he took two paces across the room and sat down next to her with a force that threatened to upend the settee. He put an arm round her and hugged her as if she was Vivi. Charlotte sobbed convulsively. She was so tired, so tired of it all. For a few hours, it had felt like a new start, an adventure, but she had cocked it up again. This, her marriage, a family. What had she got left? She wanted to be looked after; she didn't know if she could do it on her own after all. If she couldn't even cope with a bloody key card. She was supposed to be professional, efficient. What a joke.

Max held her as tightly as he dared and stroked her hair with his free hand. His cheek rested against her head, and he breathed with her. He could smell the faint fruitiness of her shampoo mixed with the underlying muskiness of follicles and sweat. After a few minutes, the paroxysms ceased, and she pulled away. This was beginning to feel dangerous, exposed.

Max said, exasperated, "I can comfort you, can't I, as a friend?"

Charlotte tried to gather her thoughts. She had to get back control of the situation. "This job is the only thing I have going for me at the moment, Max. I don't want to abuse it."

"Oh, for Christ's sake, Charlotte. We're mates, aren't we? As well as working together? I know we haven't known each other long, but it feels longer, much longer." He touched her cheek fleetingly with his hand and, recklessly, his fingers skimmed the edge of her face.

"Yes, yes." Charlotte was visibly flustered. She drew her head back, hardly knowing what to say. She couldn't trust her eyes. "You are my friend, but this, this is too much. It's… it's confusing. Too tactile. You need to stop."

She looked up at him defiantly. It had come out more strongly than she had intended; inside she was a twisted, seething mess. *Touch me*; she wanted him to do so much more, but she was also resisting what was in front of her. Why was he teasing her like this? It felt like a sick joke. She wanted to tell him how she felt, but she risked everything. It would all change and, in a split second, she would face rejection. It would end everything.

Max flinched as if he had been stung.

"For fuck's sake, Charlotte. I'm not trying to molest you or something. I… I… " He shook his head and got up, turning away. "Look, it's too late to go down to reception now. You'll never get to sleep. You can have the bed, and I'll have the sofa. It's in a separate room off this one, so it's all completely above board." He couldn't keep the icy note out of his voice. He felt insulted. Charlotte should know him better than this.

Charlotte felt on the edge of a precipice. To lose his friendship and esteem, but to speak out and make a fool of herself? Was it a risk worth taking; what exactly did she have to lose? It wasn't like she was that good, was she? His back was still turned, and she felt a desperation that she hadn't felt before.

"Wait, Max, please."

He stiffened and stopped in his tracks.

"I don't know how to say this. Don't look at me. I have… I think I have a stupid crush on you. You probably have it all the time. That's what I mean. I know you can behave yourself, but it's not you I'm worried about – it's me. I want to do my best for you, but I'm worried that my feelings are getting in the way. I know you probably don't mean to, but it feels like you're leading me on, teasing me. It makes it more difficult. The last thing I want to do is offend you."

Max turned to face her, and she took a step away.

"You don't need to say anything. I'm not naïve. It's a rebound thing. I'm lonely, you've been so sympathetic and helpful. You know what it's like when someone's kind; it can be overwhelming."

She turned and located the door. It was a fixed point that she could navigate.

"I'll say—" But she got no further. She felt Max's hands on her shoulders and was turned again trance-like to face him. He put his hands on either side of her face and brought his face towards hers. She felt his lips communicate an intensity that he hadn't dared to articulate in words. She was passive in her shock, but then suddenly her nerve endings were forced into recognition, and she responded slowly, shyly at first and then with reciprocal force. They wrenched themselves apart and she took a deep breath.

In the flickering gloom, his eyes were dark and his face mask-like. He stood like a statue marred only by the wayward shock of hair rising from his forehead. With an audacity that she surprised herself with, she reached behind his neck and pulled him to her again; this time, she kissed him back from the outset. It felt again like she was rediscovering something anew. She was eager now. All doubts were cast aside; the ache was more insistent.

Max gently levered her to the sofa and pulled her down with their mouths still locked together like they were fused.

Their bodies followed suit, melding to each other's curves, their skin radiating heat and charge. Amid the torrent of pleasurable sensations, Charlotte realised that Max's hands were deftly unbuttoning her shirt and she felt them make contact with her previously covered skin. She trembled and a spasm passed through her body as it reacted to his feather-like touch. The stroking became more definite as he gained confidence. She moaned gently, and ran her own hands under Max's shirt, feeling the sinewy muscles and the strong shoulders that held her. They both shuddered as mutual gratification matched their fervour.

Suddenly the sound of a phone rang out through the apartment, its strident noise cleaving them apart. Charlotte broke away from Max, panicky and confused. He rolled off her, his ardour slowly abating as the noise persisted.

"Who on earth is calling at this time?" He picked his phone up from the coffee table, unable to stop himself making a harsh clicking sound in his throat.

Charlotte scrabbled at her clothes, fastening underwear haphazardly, clutching her shirt together.

"Who is it? Is there anything wrong?" She looked at Max expectantly.

He looked back helplessly, "No one. Just family."

"Family?" She pulled on her shoes and raised herself upright. "Who would be calling you at 1.30a.m.?"

"It's Nell. I told you she wouldn't let go. She's been calling at all times during the last week."

There was something slightly underhand in his look. Charlotte was still breathless from their encounter, but she had seen that expression too recently to mistake it for anything else.

"You are sleeping with her still, aren't you, Max?" She already knew the response.

"I'm sorry." Max stood there, playing with the bracelet on his wrist; he couldn't meet her eyes. "You think you don't deserve me, Charlotte, but I can assure you that you are worth ten times the person I will ever be."

Charlotte felt like she was clutching pieces of herself together. It was so fucking messy. What could she say to him? He was in too deep, like she was. She arose, and this time got to the door. There really was nothing to say. It felt like she had won the lottery and then lost all her money in the same day, no, the same fifteen minutes. All she wanted was to sleep and erase the last hour from her mind.

"Charlotte," Max called after her, and then more desperately, "Charlotte!"

TWENTY-THREE

Breakfast was between 4.00a.m. and 5.00a.m. in the main hotel restaurant, a classic European buffet with a Moroccan twist. Pastries flavoured with orange or rose water and an array of smoked cheeses and olives that were authentic to that region. Charlotte had had very little sleep as Max had predicted. The hotel staff were affable and helpful, no doubt used to hapless tourists, or film crew in Max's case, but in her bemused and sleep-deprived state, she had struggled to locate the main stairwell, and then find the lift. She felt strangely calm and impervious. Nothing could really surprise her now. *All you have to do is your job, Charlotte*, she told herself. With the help of Remeil, whom she had seated herself next to, she identified the key members of the crew by sight and grabbed an itinerary for the day.

The powers that be wanted to fit in a good five hours of shooting before lunch, and apparently were trying to capture a key scene which was to figure at the end of the second season. Max's character, Helix, was embroiled in an ongoing feud with another character evenly matched in terms of superhuman strength and cunning: in a touch still unusual for this genre, his love interest. They were to fight it out in the mountains, and the cinematographer, or equivalent (this was Netflix), was keen to capture the particularly impressive light of the Atlas peaks at daybreak, hence the ungodly hour. Apparently, he and some other key members of today's film crew – the stunt team, the set design and the camera loaders – had left early so they could screen test the angles and the shadows.

Remeil was feeding Charlotte intelligence on some of the more important relationships on set when Max finally appeared, as most others were getting up to go. Charlotte registered his appearance in the corner of her eye and determinedly carried on her conversation. Max slid into the seat opposite with a glass of pomegranate juice.

"Hey, Max, hope you didn't have too heavy a night?" a wag from an adjacent table called. "Better give make-up an early warning!"

Charlotte couldn't resist glancing at Max. As usual, he looked annoyingly unperturbed by recent events, although perhaps fractionally depleted underneath his tan. He met her eyes then with a questioning look, and she quickly pulled her gaze away. Remeil had started to greet him, and she determined to pull herself together.

"Do you have a trailer?" she ventured, realising that she knew virtually nothing about what the actual shoot entailed.

Max recognised that she was trying to manage the situation. Like Charlotte, sleep had evaded him, and he had slipped into an uneasy dream only about an hour before his phone went off. Bloody Nell had left several voice messages and even sent him a photo of herself which he had deleted straight away. He didn't know what else to do, truth be told.

It had started up again fairly recently, when she had got him the barn. It wasn't the first time they had rekindled their physical relationship for a spell. She had been going through a sparse patch with Neil, and that first night he had been grateful at least that she had taken care of matters and organised everything. He supposed that that was what it was. Nell had taken the lead, and he had fallen into line. So much for being an alpha fucking male. He knew that she was selfish and exploited him shamelessly, but she also protected him to some degree, and she was so difficult to resist when he felt lonely. He realised that Charlotte was repeating the question, and he tried to remember what she had asked.

"Er, not for this, no. They want some action shots and then the rest is filmed on sets in Los Angeles of all places. Hey, Ed!"

He broke off to greet a man who Charlotte sensed had paused behind her. She glanced over her shoulder and almost fell off her seat. It seemed that Max had been gifted with a double. He was strikingly similar in physique and had a superficial facial resemblance but without Max's fluidity of expression. This man's features were slightly coarser, and his face was less mobile, although it was difficult to take him all in at present.

"Charlotte, Ed's my stunt double, and yes, we normally do have this effect on people." Max got up and went to stand next to him.

Now they were side by side, Charlotte could see more clearly that Max was marginally taller, and Ed was definitely more thickset. Facially, as she had already surmised, he lacked the vivacity of Max's features, and his eyes were a darker brown, but he looked kind, and Charlotte instantly warmed to him.

"Wow, I can see why you got the job! It's good to meet you. What have they got in store for you today?"

"Nice to meet you, Charlotte, I've heard a lot about you. It's a breeze today, just a quick jump down from the mountain, when Max is shot and falls."

"I don't know why I can't do it," Max cut in. "That bungee jump looks like way too much fun!"

"Oh, you want to have a go, pretty boy?" Ed bantered. "I don't think we're insured enough for you to have a ride!" He winked at Charlotte. "Princess here is kept strictly away from any high jumps."

Max playfully punched him on the arm, and Ed mimed an exaggerated injury. Their horseplay was interrupted by a short, rotund woman in an incongruous bright pink jumpsuit jumping on a chair and reading out instructions from a clipboard. Charlotte had been allocated a seat in a minibus carrying assistants and general dogsbodies, whereas Max was to be transported in a jeep to the film location.

"It's always like this to begin with," Max bent down to whisper to Charlotte. "I'll see you at lunch. Don't go anywhere, I'll need to let off steam. Linda always manages to wind me up big time."

"Who's Linda?" Charlotte started to say, but Max had already started moving towards the archway that led back to the reception area. She picked up her bag and sunhat and followed the other crew members out towards the hotel entrance. Stepping into the early morning, there was still a hint of chill, and the sky was overcast. Charlotte took a moment just to let the unfamiliar surroundings sink in.

They were opposite some kind of town square, and she could see walled gardens with vivid puce flowering plants climbing lazily over them. The call to prayer reverberated in the background, and Charlotte felt like she had been taken back in time. Street sellers in traditional Berber dress were setting up further along from the hotel and she could see the glint of silver in their trays. She wished for a minute that she could spend some time wandering round like a proper tourist, soaking up the atmosphere and trying to understand what Hassan had meant. Maybe later in the day.

To the side of her, several of the crew were grumbling about how long they would have to wait today to perhaps not even get a shot. She felt a tap on her arm and saw that Hassan himself was standing next to her. Affection unexpectedly coursed through her veins, someone at last that she knew. She hadn't noticed him at breakfast but perhaps he had been praying; she assumed he was Muslim.

"Charlotte, do you know where you are going?" He looked at her seriously and she stifled a grin. He was obviously taking his duties as chaperone seriously. He was so young and earnest. She felt a stab of jealousy. To be that single-minded again. There was a time, long ago, when she had been fully invested in the idea of a career, a proper career. With the wisdom of time, she knew now that she had mistaken security and comfort for happiness and contentment. And they had served her well for a while, but everything had its price, a price she appeared to be paying in spades now.

"I think so, they said that some minibuses would be coming round to the front."

"Yes, don't worry, I'll make sure you get on the right one. Would you like me to take your bag?"

"You're so kind, thank you. I can manage it though."

Charlotte felt desperately grateful. She was so far out of her comfort zone that she was practically stiff with nerves.

"Max has asked me to look after you, and that's what I'm doing," Hassan responded, relaxing a little as he acknowledged Charlotte's reliance. "He's been very good to me. Normally, the students get the shit jobs, but thanks to him, I've been able to help out on the set and I've met all the principal cast members. I owe him, big time!"

It was somewhat frustrating to be presented with evidence of Max's generosity when Charlotte was intent on focusing on his character flaws, his confession still resonating in her ears. She gave Hassan a faint smile and looked away for a minute. He was astute enough to change the subject, and soon they were laughing about the dining habits of the elderly actor who played Max's human father.

***

By lunchtime, Charlotte was thoroughly bored. The cloud had failed to lift, and they had moved onto the action sequence which was to end the second season. Max and his nemesis – his half-sister, with whom he had been having an unknowingly (on her part) incestuous relationship – were battling to the death for their inheritance on a cliff edge. They had trekked up to the midpoint of one of the more diminutive points in the Atlas Mountains. Clever camera work made the drops seem more spectacular than they actually were, although Charlotte privately thought that even this filming seemed dangerous enough. The loose earth on the unmade surfaces made the minibus's wheels spin alarmingly on the roads, little more than dirt tracks as they got progressively higher up the mountain.

The actual scene they were filming now looked hair-raising but had been cleverly designed to mask the use of Ed when Max fell away from the cliff, seemingly off a precipice. Ed was on a line which tracked down the mountain to where his team were waiting at the bottom. He was in essence bungee jumping off the mountainside with a full body harness that had been carefully colour-matched and was worn underneath the suit that both he and Max were wearing. The site had been carefully chosen because of its unusual, stepped cliff face. Although it appeared that there was a sheer drop, in actual fact, there was a mere six metre fall for Max onto a massive crash mat, while a cutaway shot of Ed would make it look as though Helix was in freefall.

She could tell that Max was increasingly feeling the strain as she noticed his hand rake through his hair with a mounting frequency. Quite early on, it had come up that he was not keen on heights and, despite the apparent safety, the scenery plummeted below them from every side with dizzying verisimilitude. The air seemed distinctly thinner at this altitude, and there was little shade although the sun was still hazy. Several times, the team who seemed to have been tasked with checking continuity errors sent in a runner to get the attention of one of the production assistants and they had to bring the hair stylist onto set to re-tame Max's ruffled locks. She could see Max rolling his eyes and, by the time a break was called, he was noticeably piqued. Finally, after 2.00p.m., the words that everyone was waiting for sounded.

"Okay, cut. Break for lunch, everyone."

The catering team had set up trestle tables under gazebos which were weighted down with rocks. There was a stiff breeze and tempers were fraying from both crew and actors, despite the welcome smell of grilling meat and piquant spices. Max's love interest loudly refused the selection of antipasti offered, and her assistant could be seen talking anxiously to one of the cooks behind the grill. Charlotte saw Max with his head down, deep in conversation with one of the directors. Clearly, neither were happy with the turn the conversation had taken and Max then lifted his hands in a helpless gesture and stepped away from the woman, shielding his eyes from the sun and scanning the barbeque. Charlotte wandered if he was looking for her, and looked round for someone she knew; the last thing she wanted was to be on her own with him again. She spotted Max 2 near the entrance to the tent queuing for the food and went and stood next to her.

Generally, both actors and cast were dotted up and down the line without ceremony. Only the bona fide A-listers were able to take first dibs of the buffet. Having failed to find her, if that is what he had been trying to do, Charlotte then wasn't surprised to see that Max joined the back of the queue without comment, although she could see others pointing ahead of themselves, offering for him to go in front.

At length, she and Max 2 managed to squeeze into a couple of spaces on the bench nearest the entrance. It at least ensured they had a cooling fan of mountain air. Both took several mouthfuls before talking ensued.

"This is shaping up to be a bit of a nightmare, isn't it?" Maxine rolled her eyes obliquely towards Max, who had managed to get a seat near the other end of the table and had sent Charlotte several pleading looks.

"What, the weather, do you mean? Yeah, shame about the lack of colour first thing." Charlotte couldn't help but notice the disappointing yellow-greyish sunrise, and the look on the main cinematographer's face had suggested that he wholeheartedly agreed.

"Well, that and everything else. Chris is so fed up that he's even suggested giving up on Morocco and rethinking the location, apparently. It's one thing after another. They shot the whole of this one scene last night, thinking it was perfect, and some muppet of a tourist launched a drone near the filming. Taking photos, apparently, although the legal advisor wasn't taking any chances." She chuckled. "Orion slapped a non-disclosure on them quicker than they could say 'we didn't mean it'. I thought they might have photoshopped it out, but the whirring sound completely destroyed the actors' concentration. Miranda looked like she was going to spontaneously combust!"

"That is a real bummer," Charlotte agreed. "Won't they keep trying a bit longer?"

"I think they might consider moving a lot of this to the constructed sets if this overcast weather continues," Maxine said. "Hey, Suze, what's the latest?"

"Oh, hi, Maxine, hi… er, are you Max's assistant?" A youngish girl with a scraped back ponytail and an intense expression looked pointedly at Charlotte.

"Yes, I am."

"I think you might want to go and have a chat with him, there's been a bit of a row. Chris and Amanda are all for pulling out, and I hear that Max is doling out final ultimatums. Of course, he's under contract, but tempers are running high!"

"Oh God, I can talk to him, but I'm not sure what I can do. Max knows what he wants."

Charlotte bolted down a couple more mouthfuls of salad and grabbed her bag. It was a scene that she had run through several times with Max at home, and she knew that he found it difficult. It was never going to be easy to act taking a bullet to the chest after rejecting a demigod and they both had thought the script at this point was rather dire. She walked slowly over to Max and hovered awkwardly behind him.

Max was moodily chewing on a piece of goat meat and didn't realise at first that Charlotte was there. The events of the morning had encapsulated what he hated most about these shoots – the unpredictability of the weather, the imperiousness of the other actors and the perfectionism of the director and producer. He just wanted to wrap it up and return to the hotel so he could sort out the events of last night with Charlotte, who he suddenly realised was standing just behind him. Fuck, just as well she couldn't read his mind.

He turned round towards her and felt himself flush under his tan. She stood in front of him, her grave stare meeting his own, and he felt a familiar burst of affection. So contrasting with Nell's beauty, her appeal was her idiosyncrasies, her individuality. He wanted to look after her, to nurture her in a way that he never had done with Nell. It wasn't about dominating her; he wanted her to care for him, to look after him too. He admired both women, but there was a reciprocity with Charlotte. With Nell, it felt like a constant fight to have the upper hand.

"What's going on, Max?" Charlotte said in a low voice. "Are you okay?"

Max pulled his sunglasses out of his jacket pocket – he was dressed in a linen suit and his character had a pair of Ray-Bans which he put on now, frowning. He grabbed a cap from one of the crew, who squawked nervously and then shut his mouth quickly when he saw who had taken it. Charlotte pulled on her own hat and glasses (decidedly less flashy) and followed Max outside the tent to where a few other couples were talking, and she could see the film crew setting up the shot again.

"It's the bloody shooting bit," Max said. "You know how I feel about this scene, and they insist on repeating it time and time again. I know I should be used to it, but I'm fucking not. Miranda wants to change the angle again now, and the words aren't right... and I can't leave my hair alone. I've had enough, Charlotte!"

"Look, just calm it." Charlotte sounded less flustered than she felt. "If they can get it today, then it's finished, isn't it? You know those words, and you make them sound convincing if nothing else. At least you're not having to do the fall, like Ed." She stalled; Max was normally so laid-back. Was he thinking about what had happened last night too?

"Ed's a fucking saint," Max growled.

Charlotte lowered her voice. "It's my fault. I shouldn't have come. It's a distraction, and you need to just focus on this. You're normally the one who can take things in your stride."

"Not really, Charlotte. Maybe I'm just letting you see the real me," Max replied more quietly. Last night had thrown him. He was used to getting his way in the bedroom, and it felt like business was half-finished. He didn't want to be the actor who threw a hissy fit, complaining that they weren't being shown to their best advantage, but right now he felt naked and defenceless. Shit, he hated heights; he couldn't believe that he hadn't shared that with anyone. Did Charlotte know? Probably. He looked at her standing there, looking steadily at him, and wished he could hold her hands. They were interrupted by the by now familiar klaxon sounding the end of the lunch-break.

"Resume your positions for take twenty-two, please," intoned the put-upon camera assistant, sounding as fed up as she could without risk of compromising her favoured position.

"You can do it, Max, just pretend you're back at home, in the garden." Charlotte leant up and whispered next to his shoulder. She wasn't even sure he'd heard but his hand found hers and gave a brief, hard squeeze, and he walked off towards the marked-out filming area near the mountain edge without a backwards glance.

TWENTY-FOUR

Charlotte found a director's chair and positioned it as far forwards as she dared so that she was behind the lead cameras that were already panning the horizon. The noise of the crew moving and chatting died away as people grabbed chairs or retired to the tent. Not that there was much of a view. They weren't allowed anywhere near the actual shooting area; a stray foot or shadow could wreak havoc. Several monitors had been set up with leads trailing back to a generator, so that the lesser crew could follow the filming. It was all a bit archaic with several seconds delay on the display.

The clapper loader stood with the clapboard and got ready to bang it together. Charlotte couldn't believe that this was still the actual method for signifying the beginning of filming – it seemed like something from the fifties.

"Take twenty-two!"

Kass, as the female protagonist was called, was filmed scanning the horizon and pacing several times. Charlotte saw they were taking the close-ups of her face. She recalled the camera directions to focus on the reflected sun in her eyes, which presumably would call for heavy editing later, and noted the photogenic way the mountain breeze whipped her luxurious curls across her face. Kass was clad in a traditional Moroccan robe for women, and she now cast it to one side to reveal her warrior's armour-plated catsuit partnered with a small, lethal looking handgun in a holster round her hips.

She was both muscular and feminine with a curvaceous figure that looked as though it had been sculpted out of sandstone itself. Her face was classically beautiful with large brown eyes and thick bouncing brown hair that hung down almost to her hips. Kass cocked the gun now, still nervously scanning left to right, and then the figure of Helix pulled himself up over the cliff slightly behind her and righted himself. Max was allowed at this point to dust himself down and run his hand through his hair as he deliberately coughed to alert Kassandra of his presence and make a play of his unperturbed demeanour. Kass wheeled round and tensed every muscle in her body. In contrast, Max's character flexed unhurriedly in front of her, and the camera shot him from below to exaggerate his looming presence.

Max locked eyes with Kassandra and laughed as her character levelled her gun at him and aimed with both hands, a slight shake detectable. Another camera panned round the scene to capture the drama from each angle while the two characters were poised, interlocked in their own fate.

"Why did you come?"

Part of the dynamic was that Kass was passionately and tragically in love with Helix, and Charlotte had to acknowledge that she had captured the melancholic tone of someone half-regretful and half-resigned to her fate.

"That's the wrong question, Kass." Helix's voice seemed to resonate from the very foot of the mountains, and Charlotte was glad to hear the confidence in Max's voice, accentuating the egotism, the hubris of Helix.

He took two steps towards Kass, and she yelled, "Stop!" Her voice was distorted by the wind. This was as far as they had got so far, and Charlotte noticed many of the crew were tense and straining to hear, on tenterhooks for the scene to continue.

Helix took a step backwards, carelessly kicking some stones with his foot towards the apparently vast drop so they ricocheted against the rocky face. Charlotte couldn't hear, but imagined the faint clanging below as they glanced off sheer rock faces and were buffeted by the wind. She found herself spellbound; the appeal of the character was undeniable. Max exuded a charismatic sexiness that was alluring, compelling and at times vicious.

His voice thinned and became more measured. "You mean, why me? Why have the fates thrown us together? You haven't guessed yet? Perhaps you aren't as clever as you think." His voice was cruel. His words were playing with her, and her body language spoke of strain.

Touching her head with the gun in her hand, she wiped the beads of sweat from her brow.

"Who are you, you bastard? What do you want with me? I've given myself to you, but you've used me, haven't you? What is this about?"

Helix laughed again but this time there was a weariness, a hollowness. "Do I have to tell you, Kass? I'm your brother; you've been fucking your brother. What a monster you've become! Like me; you are just like me."

Kass howled, though in rage or pain it was not clear. She sank to her knees and raised her hands to the heavens, then bent over her knees, her arms clutched to her and hidden. Helix laughed again, a heinous impersonation of ecstasy. He looked at Kass and smiled. She uncurled herself with the gun now in her right hand, raising it up higher with a trembling arm and fired.

Helix lifted both hands and appeared to be launched off the mountain by the power of the shot. He was lost to sight, and Charlotte felt her heart in her mouth. She knew what was supposed to happen in theory, but it all looked so realistic. There was a pause and Charlotte could feel the atmosphere palpably relaxing. Almost all of the scene was complete apart from the cutaways of Helix falling ostensibly into oblivion. There was a close-up of Helix's look of surprise, or was it satisfaction, and then the camera crackled to nothingness and the screen went black.

She strained towards the cliffs, expecting to hear the 'cut' at any point, and then the sound of Max being winched to the surface. Nothing, but a faint noise building in volume. Charlotte recognised it but couldn't quite put a finger on what it was. Then, late to the party, she identified it at last… faint screaming, a woman. Some people nearby were laughing, caught in the aftermath of a joke, others looked unsure. The noise grew louder and was joined by exclamations and shouting. Something was clearly very wrong.

Charlotte felt the muscles in her stomach tense and looked at the people standing around her expectantly. Why did they look as terrified as she felt? Then there was more calling and shouting. People running. *Shit! Fuck! Max!*

"Max!" she felt herself scream. She felt weighted, as if her legs had gone to sleep. She saw the people parting in front of her to let first-aiders through with medical boxes and she pushed forwards, forcing her way through until she came to the filming area. Security staff were cordoning off the space where Max had fallen, with fluorescent tape and chairs as makeshift barriers.

"Let me through," she blustered, "I'm Max's assistant; I need to get to him."

A security guard blocked her way. "No one through at the moment, only medics."

"But I need to see if he's okay. Is he okay? What's going on?" she rambled incoherently. A fog was engulfing her and she and was conscious of drops of perspiration forming on her forehead. "Please, I need to get to him. I need to get to him!" She knew she was shouting. People were turning and looking at her. She didn't care, she had to know that he was alright.

The guard addressed her directly. "Lady, I don't know anything at the moment either. Panicking isn't going to help anybody. Please wait patiently and I'll see what I can do."

Charlotte rolled her eyes in desperation. She could see a huddle of film crew on the horizon dropping down blankets while medical equipment was being fastened to some kind of pulley. A medic was being winched down and the rest of the entourage were being ushered into the gazebos by the assistant with the clipboard. Meanwhile, the minibuses were rumbling into life and starting to be filled. Hassan appeared at her side, but she hardly noticed he was there or the jacket he put round her shoulders. *Christ, let Max be okay, let him be okay*. She was clenching her fists so tightly that she could feel her nails cutting into her palms. Energy seemed to be building inside her like a pressure cooker. She wanted to scream.

The guard's radio crackled into life, and he started taking a message, turning away from the hastily erected barrier. It was her chance! Charlotte impetuously ducked under the tape, the jacket shed on the floor, and hared over to the group in front of her, crossing the uneven surface in milliseconds. She ran along the row of people, searching for a gap, squeezing in next to the main group.

The director turned round, eyes wild and face tear stained.

"What are you— oh, you're with Max, aren't you? Come here, poppet, he's okay."

"What's happened?" Charlotte's voice was caught between a croak and a sob. She both longed for and dreaded the answer. "Who's hurt?"

"It's Ed." Miranda's voice broke with a sob. "The poor boy's cord was twisted, and he crashed into the side of the mountain on the way down instead of making a straight drop. His head hit a protruding rock and knocked him out cold. We haven't been able to winch him in safely yet, as he's still unconscious. One of the stunt team is going down now with a medic to bring him up between them. Max has insisted on helping to winch him up."

"Oh my god, how badly is he injured?"

"We don't know yet. When he free falls, he usually hangs loose for a few seconds before regaining control. We've done it so many times before," she said plaintively. "Ed's so meticulous normally, I don't know how he lost concentration."

She was interrupted by shouts below and Charlotte looked over the edge at the ledge beneath them. She saw the blue crash mat straight away and then located Max and several others helping to lower the medic. Then, oh, she could see a limp figure carefully laid in an approximation of the recovery position. Even from this height, Charlotte could pick out what appeared to be a deep dent in his forehead and the shoulder on that side of the body hanging at an odd, disconcerting angle. She felt the taste of bile in her mouth.

A stretcher was now being passed down and the team lifted the man with great care onto it. Charlotte followed Max's tense figure as he tightened the straps with silent reverence around Ed's battered body.

"Is there an ambulance coming?"

One of the assistant directors heard her words. "Too high up – quicker getting him back ourselves. They know he's on the way. Right, let's move back everyone." His voice grew louder and more authoritative. "Out of the way. He's coming through."

The stretcher was lifted up and Charlotte could see the men straining below to create a smooth passage as it was carefully attached again to the winch and a medic. Charlotte watched wordlessly as Ed reached the surface and swallowed as she saw close-up the unsightly damage to his head at the site of the collision. The contusion had caused his eyelid to swell monstrously, and it was hard to detect any noticeable sign of life as he lay there so still and lifeless. Charlotte felt the briefest of taps to her shoulder and realised that Max had joined her side.

"Max, oh Max." She grasped his hand and squeezed it. "I'm so sorry."

Max's face was grim, and his eyes were glazed.

"I can't speak now." He managed the few words and suddenly felt a wave of nausea pass over him. He ran to the edge of the mountain and was sick. Charlotte waited till he returned to her, and silently passed him some paper napkins from her bag.

They walked towards the first tent and Max sat down heavily on a bench. Linda of the pink jumpsuit and the assistant directors came in slowly behind them, and Charlotte went over to talk to the catering team, who were in the throes of packing up.

"We need some teas with plenty of sugar."

"That's a bit difficult now," said a sulky looking youth.

"Too bad. People are in shock. I'll help you, if necessary." Charlotte itched to slap him, but her words had taken effect for he managed to drum up some paper cups of weak tea with some sachets of sugar.

Nothing was said for a few minutes, and then Miranda spoke. "Nothing more we can do here. Let's get back to the hotel, and then we can send a party to the hospital—"

"Have you let his girlfriend know?" Max interrupted. "Fiancée, I mean. He was telling me about it last night. They had just got engaged. She's pregnant."

Charlotte looked at him, shocked, but he had retreated into himself again, and was staring intently at his hands nursing the cup of tea, undrunk, in front him.

Linda exchanged looks with one of the assistants and nodded. "We'll make those calls, Max. You needn't worry." She addressed Charlotte. "Get him back to the hotel. He needs to rest."

TWENTY-FIVE

They didn't speak in the jeep. The driver was local, and they were travelling on their own. Charlotte peered out of the smeary obscured window at the sparse trees and few goats that dotted the mountainside tracks. She felt numb. She put her hand out and touched Max's arm. He felt warm and familiar, but there was no physical response. He sat there, looking ahead, a set expression on his face, unreachable.

The journey was bumpy and unpredictable. Several times they were thrown almost together; no such luxuries as working seatbelts, it seemed. Eventually they joined a more recognisable road and started passing fuel stations and roadside stalls. They drew up in traffic on the outskirts of Essaouira and young boys banged on the windows begging for change or trade; it was all the same.

Outside the hotel, the driver hurried to let them out. Max said nothing and strode inside, leaving Charlotte to awkwardly pluck some notes out of her wallet. Anything to make the driver go away. He beamed and gestured his thanks, so she supposed it had been a ridiculous amount, but never mind, it just needed to be over. Inside the entrance of the hotel, Max was nowhere to be seen. She saw some crew she recognised and hastened over.

"Do you know how he is? Have they got to the hospital?"

"They're operating now. His spleen has had to be removed. He hasn't regained consciousness yet."

Several people looked overcome and were comforting each other, collapsed on the pristine sofas in the gaudy reception, the dishevelment at odds with the marble opulence, all wet crumpled faces and bodies leaning together. Charlotte supposed they must have worked with Ed for a while. She felt like an impostor, fraudulent somehow. She felt sympathy and pain at the shock and tragedy of the incident, but it was impossible for her to share their grief fully.

"That's filming over, I guess," she overheard a man saying to a girl dressed in impossibly baggy trousers and a t-shirt with a trite epithet emblazoned across her chest. "There's no way the insurance will let them go back now. What fucking possessed Ed to do it without the full safety harness?"

"He was harnessed up, I saw him. It was the twenty-second take," the girl said with some venom and a pronounced American accent. "We were all pissed. Miranda knew it."

There was the noise of an altercation happening behind them, and Charlotte could hear raised voices. She caught sight of a brawny man exchanging heated words with the hotel security guards and suddenly heard the clear tones of the female lead through the fracas.

"Let me through, Nico, forget it. Do you think this matters? I just need a drink."

Charlotte saw her enter through the revolving door, sweeping the space with her eyes and then hesitating for a minute. She overheard the American girl say sotto voce to her companion, "It's her fucking fault; she made such a big deal of those camera angles at the beginning."

A shadow passed over the actor's face, and Charlotte realised she had probably heard what had been uttered or had got the general gist. She walked over to Charlotte, who was watching wide-eyed. Over her shoulder, she spoke clearly in the direction of her bodyguard, "An espresso martini, if you've quite finished, guys. Make it a double, plenty of ice. And one for her too." She gestured at Charlotte.

"Er, thank you... are *you* okay?" Charlotte was nonplussed.

"What the fuck do you think?" she answered wryly. "Let's sit down."

She led the way to an alcove, separated from the main reception area by some wooden screening and huge pot plants. A waiter hurried over with some olives and napkins. She plonked herself down on a chaise longue, kicking off her trainers under the low table in front. Charlotte perched opposite her with some trepidation, but now she was so near to the actress, she felt less intimidated, more fascinated. Her make-up was patchy, affected by the heat no doubt, and, beneath the heavy concealer, her eyes looked tired. She was unquestionably striking but, close to, Charlotte recognised her as a human rather than a cipher on the screen. She felt guilty now for judging her earlier.

"Call me Cat, by the way." The girl, for that's all she seemed to Charlotte, arranged herself a little like a cat, stretching and then tucking her legs under her again. Plucking an olive from the bowl, she sucked it almost distractedly, then took a long draft from her drink and focused her gaze on Charlotte.

"Well, well, what an end to the day. That's my first time for a near miss, believe it or not. That poor bastard. Ed was one of the good ones. You knew him?"

"Not really. I only met him this morning." Charlotte felt like she had been injected with truth serum. The effect of the straight talking mixed with a sip of the clearly very double espresso martini was disarming. "I thought he was Max to begin with, from behind at least."

"Yes, the junk in the trunk is equally impressive." Cat managed to keep her face straight as she replied but her eyes were dancing, and they both spontaneously burst into giggles. Charlotte put a hand to her mouth and looked nervously to the others gathered in the main lounge, but they either hadn't heard or were assiduously ignoring them.

"It's shock; relax, babe. Better to be honest than a phoney. I did know him, but not really well like Max and his gang. You do get to know your doubles – comes from having to hang out with them so much. Mine's a total douche, by the way, not much between her ears, but her figure is A-plus. I have to keep up so we can still use her. Max is the same."

Cat took another large swig of her drink and surveyed Charlotte with an interest that was unnerving. "So spill, lady. We need something to take our minds off this shit. I've been looking and listening to you from afar and wondering what the hell you're doing here. You don't seem the type, if you don't mind me saying." She deposited the empty glass smartly on the table and clicked at a waiter to bring a refill.

"I've wondered that myself," admitted Charlotte. She held back a moment, but the alcohol was loosening her tongue. "The thing is, I suppose I'm at a bit of a cross-roads in my life. You know…" She grinned suddenly. "One of those eat, pray, love moments. Except that it isn't like that in real life, is it? Everything is a bit more messy, more grey, less technicolour."

Cat didn't say anything but continued to watch Charlotte intently. Charlotte struggled to express herself.

"It's all imploding, you know. My marriage, the job. So you see, it's not so much redemptive as reductive. A lot of the time I'm realising that I don't quite know what I've got into. More and more, actually. Then I find myself having one of those 'you've completely screwed everything up and it actually isn't going be the fairy-story you once thought it was' moments."

"I hear you." Cat fiddled with the ring she wore on her right hand. It looked as if it was made of gold, some kind of Celtic design. The band was plaited together and joined with the two tiny hands. "See this? This was my grandmother's, God bless her soul. She was a housemaid to a family in New York. Raised her kids in the Bronx. Brought me up while my mum was at night school training to be a social worker. I wear this to stay grounded, to remind me that this shit ain't real, and we are helping some people to escape from their fucking awful realities." She said the last with vehemence.

"You were lucky with your family," Charlotte said. "But it's difficult with people, isn't it? They don't fit neatly into categories, and you can feel you've known someone your whole life, and then discover another side to them, or feel that you maybe never really knew them at all. You know what I find difficult to understand. That we're all thinking… talking to ourselves in our heads. Beating ourselves up, wondering what the fuck to say, how to respond. We're all probably thinking the same things, but no one actually hears us apart from ourselves."

"Girl, that's deep. But true, it can feel awful lonely. Guess that's why I'm talking to you now. And what about Max, how does he fit into all this?"

Charlotte raised her eyebrows quizzically.

"I'll tell you straight, Charlotte, I know Nell, and word is, she's fucking fuming that you're on this gig." She leant back and had another large swig of her drink.

"Is she indeed?" Charlotte could feel her guard going up again. She had started to trust Cat, wanted to trust her even, but maybe that invisible antennae had let her down this time.

Cat continued to scrutinise her steadily. "Calm it, girl. I'm not prying. You get a lot of the same in this industry: plastic on the outside and not much within. You're like me; we've come from a difficult place. We're trying to fit into a round hole… I've been lucky to get this part. Miranda is a mensch – she really is. She works us hard, but she fucking cares, and Max is sound, but then you'd know that."

"He is." Charlotte looked back at Cat, hesitantly. And then, as the drink warmed her veins, she felt herself melting backwards into the softness of the upholstery and it all came spilling out… the babies, the marriage, measuring out her life in coffee spoons, her art, the confusion. Charlotte felt herself becoming unusually voluble. It seemed important that Cat liked her, that in that looseness that overtakes you when you are on the road to being pissed and you are hallucinating connections and coincidences all over the place, there was a mutual connection.

She was trying to explain to Cat the situation, the inexplicable. "You know when there is just someone who you can talk to, someone you click with. And they aren't judging you, or maybe they don't know the rubbish that has gone before, what you are capable of?"

"Kid, we're all on our own at two points in our life: the beginning and the end. In the middle we make connections where we can. It's who you pick up along the way. Some will be for a short time, some will keep going. That's what fuels us. Feeling that we're not alone."

"How can you be so sure about everything? So certain?"

"I'm not certain. Life's a journey – different stops, different routes. You can change direction when you like – hell, that's what I intend to do. I like to listen to those who have lived. And I'm interested in people, anyone... you!"

They got more drinks, a pitcher. One of the guards came and whispered something in Cat's ear.

"He's out of surgery and he's woken up!" They ordered more drinks to celebrate.

"I should go and see how Max is."

"Leave him," said Cat. "Send him a text or call him. Let him decide when to come down."

"Are you sure? He must be upset. He likes Ed a lot." She was quiet for a moment. Had she let him down by not going after him immediately?

"If it's meant to be, then it's meant to be. I don't believe in chasing people; they come to me. Max is a big boy, and he has choices to make. Don't do the chasing, girl. You respect yourself, hear me?"

So Charlotte texted a brief message explaining where she was, and letting Max know that Ed was out of danger. Part of her felt disloyal, dishonest, but she also was resisting that moment sure to come where she knew things would end in failure. She had heard what Cat had said, but she also knew that Cat had made assumptions about her, about the person she was able to be. She didn't have that hardness at her centre. She pressed send but found herself standing up.

"It's been good to talk; you've helped." She looked at Cat, who leant back, watching her closely underneath her eyelids. *She knows*, thought Charlotte, *she knows*.

"I've enjoyed talking to you, Charlotte Seldon. Make choices that are right for you."

There wasn't really anything to say to that. Charlotte flashed an awkward smile at the actress still looking after her with a thoughtful look on her face. She knew where she had to be, and she both longed to be there and dreaded what she might find.

***

A few minutes later and she was knocking at Max's door. No answer. She hammered again, more erratically, urgently. No answer. She fumbled for her phone and dialled his number. It rang and rang and… finally.

"Whaaa?"

"It's me. Answer your bloody door."

"Alrigh."

There was a shuffling sound, and the door was pulled ajar. He turned and Charlotte followed him into the main room. He resumed his slumped position on the sofa, and Charlotte silently took in the empty bottles in front of him – looked like the mini bar had been cleared of everything – and his bloodshot eyes. He didn't look like an actor with a contract worth a cool five million. He just looked deflated and defeated in front of her, more a truculent teenager than a thirty something.

"Max, it's okay. He's okay. Conscious, at least. Don't do this to yourself. You couldn't help it."

"I know," Max snapped. His voice was louder than he intended. "Can't stand it though. Poor bastard. Saw him swinging there." His head dropped into his hands. "Where were you? Why didn't you come?"

Charlotte felt terrible. Why hadn't she come? She couldn't explain. He had stormed off. It hadn't felt like he had wanted her. She wasn't Max's keeper. She didn't want to be forced into a role. *You haven't done anything wrong*, she told herself. *Grow a backbone, Charlotte.*

"You didn't seem to want me. You disappeared, Max. I was chatting to some of the cast. Cat, actually she was really nice. We had a bit of a session, you know, sharing life stories. I needed that, I guess. It was so stressful that it felt good to unwind and let off steam. I'm sorry I wasn't there for you, but you seemed to want to be on your own."

Max had listened, incredulous, and he raised his head now, the fog of inebriation momentarily clearing.

"Cat, you say? As in Cat, the actress who carries at least six mobile numbers of celebrity journalists and has a closed line to every media show on ABC?"

Charlotte was stunned. She hadn't been expecting this animosity.

"You told me that you wanted to escape from the media attention, Charlotte! How could you be so naïve?"

In that moment, he felt so angry that he would have said anything to hurt her. Nell would have looked after him, fussed over him. Didn't she care at all? That she sat there taking it, not responding, made him go further still. He couldn't control himself; words darted from his lips like barbed arrows and the stress seemed to ooze from him in bloody waves. His anger was igniting, and it felt powerful. He had been quiet for too long. He had had enough. Was it him? The factor that linked the damage that surrounded him.

"Why are you here? You said there was something more, but what do you actually want, Charlotte? Because I'm starting to feel that you're just tagging along for the ride! You're supposed to be here for me, as my PA! What am I actually paying you for again?"

Charlotte could hardly believe what he was saying. She felt light-headed and woozy – how could her actions be so misconstrued, so wrongly represented? She didn't know where to start.

"I don't understand. I was just chatting to her. How can you say that? She was cool. We clicked. I trust her. I haven't spoken about you, just about me. Do you think that I would talk about us to her? There is no us, Max! Why are you treating me like this?"

"Treating you like this? I just can't believe that someone I am employing could be so stupid as to speak to a stranger and relax with them, clearly getting pissed, whilst I am having to go through this trauma… again!" As he said it, his soul wavered, he could hear the words excoriating, yet he couldn't stop.

"You left me!" Charlotte could hardly believe what he was saying. "Are you serious?"

His face was distorted, and she could see the child in the man. He had been rejected, and he was trying to wound as he was wounded. He was like an injured animal lashing out in its dying throes. Charlotte realised with an almost clinical detachment that she couldn't stand to be with him like this;

too much damage had already been done. She had admired him, respected him, but now he was destroying these bonds, perhaps irreparably.

"Let me know what is decided over the filming, please." She fired the words back at him. "I can see you are angry, but one thing I am sure of is that the person you are furious with isn't really here to hear it. Why don't you admit it, Max? This has been a terrible shock, but it was no one's fault by the sound of it, just a tragic accident. And that's what Bella's death was, an accident. She may have chosen to end her life, but you need to see that she was ill, as ill as if she had had terminal cancer. You did all you could with what you knew at the time. Sometimes shit happens. Why can't you see that?" She could hear her own voice rising in volume. "When you can't control something, your immediate reaction is panic. It's no one else's fault, including yours, that she killed herself. You need to stop taking it out on everyone else. We've all got our demons."

The last was said over her shoulder and she tried to convey a clarity that she couldn't quite reach. "We should be treating each other better because of today, not worse. Maybe I should have followed you, but it was hard to know what you really wanted, what was right, and you were the one who walked away. I find it difficult to deal with even myself at the moment. I barely feel that I am coping with my own pain on some days. I know that that it is paltry compared with what your family has gone through, but perhaps you need to follow the advice you gave me.

"It feels that there's a ghost haunting you. You treat yourself like some kind of criminal, but all you did was to love someone maybe too much. She's dead, Max," this she said more gently, "but we're living; that's what really matters.

You're going to end up destroying your life too. We both need to sort ourselves out. Goodbye, Max."

Somehow she got to the door and eased herself through it, leaving a dazed Max head in hands on the sofa. Everything she had said was true, but he wasn't there yet. He felt full of an incandescent rage that seemed to burn within him, white-hot, dangerous. He hated everyone, other human beings, life itself.

Why was it so hard? How had he borne it? He missed her, he missed her so, so much still. Why? Why did she choose to leave him like that? He found the grief that lay balled up inside of him, felt it flow through his veins like he was giving in to some kind of drug fix and had shot up after months of abstinence. He let the feeling wash over him, the exquisite ache that clenched at his heart.

He lay there for what could have been minutes, hours even, remembering, just remembering. Not the horrors, but the bits before when Bella had been properly present, properly his sister. Charlotte was right. He had loved her so much, beyond words, even, forever on a pedestal. When he saw her in the morning, everything was okay; her smell was his comforter, her voice when she said his name was like an embrace. He pulled a towel to his face, prostrating himself on the bland hotel bed and throwing himself into the moment.

Then, when his grief had abated, he did the thing that he never thought he would do willingly again, he picked up the phone next to the bed and dialled his home phone number. Not the house he had shared with Nell and the kids, not the semi in London or the barn in Suffolk, that proper home number, the one he had trained himself to remember when he was eight. He clung on in a blind reverie to his conviction that now it was time, time to move on, time to rescue whatever remained of his self, the self that had been stopped short in its tracks those eighteen years before. He hadn't spoken properly of his sister to his parents since then, hadn't spoken of his grief, hadn't shared his conviction of his guilt.

The change in tone told him that it was ringing in that distant Surrey semi-detached villa that he and Bella had called home. He visualised the cool hall floor and the little seat next to the phone table, the banisters opposite through which he had stared as a child. There was a brief delay and then he heard that equally adored and berated tone that he still could hear in his dreams: "Margaret Hollinsworth speaking."

He recalled vividly an image of his mother sitting at the phone table in the hall, himself and Bella dancing round her, her shushing them with her hands, laughing as she mouthed at them to be quiet, turning away as she tried to concentrate and Bella miming her expression so accurately he almost wet himself. Yet he couldn't bring himself to speak yet.

Again, tentatively this time. "Hello, Margaret here."

Another pause and he desperately willed himself to reply. There was a rustle and then, with a slightly querulous manner, the voice spoke: "If this is a junk caller, then we're not interested here, please take us off your mailing list."

He had to go through with this, it was now or never.

"Ma," he rasped. "Ma." The word stuck in his throat. He willed her to respond, to acknowledge him, for Christ's sake.

The silence bore down on them both.

"Max? Max, what's wrong?"

TWENTY-SIX

Charlotte didn't really do procrastination. All her life, she had acted instinctively. She felt strongest when she was making those choices that involved moving on, starting anew. Giving up art and moving onto teaching. Getting married to Daniel. Turning her back on teaching. She could see the opposing point of view, that what she thought was a brave new world was simply someone escaping when things got difficult or when the situation called for a bit more of her than she could give, but it was always too late to reverse her decisions.

She had taken the first steps in a new direction and now there was no going back. Sideways, forwards, maybe, but that old life was not an option. Accepting Max's job offer, and now jumping into a taxi and going home, away from Max, away from a life she hadn't known existed and back to where she knew she would find comfort and solace. It felt heady, like she was ricocheting from one idea to the other. *Better than dangling*, she told herself, *waiting for the inevitable humiliation and defeat.*

She had lain awake all night, knowing what her course of action would be, yet hopelessly running through different scenarios, if she was another person and this was another life. She dare not linger on what she felt for Max: sexual attraction, a schoolgirl crush, a momentary infatuation? It was all the same: unrealistic, unsustainable, doomed to fail.

She dressed in automaton mode, trying desperately not to think, not to feel. She couldn't stomach any food but went through the motions of sitting at a table in the restaurant and sipping at a cup of hot black coffee before she went to the reception, key card in hand. As a last thought, she got the work phone she had been using out of her pocket.

"Please give this to Mr. Collins, Room 245," she asked the maître d'. "It's very important he gets it, please," she repeated. She handed some notes over with the phone, hoping that the woman understood the significance of the gesture.

She smiled and Charlotte took this for reassurance.

"Of course, madam. Have a safe flight home."

As Charlotte went through the drill of checking out of the hotel, travelling to the airport, boarding the plane, her actions resonated through her. She was heading back to reality, back to her real life. She could deal with the aftermath of Daniel, the aftermath of her marriage, her mistakes, but she was not ready to navigate anything else. She had passed Cat in the lobby on the way out of the hotel at 5.00a.m. Cat, clad in running gear: a baseball cap, sunglasses and jogging bottoms, stretching by a potted palm. Their eyes met and Cat nodded her head, without breaking pose. She gave Charlotte a mock salute and then beckoned her. Charlotte took a step forwards and Cat called quietly, "Running away?"

Charlotte immediately understood; she looked down at her hands, still with the wedding ring intact. "This isn't for me."

"Does it have to be?" Cat called almost jauntily over her shoulder as she walked in the direction of the reception desk with her security a few steps behind. She made the victory sign at Charlotte with a wink over the sunglasses. "Good luck, bitch."

***

The taxi back from the airport was just over a hundred pounds. Charlotte couldn't help the sharp intake of breath when the obligatory ten pounds that was added on at the end had somehow jumped to twenty.

"Price a' petrol." The driver noticed her raised eyebrows and didn't offer to help her with her luggage, instead heaving it unceremoniously outside the house.

England seemed fresh and bright in comparison to Morocco. It was the beginning of June, and Charlotte was pleased to see more colour in the garden, rose buds coming into flower and the most saturated cornflower blue of a sky promising warmth later. For now, however, she felt chilly and longed for a bath and her own bed. She struggled to the front door with her rucksack and suitcase straddled on various parts of her body and was greeted with the inside of her house post-Daniel.

She had forgotten that he had been scheduled to relieve the house of his stuff during her time away. As soon as she had left the hotel in Morocco, she had turned her mobile phone off, and off it had stayed since then, an empty weapon, essentially useless but smoking nonetheless. Mercifully, there were only a few really noticeable empty places on shelves, but she saw that he had taken the sound system that he had saved up to buy at university. The bedroom television was also missing, as were a couple of chairs and a some more modern pieces of furniture that he had been keener on than her. No photos, she noticed, and strangely this hit harder than anything else. It was obvious that he wanted to blot everything out – everything with her, that is. Like it had never existed. A whole existence together reduced to shapes in the dust.

She missed him and Max in equal measures. They were like itches that needed scratching. Her hand ached to turn her phone on and contact either, but she was determined to resist the comfort that might bring. She felt the cold presence of her wedding and engagement rings on her left hand. The engagement ring had been her grandmother's, a sapphire of darkest blue. She had always thought of it as some kind of talisman: she had been found; she was looked after. She transferred this to her right hand. The wedding ring was tight, and she struggled to get it off. After a minute of tugging in vain and the alarming sensation of her finger starting to swell, she went to the kitchen sink and used some soap to finally ease it off completely. It was gold to match the other ring, and a traditional curved hoop. Daniel had had one too in tempered steel, very fashionable at the time, and she wondered what had become of it. She put hers in a jug on a high shelf; she didn't feel ready to discard it altogether, not yet.

Charlotte breathed deeply and went out to the studio. She had taken a few snatched photos of the scenery in Morocco and wanted to have a go at recreating them in oil. There was a particular one of the sun coming up over the sea she had taken just before she left the hotel on that last morning. A fishing boat had been silhouetted by the sun casting a path over the water towards the beach. It reminded her slightly of William Blake's God casting the light from the clouds for some reason. She put on her smock, and adjusted the easel, feeling her cares ease in a small way as she prepared her palette and found the thinner. She decided to paint over an earlier piece that hadn't really worked out. Quickly, she became engrossed.

Much later, she came inside and decided to catch up with emails, also completely neglected in the last week. Several from her mother; that was unusual. Still, she had been very attentive since the break-up. Strangely, Charlotte felt that they had regained a sense of affinity between them that had not been present throughout the whole of her marriage or since leaving home. Now she had been broken entirely, she felt her mother had more empathy with her. Yet it didn't feel that she felt sorry for her; more that they had been linked together in a way that only they shared. Before, there had been no commonality between them and she had been angry, maybe because she perceived that Mum had forgotten Dad, had not respected his memory somehow by finding so many new partners in succession.

Noticing one email was from a gallery but assuming it was some kind of sales or auction guide, she idly clicked on it before reading the others. It was addressed to her by first name but, as she scanned to the end of the writing with growing interest, she didn't recognise the sender's name.

The gallery was vaguely known to her, one in Cambridge that she had looked round several times and always went out of her way to look in the window when she had an appointment or shopping to do. It specialised in large, traditional pieces, and had a good reputation, she thought, amongst those who knew. Phrases began randomly jumping out at her: *knew your father... your mother has been in contact... sent a picture... can't make promises but I'd like to take a look.* Charlotte couldn't believe what she was reading. All thoughts of dinner were forgotten, and she read it several times before reaching for a glass of wine and the seldom-used landline.

"Mum, what have you done?"

"Charlotte, nice to talk to you too!" Her mother's tone was at once amused and reprimanding. "How did you get on? The photos seem to have died down at any rate."

"Oh Mum, it was pretty shit actually. Oh, there were some good bits, but there was an accident on set. It was awful. Did you hear?"

Her mother's tone changed. "Charlotte, was that you? They didn't give the name of the series or the actor. I thought it was more of a holiday you were on. Why didn't you ring?"

Charlotte rolled her eyes. Some things didn't change; her mother would not have followed the story or noticed a news report. She was pretty oblivious in general to others' goings on, unless they were right under her nose.

"Yes, that was me, or not me, thank God. Sorry I didn't get in contact. There was so much going on with..." Her voice trailed away.

"Charlotte, are you okay?" Her mother's disembodied voice crackled across the line.

The unexpected kindness threatened to undo her. "I don't know. Am I? I feel so strange at the moment, and tired, exhausted with everything. I think I've cocked up really. I came home. It's not for me. It's not what I want to do with my life. I don't know what I want to do with my life, actually. All the time, I've tried to do what's expected of me, and look what's happened."

"You silly girl, haven't you read your emails?"

"Yes, I have actually, and that's what I'm ringing about. The gallery? Phillip Brown?"

"Well, yes, I thought you might recognise the name. Bristol Phil, Daddy's friend. Do you remember, Charlotte? You might have been too young. They were at the Slade together."

"Very vaguely. But why is he contacting me? I don't paint properly."

"Well, Charlotte, why indeed? Stop being so bloody self-deprecating." Her mother's voice scolded her but then took on a wheedling quality. "I may have emailed him a few photos of those paintings you made when I was staying a few weeks back. Someone's got to look out for you."

"Those ones? But they were just for fun. That's what I do, paint for fun." Charlotte's voice died away.

"Just take them in and let him have a look, Charlotte." Her mother's voice became serious, insistent even. "We both know that you are wasting a serious amount of talent, just because you have lost your way. I may be a shrivelled up seventy-year-old who's made some pretty lousy decisions with my own life, but I know that I don't want my daughter going the same way. If you don't go and visit Phil, then… then don't bother contacting me again." The phone clicked smartly, and Charlotte heard the dull drone of the dialling tone in her ear.

She sat there for a few minutes, not fully comprehending what her mother had done. She had been press-ganged into making a decision. What was she going to do?

TWENTY-SEVEN

Two days later and she was leaning some canvases against her knees as she was being jolted along on the park and ride into Cambridge. It was a pretty undignified way to travel, and Charlotte couldn't help but reflect on the difference between this week and last. The decline, from navigating five-star hotels and fraternising with film stars, to bumming it on a bus where the suspension seemed to have completely perished was quite literally a bumpy ride. She managed to smile to herself at least.

She had heard nothing from Max since their heated conversation in the aftermath of Ed's fall. She wasn't surprised. The papers had been full of the accident on set, and she was only marginally rattled to see the headlines littering the gossip sites and even a few of the heavier papers: *Actor's Double in Horror Fall, Mad Max Stunt Double in Terrifying Bungee Failure, Award-winning BAFTA Actor in Dramatic Set Disaster*. She had been relieved to read that, despite the sensationalist headlines, Ed was on the road to recovery. There was a past picture on one website of him with his girlfriend coming out of a bar with Max. She'd had to double-take; he had looked so similar to Max.

There were even a few lines illuding cryptically to their relationship. *Max Collins, 38, was seen leaving the set with his PA, Charlotte Seldon. The two have been snapped together on several occasions this year. Charlotte Seldon, also 38, wore her wedding ring displayed visibly on her left hand but rumours have abounded that the marriage is in disarray. It is not known whether or not the two are romantically involved but sources close to the actor say that they not been out of each other's sight.* At this, Charlotte couldn't help but snort. Then the wave of humour passed, and a bleakness descended. Had Cat spoken to the press? She guessed she never would know. That was what Max had insinuated, but she had felt a genuine kinship with Cat – for an hour or so, at least. She thought, despite the toughness, that she had been insightful and kind, more real than she had believed possible. She had liked her.

Distracted by her daydreams, she tried to focus on the here and now and the rhythmic jostling of the suspension-less top deck, which definitely wasn't helping her bladder. As they pulled into Drummer Street, she began to wish she'd splashed out on a taxi; a car was out of the question with the parking in Cambridge. Still, it was a weekday, so quieter than it could have been. She awkwardly manoeuvred the wrapped canvases down the spiral stairwell and stepped out into the open.

It was the beginning of the tourist season and huge swathes of Asian tourists were intermingled with the occasional commuter or gaggle of students staying on for the summer. There was a ten-minute walk in front of her, past the yellowed buildings of Emmanuel and Caius, and she felt a few drops of rain. She could have disembarked from the bus earlier, but the journey was strangely lulling, and she had felt lethargic and protected on the bus, deciding to wait until the bus station in Drummer Street. She hugged the precious paintings to her body like a young child. They were carefully packaged together in bits of corrugated card, bubble wrap and brown tape. She had brought three to attempt to represent the different themes of her art: a landscape; a tree study; and the self-portrait she had made when had left, a wildcard.

The gallery was on the corner of Regent Street, near the Catholic church, past an odd assortment of trendy takeaways, charity shops and the odd business, property or financial mostly. She paused just before sight of the entrance and tried to straighten her clothes. She had put on a suit this morning, a throwback from her deputy head days, a bit snug around the waist but decent enough with the jacket over the top. It was a pearly grey colour and she had lightened the mood with a camisole swirled with orange and navy. If they were going to turn her down completely, then she would need a shield and chain mail.

A mother with an expensive pushchair and a toddler attached with those rope things tried to get round her and was blocked by the pictures. Charlotte realised the problem and took a step inside a doorway as the woman muttered a flustered thanks and hurried past as best as she could, the toddler wholly unconcerned and continuing his meandering way. The child was chubby and adorable, and Charlotte saw a fleeting snatch of a scrunched-up newborn snuggled up in the whiteness of the pram interior. She congratulated herself on feeling unusually removed.

Swallowing, she pushed on the front door (P. Brown, Fine Art) and a bell tinkled in the distance. There was a large period desk set back in the room, and a few oil paintings on a teal-blue wall with spotlights trained at them. Beyond this entrance, she could see a more modern exhibiting space with stark pale walls and an eclectic range of canvases, ceramics and sculptures interspersed with sharp bursts of primary colours. She breathed in deeply the faint smell of polish and the undertones of thick oil paint, linseed oil and varnish, and felt more relaxed.

There were soft footsteps and a man emerged from a doorway. He was almost completely bald apart from some tufts of greyish hair growing over his ears, over which were fixed rounded tortoiseshell glasses. By far the most noticeable thing about his appearance, however, was his vivid plum shirt which drew comparison with the inside of a fig. His skin was rather florid, and he appeared distracted. Charlotte noticed a pencil behind one ear and a sheaf of leaflets spilling out of a back pocket. As he grew near her, his pace slowed, and his mouth opened without words.

Charlotte looked back at him, aghast. What should she do? Was this Phillip? She had no idea what he looked like after all these years. He and Dad had long hair in the photos. Maybe there was a slight resemblance? She burst into introduction.

"Hello, er... I'm Charlotte Seldon. Er... I have an appointment to show some artwork. I think I'm expected?"

The man still said nothing, and slowly took the pencil down from his ear.

"Is Phillip here?" she ventured again.

The man blinked rapidly and then the floodgates seemed to open in a rush.

"Charlotte, my goodness, it's amazing! You could have been twins. It's uncanny. I feel like I've gone back in time."

He took a step closer to Charlotte and firmly took hold of the arm that wasn't steadying her package, shaking her hand vigorously. And now you're here with your own work… like a lamb returning to the fold! *Incroyable!*"

Charlotte was to learn that this was typical hyperbolic Phil! For now, she was silenced. She thought he looked like a benevolent, slightly unhinged gnome.

"Right, let's look at the little beauties then; I can't wait! I can't promise anything, mind. If I think they're good for nothing but greeting cards, then I will let you know! Charlie always said that I couldn't lie for toffee. If you're crap, my dear, then I shall send you off with the price of your bus fare." He chuckled to himself while relieving Charlotte of the paintings, hoisting them up onto the desk and slitting the tape definitively with a craft knife that appeared out of one of his copious pockets. The layers of wrapping sprang back, and Charlotte blanched as the spotlights overhead bounced off the ripples and crevices of paint.

"Hmmm, let's put you up, so I can see you better." Phil rummaged underneath the counter to pull out some portable desktop easels. Whistling quietly under his breath, he deftly upended the canvases and arranged them delicately, tilting the easels this way and that to get an angle that satisfied him. Then he went to stand a distance away, revisiting each picture several times, turning them this way and that to catch the different lights.

Charlotte watched him with bated breath. What did he think? Did he hate them? Maybe not; surely he wouldn't be going to this much trouble if this was the case. She had cast a hasty glance at the paintings displayed in this room, but they were eighteenth-century Scottish mountainscapes for the main, fashionable at the moment in boutique hotels and upmarket country renovations. There were posters advertising local showings of Claire Jackson and Simon Jones; the latter, funnily enough, was a contemporary of hers at art school and now a prominent landscape artist. She could hear Phil was murmuring now as he scrutinised the paintings.

"Hmmmm. Touch of the gothic… but I can tell you live in Suffolk. Got any more to show me?"

"Um… photos?" Charlotte thought quickly and fumbled for her phone in her bag.

She found a folder where she had photographed some of her more recent works from different points. They included an ancient mural inside the shack and a fresco she had made on the ceiling of her bedroom. Phil scrolled through them intently, occasionally sighing or *hmming* and then pausing at the various angles and close-ups of the fresco.

"Now this," he remarked, "is something. I have a few more… unusual clients, shall we say. I'm sure it won't surprise you to know that some of them *play in a band!*" This last was said in an exaggerated stage whisper. "They are going to love these little neo-classical beauties!"

Eventually, he cleared his throat and handed her back her phone. He started to rewrap the paintings in an absent-minded manner and Charlotte began to doubt herself. He had seemed so interested a few minutes before.

"So, my dear. Let's talk business. As it happens, I do have some gallery space at the moment. I can take you through and show you. Happened to shift a job lot of one artist last week and, to be honest, I was thrilled. He was a turd, Charlotte, thought I was never going to be rid. One I won't be dealing with again."

Charlotte must have looked a little apprehensive for he patted her arm reassuringly.

"Now, don't you mind me. I have a very good feeling about you. You have your father's way with colour, that single-mindedness. I'm thinking between £1500 and £2800 apiece. Ten works to begin with. I take forty per cent. Yes, I know that's high, but this is Cambridge, I have my overheads and you'll have to take my word for it that I have some very useful contacts. I'm actually going to have a word with Amanda Heaton about your work, Charlotte. Have you heard of her?"

"Yes." Charlotte could hardly speak. "Yes, she runs an interior design company, doesn't she?"

"Certainly does, and she's in high demand at the moment, too. I can see your palate fitting in with her style very nicely. She does maximalist, obviously, but I can see your skies in both minimalist and maximalist settings."

"I don't know what to say," said Charlotte honestly. "I wasn't expecting this. Are… are you sure?" She felt a little faint. It didn't seem possible that things were going so well. Was she here or was she dreaming?

Phil threw back his head and let out a bellow of laughter. "You really are just like your dad. God, I miss him. I can see some raw talent here, Charlotte. Where have you been hiding all these years? Get them packaged and sent to me. Here, this is a card for the delivery company I use. They'll collect from your house and deliver directly to me; I'll take it out of your first sale. Been using them for years. I'm going to give Amanda a ring myself."

TWENTY-EIGHT

She was going to have to turn her phone on. There was no help for it. It was the number she had given to Phil, so she had no choice. Parcelling up the canvases gave her time to think. She missed him, she knew that. She felt like she had been living his story for the last six months, and he, hers. Without fully understanding how, her focus had changed from an insularity, a feeling that she was looking backwards, to the consideration of larger horizons and the knowledge that she was more capable than she had believed.

She charged up the phone while faffing about with the packaging and, as soon as she was able, pressed hard on the on button, a dry feeling of anticipation clagging her mouth and dragging on her gut. The phone's display came to life, and she saw the familiar photo become distinct: a tiny figure (her) under the tree in the garden, timeless and remote in the tiny frame.

She had changed the homepage just before she had gone away from a photo taken by a stranger when they were in Barcelona for her birthday last year. A taut shot, both of them sitting in front of a café, glasses in hands. Charlotte was wearing sunglasses to hide the recalcitrant expression on her face. Daniel was reaching slightly towards the camera, his outline blurred and fractionally distorted, which had the effect of making him look as if he was superimposed onto the scene.

It hadn't been a great holiday, Charlotte reflected, but it was the last time that they had gone away together. Had they enjoyed it at all? It had been uneasy, she remembered. They had 'escaped' because she had given up teaching and was able to get away in the term for the first time. Charlotte thought she could relax without the hordes of children, but the city had seemed tired, exhausted, and Daniel was preoccupied. His silence over her decision said more than words ever could and they danced around one another with wary politeness.

The phone crackled into life and she could see the queue of WhatsApp messages; it seemed like hundreds, most of which were from Max. 'Sorry' seemed to feature predominantly. The round 'O' jumped from the screen like a gaping mouth. Charlotte suddenly felt the weight of responsibility. What if he was to do something silly? She hadn't really considered his mental stability before but, after everything he had been through, maybe she should. She remembered what he had said about the swiftness and the escalation. For a second, she thought she understood what it really had been like – the shock of realisation, the fear that the beloved person wasn't going to resurface, may even drag you in with them…

And the biggest question of all: if she wasn't truly interested in a relationship with him, why was their interaction preoccupying so much of her thoughts? She felt mildly obsessive. She hadn't contacted friends, wasn't really thinking about the fallout from her marriage enough. She groaned. She was in too deep.

Charlotte sank to her heels, wishing that the dog was here to give comfort. She had to think logically. Daniel! Why hadn't she heard from him? When was he bringing Jake back? She scrolled through the missed calls on her phone. There were several, although none from Max, surprisingly. Sure enough, Daniel had phoned like clockwork at 7.00p.m. for the last three nights. Their usual time. Interesting, considering that he was now apparently with the new woman. She finished preparing the paintings and texted Phil that she was ready for them to be picked up.

The message came back instantly: *Smashing my dear. Look fwd to receiving.*

Charlotte's finger hovered over Max's messages again. She was so weak. The feed was long and repetitive. He was sorry, he was very sorry, he was so very sorry. Charlotte clenched her hands tightly. Words. Words were so easy to say. She thought she had probably said too many, thought too many. Sometimes she wished she didn't think; it made things so much more perverse.

She padded out towards the kitchen and grabbed a bottle of wine from the fridge. Drinking alone. She must stop doing it. The screw top undid too easily and the wet, ice-cold slick of the bottle's sides made her mouth water. She glugged a couple of inches into a glass and gulped it down thirstily, vaguely wondering at what point you were regarded as an alcoholic. She curled up on the sofa and looked out towards the garden, towards her tree, still there, unbending and constant. Although it looked still, there was a slight tremor of the highest branches and the leaves if you looked closely. It set the greens rippling as every leaf moved independently with a mind of its own. It reminded her of children in assembly when the teachers took their eyes off them. Beyond, the horizon was lit by a beautiful pale peach glow which tinged the watery iridescence. She must have nodded off for she suddenly woke with a start.

There was a loud, insistent banging at the front door. The vibrations seemed to pluck chords inside her head as she opened her eyes groggily. The delivery company already? But it was past 9.00p.m. Charlotte felt half-dazed. Who could it be? Some kind of emergency? Daniel? Jake? She pulled herself to her feet and ran to answer the door. Before his shape had even arranged itself in front of her, Max was through it, encircling his arms round her waist with a grip that threatened to squeeze the breath from her. Her eyes accustomed themselves to the dusky light and she gasped as his hands urgently found her face and he held her still for a second, kicking the door shut behind him.

"You read the texts? I'm sorry, I'm so sorry." His voice was hoarse.

The precariousness of the situation jangled Charlotte's senses. She felt disorientated, breaking away from Max's hold even though every fibre in her body was railing against her and she could feel his fingers branded on her cheeks.

"Charlotte." His voice resonated through her. She could feel the strength of his sincerity, the unspoken plea.

"Don't say it again." She scrutinised him steadily, and he knew then that he must be forgiven, or accepted, whatever the difference was. Charlotte looked at him fully, the dishevelled hair, pleading expression and crumpled clothes. There was nothing hidden about Max at that moment, no artifice, no bravado. Across his face Charlotte could see his journey from adolescence to maturity, and even the old age yet to be. She suddenly knew what she must do. Carpe Diem. One life. One chance. She took Max by the hand; his cool, hard palm with a row of callouses on its edge. Her own hand felt weak and clammy. She gripped harder and led him towards the staircase.

Max found himself releasing his breath as slowly as he could. Charlotte seemed at once the same and different, as if she was flitting between two different selves, two points of view. The shock on her face drew some distant memory of Bella, but that darted away, pushed aside by more urgent thoughts. He had missed her so, so much. When you become used to something, it becomes a habit or a tic, a repeated behaviour; you can't even recognise it until you're faced with its absence.

He measured the steps in his pounding heartbeats. There were pictures everywhere, lining the staircase, covering the walls; he had not realised the ferocity of her obsession. Skies – beautiful, mutable, fluctuating skies of every colour, every depth and volume... and then the trees, greens, browns, blues, purples mingling with the light behind, through and beyond. His head turned as he walked, and he felt his mouth gape.

Charlotte opened the door at the end of the landing and led him through into the bedroom. He gasped. Lit by the last vestiges of a failing sun, the ceiling had been transformed into a sky whipped by wind, at the end of the day rather than the beginning. Eking out from behind a tumult of clouds, delicate rays of light touched the underside of more yellow, pink, orange-bellied cumulus, billowing with the wind, breaking through the drabs of grey. They were undulating, captured in movement, rippling through the meridian like a rent in time itself. A tempestuous, mercurial zephyr that seemed to launch the bed like a ship in an unsettled sea.

"Charlotte, I don't know what to say. Did you paint this yourself? This is spectacular. I've never seen anything like it before!" He found himself speaking in hushed tones, with a reverence for the beauty she had created.

Charlotte didn't speak. She was at a great height, looking down. To give herself voice would be to break her resolve. He could feel her tension, although she didn't turn around. Only a few centimetres separated them, yet he could almost see the emotion bouncing off her body. There was a great pent-up energy coming from her, and he reached forward with his fingers, making contact with her back. She turned slowly round towards him, her eyes blacker than ever in her paleness, inviting him to throw himself into their depths.

He put his arms around her again, drawing her to him, half-expecting resistance. Charlotte was torn between her craving and sense of the absurdity of the occasion, deeply conscious of her threadbare tracksuit bottoms, her misshapen sweatshirt, her greying underwear. She still felt unsure, hardly knew how to speak for fear of losing her nerve. Love-making with Daniel had been predictable, safe, silent. She missed it in the same way that she missed the daily routine of life before these changes, going through the motions without having to think. But she knew that that life was gone, and she had to move on or lose herself.

She found words for the first time, speaking softly but with vehemence.

"Do you really want *me*, Max? Are you sure?" The spectre of Nell danced in front of her eyes, long limbed and lovely, so perfect a shell.

"Yes." Max almost laughed, relieved by the easiness of the question. He ran his hand greedily over her hair, feeling the thick silky waves trickle through his grip like water. He hadn't realised how much he had wanted to touch her, to prove her tangibility. She felt slippery, like she would fall from his grasp; he wanted to clutch her as hard as he could, to hold on to her and not let go. "Oh yes." Then, as if he was reading her mind: "Nell and I, it really is over. I haven't seen her in weeks."

Charlotte coloured. He was being honest with her. She had to respond. "I had no business to judge you, Max, and I haven't. I know how complicated it can be. I'm not innocent in that regard either."

He didn't push it. What did it matter to him? She had slept with Daniel again? All he could think about was the here and now. He was burning up. He wanted all of her. He tried to kiss her, but she pulled away stubbornly.

"But why me? You could have anyone, anyone! I'm not in your league; I don't stand out. You would never have even picked me out of a crowd if our paths hadn't crossed." It had to be said; she had to know that this was real, however fleeting.

He looked incredulous for a second, his skin flushed with expectancy and his heart thumping in his chest like a piston.

"But that's what life is about, Charlotte, isn't it? Chances, opportunities. We were lucky. We did run into one another. Our paths did cross – literally! Why would we ignore that? Why would we fight against what seems like fate? And you do stand out to me, Charlotte."

He warmed to his theme, running his hands through his own hair as he tried to put his impulses into some kind of logic.

"You are special. Christ, that's an understatement. You are so talented, Charlotte, and I like you because you are just what you are, before I even knew about that – the art, I mean. It feels like I have always known you as well as I possibly can. It's hard to explain, but I felt you were familiar even when we had hardly spoken."

He matched her look with an intensity that seemed to bore through her, and she longed to believe him. He tried again, struggling for coherence.

"There's something between us which is important, Charlotte. You make me happy, give it all purpose, meaning. I- I can't stop thinking about you, all of you. I want to be with you all the time."

He traced his hand down her back and said more passionately, fiercely, "I need you." His hands moved further down to her hips, and she suddenly felt her inhibitions disperse like a great weight had been lifted off her. She was feather-like, ready to float away. *Everything you imagine is real. Picasso was right.* A flickering image of Daniel crossed her mind, and her conscience let out a faint cry. Max sensed the briefest of hesitation and acted. He lifted her shirt and put the tips of his fingers on her bare skin. She shivered involuntarily and turned her head towards his, eyes half-shut. Their lips clashed.

They pushed, half-pulled each other to the bed, the initial touch fuelling their impulses, the first drag of contact filling their senses. Charlotte drank in the easy perfection of his body; he was indifferent to his charms and his carelessness made him all the more attractive. Their moves were unchoreographed by habit and Max, unaccustomed to waiting for so long, was taken back to adolescence as he marvelled at her blue-white skin. His will overtook the way, so that their movements felt transient and rushed. There was an urgency, a feeling of time running out, of despair that they could not know each other wholly. Charlotte, who always struggled to lose control, did at last succumb to the intensity of the moment, a great choke rupturing her chest as she closed her eyes. Max came desperately, a poignancy oppressing him still, and he imagined the weight of his past drift upwards, heavenwards.

Afterwards, when they were lying awkwardly side by side, both too conscious of their own physicality, Max looked up at the ceiling and said, "Why didn't you tell me when we first met that you were an artist, Charlotte?"

"I suppose I didn't really think of myself as one. Not until recently. It sounds so definite, so established, and I was just doing it to escape everything else really. I wasn't trying to be good, to do it for any kind of audience. It just helped me to forget myself."

Charlotte shut her eyes and felt once more the deep misery from that sad time, when she had felt that her body had betrayed her, and she hadn't earnt the right to be thought of as fully female. She searched around for something positive, less self-indulgent.

"I'm exhibiting in a gallery. I found out today. The owner knew my dad. He was an artist too. He painted ceramics."

"That's amazing." Max kissed the top of her head, still feeling a sense of unreality. Was he really here? Had this actually happened? He let his fingers idly stroke her shoulders. "So I guess you won't be working for me anymore then?"

"I suppose not. I mean, I don't know whether or not I'll sell any, so I'm not really sure if this is the right step for me."

"Oh, bollocks. Of course it is. Tell you what, keep the money from the next few months, and how about I commission you to paint one of those in the barn?" Maybe this was real, a wave of euphoria suddenly swept through him, if he could root her to him in some way.

"Don't be silly, Max."

"No, I mean it; it's so cool, Charlotte. You know, bringing the outside in."

Charlotte laughed and it was a lovely sound. Max rolled over to face her and smiled to see her looking so carefree.

"I'm not joking. I want a piece of it, of you." He daringly ran his hand along her skin again. She laughed again and then shivered with pleasure, twitching her body from him helplessly.

"You haven't seen me in daylight, Max. I'm horrific. Varicose veins and cellulite." She was joking but not joking. Why did she still feel that she had to present the reasons why this shouldn't be happening? She tried to change the subject. "What about you? Filming, et cetera? Are you continuing in Morocco?"

"Oh, that." Max was dismissive. "The next tranche is in LA. I'm flying out next week for a month. Then a break. But I am feeling better, thanks to you." He propped himself up with his arm. "I've realised what I have been doing wrong, Charlotte. I've been so busy beating myself up about Bella, that I haven't mourned her properly. She shouldn't be a dirty little secret. I'm proud of her; I want our love to have meant something. It shouldn't have been in vain – her life, I mean." He warmed to his subject, and Charlotte could almost touch the emotion in his voice.

"Maybe I can help. All this filthy lucre, most of it just sits in bank accounts or is invested in property – I haven't cared. But now... I wonder whether I can improve facilities or support in some way. They couldn't have been much worse for Bel and, judging from the news, they've hardly improved in sixteen years. I've been coming at this from the wrong angle. It's not about me, about the effect on my life. I've been ashamed to speak out, but you've made me see it differently. I've spoken to my parents and Kirsten, and they approve. They're excited, in fact. Mum cried; we all did. Kirsten is an accountant, and she's already looking into setting up some kind of charity."

Charlotte could sense him looking at her expectantly. She sat up, clutching the slippery covers to her, and gave him a one-armed hug.

"You don't need my approval. I think that's incredible – it would be fitting to celebrate Bella and make it all mean something, have a point. Of anyone, I know you can change things. I'm so glad you're happier."

"I feel lighter," Max said, "talking with Mum and Dad. We had never properly done it – talk, I mean. They felt the same as me – we were all too busy blaming ourselves, filled with guilt. It was gruelling in some ways but at the end, I felt closer to them than I've ever felt." His voice broke, and Charlotte hugged him again.

They both collapsed back on the bed, and Max reached for her, properly this time. He leant in and stopped her protests with a lingering kiss. He ran his hands over her more urgently and she felt herself overtaken by a warmth that spread from her core as she responded and lost the power to communicate lucidly altogether.

TWENTY-NINE

They both awoke in the dawn, unbeknownst to one another. Max was first, confused by that slight paranoia of displacement. He heard the cock crowing and was taken back to his childhood, where there had been a smallholding a few doors away. His dreams had been vivid; he had dreamt of Bella and of that last sixth form holiday before they both went to university and the troubles had come. Bella had been filled with an energy that had seemed enough for both of them, and she had continually suggested outings, desperate to experience everything she could of a different country, Greece in this case. His dream had been odd, for it hadn't been like that at all in reality. He had been lying on a sun lounger, looking out to the water with a hat over his face, listening to Bella frolic with friends in the pool, when he suddenly realised that Bella was leaning over him, whispering in his ear, her long hair tickling his face.

"Max, Max, wake up, Max."

He could feel her hand on his shoulder, and he felt a deep love and peace swell up inside him and the urge to reach his arms up and pull her down in an embrace. Then suddenly the chair bed tilted, and he felt that awful bump of falling, falling, falling. He woke up with a start.

Charlotte opened her eyes slowly and sensed the tangle of longer human limbs next to her. For a moment, she was taken back to Daniel being by her side, but the breathing was different and there was a faint masculine smell which she now identified solely with Max. She lay there poised, events of the previous night flashing through her mind like a silent film. She could feel her heart beating faster as she processed what had happened between them. It was not in her character to behave in this way; she had never had a one-night stand, had only ever slept with one other man before Daniel, and that had been a shambolic freshers' week debacle.

She slipped out of bed quietly and pulled on some slightly more presentable clothes. Dare she put on some make-up? She felt bloated and unattractive. What was the point? Max could regret what he had done from the word go. There were no ties to her and nor would she present any. She made her way to the bathroom and splashed water over her face, applying her normal eye cream, serum and moisturiser and trying not to see her face.

Downstairs, the house smelt stale and unaired. It was going to be a beautiful day and Charlotte flung open the backdoor in unexpected elation at the perfection of the blue sky before her. It never failed to lift her mood. She supposed she should just appreciate the moment. She loved Max; why not name that painful, pernicious emotion for what it was? She could love him as a friend if she had to. She would make it easy for him, whatever he decided. There was a movement behind her, and she realised that the object of her speculation had also surfaced. Max yawned and stretched in front of her, like a big cat waking from its sleep. His t-shirt rose to show a slither of brown skin and she felt that pulling again from deep in her core.

Max watched her with some trepidation and willed her to act first. He needed a sign, to know that it was mutual, this jumble of confusion. As if in a trance, Charlotte stepped towards him and touched delicately the exposed skin.

"Let's go back to bed," she said. They moved through the kitchen like somnambulists with Charlotte leading him by the hand.

"We need to stop meeting like this," he couldn't resist commenting playfully. Though ravenous, he was beginning to feel undeniably aroused but, as they approached the stairway, there was a knocking sound at the door. Charlotte flinched and clutched herself; he watched her reaction and felt the house of cards come tumbling down.

"Who's that? Oh, it might be the company picking up the paintings. You had better go and wait in the lounge, Max."

"You want me out of sight, do you?" Max started to tease but he conceded the fragility of their situation nonetheless. He had no choice but to do as he was told, collapsing on a sofa and surveying the mass of packaging and packages leaning precariously against every available piece of furniture. He could hear voices, and he leant back and closed his eyes. Then something made him sit up abruptly.

"Please, Charlotte. Just listen to me."

"Get your foot out of the door. You don't live here anymore."

"Just listen. I know I've made a mistake. I want to say I'm sorry. She's tricked me. I know that now."

"What do you mean she's tricked you?"

"Please. Let me in. We can't talk here. I need to tell you something."

Max froze. Should he show himself, risk Charlotte's embarrassment but offer some protection from this evidently unwelcome visitor who he was almost completely sure was the ex-husband? Or should he give into the temptation of continuing to keep very still and hoping that the obstacle would be removed for him?

"You can stand in the hall, but that's it. Now tell me."

There was the sound of the front door being closed, and a pause as Max imagined that the two were squaring up to each other, wondering how to say whatever needed to be said. He admired Charlotte deeply in these moments; she had remained calm and ostensibly in control. But what did Daniel have to say that was so important? The next words were so quiet that he couldn't hear them, but he could definitely hear Charlotte's response, a great gasp that was caught between a guttural cry and the shock of a physical wound.

"Just go, go, *go!*"

At this, he couldn't stop himself. He levered himself up and into the hall. Both were white-faced and adversarial.

"What?" Daniel took one look at him and blanched. "Didn't take you much time, did it?" he spat at Charlotte.

"Look, mate, you need to leave. Talk when you're calmer." Max blocked Charlotte from Daniel and gestured towards the door. Daniel stared past Max a moment and Charlotte looked back at him fixedly, her eyes black holes in her face, stuck in an expression of horror and disgust.

"Please, Charlotte." His tone changed, and he pleaded. "The dog's in the car."

Charlotte felt her very soul detach and drift upwards

towards the ceiling. In that moment, she hated him entirely. That woman, she couldn't bring herself to name her, was pregnant. With his child. And he had told her that he regretted it, regretted leaving her; he wanted to come home. She felt the weight of the tears that were threatening to spill. She wanted to scream and scream until something gave inside her.

Shaking his head, Daniel walked towards the door. "I'll phone you, Charlotte. You can't ignore me. Eighteen years we've been together. Eighteen years, Charlotte. Eighte—"

"Keep the sodding dog for the moment, mate. You've given her a shock!" *You selfish bastard*, Max thought. He watched Daniel walk round to the car and saw the silhouette of Jake in the back. *Poor fucking dog.* He found himself thinking, *at least they didn't have children*, but then recoiled from his disloyalty. What a mess. He shut the door with a deliberate bang and heard the engine starting up. Took him long enough to take a hint.

He turned to see that Charlotte was still standing there. She looked like death.

"Come on, you."

He guided her to the kitchen where she sank zombie-like into a chair. He went through the motions of making a cup of tea and carried it to her, clumsily slopping it onto the floor.

She took it but put it down without drinking. He tried to put his arms around her, but she batted him away.

"You need to go."

"What?" Max wanted to be there; he needed to know what was happening, that she was okay.

"You need to go." She sat still without looking at him, and he realised that she was deadly serious.

"Okay, I will."

He grabbed his phone from the counter and pulled on the boots he had perched by the sofa. "Call your mum, Charlotte, call somebody, if you don't want to talk to me."

She couldn't bring herself to answer. It felt like she was trapped in a novel, a tragedy where all roads led to the same ending. She was doomed, nothing would go well for her ever. She didn't want him to leave, but what was the point in him staying, being part of this grief? She didn't want him to see her like this, to realise how damaged she was, how damaged she could still be.

She heard the door clang in the distance and realised that he had left the house.

***

The next few hours passed in a blur. The firm that Phil had recommended picked up the pictures and she numbly passed them to the men to pack.

"Are you alright, love?" A rotund, grey-haired man in his late fifties was driving and he had a sixth sense that all was not well. He and his mate had mouthed some expressions awkwardly at each other to the effect of 'let's do this as quickly as we can'. The air in the house felt thick with tension and the woman had clearly been crying.

"I'm fine, thanks." Charlotte just wanted them gone. The paintings too. She felt hollow. Daniel's words had scraped out her insides and the injustice was now grating against bone. After all the heartache, the longing, and to be told that he couldn't care less. That he had casually impregnated a virtual stranger. Then that he wanted her after all, their life together, ironically, without the thing that she had wanted most. But it was too late. It was all too late.

When the delivery company had gone, she determined to go on a walk, to get away from it all. She had to get out of the house, somewhere quiet, just to be. Without their history bearing down on her from every corner of the house: every book, every photo, every utensil, every choice she had ever made. She knew where she was heading. An old quarry that lay hidden along a footpath that she seldom used because it was one where Jake would run off and disappear, sometimes for hours. But now she was drawn there. She wanted to be completely alone, hidden, where she could think and escape from humanity altogether.

It was lunchtime but she couldn't eat. Her throat felt dry and sandy, and her appetite had all but disappeared. She gulped down some water and a few bites of a banana. Then she stepped out of the front door into the sun. It bore down on her relentlessly, the brightness of the noon sun hitting the back of her eyes like a fluorescent bulb. She got into the car on autopilot and started the engine.

***

Max strode up the hill towards the barn and fiddled with the keys. He let himself in and entered the alarm code, still distracted, still with that desperate sense of unfinished business. Something was bothering him. He had a niggling feeling that he shouldn't have left her. He appreciated that she wanted to be left alone but she had looked vacant and in shock. He cursed the newness of the situation, the lack of easy intimacy that meant that he was so fucking worried about respecting her wishes that he had missed the warning signs. *Shit!* He couldn't afford to chance it again.

He paced to and fro, trying to make a decision. He didn't want her to think he was losing his mind too, but there was that itching sensation that something was amiss. There was nothing to lose but his pride. He'd go back after lunch; she would have had time to calm down, and he could offer to take her to get some shopping or something.

Decision made, he felt calmer. He grabbed some bread out of the bread bin, which was pretty stale, and wolfed it down with some hunks of hard cheddar and water from the tap. Grabbing his keys, he locked up again, not bothering to set the alarm. *I'll take the Range Rover*, he thought, and sped off down the hill.

A few minutes later, the car pulled quickly into the drive of the house, gravel flicking up and wheels spinning. He registered a surreptitious swish of the curtains opposite and was tempted to flick them the V sign. He saw straight away that the battered old Volvo was not in its usual place outside. Quickly out of the driver's seat, he put a hand on the front door and realised that it hadn't been locked. He felt slightly sick. In the house, it was just as he had left it. The backdoor was wide open, and he felt a sudden blast of chill. Charlotte's phone was on the side by her charger and her bag and jacket lay discarded on the chair. *Shit*, he thought to himself, *where is she?*

He grabbed her phone and fiddled with the security screen. He could see that there were lots of missed calls, some of them his. What would she have used for a password? He idly typed in 'Jake' and gave a sharp sigh of relief as the screen sprang into life. There had been fifteen calls that morning, twelve of them from Daniel and three from an unknown number with a Cambridgeshire dialling code. He took a deep breath and pressed return call. The dialling tone went off and he sat there waiting for the sound of Daniel's voice.

"Hello? Angela speaking, Daniel's phone." The voice sounded more than a little pissed off. Max was momentarily disconcerted.

"Hey, er… can I speak to Daniel, please?"

"Actually, he's not available now, can I take a message?"

"What?" Max's assurance slipped palpably. "He needs to be available; I've got a bit of an emergency here. Can he phone me back?"

"Is tomorrow okay?" The woman sounded bored and irritated; he could have sworn he heard the sound of a television in the background.

"No, are you listening? This is an emergency. I've got a fucking emergency. Please tell him to phone now, or it'll be on his head!" Max summoned all the gravitas he could on just the right side of aggression.

"Look, I'm not his bloody secretary. He's not even home yet!" There were voices in the background, and Max strained to hear what was going on. Then he realised that the phone had been put down.

"Oh fuck," he said aloud. He pressed redial. The phone rang and rang.

He sank heavily into a chair. Should he contact the police? Her mum, maybe?

Then the phone exploded into life. He grabbed it, almost dropping it in his haste. "Yes, Daniel?"

"What? What's wrong? Is she okay?"

"No, she's gone. The door was unlocked and the backdoor

was open. Where the hell is she? I'm worried. Something's not right."

There was a wisp of sound that could have been a sigh and then Daniel's voice again, slow and with a prescient weariness.

"I'm coming over. I know where she is. I'll be about forty-five minutes."

THIRTY

Charlotte trampled through the undergrowth with a drive that was decreasing as she advanced. The path was more overgrown than she had remembered it. The air felt muggy; she could sense the heat rising from the nettles, from the earth beneath. The smell of rotting vegetation assailed her nostrils and she felt slightly claustrophobic. A prickle caught her top and she pulled away too fast, scratching her arm. She barely felt the pain.

There was light ahead, and she went faster, looking forward to seeing the expanse of space, the drop below. She started jogging, almost stumbling in her haste. Her hair fell across her eyes, and she squinted up at the sun, a black dot in the sky's membrane. Beads of sweat gathered on her neck, under her arms. She was far from the road here, far from houses and cars. There was a faint sound of crickets and the rustling of insects, grasses and moisture evaporating. One more step and she had reached the path that ran round the side of the quarry.

She surfaced from the footpath and climbed over the rickety stile, resting her weight for a minute on the wooden fence and then heaving herself over to the other side. She felt a pressing need to empty her bladder and she squatted brazenly in the open; there was no one here apart from rabbits and deer. The wire fence had been trodden down by kids or a disgruntled rambler a long time ago and she stepped over it and trod carefully along the edge of the quarry face, scuffing the dusty soil so that it rose in clouds in front of her, avoiding where the edge looked as if it was disintegrating.

A kind of path meandered round the outskirts, lined by brambles and cow parsley. She carefully followed it to the far-side, so that she was looking towards the copse opposite, and sat carefully on the jutting edge of the cliff, legs dangling below. Tufts of grass and gorse-like weeds poked through the crumbling sides, anchoring the sediment to the hill. It was safe enough, if you were careful.

Absently, her fingers found a stone and let it drop down the sides, bouncing with increasing velocity until she heard the crack as it hit the remains of the groundworks. Sometimes there was water right at the bottom; it never got very high, too dry around here. She sent another one over and it ricocheted away from the side. She suddenly felt nauseous as she remembered Morocco and Ed's broken body being lifted over the edge on the stretcher. She wondered what the bungee line had looked like as it lost control and he knocked into the sides like a pendulum.

She wondered what would happen if she slipped and fell now. All that kept her from plunging from the bank was that perfect equilibrium of opposing forces but one push, one leap and she was gone, as easy as that, like their marriage. It had stayed balanced to begin with, but the different forces had changed, pulled in different directions. She looked down and fancied herself lying there, red against the chalk. A shiver ran over her, and she took a deep breath and leant backwards so that she was looking up at the beautiful blank canvas of the sky, clearing her mind, banishing all thought. She closed her eyes, bone-tired, and sought peace.

***

"Get in, I'll drive." Max was a bundle of nerves. He had chewed a nail ragged, pacing a path in the carpet in the hour that he had been waiting. The normal symptoms – palpitations, clammy palms, and ragged breaths – had begun despite his desperate pleas to his body and mind. He had to hold it together; this wasn't about him, for Christ's sake. He pushed the picture of Bella to one side. Her broken body, the body he had chosen not to look at when it had been laid to rest in its cold wooden box.

"Are you sure?" Daniel sized him up and down. He couldn't have been further from the character of Helix at this minute in time. Daniel took a certain amount of pleasure in this fact. There was nothing quite like learning that your wife had rebounded to a film star to make you feel inadequate. Daniel had by and large regained his normal affability and was feeling decidedly guilty. He hadn't meant to land all that on Charlotte at once, but she had been so angry, so hurt, that it had made him defensive, accusative, even. He felt incredibly guilty now, of course. Not that he thought she was in any kind of harm, but he supposed you could say he was responsible for this… reaction.

"Look, it will be quicker if I drive. I know where I'm going. We can be there in ten minutes. Besides," he said as a parting shot, "I've still got the dog with me. He'll make short shrift of finding her."

Daniel drove like an old man, Max speculated as he focused on controlling his heart rate. That wasn't a bad thing in these circumstances, but it would be better if he could actually do something rather than being stuck in this metal cage with his rival. Jake was sitting between his legs, panting in that over the top way that Labradors have, and every so often he tried to scramble up onto his knee and look out of the window. Actually, to be honest, it was quite nice really, nothing like a dog to bring you down to earth.

They were driving through small country lanes and he had lost track of where they exactly were. Most of the names on the signposts he had never actually heard of, and the roads seemed to be getting narrower and more remote. Daniel finally drew up near the entrance to a farm-track. It was adjacent to an old footpath sign standing at a forty-five-degree angle by the entrance to a tall and overgrown hedgerow. It looked pretty ancient. The Volvo was tucked behind an apple tree, at a precarious angle, and Max widened his eyes as he saw it until he saw Daniel shaking his head.

"Don't take any notice of that; she can't park to save her life." He clumsily changed the subject, hastily moving his glance from the unamused expression on Max's face to his bare forearms. "You'll need long sleeves."

Max was already getting out of the car and pulling on his hoodie. *Wanker*, was what he was actually thinking.

"Through here?" Barely waiting for an answer, he started walking. The route was initially inside the actual hedgerow, and he was just a few inches too tall for comfort. The shorter Daniel fared better, although the path was scored with brambles and nettles. There was clear evidence that someone had walked through recently, with flattened patches of undergrowth and even footprints in a few boggy patches of earth, untouched by the sun. The dog was way out in front, sniffing constantly, his tail wagging like it was on a spring. This way and that, he caught a scent and then was off again.

"How long?" Max called from his position in front. He felt better now that he could actually move; he just needed to find her and hold her, that would be enough for now. He couldn't save Bella – he wasn't there for her when she needed him – but he could help Charlotte and he was determined to do so. Whatever she wanted – as a friend, as a lover – he would be there for her.

"Twenty minutes?" Daniel wished he had some better shoes on. White trainers were definitely not what he would have worn if he had planned this exhibition. Angela was very into fashion and what looked good. It had felt flattering to begin with, to be cared about that much. He wasn't used to it. Charlotte bought him things now and then, for Christmas or birthdays normally, but they were normally things he had selected, definitely not love gifts.

He wasn't stupid, he realised that Angela was trying to change his appearance, make the package more presentable. She was eight years younger than him, and sometimes it felt twice that. He hadn't minded at first but then he thought maybe he should mind, stand his ground or something. But maybe the sex was worth it, although no doubt that would change with the pregnancy. It was all so confusing. He wished he felt more sure of the situation, more definite; but truth be told, he felt stuck between a rock and a hard place.

He knew how ironical the situation was. Angela pregnant. He suspected that may have been the plan all along. Yes, he had felt trapped and even tricked initially. However, now he had calmed down, he had had a chance to think about it rationally. She had made him feel a lot better about himself and he didn't feel like she couldn't stand the sight of him. Yet she wasn't Charlotte. Was that a good or bad thing?

Earlier he had thrown caution the wind. He had had a shock, and his instinct was to go to Charlotte, to talk it through with her. But did he really want to return to her? That was the million-dollar question. He knew Max was worried about her, but he couldn't bring himself to take this that seriously. She had got into a strop, that was all. Okay, this hadn't happened for ages but, crucially, it had happened before. The first miscarriage, the row when she'd walked out after he'd told her that she was making the wrong decision over quitting teaching. Maybe quite a few times then. He trod on a root and his foot turned painfully into some black peaty gunge. *Christ.*

"So, what's the story with you and Charlotte?" He felt annoyed now. To have been dragged out here again. He needed at least to know the lie of the land. "I thought you were married yourself?"

"Not married, no," Max said shortly, "and I don't know, in answer to your first question." He felt pathetic, almost embarrassed. *If you hadn't sprung your little surprise, mate*, he thought, *it might have been a different answer.* He couldn't be bothered to articulate his antagonism. He just wanted to find Charlotte.

***

Charlotte blinked in the bright light. Through squinting eyes, she focused on the afternoon sun for the moment. She shut her eyes and she saw it again in her head, highlighting the blood vessels in relief and signalling a ghastly throbbing of being. Her head hurt and she felt queasy. She must have drifted off for a few minutes. She eased herself upright, and tensed suddenly when she heard the crunching of twigs and voices to her right. Two figures emerged from the path illuminated by sunlight, materialising patchily in front of her. In a flashback, she felt like a child again, lost and then with sight of her parents. It felt like she was in a dream – no, a nightmare. She struggled to her feet and called, but felt faint and wobbly again and had to sit down.

The dog reached her first, licking and jumping up and smashing his nose into her. She hugged him, grateful to hide her face. She felt like a fool. She hadn't needed to be found. It was all okay.

Daniel saw her at once but held back. His feet felt like they were made of lead. His whole body felt like it was dragging. He almost dreaded what he might find; the familiar sense of guilt assuaged his veins. Why did she do this to him constantly? Was he worse than other men? Sure, he missed some things about Charlotte and their old life, but was he ready to return to this? The dramatic gestures, the heightened emotions. He just wanted calm; he just wanted it to go back to normal. All they needed was some kind of stupid accident. It was so hot; none of them were thinking straight. This bloke, Max, was making a fuss out of nothing if you asked him. Typical actor types – highly strung. Actually, he could have been describing Charlotte.

Max, meanwhile, darted under the wire and was hurrying towards Charlotte, diminished and forlorn on the horizon. She was getting to her feet, and he broke into a run as he saw her swaying slightly, her hand to her temple. Daniel shook his head and started to follow him. *What are you doing, Charlotte?*

"Are you alright? Are you okay?" She filled his vision, and Max had never felt so pleased to see anyone before. She looked as if she had just woken, and her cheeks were reddened in the sun. "Charlotte," he said softly, "I was so worried, are you okay?" He put an arm behind her so that he was supporting her weight and she leant into it gratefully. He was just a man; she didn't know why she had been in awe of him. He was her support. There was no need for a plinth, no pedestal. Daniel fell back, suddenly superseded and superfluous. Apart from the first glance of recognition, Charlotte hadn't cast him even a word or look. She eyed him now, from over Max's shoulder, pulling away slightly, aware of the incongruity of the situation.

"Yes, I'm okay. I feel a bit faint, actually. So stupid; I forgot I hadn't eaten anything." *This is so surreal*, Charlotte was thinking, *both of them here. Just what I didn't want.* She did feel really strange. She pulled away from Max and sat down on the ground with a thump. The heat had been replaced with a muted hum of warmth and a haze of clouds was edging across the sun. It was humid but the sun's intensity had dulled. She couldn't move.

Max fished some complimentary biscuits out of his pocket. They were a little crushed, but Charlotte took them gratefully. He plonked himself beside her and looked out to the pit in front of him. Jake was picking his way down to the bottom and Daniel called to him to come back. He put him on the lead, pleased to be focused on something else.

"You know how to pick them, Charlotte." Max scanned the pit in front of him. Rabbits were running in and out of long-dumped farm machinery. They viewed Jake with pity. "This is extraordinary; I'd never had guessed it was here."

"It's just somewhere I go sometimes." Charlotte met Daniel's eyes and issued a silent signal of thanks.

"Let's get you back home." Max deftly helped her up and kept his arm behind her back. He didn't move it until they reached the car.

THIRTY-ONE

A bizarre, destabilising thought had begun to form in her mind, even as she got into the car. It had seemed preposterous, but she had been so distracted in these last weeks. Her routine had been so different and strange that she perhaps had not been as conscious of small changes as she once was.

Both men signalled that they wanted to come in at home, but she made it clear that she just needed to eat and sleep, sleep and eat; she couldn't really think about the order. A weariness had dulled every limb and she longed for the comfort of her bed and the numbness of sleep. She accepted Jake back, and watched as Daniel hauled his bedding and blankets into the hall, Jake scampering around excitedly at his feet and then mournfully trailing Daniel's heels as he walked towards the door. She said her goodbyes, watching the different expressions on the men's faces. Something in Daniel's of relief as he got Jake out of the car, turned to leave; anxiety chiselled on Max's features. He hung back for a few minutes after Daniel left.

"Promise me you'll talk to me. If you need to. It's up to you what you do next, but I know what happens when you bottle things up. Not you specifically, I mean. I'm in the country for a few weeks while they sort out what to do about the rest of filming. Just keep in contact, no matter what." He spoke quickly, his eyes seeking reassurance. It was as much as Charlotte could do to acknowledge the words.

"Max, don't worry. I'll be alright." She itched for him to be gone.

He stooped and kissed her before he exited, eyes open, face serious. Charlotte looked up too late and their lips missed. She knew that he had wanted something more from her, but she was in a state of flux. She couldn't think about earlier now.

Something couldn't wait. When the door was safely shut behind him, she locked it straight away, walking quickly up the stairs and into the coolness of the bathroom. The tiles soothed her bare feet, and she felt the tension begin to ebb from her body despite what she was about to do. She locked the door; probably not a good idea, but she couldn't risk Daniel coming back. The door to the bathroom cabinet was stiff and she had to give it a good pull to open it. Rummaging behind old medicine packets, toothpicks, throat lozenges, she thought there was one left: a throwback, a nod to the future from the past. Sure enough, collapsed on the top shelf, a half-empty packet, half-hidden behind some ancient lubricant, revealed itself. It seemed fitting somehow.

She desperately needed a wee so the normal furore over squeezing out enough liquid wasn't a problem. Hunched over the loo, she felt the delicious ease of her bladder emptying and swerved the stick underneath for the obligatory five seconds, replacing the cap, carefully wiping splashes and pulling up her clothes while she waited. She looked after a minute, couldn't stop herself; she was so clear what she would find. The line was so solid that it bled out into the surrounding area. There was an inevitability to the moment. She had known since that soul-piercing moment in the quarry when the incoherence of her thoughts suddenly reframed, and another possibility presented itself. A hundred little dreams were shattered and replaced. A vast chasm loomed in front of her, bottomless, unfixed. She climbed wearily into her bed, not even bothering to get undressed as she succumbed to the welcome erasing of sleep.

Exhausted, she didn't wake until gone 9.00a.m. the next day when her phone started vibrating and ringing next to her bed. Thoughts were ratcheting together in her head, clamouring for space. Charlotte felt the tug of anticipation before she gained full consciousness and recalled the seismic event of the night before. She pulled herself up remorselessly and grabbed the handset, trying to ignore the sinking feeling in her stomach. A Cambridge number, she realised now that she had missed several calls from the same number yesterday. Who could it be? Oh, Phil. She cleared her throat and pressed redial. The number flashed up on the screen and rang for only a few rings when it was picked up.

"Charlotte! Marvellous to hear from you. How's things?"

"Good," Charlotte croaked, struggling to clear her throat. Phil clearly wasn't listening or too concerned for the answer. His tone clearly indicated that he expected her to be very impressed.

"Well, I hope you're sitting down. I've managed to sell not one, not two… drumroll… but three large pieces, and I have another two clients who are very interested in the tree series. Seems that back to nature is all the rage in West London!"

Phil couldn't resist a guffaw. "I'm still waiting for a phone call back from Alison, but I've sent her the photos, and someone in her office has tipped me that she is very, very interested. I hope you are ready for a busy few months, young lady."

There was a brief period of silence as if Phil was awaiting applause.

Charlotte closed her eyes and let a faint but discernible feeling of revulsion wash over her. She tried desperately to collect herself mentally.

"Phil, that's amazing. Can I ring you back later? I've got guests who have just arrived." *Just get off the phone and leave me alone*, she thought.

"Oh? Well, okay." Phil couldn't hide the disappointment in his voice. Charlotte sensed a paternalism in his attitude towards her, which was wavering in the face of this abject failure of professionalism. His tone became more direct and forthright. "Look, Charlotte, I'm going to be frank with you. I haven't got time to piss about. I only exhibit artists who I know are going to be committed to marketing themselves and following up sales leads. Sure, call me back later, but maybe have a think about whether or not this is for you."

Charlotte mumbled a few words of apology and tapped the red button. She was bursting to go to the loo, and she felt that old nagging worry where she half-expected to see a flash of blood in her pyjama bottoms. Nothing. She had felt mildly crampy for a few weeks and had presumed that her period was on its way. How many weeks could she be? It was hard to tell with her erratic cycle.

A lot of things were making sense now: strange tastes, general lethargy, things she recognised from before. Any sense of jubilation was smothered by the flood of memories of the last time. Her insides recoiled involuntarily. How could she ever go through this again? What was she thinking? She needed desperately to confide in someone. She needed advice, but who? In the end, she settled on Claire. Yes, the cost would be paying lip service to the latest feat from one of the offspring but, on the plus side, Claire actually did know the nuts and bolts of pregnancy. Perhaps she could help to work out the dates, although there was one very awkward revelation that would have to be disclosed first.

***

"Christ, Claire, it's not *Twilight*," she retorted to her friend. It had been a lot to tell her all at once. Claire had asked many questions, especially on how she had managed to conduct tristes with two different men in little over a month. She had been careful to keep the identity of the second conquest a secret, but she could tell Claire was suspicious.

"Someone you met in a pub? What pub? I thought you weren't going out at the moment?"

"I went out with an old colleague. We met up with a friend of his." It was awful how one lie led to another, Charlotte reflected. Within seconds, she had made up a completely fabricated tale about an invented workmate and his acquaintance. The 'facts' came thick and fast.

"It was a mistake. We had both had way too much to drink. He works away from home anyway, totally unsuitable." What was that she had heard about including some truths in your lie? It was worrying how easy this was.

"Okay, okay, well it obviously is Daniel's baby judging by your symptoms. The question is, what do you want to do with this? I mean, do you want to get back together with him? Charlotte, he may be thrilled!"

"Trust me, he won't be. He's with someone else now, and she's pregnant too, remember? There's no way that this can be sorted neatly." Charlotte was pretty certain that Daniel would be shocked, yes; thrilled, no. "If it is his baby, and it does seem to match the dates in terms of how I'm feeling, I must be over two months pregnant. That's the crunch time, apparently. Twelve weeks is a bit of a misnomer. Oh, what a mess, Claire, I just want to curl up into a ball and be woken up in a year's time." Her voice wobbled. Her emotional barometer felt like was fixed on 'change', another sign.

"Have you got those injection things you're supposed to take?" queried Claire. "I think you need to take it one step at a time."

"Yes, quite a few. I couldn't bring myself to chuck them."

"Look, I wouldn't do anything for the moment. Lie low, keep painting. Talk to that gallery bloke, say you do want to sell the paintings with him, and see what happens. You'll have support from your friends anyway. What about your mum? Are you going to tell her? Do you want me to come down?"

"No," Charlotte said a little too hastily. "It's just, I'm not great company like this." She backtracked. "You've really helped me though. I- I didn't really know who to talk to. Mum's been surprising, but I don't want to push it with this. She'd probably tell me to get over myself and sign up with the child support agency."

"So you haven't told her, Charlotte? That's what I'm worried about. You need all the support you can get. Get a doctor's appointment at least."

"I will. I know, you're right." Charlotte gave her goodbyes speedily. In her head she asked herself what the point was. What would happen would happen, whether or not it was confirmed by a doctor.

She had been here so many times before, and she felt in the end that several things only made the situation worse when it all went wrong. Reaching out of her bubble meant that there were more people to let down, to see the humiliation and the failure. The less people who knew, the better. And if it all went wrong, well, what could they do? When had they ever been able to help before? When that tiny struggle between life and death was played out, there was nothing that could be done except wait and endure. Only two things in her head were clear: she had to keep painting, and there was only one person she wanted supporting her if it continued, only one person she was willing to let in. The question was, how would he respond to that invitation? And had she even enough courage to ask him?

She picked up the phone again quickly and texted Phil.

Hi Phil. I've had a think, and I definitely want to stay with you. Sorry about earlier. In shock, I guess. Don't worry, I'm going to be a model artist. I'm v. excited and I look fwd to talking thru prices.

She received a reply back within a few minutes:

That's great, my darling. I'll email through my terms, and perhaps you can pop in next week in person to sign etc.?

Brilliant. Can't wait! C u then.

She walked out to the studio and sat down in front of the window. A large canvas was sitting on the easel: her painting of the Moroccan sunrise. She had used a palette knife to create a thick textured depth to the reddish-yellow sky, but it needed more hues, scuds of orange and purple. She started squeezing out some oils and mixing in some linseed oil to thin them slightly, humming under her breath as her mind became infused with colour.

EPILOGUE

A Month Later

Things gradually felt like they had cleared inside her head; a layer of gauze had been lifted because she now saw what she could control and what she could not. There were two things she had to do, and she had to do them now before she lost her resolve. After this point, it would get easier because her choice would be taken away. No more lingering over what ifs, over what might have happened or what had gone wrong. What would happen, would happen.

She went and sat in the garden to make the call, on the old wooden seat in front of her tree where the shade cast a beckoning shadow over grass, urging her to sit down and take stock. The worn wooden slats felt reassuring and familiar whilst the tree's branches leant out in a form of embrace, containing the blue sky beyond. A muted twitter of bird song accompanied the low buzz of insects, and she could hear the distant drone of someone massacring their lawn. Summer had well and truly taken over the garden and there was a tinge of yellow to the lawn in patches and a lack of colour in other places; but the roses continued blooming determinedly, and she deadheaded them absently while the dialling tone sounded.

"Hello? Daniel's phone," a female voice answered, and Charlotte couldn't help but assess the tone and try to visualise the person at the end of the line. She sounded younger than herself; she supposed she would be. It was prejudiced and unfair of her, but she equated the slightly nasal tone with a limited intelligence or at least a lack of scope.

"Hello." She tried to answer pleasantly. "It's Charlotte, Daniel's, er… wife. I need to speak to him."

"He's sleeping." The voice became higher with a note of aggression. "I'm not going to wake him up on a Sunday. He's exhausted."

Charlotte ploughed on; she was past the point of no return. She had expected this: some comeback. In a way, maybe it was for the best. She probably needed to get the resentment out of her system, as Charlotte had, in order to reach that point where she genuinely didn't care anymore.

"Angela, I don't want to make any trouble. I know it must be very difficult for you too. It's not going to be in our best interests to fall out, and I don't want to do that anyway. I must speak to Daniel though, so would you ask him to call me back, please?"

"What do you mean?" This obviously wasn't what Angela had expected to hear. "Not in our best interests… has he told you about the baby? Is it about that?"

Charlotte sighed. Typical Daniel – he hated conflict. It had probably been much easier to pretend that Charlotte didn't know. This was quite the mess. She proceeded as delicately as she could.

"It's just... just something he needs to know. I need to speak to him. I'm not trying to take him away. It's okay."

Charlotte wondered why she was being quite so polite to the woman who had broken up her marriage, but then again, she conceded, if it had been truly solid, this possibly never would have happened in the first place. The voice was cutting into her thoughts, and she caught the end of the breathy speech.

"...just let him go, can't you. He doesn't want you anymore. I don't think it's a good idea for him to see you again. It's making me feel stressed and I don't want to harm the baby."

Gosh, she really was quite unpleasant. Charlotte wondered how much Daniel had told her about their previous pregnancies. She understood that Angela was feeling protective, not least towards herself and the foetus as she struggled to validate her position, but her manner verged on the callous. It was not Charlotte, after all, who had got together with another woman's husband. Perhaps this was why Daniel had had second thoughts. But then he thought he was getting just one baby, from a woman he had only known intimately for six months, or less.

Charlotte felt an unexpected burble of laughter surfacing from within her. It rolled around her insides and gained momentum. She tried to keep it out of her voice, but the mirth seemed to trickle into the words and her voice shook a little as she said, "Please, just let him know I called."

She pressed 'end call' with relief and then it cascaded out. She rocked herself on the bench, laughing until she ached. This must be hysteria; tears trickled down her cheeks until she could laugh no more. She just couldn't help herself;

she didn't know quite how Daniel would react, but she was very sure that two children by two different women was not what he had bargained for. An image crossed her mind of Barbara holding the two babies and she stifled another peal of laughter, waiting until she grew calmer.

Even the garden seemed to be holding its breath for her to make the next step, and a heady buzz of excitement and anticipation seemed to flow into her. Only the tree was stolid, accepting, stoical. It had absorbed her pain, her grief and now her hope. She put a hand on the trunk to steady herself and then turned and walked back to the house.

It was a waiting game now. After tidying away some more of the detritus of the last few weeks – more packaging, art materials; since Daniel's departure, the studio had overshot its space somewhat – Charlotte decided to take Jake for a walk. It really was the most beautiful day. They had reached the beginning of July, midway through the year, past the longest day. The summer solstice had been and gone and almost imperceptibly the seasons were changing again. 'As imperceptibly as Grief / The Summer lapsed away'. There was a circularity which appealed to her. She felt part of things rather than separated from them.

On cue, the dog was skittish, hovering around the front door, jumping up and pawing. She clumsily filled a bottle of water, spraying water out onto her sun-top, and pulled on some trainers. Her top kept riding up, and she ran a hand over her stomach. Did it really seem more rounded, fuller? She couldn't afford to believe her eyes, but the light bruising told its own story and the blood had not come. She was not complacent, could never be, but… but…

Charlotte grabbed the lead and set off; she had no clear

plan or route; her feet seemed to take her of their own accord. She was already feeling that slightly bloated, filled sensation and a premature heaviness that she couldn't remember from before. Was that good? She had to believe so. There was no need for a cardigan this morning; the sun was rising in the sky and would soon be at its highest point. She felt its rays warm her limbs and soak lovingly into her bones.

Half an hour later and she was ambling over the fields, feeling that irresistible sensation of freedom that she attributed to that vast expanse of sky and land in front of her. Today she had the strangest feeling; part of her consciousness felt that it was drifting from her body and could survey it with a detachment and lack of emotion. She supposed that she was perhaps in a state of shock. It almost felt like so much had happened that she didn't care anymore, as if she had finally climbed to a level higher than her fear. She had had that feeling before, when she had dreaded and worried about something so much she almost then became cavalier. What could happen now? The worst had happened already, hadn't it? At least now there would be no more secrets, no more distrust, no more uncertainty. What would be, would be. What was that Mother Julian quotation – 'all shall be well'. Just the waiting then, and she would have her painting to sustain her.

They rounded the back of the fields, picking out the path at the side through the grasses and poppies, fragile in the light breeze. The air was busy with living sounds. After the dense, immersive yellow of the rape seed, the corn wore a softer ochre, reaching up in its golden upright majesty against the vivid azure sky. Charlotte felt something close to happiness, or perhaps that was too ambitious; acceptance might have been more exact. There was the sense of a balance or harmony just within reach. It danced in front of her eyes like the bits of dandelion fluff which one never could quite grasp.

She continued walking, feeling hotter with each step, and rounded the corner onto the narrow lane that led past the barn. She slipped Jake's lead over his head; she didn't want to risk any funny business, even with the lack of thoroughfare. The avenue of trees was lit by the sunlight weaving through the branches and dappling on the ground. She could dimly hear some shouts and the laughter of children, but they were muffled by the dense foliage, only getting louder as it became lighter. It crossed her mind that Dom and Vivi must be there. She was surprised to feel a warmth spreading through her. She wouldn't mind seeing them again.

Jake pulled her up the hill, and she emerged gratefully, blinking slightly in the bright light. The sound of children was unmistakable now, and she could hear peals of mirth and imagined Max swinging Dom or pushing Vivi on the swing. The gate was in front of her on the gravelled drive and she hovered, visualising herself walking up to the entrance, greeting Max, the children, their faces when they saw her, Max's face when she told him. It was now or never, before she buckled.

She walked up to the gate and called loudly, "Hi, Max, it's me."

Her voice seemed to float for a split-second on the air before Max's voice met it.

"Charlotte!"

There was the sound of scampering feet and Dom appeared at the gate, closely followed by Vivi and Max. They both had grins plastered across their face, in close approximations of each other, and Charlotte felt the tension that had been accumulating in her stomach slowly melt away. Her eyes met Max's hazel ones before they spoke. The sun caught his irises and rendered them a ruddy amber. She couldn't pull away. The warmth in her stomach started spreading through her body, and she felt like she was swimming to the surface quickly now as the water pulled her upwards.

"Jake too," Max said as he buzzed the gate open. He looked as he always did, relaxed and yet alert, sensitive to her moods and needs. The dog nuzzled him as he held out a welcoming hand, and then ran away to the children.

"We are honoured. Look, Vivi, I think he recognises you." Jake had gone mad, running at full pelt round the yard followed by two giggling children. "And how are you?" He reached an arm out and found Charlotte's hand. His firm grip encircled her fingers and he squeezed. She hesitated for a split second and then responded, clutching him eagerly as if a hand pulled her to shore. She turned to face him, taking his other hand in hers, acknowledging his emotions by her gravitas, meeting them with equal force.

Max's heart fluttered in his chest. She looked well, surprisingly well. Her cheeks seemed more rounded, freckled and even slightly tanned, and they were echoed by the curves of her body. The attraction he felt for her was undeniable. He felt hope again. For a few weeks, he had been agonising over what had happened, so little between them, and yet what had taken place had been laden with possibilities; the road not yet taken. They had spoken on the phone a few times, yet she had evaded contact despite his every suggestion. She had been friendly, yes, affectionate, even, but he sensed